SYMBOL MAKER'S DAUGHTER

CLARE GUTIERREZ

RIVER GROVE
BOOKS

Published by River Grove Books
Austin, TX
www.rivergrovebooks.com

Distributed by River Grove Books

Design and composition by Greenleaf Book Group and Kim Lance
Cover design by Greenleaf Book Group and Kim Lance
Cover images used under license from © iStock / Getty Images Plus/Yuri_ Arcurs; © iStock / Getty Images Plus/darrenturner

Publisher's Cataloging-in-Publication data is available.

Print ISBN: 978-1-63299-538-4

eBook ISBN: 978-1-63299-539-1

First Edition

THIS BOOK IS DEDICATED TO MY SON, RUSTY WHITTEMORE.
In the very beginning of our journey, that little boy's love made it
possible to believe the impossible. It still does.

PROLOGUE

Tucked deep within a forested area near the southwest edge of England was a large mound covered in thick brush and massive boulders, not unlike various mounds in other regions. A woman hobbled from the small dugout built within the mound. Her silver hair was loosely piled atop her head, while escaped strands hung about her neck. She observed the dense cloud layers that hid the forest from the full moon slowly moving overhead. The silence felt oppressive. She knew the animals of the night—familiar with her presence—were not hushed because of her, but something else. She stood still, allowing the world to slip away and opening her mind to the messages coming to her. For weeks now, she had tried to contact Queen Elizabeth, to no avail. *She thinks she needs me no longer, but she is wrong. Now, it is too late.* Tonight, the thoughts entering her mind were for someone else. Closing her eyes, she willed the message to reach its intended. *There is a great upheaval coming to England. The pieces are already in play. You must bring the girl to me.*

England's place in the world was beginning to improve, thanks to King Edward IV. Throughout the realm, there was a cautious feeling of peace. The border between England and Scotland continued to simmer, but the king's brother, Richard, Duke of Gloucester, was an able commander who kept the area quiet.

England's throne had finally been secured. King Edward had two healthy sons—heirs to the crown. At last, Edward and his wife, Queen Elizabeth, would be able to relax and enjoy a hard-won time of relative tranquility. In the stillness of night, however, a reordering was stirring. Events were being foretold that would change the course of England forever.

CHAPTER 1

DRUE VIENETO TOOK THE STAIRS to his father's chambers, two at a time. He was medium height, strong, agile, and built for his chosen profession. He paused briefly outside the heavily guarded door, glancing in the brass-gilded mirror that hung there. The sorrow he felt was reflected in his green eyes and etched in the fine lines on his face. One of the guards opened the door for him. His father lay on an enormous bed. He was propped up on his pillow, his eyes closed, and for a brief, horrible second, Drue thought he was too late.

"Father," he spoke softly. There was no response. Drue could see the movements of his father's chest, each breath clearly a struggle. Standing at the bed's edge, Drue leaned closer to his father and spoke again. "Father, I am here."

The frail figure in the bed roused. When his searching eyes found Drue, his face lit up. He reached for Drue's hand, grasping it weakly. With every ounce of strength left in his spent body, he called to his page, asking him to bring his letter for Drue. When he had it in hand, he offered it to Drue. "This is yours, son. Your brother has gone to bring his wife—I will die tonight. Please . . ." He pointed to the document Drue held in his hand. "Read it aloud for me." Closing his eyes, he waited. The king's page, his priest, and the head of his council were all standing near the bed, attentive to any final commands.

Carefully, slowly, Drue broke the king's seal, unrolled the paper, and began reading. *I, King Vincent Vieneto, King of Padronale, do declare Drue Vieneto as my lawful and legal son, entitled to all rights and privileges thereof. Prince Drue Vieneto will stand in line for my throne, should his brother, Cicero Vieneto, and sons be deceased. If Prince Cicero has no sons, Drue is second in line for the throne, after Cicero.* Five witnesses were listed, including Cicero. The date of the notice was written and bore the royal stamp, dated six months earlier.

Immediately, Drue protested. "Father, I care not about the throne. I am doing what I was trained to do and have done for ten years. I—"

His father interrupted. "Do you ever see your mother?"

Drue nodded, and the king's eyes filled with tears. "I loved her well, Drue. I could never convince her to live with me. We have always communicated regularly, but she would not change her mind. Over the years, I gave up trying. I have been at peace, just knowing I have her love." The king struggled to take a deep breath before continuing. "Now, I am dying, and must provide clear legal direction for the future of this throne. The messages sent to the courts around Padronale simply note Cicero is my heir. Should he die before he has a son, another has been named." The king stopped talking for a moment, while he struggled to catch his breath. "I have given you what you have refused, regardless of your aversion to it." The king smiled. "Cicero has promised to not interfere with your life. But you know Cicero. He will try to get you to come home, as soon as I pass on." The king looked at Drue. "He misses you, Drue."

Drue sat on the edge of his father's bed. "I know. I miss him, too. I promise to return, as soon as my last assignment is completed."

The king nodded. "Ah, yes. England's trembling throne. It has been sturdier under King Edward. He has done well. Man knows not the changes time brings." The king stopped talking again and lay quietly, with his eyes closed. Beads of perspiration covered his face and ran down his neck. Drue picked up a damp cloth lying on the stand near the bed and gently dabbed his father's face. The old king stirred once more. "Just knowing you will be coming back gives me great peace, Drue, my son." Again, he was silent. His breathing was increasingly labored.

The door to the chambers opened, allowing Cicero and his wife, Lila, entry. Drue immediately stood and bowed to his brother. The two men embraced fondly. "Drue, you came back for Father." Cicero was nodding his approval as he spoke. His eyes filled with tears as he gestured toward his wife. "You must remember Lila." Drue bowed and kissed his sister-in-law on her cheek.

"Of course, brother. How could one ever forget such a gentle soul?"

Drue and his brother turned to their father. Cicero knelt near his father's head. "I am back, Father. I am here, Lila is here, and Drue is here. We are all together again, Father." The old king smiled faintly, his breathing becoming shallow until it slowly stopped.

"Priest?" Drue called, looking around. The priest stepped forward and listened for a breath, holding a mirror to the king's mouth and nose. He shook his head before stepping back.

"The anointing was done yesterday," Cicero responded as his wife bent to kiss the dead king's brow. She was weeping silently. "Please, wife, leave us with Father for a moment."

Lila nodded and, bowing, left the room.

Cicero watched Drue. "Dare I think you might stay?"

"I promised Father I would return for good, whenever England's throne is secure." Drue watched Cicero's face cloud over.

"The throne of England may never be without turmoil," Cicero noted dryly. "Is your family to wait until we are dying also?"

"Cicero, no. I will come when Edward's throne is secure. His son is nearly the age to rule alone. When he reaches that birthday, I will return." Drue could see Cicero held little faith such a time might ever come. Still, Cicero nodded and smiled at his younger brother.

"Very well. I am pleased to see you now. Did Father give you his proclamation for the throne?" Cicero asked, changing the subject.

"He did. Who might know of this? I would like to keep it quiet for as long as possible."

Cicero shook his head. "You have been gone too long, brother. Not two days after he completed the official document, another was already in the hands of the French and every country near us, including the Papal States." He slapped Drue's shoulder. "Although it does not name you, there is no escape now, Drue."

The room was silent, and Drue watched as Cicero gently touched his father's hand and face. Cicero was much closer to their father. Drue could find no fault with that, as he himself was absent most of the time, doing dark things to keep his father and Cicero safe. When Cicero stepped away from the bed, both men left the room.

The dead king's esquire still sat quietly nearby, tears dripping off his chin. Several other witnesses to the death of the king tactfully withdrew. Drue was deeply saddened by the death of his father. He was determined to stay for an extended visit this time.

THE KING HAD ONLY JUST BEEN ENTOMBED when a man discreetly approached Drue. "Your Grace, I have a message from Lord Bruce."

Lord Bruce was one of Drue's most trusted friends and would not have interrupted Drue's visit with his family needlessly, as those visits came seldom and were treasured. The man handed Drue a small packet.

Drue opened the worn document and read, *Drue, you should return posthaste. Keaton has men about looking for you. You are known to roam throughout the realm, but by next week's end, Keaton will realize you are not in the country.* Drue ordered the man be given food, allowed to rest for a short while, be provided with a fresh horse, and be allowed to leave just before the gates were closed for the night. "Young man, when you have eaten and rested, please tell Lord Bruce I will be on my way at first light." Drue watched rider and horse cross the courtyard toward the barracks, and then set off himself, to meet his brother and Lila to dine.

After everyone had finished eating and the table was cleaned, Drue cleared his throat to speak. "It seems I have been missed, and the individual searching for me will soon realize I am no longer in England. My absence will cast doubt on my undertaking when I find it necessary to act. As yet, my relation to you is unknown. I must leave here at first light. When the time is right, I will return. I protect you and your kingdom, Cicero."

With a sad smile, Lila slipped her hand over Cicero's. "If you must leave, leave with my blessing and Cicero's. Promise us you will stay safe, Drue."

Drue stood to leave and embraced his brother. "Take care of yourself. Very few countries lay quietly. England could well rise up again and throw off its crown."

When the sun's first rays spilled over the small kingdom of Padronale, Drue was already well on his way to board a ship that would carry him back to English shores.

CHAPTER 2

RUE SLOWLY WALKED THE FAMILIAR STREETS of London. He had lived in England for five years. During that time, he had made it his business to know the land and its people. He knew every river, valley, trail, road, forest, and village. Different from Drue's land yet beautiful in its own right, this land called England. He had grown fond of the rolling green hills, streams, gorges, coves, and forests. Traveling quietly, without notice, assured few people knew him.

On this night, drawn to London by an inner voice he never questioned, he waited for some direction, some sign that would indicate his next move. At that very moment, a man and his three companions stepped from an inn onto the street.

"Lord Drue! There you are! We have been looking for you, for days now." The man, Lord Keaton, strode up and grasped Drue's arm in a familiar way. Drue did not pull away, although it took great effort not to do so. "I have something I wish to discuss with you. Come." Keaton nodded toward another inn nearby—one known for its singular reputation. Patrons who entered the establishment were not there to make merry, but to speak to each other of private matters. Matters that never left the building carried away by gossip. Keaton led Drue to the inn, his companions walking on without salutation.

Once inside, Keaton chose a corner away from most of the tables, and Drue followed his lead. They sat together in the dimly lit corner, waiting until their order was taken before speaking. "Do you ride for anyone in particular these days?" Keaton asked, studying Drue through narrowed eyes.

"No," Drue answered. He in turn studied Keaton.

"Still a man of many words, I see," Keaton noted dryly. "I need the services of someone like you. Someone who knows this land well and does not talk of what he knows."

Drue remained silent, allowing Keaton to continue.

"There is a certain Lord Weldon. I have been given information that there are those who believe he is devising a plot to overthrow King Edward. I have been hired to rescue Lord Weldon's only child, a daughter, and bring her to safety. She is an innocent." Both men were silent while the man bringing their drinks served them.

As the server walked away, Drue leaned back in his chair, his gaze wandering the room. *Was this the girl?* Finally, he spoke. "What part am I to play?"

Keaton smiled at Drue. "There are men sailing from Burgundy, paid with French money, en route to Weldon's castle. It sits along Bristol Channel, an area I am not familiar with. You are, I believe?"

"Yes."

"I need to reach the lady before the men can take her. I expect to move soon, in two days. If I did not truly need your services, I would never ask the likes of you for help," Keaton admitted, taking another drink of his brandy. "You are a talented guide and swordsman. I have need of both, and I need the best. Can you help?"

Drue waited a moment before answering. "I can. Where do I meet you, and when?"

When Keaton relaxed in his chair, Drue could tell he was relieved. "Day after tomorrow. On the road headed northwest of London, near Windsor. Be there early morning."

Drue drained his mug and stood. "I will see you then." He walked away without looking at anyone. As he stepped out of the building, his mind left Keaton and returned to another request. *I got the message, but what girl? Is this her?*

CHAPTER 3

Λ LONE IN THE DARKENED CHAPEL, Lady Margaret Beaufort knelt. Small of stature, dark-haired, and soft-spoken, she knew her appearance belied the spirit and strength of conviction residing in her heart. She took in the space that surrounded her. This was the room where she felt most untroubled. A gift from her present husband, the chapel was private and tranquil. Light filtered in through a stained-glass window, casting soft colors on a large statue of the Blessed Virgin holding the Christ Child. A rugged cross stood near a small altar, in front of which there were two kneeling benches. The only pew—with room enough for two people—was placed off to one side.

A devout Catholic, Margaret spent hours every day praying for her son, Henry Tudor. Seldom a thought was formed, a spoken command issued, or a plan carried out before she had prayed. Every move she made was carefully planned out first. Well, nearly all. She had never planned on having a child or getting married even once, let alone three times. Rather, she had hoped she might spend her days in a convent. It was not to be. On this particular afternoon, her mind wandered back through the years since her son's birth.

Margaret was the richest heiress in England. She was given in marriage at the age of twelve to Edmund Tudor. Although most girls given in marriage so young were allowed to live with their parents until they were of a more mature age, Margaret was not. She was taken to her husband, whose first order of business was to consummate the marriage so it could not be contested. The Tudors could claim a bloodline to the throne of England—weak, but a line nonetheless. Edmund Tudor was a half-brother to the old King Henry VI, the man on the throne before the sitting monarch, King Edward IV. It was King

Edward who, with help from his brothers, was rumored to have murdered the old king.

Well educated, Margaret Beaufort understood the battle of King Edward, a York, against the now deceased by fair or foul King Henry VI, a Lancastrian. Edmund Tudor had been a cornerstone in plans to overthrow King Edward and place the aging King Henry's wife, Margaret of Anjou, and her son on the throne. Fate would see Margaret end her life alone, in obscurity, far from English soil.

Unable to read the pages of fate, Edmund Tudor carried on a private war against two Duke of York retainers, passing very little time with his new wife. Although that time would prove well spent. By the age of thirteen, Margaret Beaufort Tudor was pregnant. Mere months before the child was born, Margaret was widowed when Edmund was captured and died soon after his release. Severely weakened by fighting and imprisonment, he was not able to survive the plague sweeping the town. Alone, heavy with child, unable to return to her mother's home because of inclement weather, Margaret was forced to travel to her brother-in-law Jasper Tudor's home, Pembroke Castle.

There, at only thirteen years of age, a child herself, Margaret delivered a boy. That boy, christened Henry Tudor, was now the only living male who might have a claim to the throne. The delivery was traumatic—she never bore another child. When King Edward and the Yorkists took control of England, Margaret's small son was taken from her. At four years of age, he was put under the wardship of one William Herbert, then Earl of Pembroke, who bought the boy from King Edward for one thousand pounds. Herbert provided him with a brilliant education and groomed him for marriage into the Herbert family. Fate had other plans. When young Tudor was twelve years old, Herbert took him to watch the battle of Edgecote, to witness in person the realities of war. Men were being hacked down and slaughtered by the hundreds.

Margaret would later learn that, in this same battle, Herbert lost his own life. From that moment, Margaret knew that Henry Tudor would never forget how fragile the line was between winning and living, and losing and dying. Henry was forced to flee for his life with his father's brother, Jasper Tudor. Alongside Jasper, Henry Tudor eventually found his way back to his mother. The reunion did not last long.

Two short years later, Henry and his uncle were again fleeing for their lives. Edward was now firmly entrenched as King Edward IV. Henry was the last one standing who could be a credible, albeit shaky, threat to King Edward's throne. The word was out. King Edward was looking for Henry. The Tudors hastily made arrangements to sail for France, leaving Edward the indisputable king of England. Margaret comforted herself with the knowledge that Henry Tudor and Jasper had formed a deep bond. That bond would last as long as both lived.

The years had been long and difficult, but Margaret believed with all her heart that her son was meant to be the king of England. After all, had she not spent years praying for his safety? Had he not managed to escape with his life each time it seemed he would be caught? Still, as she knelt and prayed on this day, and as much as she hated to even think it, she was discouraged. King Edward had two sons, a brother, and a nephew. A sitting king with four heirs—Margaret could not see how Henry would climb over such a heap, but climb he must. Unless . . . Was it possible plans for Henry had changed? Perhaps he was meant to reclaim the Tudor lands and titles, but not take the crown. Perhaps she herself should focus on such a move. Perhaps . . .

"Margaret!" Lord Stanley's voice shattered the stillness. "You and I are to report to court. You will be a lady-in-waiting for Her Majesty Queen Elizabeth."

Margaret stood, whirled around, and stared at her husband. Lord Thomas Stanley had agreed to marry Margaret after she proposed they unite forces for the betterment of both. He was a respected lord of considerable wealth, but more importantly . . . a man. Lady Margaret was no fool. A woman alone stood little chance of convincing anyone to help the cause of Henry Tudor, even a woman as rich as herself. Lord Stanley could help. He agreed to the match.

Never one to commit to any cause too soon, Stanley could see Edward was firmly on the throne. Margaret's son would have a long wait, as it became clear to her that Stanley intended to stay safely on the good side of the king.

"Surely, Thomas, you jest. I would never agree to serve that witch. Never!" She lifted her chin in defiance.

"Oh, but you will, lady," Stanley calmly replied. "It took a great deal for me to convince His Majesty that you and I—both of us—would be very willing to serve in whatever capacity he saw fit. You are the mother of one Henry Tudor. Remember? Edward could have you sent to the Tower, if he so chose." Stanley paused, appearing pleased with the gasp that escaped from Margaret, who had not considered such a possibility. "He has done that very thing to more than one of his old advisors. They do not leave the Tower, Margaret."

Margaret could think of nothing to say. She wanted to turn on Stanley, but she knew only too well he was correct. She also knew he was not loyal to anyone but himself. Not to King Edward and certainly not to her. Their marriage was one of convenience for them both. She was able to keep her wealth, and he was able to enjoy it.

"When will this happen?" she asked, quietly.

"We leave in two days. Pack what you will. Most of Queen Elizabeth's ladies are very young. I am quite certain they welcome your wisdom." Stanley could not keep the sarcasm from his voice.

"And you, husband? What will you be doing?" Margaret's voice sliced the air between them.

"I have been assigned to his Privy Council." Stanley's tone softened. "It is a good thing, Margaret. I will share all I can with you. One never knows how life might turn." With that, he left the chapel.

Margaret knelt again. "Please, God, please. Your plan for Henry has become my plan too." Surely, all these things could not have happened to her if they were not in God's plan.

HENRY TUDOR STOOD WITH HIS UNCLE JASPER on the deck of yet another ship, staring at the ocean before him. There were four male heirs to the throne. Even if something should happen to Edward, Henry's journey to take the crown seemed to be in vain. "I think I am finished, Jasper." Henry spoke quietly, the sound of defeat edging into his voice.

Jasper was the brother of the father Henry had never known. To Henry, Jasper was his father. But try as he might, Henry could not hide his feelings about what had become an obsession for his mother. She insisted Henry belonged on the throne of England, more than any other man. Her answer was always the same—it was God's will that Henry be king. He turned toward his quarters.

So far God has not made such a claim very clear to me. In fact, it would seem God wants me to rethink my quest.

In what Henry could see was an attempt to bolster him, Jasper protested, his hand on Henry's shoulder. "Henry, you must not give up. Kingdoms are not always won overnight, or even in years. Your time is coming, I am certain. Your mother feels it also." Henry could tell it took all Jasper could muster to continue speaking with conviction for Henry's cause.

"My mother is working to allow me to return to England with Edward's blessings. Do you really believe that could ever happen? Mother is wrong about this—King Edward has no doubts I represent a threat to his throne." Henry walked toward his quarters. "If he thinks I am harmless, why does he try to bribe, trick, or force my return? He will not rest until I am dead." He could hear the flatness in his voice, the defeat. "I am through with this game, Jasper. I fight for the crown of a country I hardly know, pushed by a mother I hardly know. I think to abdicate any claim to the crown and make it very public. Maybe with the blessing of the pope, the king of France, Spain—whoever has the most power just now. Certainly not poor England."

Jasper was quiet. After all, Henry thought, what could he say to that? Sighing, Jasper finally answered. "You have to stay strong, Henry. We cannot know what will happen. We must deal with each day as it comes."

"I have a hard time remembering that. I barely know my own mother. I have never really lived in the country you and Mother would have me rule over." Henry closed his eyes for a long moment. "I am tired of running. I do not know how long I can keep this up. Maybe it is not meant to be mine. How long am I expected to stay in this fight?"

"As long as it takes," Jasper answered, looking at Henry. "You will be forced to fight for that crown, Henry. Of that I am certain. I am not in favor of you returning to England as anything less than a king taking what is rightly yours. I fear you might return with Edward's blessing, and at his command be housed in the Tower, to be executed. That must not happen. My sources tell me the men willing to follow you are not giving up. Neither will you."

"Uncle," Henry replied, "despair is an ugly wound. I know you are trying to find some way to close that wound, or the cause will be lost for you, and for Mother as well."

They had been lucky to escape once again. Leaving England and sailing to France, a storm blew them off course and they wound up in Brittany, an independent duchy. Henry knew they were being used as pawns in a power play between England and France. The Duke of Brittany, Frances II, welcomed them, but Henry knew Duke Frances would resist King Edward's bribes only so long. He dared not share with Jasper the endless nights he lay awake, trying to see some way he might claim the crown of England. For Henry, the days were as dark as the nights.

CHAPTER 4

ALONG THE SOUTHWESTERN COAST OF ENGLAND, where it banks the Bristol Channel, there are places where the land ends at sheer bluffs whose craggy faces droop into the sea below. Perched atop one such bluff, at a higher elevation than the coastline on either side, was Lord Weldon's well-maintained castle. Though well manned, the castle's ability to withstand an attack had never been tested. The rear of the castle courtyard ran along the cliffside. Inside the walls of the estate were nestled a few small huts, stables, a tiny garden, and several trees. A spring provided water for plants and livestock. Over time, huts had appeared outside the citadel, mingling with livestock pens and other signs of a growing hamlet.

Weldon had fought several times for the cause of King Edward and held great pride in regard to those efforts. Fearless in battle, he was well known to the king's soldiers and had earned a well-deserved reputation for being a kindhearted lord who provided as best he could for those living on his estate. At home, Weldon was a gentle man, slowly declining in health. His wife had died of consumption ten years earlier. When Lady Weldon died, many felt Lord Weldon would follow soon. He might have, but for his only child, Nicola. Left without a mother at the tender age of seven, Nicola was gently moved along in life by her father and his staff. The girl had her father's quick wit, her mother's light skin, dark eyes and hair. Lord Weldon's loneliness was manageable during the busy hours of daytime, during which he spent a great deal of time and effort educating the girl. Nights, however, proved more than he could manage.

In an effort to find peace, Weldon began toying with stone setting, gold etching, and other jewelry designs that required his full concentration. What began as an activity to fill long sleepless hours became a passion. When he did sleep, Weldon had visions of elegant designs. He began to sketch them, create them, then destroy the prints, saving the originality of his work. One of Weldon's creations found its way into the hands of King Edward's wife, Elizabeth, when Weldon left it and several other pieces with a well-known stonecutter. Weldon hoped the cutter could tell him if the flaking of the stones on the pieces had been done correctly. The cutter not only praised Weldon's work—he gave one piece to Queen Elizabeth as well. That exposure thrust Weldon's reputation onto the market of unique jeweled pieces coveted by English, Spanish, and soon, French royalty. His hobby garnered acclaim . . . and money.

At one time an attractive, muscular man of average height, whose easygoing demeanor was soothing to others, Weldon was now frail and fidgety as the dreams he had dealt with for years became much more than pictures of designs. His green eyes, reddened from lack of sleep, were filled with worry. Tonight, lying on his chamber floor as was now his habit, drenched in perspiration, barely breathing, Weldon forced himself to relax. Slowly, he unclenched his fists. For several moments, he lay as if death had finally come. Outside, darkness still covered his land, but it would soon fade. The bed across the room was undisturbed.

He took meticulous measures to be certain no one would know what went on in his room at night. Rest was becoming impossible, but his bed could not look like a battleground. There must be no indication anything was amiss. It should look like a place of rest. To this end, he lay on the floor, where he tossed and turned. *It's the dreams. They speak of that which is treason.* The thought made him shudder. Weldon slowly got up from the floor, folded and put away the blankets, crossed the room, and slid under the covers on his bed. Staring at the ceiling, Weldon felt the familiar wave of helplessness wash over him again. The scheme had already begun. There would be nothing he could do to stop it. Now, he needed to protect his child—his only child—seventeen-year-old Nicola. When his page came into the room to clean as usual, he found Weldon's bed slept in.

Never had Weldon ever discussed how he came by his designs, nor had he ever left any sign of the sketches. In the beginning, he was afraid they would be copied if found and his work would lose its value. Then, the unthinkable happened—the dreams changed. Suddenly, the consequences of someone finding sketches of his latest designs would mean certain horrible death for him and for his child.

Despite this knowledge, Weldon dressed and made his way to his workshop.

He was being driven to create designs for a cause he could not share. And no matter what he tried to do, the dreams came, again and again, the images within them a sign of things to come. Weldon was certain of it. They gave warning of great turbulence for England, and always with the same etches. It was as if his hands were possessed. The designs became more and more defined, as he worked. One was large, and one small, but with the same symbols and priceless stones. Hammering the gold leaf carefully, he worked for several days, creating two identical pieces unlike any he had made before. With both pieces completed, he was uncertain what to do with them.

His thoughts turned to an old friend. She would confirm what he believed the symbols predicted. She could also notify the Guardians. He needed help with Nicola.

FEW TRAVELERS CAME THROUGH THE THICK PATCHES of forest not far from the Bristol Channel, but that was where Weldon rode today, his daughter at his side. Those who dared to venture beyond the safety of the common roadway nearly always found themselves lost. The majority eventually made their way back, but tales of the darkness, eerie loss of direction, and legends of people disappearing insured that few men dared stray from the safety of the road. Weldon, however, knew this place, and did not fear it.

He also felt fortunate to know the old woman. Scarcely had anyone ever seen her—or her home within the mound. She spent her time studying the stars, making healing potions, and waiting. Years earlier, Weldon had stayed with her for three weeks. For a long time, he did not return, though he was certain she was aware of his dreams. When he began to have disturbing visions of England's throne, he came several times to seek her knowledge.

For this last visit, he brought his daughter, Nicola. Uncertain if the old crone was still alive or if he could find her again, Weldon desperately needed her confirmation to understand what was happening. As if she heard his very thoughts, he dreamed of her home. The images were so crisp that, even when they left the road behind and entered the dense forest, they found the mound without difficulty.

At first, frightened at the sight of the old, bent, and wrinkled woman with the unkempt hair and gnarled hands, Nicola held back. However, Weldon introduced them, and as the woman turned to speak to her, Weldon could see Nicola's apprehension fade. He nodded to a chair across the room, indicating Nicola should wait there for him. After handing the symbols to her, he listened with foreboding as the woman confirmed what he believed he had created and the danger that would come his way.

Weldon and Nicola were back on the road when Nicola asked, "What does that lady do by herself, Father?"

Weldon replied, "You might have need of her knowledge someday. But under no circumstances can you tell anyone about this visit nor about that lady. Never. Do you understand?"

Several weeks went by, and still the pieces sat safely hidden in his chamber, tucked beneath a loose stone near the fireplace. The story revealed itself to Weldon as he studied the symbol, just as the old crone indicated it would. The broken crowns meant a king would not complete his rule. Only one crown was whole. The colored stones set within the crowns meant which king would survive. Weldon trembled at the implication if these symbols were ever discovered by outsiders. His habit of destroying all evidence of his workings was now an act of self-preservation. Feverishly, he folded the symbols within a soft protective pouch and returned them to the secret hiding place.

That night's visions, however, had nothing to do with designs. Weldon felt a threatening chill. The dreams now revealed there would be a vicious attack because of false rumors of treasonous activities. He had been accused of predicting the fall of King Edward. He saw foreign soldiers pouring over his castle walls. Some of his men lay dead. Worse, he saw his daughter running from them to him. If the symbols told the story, blood would drip from the crown of England. If Weldon did not move quickly, the message on the symbols would be for naught. The last image Weldon saw revealed who betrayed him.

CHAPTER 5

I N ᴄHᴇ ꜰᴀᴅɪɴɢ ʟɪɢHᴄ oꜰ oɴᴇ ᴇɴɢʟɪꜱH ꜰoʀᴇꜱᴄ, five armed men, known as the Guardians, slowly slogged forward through a vicious downpour. As they were forced to leave the road for cover provided by the thick vegetation of the forest, their travel was a hazardous ordeal. The men knew if they made it to Lord Weldon's castle early enough, they could rest and eat before escorting his one treasure, Lady Nicola, to safety. Simple enough, yet even so, each man understood the potential unexpected surprises characteristic of such a task. Unfortunately, the storm raging around them drowned out the sound of oncoming riders. When the first arrow struck the lead Guardian, he fell, and the men following him were quickly cut down as well. All but one. When that last man finally died, after a gruesome interview, the ambush leader, Lord Keaton, and his men had the information they needed.

Lady Nicola and one companion would be riding a cliff road. Keaton had no idea where the cliff road was, but he knew Drue's knowledge of England's landscape was unmatched. Drue knew where a river cut deep into the land's side, releasing waters that thundered over the edge into a plunge pool and eventually into the sea. The falls hid a cavern that opened back to the land behind the falls. On the face of the cliff, hidden by dense brush, a trail led upward from the falls.

IN ᴄHᴇ ᴇᴀʀʟʏ ᴍoʀɴɪɴɢ ʟɪɢHᴄ, Weldon stood at the window, staring. His eyes failed to see the garden below, the courtyard, or anything else. In his mind's eye, he saw the images. Last night was the first time he had ever seen such things—visions of fighting, pain, and death. Worse, he knew well the location of the envisioned battle. It was his own castle, his home!

This cannot be, he thought. *What is this that I see?*

For hours, he paced in his workroom. Slowly, the message had become clear. Weldon knew what he must do. Intent on saving all he could, he called the captain of his guard and the chief groundskeeper. Neither man questioned Weldon. Both had worked for him many years and knew he had an intuition of sorts. His sense of what would come had never been wrong. He knew when storms would hit, when crops would fail or be bountiful, and when the illnesses that plagued England would come. And now, he was greatly distressed over his people's safety and that of his daughter.

He first gave orders for those living within the castle walls to be moved to the surrounding areas outside the castle perimeter. Weldon's experience had shown that people living within the walls of a captured castle were treated with little pity, while those living outside the walls were able to escape, allowed to leave or live and work with the new lord of the manor. His daughter and her ladies were to be guarded carefully, without alarming anyone.

Both men left Weldon to carry out his orders. When his chambers were empty, Weldon destroyed all evidence of anything he had made—papers, metal scraps, tiny stone chips, all he could find. He melted down every mold and stored the precious stones in bottles of the same color. When finished, he looked over the room carefully, again and again, making certain every item was in its place. There was no mistake; the men coming would be looking for anything that might foretell the future of England. The very symbols he had made would tell the story. That reality made breathing difficult. The traitor in his house must have found the symbols. How anyone could understand what was on the pieces did not matter at this point. It was all beginning.

With dread, Weldon knew he and his daughter would be the main target of the coming attack. The objective would be to retrieve the jeweled pieces with their strange symbols. Symbols he now understood, but chose not to share with anyone, lest innocent people be ensnared. Weldon knew nothing would protect him, but he could protect Nicola and the symbols. Weldon retrieved the pouch from its hiding place and silently slipped into his study, where he tucked it inside of a special nook hidden within his desk—the very place where Nicola had hidden treasures as a small child. Inside the nook were rocks, a feather, a map, and a dried flower. Removing a child's pickings, Weldon pushed the pouch deep within the nook, then replaced the child's items. Back in his chambers, sitting in his chair near the fire, Weldon waited.

His intuition had kept his people safe all these years. Weldon prayed he could do so a while longer. He shared his belief with his men that an attack was coming, but never spoke of what drew the attack. The men went to work, each intent on saving as many people as possible. Families had already been moved outside the castle walls, basic provisions sent along with them. Weldon knew there would be a fight . . . a fight he would lose. Most of the livestock had been moved outside, but for Weldon's prize horses. Not a reason was given to his people behind the moves, for they knew Lord Weldon took care of them and simply did what was asked of them.

Late into the night, Weldon searched his rooms and workroom one last time. There could be nothing left to hint at his last creations. Once more he became a commander, playing every potential scenario over and over in his mind to be certain he had taken every precaution. Only one thing remained. He called for his old friend, the priest of his castle. After giving his last confession, he gave the priest a message for the Guardians. When the time was right, Weldon would pass every bit of information on to his daughter.

CHAPTER 6

THE SOUND OF FOOTSTEPS ECHOED OFF COLD, damp walls, creating an eerie tempo for Nicola's thoughts. Shivering not so much with the chill of the dank dungeon as with fear and dread, she followed a silent guard. Two more guards walked behind her. It did not escape Nicola that she was the only living relative of the man currently held prisoner in his own castle. A feeling of doom overwhelmed her, its presence growing in strength the deeper inside the dungeon they moved.

Nicola understood little of what was happening. The events rolled one onto another so swiftly she could hardly remember what the day was. Foreign men were clearly in control of her home. The invaders wore unfamiliar colors and spoke French so rapidly that she could only pick out a few of the words. Her world had shattered. The events closing in around Nicola left little doubt that she herself might not survive.

After rounding a sharp corner, the lead soldier stopped. The door before them was solid except for an eye-level slit and an opening at the bottom large enough to push a shallow bowl through. When the door opened, creaking with the effort, its formidable thickness was revealed. One small, barred window near the top of the cell allowed a shaft of light to slide across the floor.

"Nicola!" her father's feeble voice called to her as she stepped inside. He weakly limped across the space toward her.

"Father!" Nicola cried, falling into his arms. Arms that were once strong and protective were barely able to grasp her. His beaten, bloody face bore burn marks, and one eye socket was sunken. Numerous oozing wounds were visible on his torso through the ragged remnants of his shirt, and his face was filled with deep sadness. Nicola shuddered when she heard the door behind her slam and the lock secured.

Her father held her tightly—she had never felt as precious to him as she did in this moment. The guard watched briefly through the slit in the door, then turned and walked away. As the sound of his steps faded, her father whispered into her ear, "Listen carefully—do not speak. I am accused of treason. I swear to you that what they say is not true. Quickly, find the packet I've hidden in your special place. Hide it on your person. Hide it well. You must take the larger piece to Henry Tudor, in Brittany. He has to know what is going to happen. The smaller one, deliver to his mother, Lady Margaret. No one can ever know what you carry. Ever! Leave tonight. You have to take Allie. Ride the cliff road, to the falls. Wait for the Guardians there. Go quickly, now, with Allie. Know that I love you, more than my very life, little Nicola." He grasped her tightly one more time. The sounds of the guards returning put an end to any conversation. A guard opened the door and walked toward them. As her father stepped away from Nicola, he told her, "Do what the commander of these men tells you, Nicola. You will be safe with him. Promise me you'll do as I say." Nicola understood that the command, given in the guard's presence, would provide cover for his whispered request.

Her tear-filled eyes met his. "I promise."

The guard spoke hesitantly, looking into Nicola's eyes. "You must leave now." With a shake of his head, as if to brush the image away, he bowed slightly and stood waiting. Nicola kissed her father's bloody cheek. Unable to hold them back any longer, tears escaped down her cheeks.

The guard glanced at her father, then cleared his throat uncomfortably. Weldon simply nodded at Nicola, as he gently pushed her toward the waiting guard.

Nicola walked away from the cell that held all she cared for in the world. When she touched the guard's arm, he started. "Will I see my father tomorrow?" Nicola softly asked. The man could not meet her gaze. His eyes moved to the floor briefly, then fixed upon some invisible point ahead. Without warning, Nicola turned and ran back to her father's cell. "Papa!" she called out.

Her father was on the floor, leaning against the wall. Struggling to stand, he limped to the door. Nicola slipped her fingers through the small observation window. Her father's fingers touched hers for one brief moment before the guard pulled her arm away.

In that instant, Nicola knew she would never see her father again. The pain in her heart made her feel as though she herself might be dying. Breathing suddenly became difficult. Nicola ran. She ran through the dark hall while the guards trotted to keep up.

When she burst through a side door, she found herself in her father's familiar courtyard. Nicola resisted the urge to look around the grounds. *I cannot bear to see this place of refuge turned into a garrison.* For the first time in her life, Nicola felt consumed by fear. Gasping, she stopped. Unable to hold herself together any longer, she leaned against the wall and vomited. The guard stood silently, watching her. "Sir, how long will all these men stay here?" Wiping away the dribble from her mouth, she waved her hand toward the men in the courtyard and the guard.

"All night, m'lady," he responded.

"Thank your lord for allowing me to see Father." She hesitated a moment, before asking, "Will I be allowed to see your lord in the morrow?"

"Yes," the soldier replied. "I am to escort you."

"That is not necessary," Nicola noted coldly. "I grew up in this place. I know my own home." Before he could answer, several soldiers approached with a group of her father's men, shackled and bloodied. While the soldiers were talking, Nicola slipped away and ran inside the ground floor of the castle and up the stairs, taking two at a time.

Reaching her rooms, Nicola nodded to the guard stationed at her door. As she stepped inside, the door was secured behind her. Her entry chamber was deserted, though soft talking could be heard coming from the sleeping area. Nicola hastened to her father's study. As quietly as possible, she stepped to her father's great desk. Sliding her hand into the nook where she once hid a little girl's treasures, she grasped them and then pulled them out. Reaching inside once more, as far as she could, her fingers felt the soft material of a packet. After pulling it out, she quickly secured it beneath the gathers of her gown at her waist. She returned the other objects of an innocent childhood deep within the nook before walking through to her bedchamber.

Only two of her ladies were still anxiously waiting. "You are dismissed." Nicola nodded to the older one. "You may do as you like this evening. Do not be late in the morn. Allie, can you stay a little longer? I do not wish to be alone this night."

"Of course, my lady," Allie readily agreed. Allie was near Nicola's age and had been with Weldon's family for years. Slow to learn, she had quit trying long ago. Instead she filled her days gossiping and entertaining the house staff, frequently finding herself at odds with the man in charge of the staff. Nicola came to her rescue at least weekly.

The older woman grabbed her cloak and followed Nicola to the door. She had been with Nicola's mother and now provided the same shoulder for Nicola whenever she needed it. Nicola hugged her, whispering into her ear, "Do not return to this place. It is not safe. I will be fine." As the door opened, the woman hesitated, then turned away. The guard allowed her to leave.

As soon as the door had been locked from the outside, Nicola slid a safety bar into place on her side of the door. She turned to Allie. "Allie, come quickly, we must leave," Nicola whispered, already pulling a heavy wool cloak over her head and shoulders. Allie stood staring, shaking her head, while Nicola slipped all the coins she kept hidden inside a trinket box into a deep pocket sewn on the inside of her cloak.

"No, Nicola, we must not leave," Allie whispered back. "Just where would you have us go? What are you thinking of doing?" Allie started for the chamber door.

Grasping Allie's arm, Nicola spoke into her ear, the firmness of her resolve comforting even to herself. "Allie, I asked you to be quick about it. We are leaving now."

For a short moment, Allie stood staring at Nicola.

"I do not think I will survive if I stay here," Nicola added.

"Yes, my lady." When Nicola released her arm, Allie pulled one of Nicola's cloaks on and followed her.

"Do not speak until we are away from this place. Just walk calmly by my side. We must do nothing that warrants attention." The two women walked through the study and, in minutes, were moving down a narrow staircase leading from the study to the outside. Nicola led the way toward an old garden shed located near the stables. The few staff left within the castle grounds were packing and departing, unhindered by the soldiers. As Nicola and Allie approached the shed, a man stepped from the shadows and motioned to them. Carefully surveying the courtyard, he led the women behind the shed. Two saddled horses were waiting.

"My lady, stay on the trail; let your horses take you. They know the path well." The man took Nicola's hand in his and kissed it. "You will not return."

"Bless you, Jamie. You are dismissed. Father will no longer need your services. If possible, you should leave this night," Nicola softly replied.

Allie looked back toward the castle. "Nicola," she whispered, "we should not be riding alone. It is not safe. And where will we go?"

"Come, Allie." Nicola left without looking back, riding toward the cliffs that bordered the back of her father's castle. Praying it would stay light a little longer, she turned the horse toward the brush clinging to the cliff edge.

"Nicola, you cannot think to ride this way." Allie hesitated, holding her horse steady. "We will fall onto the rocks below! What is happening to you?"

For several minutes, Nicola was silent. Trusting her horse, she held the reins loosely. Firmly, with confidence she was not feeling, she replied, "Allie, I mean to flee to safety this night. If I stay in my rooms, I will die. I would rather chance dying on the rocks below than die being raped. The men who now live in my father's house are not men of honor. I forfeit my life if I stay. I need you with me, Allie." She started to say more, but the ache in her heart would not let her give voice to what she felt. She knew her father was nearly dead already.

Allie's eyes widened, her lip trembling as she sat frozen, staring at Nicola. Nicola continued, "Just follow me. You are riding Father's horse. He knows the trail well. We must leave now. Please do not leave me alone, Allie. Come quickly." With that, Nicola calmly rode through the brush. Her horse did not hesitate. Allie heeled her horse and the animal walked into the foliage, following Nicola.

The route the animals took was a narrow passage, the trailhead hidden by outcroppings of brush and other vegetation. The brush cover gave one the impression that the edge of the cliff was immediately beyond and dropped straight downward. Her father had taken her down this same trail several times. The first time, she was terrified. Her father had insisted she follow. The trail was safe, and well hidden—the safest escape from the castle, if ever needed. Only a few of his own men knew about it, and they had been killed in the initial attack the day before. With their deaths, the escape route would remain unknown.

Letting her steed slowly pick his way, Nicola kept an attentive eye on the trail. Leaning down to pet her horse's neck, she softly encouraged him. "This is a special ride, my friend. Take care." Silence around the two women was only broken by the sound of their horses and the waves crashing below. Sunlight slowly began to fade. As darkness bled down the cliff face, the trail was slowly engulfed in black. Somehow, she must get Allie and herself to safety before the entire trail was darkened. Nicola prayed. She prayed that the Guardians her father spoke of, whoever they were, would come and she would know them. She prayed her father would die tonight, before the awful men holding him could do more harm.

Nicola glanced back at her friend. Allie had regained her composure and nervously nodded to Nicola. As the sun continued to dip, Nicola grew anxious. *How can we do this in the dark?* To the right, the cliff wall rose upward, fading beyond view. To the left, there was nothing but emptiness, plunging to the shore below, where sharp-edged boulders lay. The howling wind and the waves surging over the rocks were constant reminders of where she and Allie would wind up if their horses stepped off the edge.

As darkness spread across the cliff face, the ride was becoming more dangerous. "Allie, we have to get off. Let the horses walk as they will. If they step wrong, we won't be taken with them." After pulling her horse up, Nicola slipped off to stand at the horse's side. There was little room to stand, and her horse was clearly not comfortable. He tried to move forward. Speaking to him softly, petting him and slowly sliding alongside him, Nicola carefully made her way in front. Loosely holding the reins, she began to descend, again. The horse settled. Allie followed suit, staying close, and they moved steadily downward.

CHAPTER 7

By now, the sun's light just barely grazed the cliff trail. The sound of someone approaching drifted to the women. The narrow trail would not allow anyone to pass. The sound came closer and closer. "Nicola, what do we do now?" Allie whispered hoarsely, frightened. Nicola was frightened too, but there was nothing she could do. Just then, a man's voice came to her. He spoke so softly that she could barely hear him.

"Lady Nicola?"

"Yes?" Nicola answered.

"My name is Lord Keaton. We are the Guardians. We can take you safely the rest of the way." The voice was firm, confident. As he came into view, Nicola could see the man was tall and muscular, and he carried himself with an air of confidence and control. Relief washed over Nicola.

"Who is it?" Allie's voice trembled.

"I do not know, but they have offered to help," Nicola replied. Gladly, she handed the reins to Keaton when he came nearer. He bowed and, with a wave of his hand, sent her ahead. And so they walked, one man in front of Nicola, who was followed by Keaton leading her horse. Allie followed while another man, leading Allie's horse, brought up the rear. Their descent was much faster. The sound of the waterfall that marked the trail's end grew louder and louder, until nothing else could be heard. Following the man ahead of her, Nicola maneuvered behind the cascading water. The party continued farther back, deep into the cavernous tunnel, coming to an area where the sound of crashing water plummeting down the cliff face was not so intense. A fire was already blazing.

Voices bounced off the walls as the man with Nicola's horse called to someone near the fire. In short order, a meal was cooked, everyone had eaten, and sleeping places for the women were prepared. Keaton, though clearly the leader of the Guardians, had only introduced himself. The men had moved closer, some sitting or leaning against the cavern walls.

Allie sat down near the fire. "Nicola," she whispered, "you do not know these men. We should go back, please. Why are we doing this?" Allie looked around fearfully.

Nicola could not eat. She sat in silence, staring at the dancing flames.

When she finally spoke, the sound of her voice filled the cave. "I do not understand any of this. However, I am certain I would not be allowed to live, Allie. I am afraid of the men in my father's house." Nicola looked at Allie, then back at the fire. "I saw my father. It was awful. He had been tortured, horribly." Nicola shuddered at the picture embedded in her mind.

"He could not have been tortured. No, you're wrong," Allie insisted, no longer whispering, her face anxious. "He was not tortured!"

Keaton whirled around toward Allie, but she was watching Nicola.

"Allie, I saw him. His face was bruised and bloody. He could open only one eye and he had burns all over. I could see other places on his body where he was beaten severely. He could hardly walk. He *had* been tortured." Tears slowly made their way down Nicola's cheeks.

"No!" Allie stood up, her voice rising and bouncing off the rock walls. "That can't be. They promised he would not be harmed."

"Allie, I saw him. I . . . saw . . ." Nicola's voice faded, her head jerking up. The cave was silent but for the sound of the water in the background. Every eye was on her.

Nicola recoiled. Her voice incredulous, she responded, "They *promised*, Allie? They *promised*? You knew these people? You knew this was going to happen? They are going to kill my father, Allie! You knew it?" Nicola lunged at Allie, grasping her shoulders, shaking her and crying. "*You* are a traitor living in Father's house. You! You were my best friend! How could you do such a thing?"

"You were always his favorite!" Allie burst out, desperately struggling to break away.

"I am his daughter, Allie. His *daughter*!" Nicola shouted.

"You think you are his only daughter?" Allie snapped.

"What are you saying?" Releasing Allie, Nicola pulled back.

"I am saying what you already know, if you look in your heart," Allie said with satisfaction as she straightened up. She smiled coldly at Nicola. "You *know*."

Nicola advanced upon Allie and slapped her, as hard as she could. As Allie staggered backward, Nicola pressed forward and slapped her again. One of the men stepped between them. He held Allie while another pulled Nicola away. Nicola struggled to get at Allie. Unable to break free, she clung to the man's arm, glaring at Allie. "That makes what you did even worse," Nicola responded. "You had your own father tortured and killed! You are dead to me, Allie. Dead. I never want to see you again. Do you hear me? Never!"

Allie collapsed onto the ground, sobbing, and Nicola turned away without looking back, even when Allie crawled toward her, her desperation evident. "Nicola, please," she begged, and Nicola, by then, could not resist looking at her. One of the men was grasping her shoulder, holding her back.

"Stay away from me," Nicola said flatly. Turning, she ran toward the horses, her only thought to get as far away from Allie as she could.

Keaton stepped in front of her. "Lady Nicola! Stop!"

"Leave me be. I will not stay in the same space as her." She tried to shove the man aside.

Keaton stood strong, refusing to allow her to pass. "You have no knowledge of where you might go. Men are searching for you as we speak. It is far too dangerous for you to leave. You will wait until daybreak. It is black outside." His voice was firm.

"It is black in here also," Nicola responded, glowering at the man.

Ignoring her, he continued, "You must wait. You will remain here this night." It was clear Keaton had no intention of allowing her to leave. The only sounds in the cavern were the waterfall and Allie's sobs. Nicola could not stand to look at her. The betrayal was too cruel.

Despite her distress, Nicola had noticed one man, standing out of the light from the campfire, watching the drama unfold. He watched Allie, whom Nicola had seen look repeatedly to Keaton. Nicola could see the unease written on Keaton's face. What worried him so? What did he know that she didn't?

Allie had stopped crying. She sat hugging her knees, swaying back and forth. Around her an aura of finality swirled. Her sleeping pad was moved near the falls, away from Nicola. Another of Keaton's men sat close to Allie. Nicola returned to the fire and sank down against the cold rock wall. Keaton squatted down in front of her. "You haven't eaten, lady?"

"I have no appetite." Nicola's voice was flat. She felt only numbness.

"Lady Nicola," Lord Keaton said quietly, "you have a very long road before you. That same road lies ahead of each of these men. You cannot think to quit. This was a terrible day for you. There will be others. Remember, you do what your father asked—for your father, for us, and for so many more."

Nicola sat staring at her hands. When she spoke, it was with a calmer voice. "I must trust you and your men. My father did. You call me by name, Lord Keaton. Who are these men?"

"We are the Guardians, at your service," Keaton replied. Short, wavy black hair grazed the collar of his tunic. His mustache and beard were well trimmed. Light brown eyes watched her as she studied him. His speech, expression, and conduct spoke of education and polish. He was very unlike the soldiers who manned her father's castle. Slowly, his eyes narrowed. "At your service," he restated.

A feeling of uneasiness brushed Nicola. The urge to escape that sensation made her look away. She glanced around at the others. "All of you are Guardians?" Nicola asked. She needed to break the moment.

"Yes, every one of us." He continued to watch her closely. "There are others," he added casually.

Lord Keaton sat down next to Nicola, stretching out his long legs and leaning back. "By the time you saw your father, I believe he knew Allie was the traitor who provided valuable information to the men who overtook your home. Information such as how many men would defend the castle."

Another wave of anger over Allie's betrayal rushed through her. That betrayal had unimaginable consequences. Nicola's father was dead, most of his soldiers were dead, and the people living around his castle were most likely in danger because of the accusations leveled against her father. Her home and all its lands would be confiscated by the crown, in King Edward's name. All because Allie told lies about her father to someone. Her tales painted Weldon as a traitor. Nicola realized that she herself was a fugitive riding with men she neither knew nor trusted. Allie had destroyed all Nicola held dear. Nicola sighed and leaned her head back against the rock. It felt strong. *So much stronger than I.* "Father insisted I bring Allie." Nicola shook her head. "His heart surely broke, if he knew she had betrayed him."

"I imagine so," Lord Keaton offered.

"But why would he want her to be safe?" Nicola blurted out. "He insisted I take her with me." Her voice was bitter.

"He was not concerned about her safety," Keaton replied simply. "He wanted her out of his house to be certain she did not endanger anyone else." Lord Keaton paused for a moment. "You must understand how someone like Allie thinks. Once they have a taste of the attention they receive, they are just as likely to make things up, to keep the feeling alive . . . to feel important. She could not know that once they had gotten all they needed from her, they would dispose of her. They would never leave anyone alive who might tell others of the atrocities committed against Lord Weldon. One reason why you are no longer safe."

"I will not have her with me," Nicola said with finality. Closing her eyes, she tried to remember every detail of the day leading up to the attack. When men first invaded her father's castle, she was outside with Allie and the rest of her ladies. Thinking back on the scene, Nicola became conscious of the fact that Allie had not appeared surprised or concerned.

Nicola, on the other hand, had darted into the castle, running to her father. She had found him in his study. He had already ordered the castle secured, with guards positioned at the living quarters and his staff moved to a safe house. Cloaked in unfamiliar feelings of danger and a pending battle, Nicola had not voiced her fear. There was no time to talk. She had simply followed her father's order to return to her chambers and secure the door. From there, she had listened to the sounds of fighting. It seemed to go on forever, until suddenly it became quiet.

Now, staring at a dying fire through a long night, Nicola struggled to understand how her father could have had so much done, unless he too knew the men were coming. *Why did we not leave if he knew they were coming?* So many questions whirled in her mind. *How did Father know about Allie's betrayal?* As of yet, she still had not been able to even look at what she carried tucked away in the folds of her clothing. Questions without answers. Her thoughts kept returning to Allie. Was it possible to hate someone she once loved? Knowing her father was the victim of a betrayal crushed any feelings of sympathy for her childhood friend. Nicola could not think of Allie without seeing her beloved father. Nicola heard the rumors her father had once "wandered afield"—as the lady cleaning the kitchen described it. Until tonight, Nicola had given the tale no credence. *Allie had betrayed her own father, if the tale was true.* The very thought was revolting. Worse, who might Allie's mother be? Was she a traitor, too? Nicola knew Keaton was right when he told her Allie would probably be killed after it was clear she had lied about Lord Weldon. Just the thought of her father brought his image to Nicola again. Beaten, dying, holding her for the last time. Nicola could never forgive Allie's treachery, and just like that, she pushed Allie from her mind and heart, forever.

Nicola wanted desperately to talk to her father. Too late for that now.

With dawn's first hint of light, Nicola was up and pacing. No closer to understanding everything that had happened, Nicola felt a chill of isolation. She was at the mercy of these men. Knowing her father had trusted them gave her little comfort. She could not shake the feeling of danger the men seemed to evoke. Something was amiss.

She needed to find someplace quiet and safe to think. There had to be someone who could tell her what had now begun, someone to explain this burden. Nicola wanted to talk to Lord Keaton, but something she could not explain stopped her. Some feeling like nothing she had ever experienced. It was as if she had suddenly taken a black shroud to cover herself. Nicola knew she should look at what her father had given her. Even if privacy were hers, she could not bring herself to do so. Not yet.

HIS MEN WERE SOON STIRRING, GOING ABOUT the business of breaking fast, closing the camp, and making haste to travel. Lord Keaton knew what must be done before the cavern was left empty. He did not relish the idea. To have even one person aware of Nicola's escape with supposed protectors would put everything in jeopardy. Nicola could not be allowed to complete her mission, whatever that was. He could not risk her rescue. He knew she must be protected until he knew what her mission was, exactly.

At the beginning of this undertaking, he had chosen each of the men currently traveling with him for a particular reason. Not all were men he would trust with his life—he chose them because of the skills they possessed. Still, he was quite certain none of them had ever been asked to do what he would soon ask of them.

He glanced back at Allie. Her eyes followed him, begging for mercy. Nicola was already up and ready to leave. She stood by her horse, leaning into him, her eyes closed. *Best get on with it*, Keaton thought. He instructed one of his men to begin moving out with Nicola. Nicola was helped onto her horse. She rode out without looking back.

Allie tried to call to Nicola, but she was quickly silenced. Her head lolled forward as her body collapsed onto the cavern floor. "Hide the body. We cannot have anyone know of this," Keaton ordered. He was about to walk away when one of his men, Garrett, stopped him. Garrett had blonde hair and blue eyes. His face was covered with a full beard, trimmed close to his chin. A skilled swordsman, Garrett, Keaton knew, was the sort who fought for the highest bidder, never caring for causes. Money allowed him to live the flamboyant life he loved, a life the low station of his birth would not have allowed. He eyed Nicola as he spoke to Keaton.

"The time that lies ahead of us is dark. It calls for men of some conviction. You and each of us with you are such men. You, sir, command what must be done to see this thing completed. It is quite clear Lady Nicola knows nothing of what she is now a part of. Our job has grown much harder."

For a moment, there was silence. Sir Keaton nodded, watching Nicola ride away. Garrett turned to assist with the disposal of the body, but it was already gone. Thus far, Garrett had always carefully avoided any of the unpleasantness that came with working for Keaton. When a second man walked toward him, Garrett refused to acknowledge him and simply changed course toward the horses, avoiding the man.

It was obvious to Keaton that this man, named Drue, cared little for Garrett and took no notice of him. He walked to his horse without speaking. Drue was the latest addition to the group Keaton had put together, and as yet he had not been accepted by the others. Unlike the rest of the men, Drue seldom joined in fireside chatter. He preferred to stay to himself, sitting or standing at a distance, listening. Keaton had taken him on only because of his keen knowledge of the land. He needed someone with that knowledge, as his men would be traveling much of the time under cover of darkness. This country was not their home.

Keaton easily caught up with Nicola's group and they rode in silence for several hours. Nicola turned once to look behind them. No doubt looking for Allie, although she made no comment. From Nicola's outburst, Keaton knew Nicola's anger and pain was such that she now had little regard for Allie.

"When we stop for the night, will we be in a safe place?" Nicola asked when he rode up next to her.

"Yes, my lady. We are going to ride for a long time this day, but when we stop, we will be at a safe estate, unknown to any but the men you have with you. There, you may rest without worry of danger. I know you must be tired."

"Some," Nicola answered. "I rather believe I need time to think, more than sleep. I would speak with you; I have a great many questions."

"Of course," he replied. "When we stop and you have rested. We will have time then."

Perhaps Garrett was right. Maybe Nicola knew nothing of what her father was rumored to have done. If this was the case, what would he do with her? In truth, he did not fancy the answer.

CHAPTER 8

L AREAU WAS PLEASED WITH HOW THE BAND of Frenchmen in his charge overran Weldon Castle. It had been easy. Lareau was tall and tough-looking, seldom smiled, and kept his brown hair tied neatly at the back of his head. Having spent his career in the service of France, he found each mission was different from the next. However, now France wanted him to work for the Duchess of Burgundy, who happened to be King Edward's sister. The duchess intended to dredge up proof that Lord Weldon and his daughter were working to put Henry Tudor on the throne. If that proof were found and exposed, it could put legitimacy to Tudor's claim. None of those things mattered to Lareau, as long as what he did was for France, and for the money. This mission promised to be little trouble, thanks to the information received from a spy recruited from within the household of Lord Weldon. All that remained was to determine exactly what it was that Weldon knew. That was proving much more difficult than he had imagined.

In the morning following the initial invasion, Lord Lareau was breaking fast. For a change, he had slept well. Lareau planned to put the whole mess behind him as soon as possible. The spy had been easy enough to recruit, as soon as she was approached by the man Lareau sent. Lord Weldon himself had proved much stronger than anticipated, refusing to talk even after intense and cruel torturing. Clearly, he would not talk, but it also did not look like he would live much longer, and that fact would necessitate using the daughter. *We shall see how he holds out once he sees his daughter in pain. Not a thing I care to do, but we need to know what he knows and from where he got the information.*

Lareau closed his eyes, thinking. *By this evening, I should have what I need. The spy will have to disappear, as will Weldon's daughter. With Weldon and his daughter dead, I could have a stronghold in this castle. And France will have a location to stay on English soil, unknown to Edward. Perfect.* As yet, Lord Lareau had not seen the daughter. It was time. After finishing up his meal, he stood and headed for the dungeon.

One of his guards met him at the door leading into the dungeon depths. "Your prisoner is dead," the man informed Lareau quietly.

Lareau frowned. "Dead." *This moves everything forward. I have to find out what the girl knows.* "Take Lady Weldon below. Hold her there." With a second plan in mind, he strode toward Weldon's study. There were still mounds of papers to review. Maybe, just maybe, Lareau would not need the daughter after all. She would just conveniently disappear.

A knock at the door of the study startled him. He had lost all track of time. Glancing at the window, he was surprised to see it was already midday. "Yes?" Lareau stood and stretched his back. Digging through mounds of paper was not a familiar task.

His captain entered. Without preamble, he announced, "There is an issue, my lord. The Lady Nicola and Lady Allie have both gone missing. Our men have helped themselves to the horses, so I cannot discern if they have departed on horseback or on foot."

Lareau sank back down into the chair. This was a catastrophe. "Find them! Question everyone. Is that clear?"

"Of course. I have already begun." The man turned and left Lareau alone. Suddenly, the day turned dark. Lareau had no more information now than he did when he overran Weldon Castle. His whole purpose was to get information to the Duchess of Burgundy. For the first time in his colorful career, he had failed—unless he could find the two missing women. *Rumors, it's just rumors. That old man was no visionary. But why would the daughter run? And with Lady Allie?*

Lareau made his way to the daughter's rooms. The furnishings were modest but well cared for. A quick glance at the armoire gave no indication of missing clothing. In fact, he found the trunk to be full, and several travel bags were neatly stacked next to it. Nothing in the room gave the impression of a planned trip, or any trip, for that matter. Carefully, he began to search the rooms. He found her small box of jewelry—in it were some rings and bracelets and a gold chain. Although they were not expensive pieces, they were beautifully made. He was tempted to take them but set them back in place. Lareau knew there would be others taking the castle. It must appear undisturbed. Cursing, he slammed the doors closed and left the room as he found it.

CHAPTER 9

Lord Keaton took Nicola deep into the forest. Late evening found her entering a small, well-hidden castle. Its walls, gates, and every other detail appeared to be built with defense in mind, rather than comfort, but that gave her a welcome sense of safety and security.

Nicola followed Lord Keaton up several flights of stairs to a modest room. The door had two metal bars that could be slid into place, securing it from inside. From a narrow window, one could see the grounds below. A few candles and a fireplace provided light and heat, and a sturdy bed nearly filled the space. It was covered with a bulky padded mattress, heavy blankets, and pillows. Dense rugs covered the floors and walls to keep out the cold from the thick stone walls and floor. A small chest and one chair took up the remaining space. A door on one wall led to a tiny privy.

"There will always be one of us near," Lord Keaton explained as he and Nicola entered the room. "Only my men and I know you left your home. I would like to keep it that way. There are no women here to assist you. I have sent for a bed gown. In the next several days, we will have more gowns."

"Which of your men wear gowns?" Nicola asked as she casually glanced around. "That is . . . if my presence is to go unnoticed?"

Lord Keaton smiled. "I have one man who likes to buy gowns for his ladies. Some of the gowns will come to you. Easy. We will dine soon. Until then, try to rest. Is there anything else you might need?"

"No," Nicola replied. "Thank you for your care and kindness, Lord Keaton."

"It is my pleasure, Lady Nicola." Keaton bowed as he backed out of the room.

With the closing of the door, Nicola slid the security bars into place and immediately began searching every inch of furniture to find a hiding place for the small bundle hidden beneath her gown. She finally found a loose board on the underside of the chest. Gently, she pulled her dusty, crumpled gown off. Safely nestled at her waist was the wad of cloth she had tied in place. Hearing footsteps outside her door, she resisted the urge to examine the bundle and instead hurriedly tucked it under the loose board and pushed the board back up. Although the door was secured from within, Nicola knew she would be expected to open it quickly, should someone knock. The footsteps passed, while Nicola rushed to pull her gown on again. She waited several moments, listening. Again, steps could be heard passing her door. When all was quiet, she lifted the lid on the empty chest and was relieved to see the base was intact. Her little bundle would not be visible to anyone looking inside the chest.

Exhausted, Nicola lay on the bed, trying to make sense of the past two days. When she closed her eyes, she saw her father. She could still hear the urgency of his whispers and see the mess someone made of him. He would not have remained alive, if he had given them what they searched for, that which he had given her. It must be important. The men with her now were all soldiers, serious and dedicated to some cause she knew little about as of yet. Since she was unable to look at what her father had given her or understand the events that engulfed her, her mind felt scrambled. Her father had been tortured. She knew in her heart that he was already dead. But why would he put a child in harm's way? How could she continue with whatever job was thrust upon her? The heavy feeling of danger still clung to her. Eventually, fatigue took over and she slept.

Persistent knocking at her door awakened Nicola. For a moment, she looked about groggily. Lord Keaton's voice called to her through the door, and she stumbled to it and opened it. "Forgive me," she said. "I must have fallen asleep." Trying to focus, she looked into the face of the man who now had her life in his hands.

"You rested. I'm certain you needed it, lady, but you must eat something. Come. Join us downstairs. It is warm and you are welcome there." He nodded slightly, holding the door open. When Nicola hesitated, he gently nudged her, "You should know the men who would serve you, lady. They should know for whom they ride." Keaton reached forward to brush Nicola's hair back. She resisted the urge to lean away from him. Instead, Nicola stepped into the hall.

Lord Keaton followed her down the stairs and into a larger room that functioned as a meeting hall and dining room. The light from candle sconces mounted on the walls and from the flames of a large fireplace made the area comfortable. That feeling did not extend to Nicola. She felt humiliated by her appearance and ducked her head in order to smooth her hair. When she looked up, the men were watching her in silence. Her cheeks felt flush—there was nothing to say.

"Fear not, lady, we have seen much worse, though none prettier," one man boldly spoke up. Most of the men nodded in agreement, trying to encourage the young woman who was now the focus of their mission.

"I doubt that," Nicola responded, with a forced smile. "But I thank you for your kind words. It would seem I have intruded into your world. One that had not the issues women bring with them, I feel."

At this, several men nodded in friendly agreement. Another man stood, gesturing at the hearth. "Come, sit by the fire and eat with us. We shall all become great friends, I am certain." He grinned at Nicola. "I am called Harding." Harding was redheaded, green-eyed, and dimpled. Average-sized, he too was dressed like a soldier. In fact, every man in the room looked capable of fighting, and fighting well. She had not examined the men in the beginning. The darkness and Allie's horrible tale had filled her mind. Seeing Harding's easy smile made Nicola feel more at ease. She vaguely remembered him sitting near the fire when she first entered the cave. Grateful for the welcome he extended, she managed a half smile. Someone handed her a bowl filled with chunks of meat, and someone else handed her a piece of bread. Nicola tried but could eat very little. The cool wine she drank on an empty stomach began to dull her senses quickly. Barely able to stay awake, she slowly stood and looked around to find Keaton standing off to one side, speaking with one of the men.

"Lord Keaton, please excuse me—I wish to return to my room." With a few quick steps, he was at Nicola's side. "I must rest," she added apologetically.

"Of course, lady. Come." He took her elbow and escorted Nicola to her room. Inside, a small tub sat in front of the fire. The water in it was barely warm, but to Nicola it did not matter. "Lock the door, lady. Sleep well and long. There will be time to talk in the afternoon. If you have need of anything, simply ask any of the men in this place. Rest, Nicola. You need to rest. Bar the door as soon as I leave." Bowing, he left.

Nicola closed and secured the door. When he had gone, she felt relief. Her hair and gown were a mess, and the horrors of the last days were etched upon her. There was a package lying on the bed. Inside it, she found a bed gown and robe. Once she was bathed and dry, she pulled the bed gown on, slid beneath the covers, and slept.

Sounds of activity outside Nicola's bedchamber were muted by the thickness of the walls and coverings. When she finally woke up, the darkness surrounding her told her it was still night. Taking care to move quietly, she visited the privy, then returned to bed. She tried to sleep again, but thirst would not allow it. Wrapping the robe loosely around her, she tiptoed to the door and gently slid the bars aside, slowly opening the door to find Harding and Garrett walking past. The sun cast a soft glow on the first-floor level of the castle, as it began its slow journey toward darkness. "Is the day nearly past?" Nicola blurted out. "I slept all day."

"You slept because you needed rest. Simple." Garrett's accent gave hints of his Irish background.

Nicola's father frequently admonished her to be attentive. "Look around carefully, child. You must see and feel every detail." It had become a habit. Just now, standing with Garrett and Harding, Nicola had a feeling she could not explain. She felt she had misread their friendliness toward each other that first night. None of the men really knew one another very well. *They are the Guardians, of what, I am not certain. Father, what have you done to me?*

Harding smiled at her. "Come, you must be quite hungry." Not waiting for any response from Nicola, he took her arm and all three walked to the main hall. To her relief, the hall was empty. Harding left Nicola sitting at a table. When he returned, he brought with him wine, fresh bread, and a bowl of thick stew with chunks of meat and vegetables. Its aroma made Nicola's mouth water. This time she ate.

Garrett stayed with her, while Harding left in search of Keaton. While she ate, Garrett talked about the castle's structure. The castle and thick forest surrounding it were all that remained of a large estate. They were east of Weldon Castle. "This castle has an unusual feel, rather like a dungeon," Nicola observed. A slight shudder passed through her. A picture of her father as she saw him that last night flashed through her mind.

"'Tis not anything like that, lady," Garrett quickly corrected her. "This place was built to withstand any attempt to overtake the castle, and to protect those within these walls." He sat watching Nicola eat. "This all must feel very frightening to you, Lady Nicola."

Nicola looked at Garrett before allowing her eyes to wander the room. "Not frightened, my lord. Confused." Keaton and Harding entered as Nicola pushed her empty bowl aside.

"Lady Nicola, how nice to see you this afternoon," Keaton said, smiling, as he surveyed Nicola. Still dressed in a sleep gown and robe, she found herself blushing deeply at his attention.

"I believed it was still night when I awoke, Lord Keaton," she tried to explain.

"Come, I will take you back and you can dress," he added quickly, "unless you find your present attire quite sufficient."

Nicola's eyes narrowed. "You are mocking me, Lord Keaton." With that, she stood and walked away. She moved quickly up the stairway, forcing Keaton to walk faster to catch up with her.

"I am moving you, lady, to a larger room with more window light." His comments were curt. He opened the door for her and bowed. Without further comment, he turned and walked away.

Nicola's temper was still raw. In the space of a few minutes, she had understood she was essentially a captive, for now. Another package lay on her bed. Inside there were two gowns and a shawl, elegant and finely made. Included in the package were underclothes and stockings. *Well done, Keaton. But why are you moving me?* Nicola could not shake the feeling that she was in danger. She dressed quickly, then left the bedchamber in search of

Keaton. As she pulled the door closed behind her, Nicola promised herself she would explore every inch of the castle just in case she found it necessary to hide. *Lord Keaton tells me I am safe here. Yet . . . I once believed father's castle was safe.*

CHAPTER 10

After descending the stairs as quietly as possible, Nicola paused a moment before entering the dining hall. There was no one about. She walked the perimeter, trying several doors. A low hum of voices came from beyond one door. Carefully, she opened it, glanced behind her, then calmly stepped into the room. She stopped immediately. Garrett and two other men were sitting around a table laden with papers. Talking ceased and all eyes shifted to her.

Nicola spoke first. "I beg your pardon, Sir Garrett. I was to meet Lord Keaton, but I am not able to find him."

She turned to leave, but Garrett's voice stopped her. "Wait, Lady Nicola. You have been and will continue to be assisted by these men—it is time you knew their names." Nicola felt Garrett's disapproval and had no desire to give him cause to distrust her further. Though she felt an intense wish to vacate the room, she understood that it would be better to know the men causing her unrest.

"Certainly, my lord." She turned back toward the men, now all standing.

Garrett nodded toward the man on his right. "You have already met Lord Harding."

Harding nodded to Nicola. As before, his green eyes spoke of mischief and his smile was warm, welcoming. "Lady." Nicola smiled back.

Next, Garrett introduced Drue. Nicola remembered Drue. Drue was darker, with black eyes. His black hair was cut short and graying at the temples. He stepped closer without making a sound. His movements were fluid, calculating. He nodded and spoke, "At your service, Lady Nicola." His voice was quiet, without emotion. Nicola felt a chill run up her spine. *This man answers to no man or cause. He looks dangerous.*

Across the room, Garrett pointed to where a fourth man stood, slightly apart from the other three. "This is Lord Carnell." Carnell was the shortest of the men. He had scraggly dark auburn hair that stood out all over his head in disarray. He stepped up, stood closely, and spoke. His voice was quiet, his manner easy. Deep blue eyes looked into Nicola's dark eyes. "Welcome, lady. Your father spoke highly of you."

I doubt that you knew him—the thought flashed through her mind. Surrounded by men she barely knew, Nicola felt intimidated, but she was determined they would not know. They must see her as strong, able to take on whatever it was her father expected her to do. "I know I have much to learn, but I trust those around me to assist me. My father was a gentle man, a gifted craftsman, and fearless knight. In his honor, I promise to represent him well." When she had finished speaking, she could see no change in any face, not even Garrett's. She curtsied, then left the room, closing the door behind her. Only time could prove her worthiness to these men, or, of more concern, their worthiness to her.

Outside the room, taking a deep breath, she leaned against the wall. She could hear the hum of voices beyond the door pick up. *Comparing opinions, I am certain. Well, with Lord Keaton, that makes five. Five men to keep me safe. Time will surely tell whether they do so or not.*

Nicola continued exploring the castle. She found the kitchen, a large supply room, and, to her surprise, a well-stocked wine cellar. She also found a study with two bookcases. There were books on other countries and their leaders, maps of various countries, and a Bible written in Latin.

The halls were still silent and empty when Nicola climbed the stairs. She opened every unsecured door. She found where the men slept, two to a room. She discovered a room of weapons. She found a room set up for only one occupant and recognized it as Lord Keaton's by the clothes hanging about.

The last room she tried was locked. Nicola was wandering back toward her own room when she heard Keaton's voice downstairs. She hurried to her room, slipped inside, and waited, listening. Eventually, she heard people coming up the stairs. She was sitting in the chair when Keaton knocked on her door. "Nicola?" he said.

"Yes." Nicola walked to the door and opened it.

Keaton, Harding, and Carnell were standing outside. "We are moving you now. Come, I will show you where you will be staying. The furniture will be more comfortable, I think." He started to walk away.

"If it pleases you, Lord Keaton," Nicola stopped him, "I would prefer to pack my own clothes. There are not many, as you know, but it would seem more . . . well, more proper if I moved my own gowns and other clothing."

"Of course, lady. I did not think. Please, let me show you where you will be, and we will wait downstairs until you are finished." Keaton then led her to the one door that was locked. When he unlocked it, the door opened to a sizable room, with a large window near one corner. By the window was a small table and two chairs. The fireplace was in the center of the wall, and an ornate armoire sat farther along the wall at the next corner. The bed was the same as in her previous room and stood opposite the fireplace. The floor and open walls were covered as well. A larger privy was located at the end of a short hall from inside the room.

Nicola stood silently, surveying the space. She finally turned to Keaton. "This is far more than my needs require. It is beautiful. Thank you, Lord Keaton."

He smiled. "For certain." He looked around the area with satisfaction. "Now, Nicola, just come for us when you have finished."

Nicola returned to the first room, again placed the pouch with her father's jewelry at her waist, and began to remove the gowns from the little chest. Laden with her gowns, she made the short trip to her new room. Fearing someone might return before she could hide it, Nicola kept the pouch with her. She rejoined the men downstairs.

Following her, they went upstairs and rearranged the new room to include another chair and table. Wood was neatly stacked near the fireplace, candles were set in each sconce, and two rugs were added to the floor, covering it completely.

"I appreciate all you have done to make me comfortable. You should know, I need little and complain less. I will not be a burden." She made her sincerity known to them. Even Garrett smiled slightly.

"There are still a few hours of daylight, lady. Come walk with me, and let us talk. It is time." Lord Keaton stood at the door of her room as the men began to file out.

"You did not look far enough, lady. When next you explore, let me know," Garrett whispered as he passed her. Shocked, Nicola watched him walk away. *Did he see me? He knew where I looked. I must take care with Sir Garrett.*

Keaton walked with Nicola around the grounds of the castle, talking about his men. "I hope that you will feel comfortable enough to share what your father must have shared with you," he said at one point. "The more we know, the better we can protect you." He casually asked Nicola questions as they walked. She knew much about King Edward's fight to gain the crown, including the rumors of the death of King Henry VI. However, she knew very little about Lady Margaret and Henry Tudor, and she told Keaton as much.

"Your father has shared with you more than I thought he would have," Keaton said gently. "He must have trusted your discretion and intellect. But I wish we knew a little bit more of what his plans were for you, specifically." When Nicola remained quiet, he began to talk about the throne and the perils of occupying such a station. He spoke of the years of unrest, bitter fighting, and great loss of life over the throne. All the while, Nicola listened, trying to see how anything her father might have done could have impacted what Keaton was telling her. She could not make any solid connections.

As dusk threatened, Keaton escorted Nicola to her room. Once alone, Nicola began searching for a new place to hide her father's pouch. This room was furnished with heavy, well-made furniture. None had loose boards that could be pried away—nor were there loose stones near the fireplace. Looking around the room again, she realized the desk was just like her father's. She remembered how his desk had a wide space between the central drawer and the back of the desk. Pulling the drawer out, she smiled when her fingers touched the ledge meant to support a longer drawer, just like her father's. Perfect, with just enough room for the small pouch. Relieved, Nicola stuffed it inside the space and replaced the drawer. This time though, she could not just walk away.

After checking the security bar on her door, she returned to the desk. For several minutes, she stood staring at the desk, hesitating. Taking a breath, she pulled the pouch out and opened it. Two pieces lay in her hand. The larger was meant for Henry Tudor. The second was smaller, meant for Lady

Margaret. Studying the symbols, Nicola frowned. *Black, gold, and brass. An oak leaf and a herder's staff—what can that mean?* The message of the etching and stones made no sense, and the warning on the symbols evaded her. She did not understand what it all meant, but she knew someone who would. *The crone would know. I must get to her.*

Fearful someone might come knocking, she replaced the pieces and tucked the bundle back into its hiding place.

CHAPTER 11

*T*HE SUN WAS JUST RISING WHEN NICOLA woke up. She intended to go downstairs before someone came for her. Once dressed, she took a deep breath, opened the door, and stepped into the hall. Sounds of activity drifted through closed doors along the hall. She reached the lower level, where the light and smells coming from the kitchen drew her forward. She walked into the area to find Harding busily preparing the morning meal. He smiled with surprise when he saw her. "Hungry, are you?" he said cheerfully, waving to the pans already set out. "Help yourself."

To her surprise, the table was laden with eggs, a grain cereal, cheeses, cooked fish, and fresh bread with butter. Wine and cider completed the menu. Harding grinned affably. "We move around a lot. Learning to cook is part of learning to survive." With that, he handed her a platter and returned to his fire.

Nicola took bits of all offered, poured a small tin of cider, and headed for the great room. Choosing a seat farthest from the head, Nicola sat down. When all were present, she heard Keaton speak to Drue, who sat to his left, spooning eggs into his mouth. "Drue," he said, "I will need you to ride to the blacksmith south of here. He has a package for me. Pick up anything else you think we might need." Nicola was curious as to what might be in the package but gave no indication she heard or cared what was said. The talk moved to politics. Nicola quietly finished eating, gathered her dishes, and walked to the kitchen to clean them. She returned to her room. It was tempting to look at the symbols again, but fear of discovery held her back.

Nicola stood at the window in her room as morning faded, watching the courtyard below. It was now near midday. She watched as Keaton and another of his men walked away toward the stables, their heads close together. Keaton seemed to be arguing with his companion. Earlier she had heard him send Lord Drue to retrieve a parcel, and, to her knowledge, he still had not returned. That meant three of the men had kept themselves busy. For the past several days, Garrett and Carnell had spent afternoons in the courtyard, practicing with their weapons. The castle had no staff. *I should look around again. Something is very wrong with this place. There is no one here. Only me and these men. No servants, no staff? Why?* Opening her door, Nicola listened. Silence filled the dark halls. She hesitated but a second before slipping downstairs.

Nicola wandered through the kitchen and storeroom. Nothing had changed. She next entered the dining hall. She knew that room well. Without stopping, she headed toward a smaller room off to one side of the hall. She had been unable to open that door when she tried before. Today, the door was cracked open. There was no sound coming from inside. Looking cautiously around behind her, Nicola pushed open the door and stepped inside. She had already tiptoed deep into the room when she saw Garrett and Drue. Drue was leaning over Garrett's lifeless body, which was slumped against the wall. Nicola gasped, and Drue spun around to find her staring at him. "Nicola, come here," he ordered, straightening himself up.

Terrified, Nicola began to back away slowly, step-by-step, keeping her eyes on Drue. She kept her hand over her mouth to silence a scream as she continued to back away. Drue walked slowly toward her, wiping his hands on a cloth tied around his waist. "Nicola," Drue spoke again as he continued to move toward her, "come here."

Bumping into the door, Nicola whirled around and fled. She reached the stairs and, grasping her skirts, ran up them, two at a time. She burst into her room, slammed the door, and slid the lock bar in place. She was trapped. Fear sucked the breath from her. Standing as far from the door as possible, she waited. Minutes passed, but no one knocked on her door. Gradually, her breathing slowed. The fear stayed. *What has Drue done? I fear he killed Garrett. What kind of men are these Guardians?* Nicola heard the footsteps come to her door and someone calling to Drue from down below. There was no mistaking the sense of gravity from the caller. *The body is found. I have to leave this place. I am in danger.* She sank onto a chair near the window, trembling. *Why would Drue kill one of his own? I could be the next. As soon as it is dark . . .*

Nicola realized she was truly alone. Alone and certainly without protection.

HAVING RETURNED TO THE CASTLE, Keaton walked upstairs to escort Nicola downstairs to eat. For Keaton, Nicola was an enigma. It gnawed at him. Her father had proven to be innocent of any wrongdoing, but something about her escape from Weldon Castle at her father's command combined with her occasional demeanor sat wrong. He was reasonably certain she knew nothing about the storm brewing around the throne, yet she seemed set on doing whatever she was asked by her father to do. Worse, she had seen his men and Lareau's men. She was a problem that needed to be removed. Keaton would have to take advantage of the first opportunity, the sooner the better. He stopped at Nicola's door, his hand raised to knock, when someone called for him from downstairs. The urgency in the voice made Keaton hesitate. He turned and then headed for for the dining hall below.

Downstairs, Keaton found Carnell at the door of the room beyond the dining hall. Carnell stood to one side. Slumped against a wall was Garrett's body. His eyes, wide as if in disbelief, stared back at them. Keaton frowned. He glanced at Carnell. "What happened?" Garrett was the only man among them who could speak to the court of Richard. He had fought for Richard, and Richard would never forget him. But they had lost that link.

Carnell shook his head. "He did not show at the corral. I looked for him and found him like this, just now. I heard nothing, nor did anyone come from the room. There is no blood, no signs of a fight. It is as if he just fell back and died. He is not even cold yet." Carnell looked back at the body.

"I would say he was poisoned," Keaton announced grimly. "Gather everyone! Here. Now!"

"Drue is not back yet," Carnell reminded Keaton.

"Then get Harding." After looking over the room again and finding nothing amiss, Keaton strode out, taking the stairs several at a time.

Keaton pounded on Nicola's door. She cracked it immediately. Before she could speak, Keaton pushed his way inside the room. He made a quick search of the room and found nothing unusual. Nicola watched him, frowning. She intended to speak, but he stopped her, grasping her arm and pulling her toward the door. "Come with me." Nicola attempted to resist, but he did not give her any other choice. He jerked her around to face him, as he roughly pulled her close to him. "If you resist again, I will hit you. Do you understand me?" he hissed, pulling the door open and shoving her out of the room. He walked behind her, without speaking, down the stairs and into the room where Garrett's body lay.

Barely inside the room, Nicola stopped walking and stared at Garrett's lifeless body. *Drue is not here. I must not let anyone know what I saw. I care not to have them focus on me. Let them turn against themselves.* When she spoke, her voice was trembling. "You are wrong, Lord Keaton, so wrong."

"Tell me, lady," he challenged, "what am I wrong about?" Keaton knew this killing was not the work of any of his men. He could not imagine Nicola would have access to Garrett, yet someone did.

"You are wrong," Nicola repeated. "This is not a safe place for me." Nicola looked at the men circled around.

Ignoring her comment, Keaton turned her around to look directly into her eyes. "This thing you have been asked to do for your father, what is it? You will tell me now." His voice was cold and sounded foreign to him, not his own. Events were moving too fast. He could not allow Nicola to live and risk losing more men. But first, he needed to find out what she knew, if anything.

Nicola hesitated. "I'm not certain," she replied quietly. She shook her head. "I simply do not know." Fearfully, she looked back at Garrett.

"What happens if Edward is not king?" Keaton asked, grasping her arm tightly, trying to force information from her. Nicola's eyes widened. Before she could answer, he put a finger over her lips. "If Edward were not king, who then?" He thought to trick her into telling what her father must have envisioned.

"He has two sons, a brother and a nephew. Any one of them." Nicola was watching Keaton through eyes widened and serious.

"And if none of those people were king?" Keaton prodded her. "What did your father know?"

Jerking her arm free, she demanded, "How can you even ask that? There are four people after Edward in line for that throne. To even talk that way borders on treason! What are you trying to do to me?" Nicola's eyes narrowed as she glared at Keaton. "You are trying to cast a shadow upon my father's reputation! My father was loyal to King Edward. He rode for him, fought in two battles for him. How could you think that way?" Nicola asked defiantly.

"You tell me, Nicola," Keaton answered coldly. "Your father and I have always been close. For a long time, the Guardians have worked for him and for others. Your father had hoped you would not have to be entangled in all this, but when he realized Allie was an informant, he had to move to protect both you and the crown . . . and his dreams." Keaton stepped closer to her. "You must not be afraid." He forced his voice to soften. "You cannot be afraid, lady. You must trust us."

"Not be afraid? Trust you?" Nicola's voice was bitter. "Have you taken leave of your senses?"

"Nicola, if anyone can do what he asks of you, it is you. Must you be careful? Of course. Will you have protection? Yes. Will this be easy? No, but you *can* do this." Keaton demanded she look at him. "If your father thought you could not complete this, he would never have asked you to do what you must do." Nicola stared at him in silence. "You must know, Nicola, your father knew this day might come. Allie was not his daughter, nor did he have any other children. He was never able to. He married your mother when his friend—the man who was her husband, and your father—died in battle. He refused to leave your mother alone with a newborn. He married her. They grew to love each other dearly. For all practical purposes, you were his daughter. All his properties and papers so state."

"Properties that now belong to the man who occupies my home," Nicola replied coldly. She stepped back. "And you, Lord Keaton? How do you know these things? How do you know anything about my father? How do you fit into all this?" Nicola asked. "If you were so close, why had my father never mentioned you? Why had I never seen you at my father's home?"

He was surprised by her questions and answered a little too quickly. "Just as I told you, we were always close. He was like a father to me. I kept in touch with him even when I left to fight for other men and their causes. I joined the Guardians while fighting in Italy." Keaton looked around the room. Silently,

Harding and Carnell sat listening. "Your father was against it at first, but grew to understand, later." He looked back at the lady still glaring at him. "You must trust me. The men who ride for me are loyal to a fault. You can trust us." Watching her expression, Keaton could tell Nicola was not going to share anything with him. He had to think what needed to be done next. Somehow, he would find out who had killed Garrett and why. Talking with Nicola now was pointless. Taking her arm, he turned her toward the door. "You should return to your room and get some rest. Try not to think on this. Lock your door. In the morning, we will talk with everyone." He escorted her up the stairs. "I am sorry I have no one here to assist you."

Nicola shivered. Her fear was like a stone in her stomach. "I do not need assistance from any woman, Lord Keaton," she answered curtly, increasing her pace. As he opened her door, she added, "I do not understand why Father never spoke to me of these things or of you, if you were so close." She walked past Keaton and stepped into her room, closing the door before he could follow.

CHAPTER 12

INSIDE HER CHAMBER, Nicola sat near the fire, wishing her father was with her. But he was not. *Because of Allie, this thing I must do, I must do alone. These men with me . . . they stop speaking when I am near; they watch me with suspicion. These men are guardians of nothing.* She sat staring at the dancing flames, remembering the last time she saw her father. *Father's final command becomes more difficult. I am alone. No one can suspect I know anything. If I become of little use, I will surely be put to death.* She wiped a single tear from her face.

KEATON STOOD LOOKING AT THE CLOSED DOOR. He would have kept his thoughts to himself, but Nicola was so unsure of what was expected of her that he said more than he intended. His decision was made. He had no intention of protecting Nicola. *Lady Weldon is not the keeper of any information. I think the Duchess of Burgundy and Lord Lareau made a very bad decision taking Weldon's castle. A decision based on the information I gave to them. His daughter knows nothing. What now?*

Deep in thought, Keaton returned to the lower level, thinking about the nights he had spent with Allie before all of this. He had showered her with little trinkets, sweet-talked and bedded her. She was a virgin, impressionable and inexperienced. Keaton shook his head. She had fallen in love with him. When she began to whisper of Weldon's work, he listened. She seemed to know so much. Yet Lareau had sworn his search of Weldon's study and even the torture of the old man himself revealed nothing—Weldon appeared to have no idea what Lareau was seeking. He was not even able to make something up to ease the pain of torture. Keaton had to face the fact Allie had lied about it all. The secret messages to Henry Tudor, King Edward's troubles with his wife and the crown. All the wild imaginings of a girl trying to impress a man. *And I fell for all of it. Worse, I passed false information to the duchess. Lareau took the castle with nothing to gain. Nothing.* It was a bitter admission.

When Keaton reentered the room where Garrett still lay, Harding stepped forward. "Why would you think to bring her in here? So she would be afraid of us? You think she would share anything with such men?"

"No, he hoped she would not know who to trust. Is that it, Lord Keaton?" Carnell asked coldly. At that moment, Drue entered the room, slapping the dust from his riding gloves. His stance changed as he strode to Garrett's body. A deep frown creased Drue's forehead and he looked hard at Keaton. Keaton simply shook his head and resumed angrily pacing around the room. Finally, he replied to Harding. "Both. I hoped she would not know which of us to trust, and that she would be afraid. Both! Perhaps then she will talk. She is not prepared for all this. Especially if she is not certain which of us she can trust." Keaton stopped speaking, looking at each man. Carnell and Harding did not appear to see how this might help them.

Only Drue smiled briefly and nodded his head. "Of course that means she could only trust you. You will have to kill the three of us, then?" Drue stated. "Excellent plan, Lord Keaton." He looked back at the body slumped against the wall.

"That was not my plan," snapped Keaton. Both Carnell and Harding looked from Keaton to Drue and back at Keaton. They looked at Garrett and each other. The idea took root.

Carnell cleared his throat. "We know that Drue could not have killed Garrett. He just returned with the supplies we needed. Supplies he could only have gotten from the blacksmith, three hours' ride from here. That accounts for at least seven hours. Garrett was alive five hours ago. And I know I did not kill him." He looked at the remaining two men and waited.

Harding spoke up next. "Well, I know I did not kill Garrett. Keaton, what have you to say?"

"Do not be empty-headed. I was with Lady Nicola. I can speak for myself and for the lady. You found him, Carnell." He looked keenly at Carnell, then at Drue. Drue returned his stare, without comment or wavering. Keaton looked away. "Perhaps we should try to uncover just what Lady Nicola does or does not understand."

Drue poured himself a goblet of wine, and Keaton took the opportunity to speak further on the matter.

"Lareau made certain there was nothing on Weldon's person. Nicola was not left alone with him outside his cell. He had no secret papers on his person. An aggressive search revealed nothing in either Weldon's or Nicola's rooms." Keaton was frowning. "One of you take food up. Taste it first, in her presence. In the morn, we will gather together to discuss our next move, with her in attendance. Let us see what that tells us."

Both Carnell and Harding agreed readily. Harding suggested Drue would be the best choice to take her dinner to her. All, including Drue, agreed.

CHAPTER 13

Lord Stanley watched the court begin the dance of loyalty. King Edward was dying. Unexpectedly. His oldest son was not old enough to assume the throne on his own. That would mean Richard, the king's brother, would surely assume the role of king, although technically he was the protector of the king-to-be. Weaving his way through the throng of people pressed outside the king's chambers, Stanley searched for his wife, Lady Margaret, the mother of Henry Tudor.

Stanley knew well that the goal of Margaret's life was to see Henry crowned king of England, though he had once pointed out to her that Henry would have to get past five contenders—Edward, his two sons, his brother Richard, and Richard's son—before Henry would have a chance. The list was about to shrink by one. Margaret had insisted that she could feel a change coming. She believed Henry was the rightful king. Stanley's mind raced. Soon Edward would no longer be alive. The court of Edward was peppered with enemies. Who among them had the strength to prevail, and would it be someone Henry could topple?

The king's entire court was assembled outside the king's chambers. Some weeping, most waiting. King Edward, everyone knew, was probably dead. Lord Stanley found his wife standing against a wall, watching the crowd milling around. "Come, wife. We should return home. I doubt dowager Queen Elizabeth will have need of your services any longer. We should be away from the mayhem that will surely come from this most untimely death." Taking Margaret's arm, he led her outside.

"It is God's will," Margaret stated flatly. *Henry is one step closer to the throne.*

"I'm sure," Lord Stanley responded dryly. "And now God wishes to watch how the dead king's relatives line up at the table, each pushing to the front. One can see just how shallow the loyalty for Edward runs. See them looking from one to another, gauging each as friend or foe."

"You make light of this," Margaret whispered. Lord Stanley did not reply.

Thomas Stanley, Earl of Derby, accompanied by his wife, Margaret Beaufort, returned to his estate. As was his custom, Stanley played the waiting game before he openly pledged for either side. There remained four possible candidates for king of England—Edward's two sons, his brother Richard, Duke of Gloucester, and Richard's son. Stanley would wait until the royal dust settled. He knew Margaret, however, would not wait. He knew she would send word to Jasper Tudor. Whether Gloucester ruled in young Edward's name or as the king, she believed that Henry should gather his supporters. Stanley had no doubt that a real fight was finally brewing.

Tucked away in Brittany, Jasper read and reread the letter from Margaret. King Edward was dead. That meant the Duke of Gloucester, acting for young Edward, was now in control. Jasper knew the duke well. A staunch ally of King Edward, he was nevertheless human. Jasper also knew the workings of men in power. Clutching the letter, he knocked on Henry's door, telling him, "I have news from your mother, Henry."

Henry rolled over in bed, covered the woman in bed with him, and answered. "Enter, Uncle. We were just visiting." The woman giggled. Henry waited for his uncle.

Jasper opened the door. "Leave us, now," he ordered the woman. Henry looked at Jasper with raised brows. When the woman did not move, Jasper added, "If you do not leave dressed now, I shall remove you in your skin. Move!"

Henry caught the tone of urgency and nodded to the woman. She left the bed and hurriedly dressed, then slipped behind Jasper and out the door, which Jasper closed and locked. "Henry, listen to me. It seems your challenge will again include a waiting game."

Henry fell back on the pillows. "Again, Uncle? This is supposed to be news?"

"I am not finished, Henry," Jasper spoke forcefully. "King Edward is dead."

Henry suddenly sat up again. "Is this true? How do you know?"

"Your mother sent a letter. He is dead." Jasper handed the letter to Henry.

Henry scanned it, then looked at Jasper. "Richard is to act in young Edward's stead, until the boy is old enough to rule on his own. That does little for my cause. I would have to defeat Richard, then both sons, and of course, Richard's son. Four! While you and I are a force to be reckoned with, Uncle, we hardly could manage such a challenge."

Jasper stood looking at his nephew. "No, we could not, but we could begin to muster men, quietly."

Henry lay back down, staring at the ceiling. "This thing you are hoping for, it lays far out of reach. Too far for the two of us, I fear. Yet it does change the picture. How can we stay abreast of what is happening?" Henry got out of bed and began dressing. "It is not safe to hope Mother can find a way to get information to me. If she were caught, she would be accused of treason. Do you know anyone else close to our cause?"

Jasper smiled at his nephew. "Of course. Your father and I had a very active lane. It still exists, and I can easily start it back up. I will do so today. I intend to ask they keep us posted on all that happens in fair England." *I see he talks of giving up, but his heart will not let him . . . at least not yet.* Jasper nodded toward the bed. "You should save some of your energy for the expedition coming." Not waiting for a reply, he left Henry's room.

CHAPTER 14

L ORD LAREAU, STUCK IN WELDON CASTLE, paced the floor
while his commander waited for direction. Both Allie and Nicola had
disappeared. *Should have locked her up with her father. But Lady Allie too? Where
could they go? Every man is accounted for, as are the horses, finally, as much as possible.* A search of Lord Weldon's study and bedroom only provided greater
cause to question the attack on the castle. There was nothing to indicate Lord
Weldon was a traitor; in fact, everything indicated he was very loyal to King
Edward. Even Lady Nicola's rooms held no clue. "I have no fondness for this
useless chase the duchess planned for us. We leave in the morn, at first light.
Nothing in this place is to be taken. Tell the house staff we will return in three
weeks' time and expect things to be as they are when we leave."

His commander raised his eyebrows, his frown evidence that the man
neither agreed with nor understood Lareau's order. Lareau explained,
"They need to keep the place as it is. It is possible the ladies we seek might
return. Where else can they go? Two women alone?" Lareau asked. "I will
determine our next move after I hear from King Edward's man. You just be
certain you spread the word that we seek information regarding the women
and will pay well for that information."

"Yes, my lord. If they live still, we will find them." The man nodded
briefly and turned to leave.

"Wait. *If* they live?" Lord Lareau stood expectantly. "What are you
saying?"

"Only that we have searched every room, hall, hut, and hovel. Nothing.
No one has seen either woman. It is now widely accepted that they were both
killed, along with the father."

"Would that were true," Lareau muttered.

"What can it matter if the Lady Nicola lives? It would seem the stories about Lord Weldon were false. We both have searched his study, his rooms, the lady's rooms, and found nothing. Nothing that would indicate he stirred a rebellion."

Lareau began pacing again. "You may be right. All we found were writings supporting King Edward. Perhaps Allie lied, and we were fooled because her information about the castle and soldiers was accurate. She knew nothing else because there was nothing else to know." Lord Lareau stopped at the window and stared at a vacant courtyard. "This may have been just another blunder by the king's council or Lord Keaton. No matter. Neither woman can be allowed to live and tell of the acts committed at this place. Dispose of Weldon's body discreetly."

His commander replied, "The body has already been removed and well hidden. The survivors of Weldon's men have been patched up and cared for. They are farmers. Simple men who understand nothing of what happened. The ones killed during the fight were soldiers—those have been quietly buried. You would not know what has transpired in this place, if you were not here. If any of the people living around tried to tell of a raid, none could believe them. The castle and grounds are untouched. I had Weldon's cell cleaned of anything that might tell the story."

Lareau nodded. What seemed like a low-risk venture that could net huge returns had turned into a colossal mess. He had no reliable information to help Edward. Worse, he had lost what he hoped would be a hidden post for France, on England's own soil. That was the greater prize. It now appeared his misgivings about working for the Duchess of Burgundy were well founded.

The moon hung low and night was well on when a horse raced through the castle gates. Lareau was awakened by the commotion below his room. He had risen and started for the window when someone knocked at his door. "Enter," he said, pulling a robe over his nightshirt. The door opened to his commander accompanied by a man wearing King Edward's colors. "You have news?" Lareau asked quietly. *Of course the duchess has spies in Edward's own court.*

"Yes, my lord. King Edward has died. The Duchess of Burgundy calls you back. She would rather you not be on English soil, until Edward's son is crowned." The messenger waited.

For a long moment, Lareau was silent, stunned by the unexpected news. "Ah, Margaret of York, the dowager Duchess of Burgundy. Her request is our command." Lareau turned to his commander. "We will depart as planned, but our course has changed. We will return to Burgundy . . . for now. The men will be sent ahead." Lareau nodded toward the messenger. "See this man is fed and provided with a place to rest."

When his room was empty, Lareau wandered to the window again. "No matter. Margaret of York knows well what is at stake with her brother's death." Lareau stood a long time staring out the window, contemplating how quickly the world could turn. "I doubt Richard, Duke of Gloucester, will be pleased to remain the protector of King Edward's son until the boy reaches an age to rule on his own. 'Twill be a deadly game we see, I fear. It would seem an old man's dreams are of little consequence now. If he ever had such dreams. The king has two sons, a brother, and a nephew. England's throne is secure in that family. But which man will wear the crown is still a question."

Lareau called for his commander again. "Find two men you can trust. One is to go to court, observe what is left of Edward's council, and report back to the duchess. The second is to ride to the Duke of Gloucester. The duchess will want to know what his plans might be now, seeing the eldest of Edward's sons is only twelve years of age. This second man is *not* to offer an opinion, only observe. Both men are to keep a keen eye out for Lady Allie and Lord Weldon's daughter. If either man finds the ladies, they are to be put to death and the bodies hidden. Clear?"

"Absolutely. Men will be sent immediately." The commander left to make the arrangements, leaving Lareau alone with his thoughts.

CHAPTER 15

As evening surrounded Keaton's castle, riders erupted into the courtyard below. Men called out, their voices ringing with urgency. The noise awakened Nicola. She ran to her window but was unable to tell what might be happening. After grabbing a robe, she carefully opened her door. An excited rumble of men's voices rose from below. She looked around before noiselessly making her way downstairs to the great room. Standing hidden against a wall in the shadows, she listened to the talk coming through the open door. An unfamiliar voice asserted, "It's true, Lord Keaton! He is dead!"

"What happens now?" Carnell asked. "Surely Prince Edward, the eldest son, is too young to govern. Who reigns in his name?"

Lord Keaton answered, "I have never seen Edward's will, but I am certain it would be Richard of Gloucester, his brother, as protector."

"That may help us," Harding observed.

"Not necessarily," Drue argued.

"How so?" questioned someone else.

Nicola stepped into the room. Every man stood respectfully, but silence ensued.

"Please, do not stand for me. I am one of you now. Neither better nor worse." She stood a moment at the doorway, looking pointedly at Lord Keaton. Keaton nodded to her and indicated a chair nearby.

"No thank you, Lord Keaton. I heard the horses come into the courtyard." She frowned slightly. "The last time I heard horses enter a courtyard, they brought with them pain and death. That is not the case today. I see you are not readying to fight. Please excuse my interruption." She curtsied, turned, and left the room, closing the door behind her, and hid herself outside in the shadows. For a long moment, she waited, but the room remained silent. She knew they were waiting for her to move beyond hearing before resuming their discussion. As she continued to listen, she heard Keaton's footsteps as he walked to the door and opened it. Nicola held her breath, standing against the wall, hidden in the shadows, until Keaton closed the door. Nicola then stepped out of the darkened hall and crept closer, listening to the voices beyond.

Again, the throne was changing hands. The issue of just which York might be named king and how this might increase the instability of the throne took the attention of the men from the Lady Nicola to the crisis looming ahead.

"With King Edward dead, who comes forward, I ask again?" Carnell pushed. "Duke of Gloucester has little following. In some areas, none at all."

Keaton spoke next. "Gloucester certainly has a solid reputation as a leader and commander. Right now he is north, holding the border. He has strong support there. However, I am not certain how that would translate to viewing him as king. The question should be, will Lady Margaret be able to gather men for Henry this quickly? There are still four legitimate males in line for the throne. Perhaps it is time we get to Henry Tudor and squelch any ideas he might have. He must not be allowed to take advantage of this unrest. A damnable time for Edward to die!"

"We should not move against Henry yet," Harding insisted. "Not without checking with the councilors who take over for whoever rules, or at least word from Richard."

Keaton plans to get to Henry Tudor only to stop him! They are not here to help me. Stunned, Nicola tried to remember everything her father had said that awful night, and what it might mean. Her mind raced. Out of the disarray, she remembered something once more. There might be one who could help her. One who knew the story the symbols told. *The old crone.* She had never forgotten the ancient, shrunken old woman. Nicola had accompanied her father on one of the visits and, looking back, she remembered how troubled her father had been. Lord Weldon and the crone had spent a long time in quiet conversation. When she and her father rode away, it seemed he had gotten whatever advice he needed. The old crone and her father were friends, it was plain. *The crone would know. I must find her. Tonight, I leave tonight.*

Silently, Nicola climbed the stairs. Inside her room, she secured her chamber door. Crossing the room, she stared at the darkness now filling the courtyard. To find the crone, Nicola first needed the map to the hut that her father had drawn for her. He had purposely drawn it in such a way that it looked much like one of his jeweled pieces, and it was even inscribed with the words "little one." She had believed it was a childish game with her father. Until this moment, Nicola never dreamed she would ever use the map. She needed to go back home. Back to a place inhabited by Lareau and his men. *I know my home and my own room. I can do this.*

Nicola changed into the heaviest of her gowns and grabbed her heavy cloak. She gently touched the pouch with the symbols, hidden beneath her gown—the only tie to her father that was left. She stuffed all her saved coins into her cloak pocket, looked around the room one last time, and then slipped, like a shadow, unnoticed, from the room. At the stables, her soft call was answered by her horse, and they were off, leaving Keaton's castle.

LORD KEATON STOOD AND YAWNED. "We could talk all night and not settle the course before us." He looked out the window at the grounds beyond. "Humph, in truth, we *have* talked all night." Keaton was hungry and tired. It was far too early for Nicola to be up. The men headed to the kitchen. Keaton felt a twinge of guilt that neither he nor Drue had thought to bring food to Nicola. *The next time I come here, I will be certain to have staff. Though it matters little. She will not be around the next time I come here.* He set aside thoughts of Nicola and wandered into the kitchen, his men trailing behind.

Keaton began formulating a plan with his men. "Richard of Gloucester will be headed to London. The time has come for us to ride north. Richard will need us to hold the border to contain any uprising. There will be support for Henry's cause there." Keaton frowned. His thoughts again turned to Nicola. *Unfortunately, Nicola has no idea what her father expected of her. Her time is done.*

The meal was a silent one, and Keaton remained lost in his own thoughts. When everyone had eaten their fill, Keaton stood. "Harding and Carnell, you head north, toward the border. Scotland has promised men for Henry Tudor. Time to find out if they are in earnest. We may be able to hold them back while it is decided who will actually occupy the throne." Drue he directed to ride south. "The mood in the south could turn against either young Edward or Richard, with very little effort involved." Keaton hoped Drue's knowledge of the land and of England's people could keep the south quiet, at least until young Edward was crowned. "Drue, start gathering support for young Edward on your way. There will surely be men to be had where Edward was much loved."

"What about Lady Nicola?" Carnell asked. Keaton had known Carnell the longest. Both Keaton and Carnell had lost land during Edward's reign. Carnell and King Edward's brother George, Duke of Clarence, were bitter enemies. Carnell had no use for George, recognizing him as shallow, self-centered, and scheming. It came as no surprise when George was found guilty of treason by his brother, the king, and was sentenced to die. When given the choice of the manner in which he would die, George chose to be drowned in a vat of wine. Though that may have been the most fitting end for him, King Edward had grown ruthless to maintain power. It made sense that Richard would also do whatever it took to keep young Prince Edward from the throne.

Keaton's thoughts turned to the lady housed above. To have someone running around with information, anything that might suggest the throne was not secure, would spell death for that person—whether he carried it out or someone else. Nicola was in danger from Richard's men as much as she was from his men. He felt a little sorry for her.

"The lady is in danger," Carnell flatly observed, as if reading Keaton's mind. Keaton frowned. While he agreed with Carnell, he had already made his mind up regarding Lady Weldon.

When Keaton remained silent, Carnell turned away. Keaton imagined he had heavy questions weighing on his mind—whoever had poisoned Garrett certainly had to be one of them. With everything else going on, that incident seemed to have been forgotten.

Again as if reading his mind, Carnell turned to Keaton and quietly stated, "Garrett was killed by one of us, Keaton." Keaton turned sharply to Carnell but did not respond. Things were beginning to unravel quickly. He nodded toward the stairs, and they climbed toward Nicola's room.

Carnell was reserved and seldom spoke out. The fact that he had spoken up took Keaton by surprise. Like the rest of the men, Keaton included, Carnell was always dressed for a fight. His clothes were slim-fitting, allowing for quick movement, his sword and dagger were in place, and a gun was tucked in his belt. Carnell was a dangerous adversary.

Garrett's killer had to be either Harding or Carnell. To Keaton, the greater question was why. The sudden death of Garrett could not have come at a worse time. Keaton needed every man he had. The throne needed to stand safe for one of King Edward's heirs. Just which heir was unclear, but that detail mattered little. To this end, it was crucial that Keaton defend England's throne from an invasion by Henry Tudor. Henry was the only formidable contender. People cared not that Tudor had only lived a few years in England, was rumored to not speak English well, and probably knew very little of the intrigue surrounding the throne at this very moment. Many of England's people still harbored doubt over Edward's claim to the throne and remembered old King Henry. That doubt could easily transfer to any of Edward's heirs.

"This is not a conversation for this time." Keaton stepped onto the second-floor landing. Without answering, Carnell followed. When Keaton and Carnell reached Nicola's rooms, Keaton knocked lightly. There was no answer. He called to her, "Lady? Are you awake?" Only silence. Frowning, he carefully tried the door. It was secured from inside. Hastily searching for something to batter the door down, he hoisted a large marble statue. After several tries, with both Carnell and Keaton wielding it, the door finally gave.

Her room was cold. Neither fire nor candle had been lit. Keaton lit a candle and surveyed the room. A gown had been carelessly tossed on the bed, and a quick inspection proved that the other gowns were still tucked in the chest. The satchel he had given to her sat empty on the floor. Gathering his wits, he asked, "Horses. Did she take a horse?" Without waiting for an answer, he headed for the door and raced down the stairs.

Carnell called after him. "Keaton, wait, she left a note." Keaton grabbed the note and read it twice. *Lord Keaton, I no longer have need of your services.* "She releases us? She really believes she can do such a thing?" Keaton was fuming. "Where could she go? To London? Now I am forced to ride to London. Fool! London will be a town on edge. Everyone new will be suspected of something. Asking questions about the whereabouts of anyone could send her to the block." Keaton shoved the note into Carnell's hand. *That would take care of her for me. The sooner the better. Damnation! On the other hand, the lady is not as simple as we imagined. She has a fire within her, one that could burn Edward's throne. She just does not know it yet.*

Not knowing where Nicola was ate at him. *Women do not do well when left on their own. She could be the one who topples the throne before Edward's son is even crowned. At the same time, she is not worth taking a chance in terms of having me or any of my men ensnared in Richard's call to arms. All of England will be fearful of every stranger.* He couldn't worry about Nicola—in fact, he would be hard put to keep his men out of anyone's mind. Keaton's thoughts turned to Lareau. Surely Lareau would be on his way back to Burgundy. *I would like to be on my way back to France. This has turned into a nightmare happening in the light of the sun. My demon has the face of a mocking King Edward.*

DRUE LEFT SOON AFTER EVERYONE HAD EATEN, riding south as Keaton requested. At least that was what he intended Keaton to think. Drue had other plans. As darkness fell the evening prior, he had noticed Nicola's horse was gone. Drue knew that neither Keaton nor any of his men had noted its absence yet. Although uncertain about her precise time of departure, he knew she was hours ahead of him. Drue rode in pursuit of the missing horse, certain he would find Nicola at the same time. Out of sight of Keaton's castle, he changed directions and rode hard toward Weldon's castle. Keaton would discover Nicola was missing and, shortly after, would find that her horse was gone. He would come after Nicola. Drue planned on getting to her first.

AT KEATON CASTLE, CARNELL made ready to ride north as directed, seeking to thwart any support for Henry Tudor's campaign from Scotland. Harding would be at his side and had a formidable reputation as a talented swordsman. His lively green eyes and ready smile seemed at odds with his steel nerves and cold determination when it came to fighting. His easy, convincing manner would be valuable in gathering men willing to take up the fight against Henry. Carnell was every bit as drab as Harding was lively. Harding spoke his mind without hesitation and was more than willing to back his mouth with his weapons, if need be. Carnell planned to keep him out of the conversations as long as possible, taking advantage of the situation to bolster his personal hopes for a position in Richard's court. However, he recognized Harding would be of great help if he found himself in need of immediate support.

At the last moment, Keaton decided to ride along. The north would probably provide the least support for young Edward or Richard. If Nicola were still alive in London, she stood little chance of surviving. Better for Keaton. Carnell was not pleased, but he kept his opinion to himself. The men rode in silence for a long time. Eventually, Keaton spoke. "I think Lady Nicola knows nothing. Lord Weldon never spoke an unkind word or moved in an unkind manner toward King Edward. It is well known that Weldon supported and fought for Edward." Keaton turned to Carnell. "Why the attack on Weldon and his people?"

"Aye, why indeed? The attack was an error in someone's judgement, Keaton. Bad information, it would seem." Carnell ignored Keaton's black look. "With four living potential candidates for the throne of England, none of which are Henry, Lady Nicola has no purpose." Carnell knew it was unreasonable to think Henry could ever get past all four heirs. "Lady Nicola walks a dangerous path, wherever she is."

Keaton merely nodded in agreement, but there was something else churning behind his eyes that Carnell did not quite trust.

CHAPTER 16

FOUR WEEKS BEFORE HER HUSBAND FELL ILL, Queen Elizabeth sent a secret message to her brother, young Prince Edward's keeper. *You must keep Prince Edward safe. I have had a premonition of great danger for him. Please, I beg you, take care.* Only five days ago, her message was finally answered. Of course, her brother pledged he would take every precaution for the prince. Her fear told her it would not be enough. King Edward lay dying. Who could have imagined how swiftly her life would change. She looked at the man she had loved these past years. The queen gently brushed King Edward's hair aside. He was burning with fever, barely conscious. "Thank you," he whispered.

"For what?" Elizabeth asked, frowning. She leaned closer to hear his words, as her lips touched his forehead.

"For loving me. For believing in me. You have always been my gift, my strength." He smiled weakly. "Care for our children. Provisions have been made."

Elizabeth did not answer. There was no need. He had already faded beyond her grasp. King Edward was dead. A great wave of fear overwhelmed her, and she lay her head on Edward's chest and wept. Eventually, the silence of the room stirred her. Again, Elizabeth felt the cold of danger. Shuddering, she rose, opened the door to the crowd gathered outside of it, and gracefully stepped out of her role as queen.

Her first concern was for her sons. Her dead husband's brother Richard, Duke of Gloucester, was in northern England, leading the king's military against Scotland. He had always been Edward's strong and steadfast champion. King Edward believed his brother Richard was best suited to govern in his son's name, should young Edward become king before he had reached an age to rule on his own. But Elizabeth knew only too well how the wheel could turn. She would take no chances. Her premonition of impending danger grew stronger.

Elizabeth's stride quickened, as she hastened to where her younger children were huddled. Her two older daughters were with the crowd outside Edward's chamber. Elizabeth knew they would soon join her. But now, she had to do all she could to protect King Edward's heirs. Young Edward and his brother Richard would most certainly be in danger.

While it was true that King Edward had named his brother Richard to govern in young Edward's name, Elizabeth hoped against hope to convince the dead king's council that, with their help, Prince Edward could rule effectively while he came of age. She began her campaign.

Elizabeth was a very smart and politically astute woman. Although Richard had always been extremely loyal to King Edward, Elizabeth knew the lure of power, especially the potential authority and strength of a king. She began crusading for the coronation of young Edward to happen quickly. Her brother would be en route with Edward even now. She sent word to the council, suggesting young Edward would be able to rule on his own, with their help.

Upon hearing her proposal, Gloucester concurred with Elizabeth, agreeing to move forward with the coronation. However, as Elizabeth feared, his initial response changed, or more likely was insincere from the beginning. She assumed he recognized the probability of her influence on young Edward, or he suspected that Elizabeth's family, the Woodvilles, would move into power. Elizabeth knew that, in his heart, Richard believed he would be a good king. Yet she wondered about Richard's wife's motivations. Anne Neville was keenly aware of how little time Richard would have to make a decision and move on it. She began her own campaign on Richard's behalf. Standing so near the throne, why should Richard step away? This could be his only chance to take the crown. The once secure throne of England was again beginning to weaken.

A crisis was underway. Elizabeth was forced to seek sanctuary for herself and her children behind the walls of Westminster Abbey, again. She reached the Abbey only moments ahead of Richard and his men making their way to her chambers.

RICHARD QUICKLY SENT WORD in writing to Edward IV's council. He would be young Edward's protector as per King Edward's will, though he purposely placed no termination on the time he would act as the protector. He recognized that would cause grave concern to council members already discussing the dowager queen's proposal. Richard also knew his proposal was far more sinister. The councilors would lose ruling power. Richard's claim was voted down by the councilors. Young Edward was named King Edward V. In response, Richard of Gloucester simply seized Edward V before he reached London, then escorted him to his mother. Edward's uncle and guardian, the dowager queen's brother, was accused of treason and executed.

Meanwhile, Richard's wife, Anne, had witnessed her father's climb and horrible plunge from favor with the deceased King Edward IV. The throne loomed so close, as did the capacity to keep her family safe. She succumbed to the potential of overwhelming power that would come to her if Richard of Gloucester were crowned the king of England. Anne did the only thing she knew to do—she continued to push Richard to stake his own claim on the throne. Her father's obsession had become her own. Ultimately, Richard refused to accept the council's decision—he simply took command and claimed sovereignty.

THE NEXT SEVERAL DAYS WERE FILLED with unspeakable dread. Elizabeth tried, unsuccessfully, to keep her sons safe. Gloucester claimed his control of young Edward was to secure his safety, and he ordered the young prince to be taken to the Tower, in keeping with the practice to ready him for his coronation. While this was indeed customary, Elizabeth already knew the terrible storm brewing. If young Edward's coronation went ahead, Richard's powers as protector would cease. With Edward's reign to be followed by any sons he might have, followed by his younger brother, it would take a miracle for Richard to ever come this close to the throne again. Richard had not planned on this opportunity, but Elizabeth knew he would take it. The dowager queen's mother and King Edward IV were both dead. She stood alone for her sons. That would never be enough. Tears filled her eyes, blurring the figure of her oldest son as he disappeared down the hall, surrounded by Richard's men.

Elizabeth's son was not fooled by the pretense of the protection offered by his uncle and by the Tower, and he resisted. Elizabeth watched as Edward shoved the guards away. If there were ever any doubts in Richard's mind about his nephew's future, young Edward's tough response to his uncle had just sealed his fate. Elizabeth knew that Richard could never allow Edward to be free.

The evening Richard came for King Edward IV's son, Elizabeth knew the die had been cast. Try as she might, she was not able to keep her son safe and out of Richard's grasp. He would be held in the Tower, never to be released. In her heart, she knew it was a dismal future. The news of the prince's imprisonment would soon reach all of England, and beyond. The Duchess of Burgundy was aghast, but that was of little comfort to Elizabeth, who recognized the prince could never be released if Richard was to keep the crown. The general populace of England was still in disbelief. Though few understood the political arena, they all understood it would mean more fighting. Each civilian kept his loyalties to himself. Survival of the least noticeable.

CHAPTER 17

*T*RAVEL FOR NICOLA WAS DIFFICULT. Dense tree cover allowed only slivers of light from the moon to slip through. Overgrown brush and fallen logs made the terrain dangerous, forcing her horse to use the road. When Nicola had ridden through this area only days before, darkness had distorted the features of the forest just as it did now. Nothing looked familiar. She had no idea where she might be. Determined to return to Weldon Castle, she allowed the horse to pick its way, praying he would take her back to his stable. Nicola had to find the trail to the waterfall before the horse was too close to the castle. By taking the cliff trail, she could avoid alerting the men now occupying her home.

Several hours had passed when Nicola first heard the sounds. The unmistakable jingle of bridles and clanking gear gradually grew louder. From the noise, she felt it must be a large company of men headed toward her. She turned her horse away from the road and was working to move as far away from it as she could. When she heard yelling in her direction, coming from her right, she froze. "Stop right there!" a man's voice commanded her. Another voice on her left added, "Stay just as you are."

Fear filled her. A woman riding alone in the dark made for quick entertainment. Left with little choice, Nicola sat and waited. When the contingent of men made it to her, she was amazed at its size. More men appeared from the woods around the road, easily surrounding her. She would have to make something up quickly, but whatever story she told would have to carry some element of truth in it somewhere. Her life depended upon it.

One man rode up close to her. From the way the rest of the men moved to allow him room, she surmised he must be the leader. He asked for a light. A torch was soon provided. He studied her for a long moment, and his eyes moved over her horse before slowly returning to her. She sat still, praying she could keep her fear from showing. At last, he spoke. "I am Lord Braggio," he told her, his voice firm and challenging. "You travel alone, lady?"

"Not by choice, my lord," Nicola lied, meeting his gaze. "I traveled with a companion. She died with the sickness. The four men who rode with me did not care to stay. I chose to save my pride. Rather than have it known I was deserted by my guard, I released them." Nicola paused. Quietly, she added, "I was left alone. I hid for seven days, for fear I too might have the illness."

Braggio was a tall man with a commanding presence. He and his men wore full battle gear. Although the hour was late, neither the men nor the horses appeared worn. Nicola reasoned they must have come from nearby. While Nicola did not recognize the men or their colors, it was possible Braggio might know her father and what had befallen him. She prayed he did not—in the event he was an ally, it would be useful. But, in the event he was not, it could mean her death.

Braggio was still for a long time. At last, he smiled. "You expect me to believe you stayed alone in the forest? Alone for seven days? Lady, I believe your story needs work. Perhaps you would try again." His voice dripped with sarcasm.

Nicola knew he was trying to decide just what to do with her. His manner was not particularly threatening, so she took a chance, calmly replying, "There are many places to hide on this land. There is a rocky point, not far from here, that offers some shelter. A place nearly inaccessible and probably not known to many. From that place, one has a clear view of the many roads in this forest."

Now, the man's voice was quiet. "Please tell me how you found such a place. Or have you imagined this place?"

The man's stance had relaxed; he no longer appeared as threatening. Nicola purposefully waited a moment, then answered quietly. "No, my lord. I had a brother. He loved a friend as a brother. The two spent many hours at that place. Frequently, they allowed me to accompany them."

The man sat straighter in his saddle. "And your brother? Where is he now?"

Nicola looked directly into the lord's eyes. "He left to fight for King Edward. He never returned," she said softly, and sat quietly waiting.

"Where are you bound, lady?" Nicola guessed that the man had most likely made a decision about her by this point. She prayed he would let her go on alone and chose her next words carefully.

"I was told I could find shelter in a castle a day's ride from here. It is said the lord of that manor is kind. I hope to find a place to stay. At least until I can decide what next to do."

"The man of that place is indeed a kind man. It is a full hard day's ride, lady, slower if you ride at night. Wherever the rode splits, stay to the left. I would rather not leave you alone, but I am called to arms and cannot take you." He rode closer and extended his hand. When Nicola placed her hand in his, he bent to kiss it. "God go with you, lady."

Tears filled Nicola's eyes. She was safe again. "And you and your men. Pray you are not long away from your home."

The man nodded and pulled his horse aside, allowing Nicola room to ride on. His men did likewise, though several watched her ride past, their heads turning to follow her. "If any harm comes to that lady, I will take the man or men responsible. They will be skinned alive and left tied down to die with the sun burning, while fowl and insects feed on them." He spoke loud enough for everyone to hear, including Nicola. Immediately everyone faced forward.

Nicola shuddered with his threat. His bearing told her he would be good for his word. Perhaps the man knew her father, but it seemed he did not know what had befallen Lord Weldon and Nicola. Grateful that he had allowed her to leave unhindered, Nicola rode on. Her mind left Braggio and returned to the problem of getting into her father's study undetected.

LORD BRAGGIO WAS ALREADY MOVING ON, but his thoughts were on the young lady he had just encountered. Though the moonlight was weak, she looked to be a pretty little thing, with great spirit. He smiled to himself. *Not a very good liar, though.* There was something about her that made him want to protect her, but his job lay elsewhere. Maybe his mind was simply tricking him, distracting him from thinking of what lay ahead.

Tudor would most certainly have to fight for the crown. The outcome of that battle was any man's guess. Again, he thought about the young lady. He had not asked her name. She looked to be of higher birth, was well-spoken and elegantly dressed. Moreover, she looked too clean to have been hidden away in a cave. She did look exhausted. From whom did she run? He would like to know her better. *Little chance. Not likely to see her again, with what is coming for England. I only hope to get home one day.* Braggio knew he and his men would be very lucky to survive any battle against Richard and his men. Better to be killed in battle, though, than be taken prisoner. All of Braggio's men were experienced soldiers. *We are just too few.* It did not look well for any of them. But Braggio was a man of honor. He had sworn allegiance and vowed to fight by the side of his prince. He and the men who rode with him would keep that vow.

Long after daybreak, a rider broke through the woods lining the road. "Lord Braggio," the rider called, "men are coming, not a day behind! I have been following them for two days. They ride for Lord Weldon's castle. They were sent by the Duke of Gloucester's wife, Lady Anne Neville. They ride hard. They could catch up with you by midday." The man sat quietly, waiting, as Braggio considered the best approach.

"They are not aware of us?" Braggio asked.

The man shook his head. "No, my lord. They are not."

"Then we should not interrupt them." Braggio smiled. Though he aimed for modesty, he knew himself to be an excellent tactician and seasoned soldier. "I do love this game," he noted under his breath. To his men, he gave directions. "We are moving off the road quickly and quietly. Far enough to not be detected by anyone riding by."

Braggio led his men deep within the forest. When he stopped, his men immediately dismounted. In groups of three, the men moved into place along the roadside in positions that allowed them to watch Gloucester's men without being seen. Braggio rode a short distance farther, and he began to see evidence of recently disturbed brush and tracks. *Another rider was here, not long ago. A lone rider. Could it be one of Gloucester's men?* Braggio sat still, listening and waiting. Drue rode into view. They dismounted and exchanged a warm greeting.

"You are avoiding someone, my friend," Drue noted.

"And you ride alone, as always," Braggio replied. "I heard you were riding for Keaton. You do know he is backing young Edward?"

"I rode *with*, not *for*, Keaton. We have parted ways, although he may not know it yet," Drue corrected him, adding, "There is a lady."

"You ride for a lady? Since when do you follow any lady?" Braggio laughed.

Drue watched him through narrowed eyes. "I ride for Henry Tudor, as always. The lady happens to be for Tudor also. And is in over her head, I believe." Drue shook his head and kicked at a dirt clog. "It is a rather long story, but the short version is I believe she knows more about her father than she wants to reveal. He may have given her information before he died. She is clearly trying to protect that."

"What kind of information?" Braggio asked. "You prick my interest. Can I or my men help?"

"Hmm. You always want to help a lady, I know. But not this one," Drue added dryly. "I will let you know if I have need of your services."

Drue was walking toward his horse when Braggio asked, "This lady, does she ride alone?"

Drue stopped dead in his tracks. He turned very slowly and faced Braggio. "Why do you ask?" His voice was level, but knowing him well, Braggio knew this was not any ordinary lady.

"I met a lady riding alone, only today, shortly before dawn. It was still dark. When I asked about her circumstances, she lied. She insisted the lady who was her companion died of the sickness, while the men with her refused to stay. She said she released them, rather than admit they could leave anyway. She was bound for Lord Weldon's. I gave her directions. If she stayed the course, she should be there by now."

Drue nodded in agreement. "She should."

"You should know, Drue, we are less than a day from a group of men who belong to the Duke of Gloucester. They talk of having been sent by Lady Anne Neville. They were overheard saying they are bound for Weldon's castle." Drue had turned to listen and now was mounting his horse. "Can I help?" Braggio asked.

"You already have. I owe you." Drue circled his horse around. "I will be in touch. Good luck to you and your men."

DRUE RODE THROUGH THE FOREST, directly toward Weldon's, praying he would beat the men coming behind Braggio. He knew he would have to move quickly to get to Nicola before she could leave again. While he understood that Nicola intended to protect information given to her by her father, whatever that was, he did not know why she would return to Weldon Castle. That men riding for Anne were also headed toward Weldon Castle would mean Nicola was in danger. Anne would have heard the rumors about Lord Weldon and sought to keep Richard safe. Drue believed the worry stirring this hunt likely grew from the rumor that Lord Weldon had foretold the future of England's throne. How the rumor was born and grew so quickly was any man's guess. Lord Weldon was already dead. Nicola Weldon would die if she were caught.

CHAPTER 18

By midday, Nicola had reached the road leading up the mountain to her father's castle. The road was already being reclaimed by vegetation. She could see no tracks made by horses or carts. All was quiet. When she neared the castle, she entered the forested area along the road so that she would not be seen. Painstakingly, she zigzagged, searching the ground, moving deeper and deeper into the thicket until at last she found a faint trail. The cavern waited ahead, behind the waterfall.

Nicola looked around. It was just as they had left it. Remnants of a fire long cold was the only evidence anyone had ever stopped there. There was no sign of Allie, but the memory of what happened in this place made Nicola shudder. After securing her horse inside, Nicola began climbing carefully up the trail toward the castle. Nearing the top, she crouched low and crept forward. Cautiously peering through the brush, she could see a deserted courtyard. There were neither animals nor people about. Grasses and weeds were beginning to invade the area. Only the sound of crashing waves behind her and birds flying overhead broke the silence. The invading men were gone. The people who once lived within the protection of the walls were gone. With the first feeling of relief she had felt since the attack, Nicola scrambled back down the trail to bring her horse up. She would be safe again.

As the daylight began to fade, Nicola led the horse through the brush at the cliff's edge and past the deserted stable. She crossed the courtyard to the place she had once called home, then stood at the back wall, running her hands over the smooth rocks. They felt strong, like her father once was. "Maybe nothing ever stays the same. Maybe that is the way it is supposed to be." Her voice faded in the gentle breeze.

Continuing along the wall, Nicola searched for the door hidden from view behind several large rock columns extending beyond the wall. Her father's horses had stayed in this place, beneath the main living area, many times. Her hands felt the wide wooden door and she pushed. With a great moan, the door began to move inward. It took several more tries, but Nicola eventually opened it wide enough to allow her horse entry. The horse readily walked inside.

Using all her strength, Nicola pushed the door closed behind them, then looked around. It was musky, but safe. Several large windows just below the ceiling allowed light and air into the area. The sound of water bubbling from a spring near the stall echoed softly. The water trickled through a low trough sitting against the west wall, and from there it seeped into a small pool outside. Nicola removed her saddle and dragged it to a corner. Her horse immediately headed toward the trough. She found a cache of grain, filled the feed sack, and hung it up for the horse. Remembering the violence this home had witnessed, Nicola shivered. She would need to leave soon. It was not safe to be found here, beneath the dark cloud of suspicion that smothered the castle.

After opening a door and ascending the stairs leading to the main floor, Nicola crossed the great room and stepped outside onto the grounds. With a deep ache in her heart, her eyes perused the courtyard, searching for any sign of where her father was buried. She could see nothing. It was as if that life had never existed. She returned inside, where the living quarters of the castle were dark and deserted. She felt like an intruder.

Nicola slipped into the kitchen, looking for something to start a flame. She badly needed more light to see. Using a flint stone, she brought a small candle to life. With candle saucer in hand, she climbed upstairs to her rooms, her mind drifting back to the day her father had given her the map to the old crone's hut. She tried to remember where she had hidden it.

Nicola entered her father's sleeping room. The men who killed her father must have searched his study. Yet nothing was strewn about, no drawers were left open, and nothing was broken. Whoever searched the room seemed intent on finding information but not bent on damaging anything. Perhaps Lareau had come to suspect her father's innocence. Nicola tried to shake the feeling of despair, walking around the room and picturing her father there with her. She moved to her father's study. Nothing. As she stood trying to think where the map could be, she heard the sound. It was the sound of a door closing, and it echoed from below, up through the empty halls. Startled, Nicola froze.

Panic struck. Snuffing out the candle, Nicola could barely breathe as she listened. The steps sounded louder and closer, steadily moving up the stairs. Whoever it was made no effort to be quiet. *No one knows I am here. I must hide.* Her heart raced. If it was Lareau, she was in grave danger. The steps continued, slow and deliberate. As they proceeded along the hall, Nicola scrambled beneath her father's massive desk. She listened as each door along the hall creaked open. It took a few moments before a door was closed and another opened. *The rooms are being searched.* Nicola was beginning to sweat. When the door to her father's study was opened, she began to tremble. She listened in horror to the footsteps as they entered the room, stopping at the candle she had just blown out. Shocked, she heard a man speak. "Lady, I know you are here. Reveal yourself. I have little time. It will go worse for you if you keep hiding. You know I *will* find you." It was Drue's voice that she heard, quiet but firm. "There are some things worse than dying, lady."

Nicola closed her eyes, the picture of Drue leaning over Garrett's body vivid in her mind. She crawled and stood to face him, expecting him to kill her too. His body was silhouetted against the moonlight coming in the window. He too remained still and silent for a moment. Nicola waited.

"Come with me. Quickly—we have little time." Drue's voice was softer, though he remained where he stood. "I did not come to harm you." Nicola started to move around the desk toward Drue. She turned slowly as her eyes took in the shelves, tables, and books. Darkness now gave everything an oddly comforting feel, as though nothing had ever happened to her father or to this place. But then there was Allie. The hatred she felt for that traitor to all she held dear rushed through her. "You have to let it go." Drue's voice behind her broke through her dark thoughts, and she gasped at his ability to read them.

"No! I will never let it go," she said, no longer able to restrain her impulses. "I will hate Allie forever. Forever!"

"Then you have abandoned your father's request," Drue stated flatly. He remained still.

"I have not!" Nicola denied. "I would never do such a thing."

Drue answered quietly, "Lady Weldon, you cannot have both. You cannot carry the burden of anger and hate at the same time that you carry the burden of the cause your father entrusted to you. The weight of the two loads will consume you. One must go. Only you can choose which to set aside." He took one step closer to her and continued. "It now matters little what Allie did. Allie invented what she felt she had to, to get the Frenchman to listen. Once the game was started, she could not leave the board—the die was cast."

Nicola's shoulders drooped. Defeated, she turned and walked toward Drue, resigned to be returned to Keaton. "Your horse?" Drue asked.

"Below," Nicola answered, without looking at him. Had she known he was in the castle earlier, she could have joined the horse. Drue would never have found them. Too late now.

"Below?" Drue nodded toward the open door of her father's study. "Your horse is below?" Nicola nodded.

"Show me," Drue commanded.

"I must find something first." Nicola turned to Drue, trying to bargain for time. "It's important."

"There is no time for that now. This room has been searched by men who do such things for a living." He lifted his arm, making a ghostly sweeping gesture. "Anything of worth, including information, is gone by now."

"But I must . . . it's a—" Nicola began.

Drue interrupted. "There is no time, lady. Now, at this moment, you are the object of a very determined search party sent by Lady Anne Neville. She would eliminate anyone not in favor of her husband, Richard of Gloucester. Show me where your horse is, now." His voice was firm.

With one last glimpse of the darkened room, Nicola picked up her cloak. Drue stopped her. "No." Drue took it from her. "Another one. The heaviest one you have, but nothing anyone would recognize," he added. She left the room. Drue followed her to her own chambers. After opening a chest, she pulled the thickest woolen, hooded cloak from the bottom of it. Carefully, she folded the first cloak to the bottom and closed the chest. Drue gave her a quick nod, then followed her as she moved down the stairs and beyond to the lower level.

When she opened the door to where her horse was standing, Drue was taken aback. "Your horse is here, within the walls?" Drue glanced at the water and the stall, all invisible from outside unless one was aware of its existence. "You have always known about this place?"

"Of course. This is my home," Nicola replied quietly. She stopped walking and turned to Drue. "How did you know where I was?" Before he could answer, she added, "Why take me back to Lord Keaton? Please let me go."

"I am not taking you to Keaton," Drue replied. "You're going with me. We should move quickly, Lady Nicola." He added, "Your tracks led me to this place."

"Are you going to kill me?" Nicola asked. She looked Drue in the eye, hoping to see the truth in his face.

Drue frowned. "No, I am not. I did not come to harm you, Lady Weldon."

Nicola left the hidden stall. A strange feeling came to her, an image of a meadow and chapel floating across her mind. Startled, she nearly stumbled. Nicola ignored the feeling as it washed over her again. This was not the first time, but she refused to allow it to stay. Drue gave no indication he had noticed. With the animals saddled, he led them outside and pulled the door closed. When both were mounted, he started to lead them out of the castle.

"No, this way." Nicola turned her horse and rode to the brush line at the cliff edge.

"Wait, Nicola!" Drue stopped, dismounted, and retraced their steps, brushing away the tracks that led from the castle to the brush. Nicola watched him, asking herself how leaving with him could be safer than with Keaton.

She knew she had no choice. "Your horse might not care for this trail. I will go first. Do exactly as I do." Not waiting for an answer, Nicola gently heeled her horse. He readily stepped through the brush and began the descent. Drue had a harder time getting his mount to follow, but the horse finally stepped through. The two reached the waterfall, where Drue rode around Nicola and took the lead.

CHAPTER 19

"WHERE ARE WE GOING?" Nicola asked as they emerged from the cave behind the waterfall. She refused to look at him, for fear he would see the tears that filled her eyes.

"London. Some place to start." Drue looked back at Nicola, and she knew she must look frail and alone to him. "Lady, what did your father want you to do?"

Nicola was silent for a long time. Drue did not push her, instead staying alert to any sounds that might indicate they were close to other riders. Suddenly, Nicola reined in her horse. Drue stopped and turned back to her. "What are you doing?" His voice indicated his irritation. "This is not the time for you to be independent. I have no intention of taking any chance that we might run into Keaton, Lady Anne's men . . . or any number of men out gathering support for young Edward, or for Gloucester."

"I do not wish to travel with you." Although she tried to sound determined, her voice wavered. She was not certain what she would do if he left her, but she did not trust him any more than she trusted Keaton. Nothing looked familiar, but she had to try. She felt like one of the puppets the monks used during celebrations of the church.

"I do not remember asking you whether you did or didn't," Drue remarked. Nicola's shoulders drooped, and she simply followed him deeper within the forest. Drue hardly spoke to her or even acknowledged her presence. When she spoke to him, he did not reply, although when she had fallen slightly behind, he was quick to insist she keep up. Finally, Drue stopped and dismounted, informing her, "We will stop here." Nicola had already started to dismount when he ordered her to stay atop her horse.

Frowning, she sat waiting for him. "Why?" she asked.

Drue did not answer.

"Is there something wrong? Why is it that you do not speak?" Nicola prodded. When Drue remained silent, Nicola became irritated. She could see he was removing large pieces of something from the bags behind his saddle. "What are you doing?" Nicola demanded. Still, he was silent. *I need to find the crone. I have neither the time nor patience to wander around with a man I do not trust. A man able to kill but unable to provide me with simple responses.*

Drue walked to her horse first. Petting and speaking to it quietly, he began to cover its feet with the materials in his hand. When he was through with all four hoofs, he began to wrap the bridle bit and anything on her saddle that might clink. Finally, he addressed Nicola. "You are to be quiet, from now forward. Silent. Do not make a sound. Can you do that?"

"Yes!" Nicola snapped. "I can be silent!"

"You do have *some* talent," Drue replied curtly. He began the same process for his mount.

"And you, Lord Drue? Do you have any talents I should know about?" Nicola responded, as the vision of Garrett flashed before her.

Drue stopped working and straightened up. He turned and slowly walked to Nicola, stopping at her stirrup. "It did surprise me, when you did not say anything to Keaton. I am an assassin, if you must know." His voice was even. "I am very good at what I do."

He likely would have kept his profession from her, but when she pushed him, he had responded. At any rate, she had seen him with Garrett, so she was not entirely surprised. Drue turned on his heel and returned to his horse. Neither he nor Nicola spoke as he completed his work. After patting his horse, he walked back to Nicola, lightly tapping her foot. "When I stop, you stop. Your horse is well trained. He knows what to do. It matters not what you might hear; you must not make a sound. It could mean your life." His voice had softened, but Nicola felt he was angry with her.

"Yes," Nicola answered. *If he is going to kill me too, why does he not just do it?* Her eyes followed him back to his horse. She looked behind her. Blackness interrupted by blurred images of trees and bushes was all she could see. It was evident Drue knew where he was and where he needed to go. Nicola was caught. There was no going back, and the fear she had first felt around Drue proved to be warranted. *Every turn takes me closer to danger. What am I supposed to do now?* Even as the thought slipped through her mind, another quickly followed. *I must be stronger. The time is coming when I will make my own decisions.*

Drue and Nicola moved forward as if they were ghosts. She could barely hear the horse she rode. Drue took them around trees, skirted brush, and looked for softer earth, as the two horses moved painstakingly slowly.

At first, Nicola thought the sound she heard came from Drue. Just as she started to reply, she heard it again. It was a man's voice, coming from somewhere close to her right. Drue stopped moving. Nicola's horse stopped as well. In the surrounding stillness, Nicola could hear the voices of several men. Straining to listen, she realized she knew those voices. The men were Keaton, Carnell, and Harding. Drue sat as if made of stone. Instinctively, Nicola followed suit. The voices of the men carried through the darkness, sliding around trees and brush to the two lone riders hiding just beyond Keaton's view.

"Tomorrow as the sun sets, we will be in London. Ask about Edward's coronation, certainly, but ask for information that might lead us to Lady Nicola. If she lives, though I doubt she does, we must find her before she finds Lady Margaret. Remember, if you see her, she disappears. I wish no contact with her. Get rid of the body." Keaton spoke angrily. He looked pointedly at both Harding and Carnell. "I think somehow Drue killed Garrett. I know I did not. Nor do I believe either one of you would make such a stupid mistake."

"Stupid?" challenged Carnell. "How is Garrett's murder without thought?"

"We were five, now we are four," Keaton replied.

"Of what use is Drue?" Harding spoke up. "I have good friends in Scotland. You two are friends. Why is Drue even with us?"

"Drue," Keaton responded, "knows this land—every foot of it—better than any man, better even than Edward did or his brother Richard does. He knows the best place for us to lie in wait for Henry, what shores are the easiest for us to defend. Drue knows this land better than even Jasper Tudor." At this, both Harding and Carnell were silent.

For a moment, no one spoke. Finally, Keaton continued, "Drue has no love for either York or Tudor. He likes the assignments. He likes the kill."

DRUE CAUGHT THE GASP BEHIND HIM and smiled. He knew Nicola had overheard the exchange. *'Tis always better to know with whom you ride, lady.* Without comment, he quietly moved past the men, and Nicola had no choice but to follow.

CHAPTER 20

EVENTUALLY, THE MEN SETTLED DOWN for the night. Keaton lay without sleeping. He heard first Harding, then Carnell begin to snore. Staring at patches of sky and stars visible through the treetops, Keaton wrestled with the idea that Carnell must have killed Garrett. Drue, Keaton knew, could not have. Drue had ridden in after the fact and carried with him all the supplies from the hamlet two hours' ride away. He also knew Garrett was poisoned, and the only one of the men in proximity to Garrett was Carnell. *If he could get rid of Garrett so easily, without my order, and stand by while I try to figure out what happened, he could just as easily kill Harding or me. But why, when he knows we need every man we have? Where would his advantage lay?*

As the night wore on, Keaton decided Carnell could be a spy for Jasper Tudor. Why else would he kill one of Keaton's men? The realization made him angry, then gravely concerned. *Who else wears a mask? How do I deal with this now?*

By the time the sun's first rays broke through, Keaton had a plan.

While the men sat around breaking fast with dried meat and hard cheese, Keaton announced they were changing their plans. "We are not going to London. Instead, we go to find Drue. He is headed south and should be easy enough to locate, once we get closer to the coast. I have a new course of action for us." Keaton suspected Carnell's loyalty lay with others. Time to see if he was correct.

Harding frowned. "What about the northern border? I know you planned to go to London after Lady Weldon, but I think she will find herself in a cell soon enough. The Scots are going to be against young Edward. We stand a better chance of holding the Scots back from gathering a larger force if we are there. The Scots know you and Carnell, Keaton. I think you could get them to listen to reason and give the crown time to settle. Do we not waste time going after Drue?"

Keaton stood staring at the dying fire. Carnell made no comment, until Harding pushed him. "Carnell, how do you feel about this change? Should we not ride for the northern border and try to garner support for young Edward, instead of losing precious time searching for Drue? Besides, Keaton, you yourself said Drue knew this land better than anyone. How would we even know where to find him?"

AS TALK BETWEEN THE MEN GREW HEATED, Carnell placed his last piece of cheese in his mouth and chewed while considering his options, and thereby the best way to answer Harding's question. He was unwilling to turn back toward London or ride north, accompanied by Keaton. If they were successful in stopping the flow of men from Scotland going to Henry Tudor, Carnell wanted it known *he* had made the difference, not Keaton. Having Keaton around would overshadow anything he might do. Refusing to do anything that might jeopardize his one chance at a place in what he believed would soon be Richard's court, Carnell made a quick decision to side with Keaton's idea to find Drue. While he would be perfectly happy letting Drue wander around out of the way, in the southern reaches of England, Carnell would do whatever was necessary to keep Keaton from Richard or young Edward, until he had his chance to show both potential kings what he could do for them. "Lord Keaton has led us well so far, Harding," he said. "I suggest we see where he is taking us now."

Harding sat quietly, looking slightly stunned. Without another word, Harding walked to his horse. He glanced back briefly before mounting, and rode away without looking back.

"You killed Garrett!" Keaton whirled, snarling at Carnell, as he drew his sword. "You picked the wrong side, Carnell. Tudor does not stand a chance." Keaton began to move slowly, deliberately around the fire. "You always did like to gamble," Keaton added bitterly.

Carnell tried to process the accusation. But there was no time for that. "So be it, Keaton. I intend to take a place in the court of England. A court that will soon belong to Richard. You are not a part of my plan." Carnell quickly drew his own sword. Neither man spoke as sounds of steel clashing reverberated through the surrounding forest. Keaton was a superb swordsman, but Carnell fought with more than his anger on the line. His future plans had never included Keaton. Now, more than ever, he needed to put the threat of interference by Keaton behind him.

Carnell drew first blood. The red stain on Keaton's side grew, but Keaton fought on. The tip of his blade caught Carnell's sword arm, leaving a great gash. Carnell's sword fell to the ground. He drew his firearm, but, forced to use his left hand, he shot wild, missing Keaton entirely. Keaton moved in quickly. His aim was accurate. So was the pitch Carnell made with his smaller blade. The wound to Carnell's chest bled profusely as he sank to the ground. Carnell's blade disappeared into Keaton's belly, up to the handle, and the wound on Keaton's side was now gushing. He too sank to the ground.

CHAPTER 21

BEHIND THE WALLS OF THE SANCTUARY, Elizabeth waited with her remaining children. It was quite clear that Richard did not plan on having any coronation but his own. Elizabeth refused to believe Richard would actually have young Edward killed, but neither did she care to have him waste away and die in the Tower. Her youngest son would most certainly become a prisoner in the Tower too. He would not survive either, if Richard was made king.

On this evening, with shadows lengthening, she met with an aging priest, one who had shown her family kindness before, and continued to do so, especially now, when they were essentially prisoners. With neither her mother nor Edward to offer encouragement, she felt dreadfully alone and defenseless to change the course of events.

"I must find some way to keep Edward's line on the throne. Surely there are those who would support Edward's fight for his father's crown, the crown that is undoubtedly destined to be his."

The priest lowered his eyes momentarily. But it was long enough for Elizabeth to feel the stab of fear.

"I have heard, my lady, of men who are ready and willing to rescue Edward from the Tower. It should be done carefully, without loss of life, as it cannot appear to be simply an uprising." The priest spoke quickly. "I will speak with you again, lady. Have faith." He kissed her hand.

As she watched him walk away, the tears that filled Elizabeth's eyes spilled over. She seldom gave way to feelings of great sadness or fear. On this night, she felt both. Yet if the plot were successful, she and her children would finally be safe. Slowly, Elizabeth turned and walked from the narrow gate separating her from the outside world and entered the bowels of the sanctuary. Her daughters were sleeping, all except the eldest.

"Lizzie, can you not sleep?" Elizabeth asked, brushing the curls from Lizzie's face and kissing her forehead.

"Can anyone help us? Are they going to kill my brothers?" Lizzie's voice broke. "Would Uncle Richard really do such a thing? He said he was keeping both boys safe. Is that what he is doing?"

Elizabeth sighed. She sat on the bed she shared with her eldest daughter. "I think the thought of becoming more than an advisor to Edward and the chance to become the king are moving Richard in a direction he would never have dreamt of, were your father still alive." Elizabeth stared at the bars separating them from the halls beyond. The bars were for safety but gave the impression that they resided in a prison. She looked down at the eldest of her children, so sweet and innocent. "I am fearful for their lives, Lizzie. I do not know what might happen to them."

"I want to see them." Lizzie sat up suddenly. "Why can I not see them?"

"We are not allowed beyond the walls of this place, Lizzie. If we step beyond, we give up the protection the walls provide." Elizabeth's voice was bitter. "There is an undercurrent of unrest that is going to boil over. There are those who would try to rescue your brothers. Pray they are successful. If they fail, surely my boys will die." Elizabeth stood and walked to the wall, where a small window allowed the rising moon to shine into the cells. *Who could have ever dreamed this is how my family would find themselves. The life of a king is perilous, as is the life of his children. Perhaps it is time I asked the old crone for help. I must call on her.* Elizabeth stepped back to Lizzie and kissed her cheek. "Sleep, daughter. We will pray for your brothers and pray Richard keeps his word. There is nothing we can do within these walls. You must not let the little ones know our worries. They are much too young to understand. Like you, I cannot believe your uncle would bring harm to his own nephews."

Lizzie nodded, slightly comforted, then rolled over. Elizabeth pulled the blankets closely around Lizzie's shoulders. After patting her, she stood up and walked to the window. She waited motionless, until the even breathing told her Lizzie was at last asleep.

Quietly, holding a shawl over the latch to muffle the sound, she slipped out of the cell. Carrying a small lantern, she stepped into the alley between her building and the great walls surrounding the monastery. She walked its length, then stopped where the wall turned. She set the lantern down and took out a feather, strip of paper, and bit of lint from the cell. Very softly, in a voice that would not carry to the wrong people, she whispered, "Can you hear me? I have need of your services once more. My son is in danger. I need your help to see he is liberated. I call on the winds to carry my message to you. I call on the winds to touch the minds of men of like thinking, to protect Edward." After setting the paper, feather, and lint on fire, she waited until all had burned out. Looking around at the darkness, she stepped back against the building wall and waited.

Tucked away in her bed, an old lady was suddenly awakened. She sat upright. In the silence surrounding her, she waited for the message to come again. As the whispers reached her, she sat very still, her eyes closed, and listened. "Ah, you seek help. You never wanted it before, but now you do. I know your mother is dead, your husband is dead, and you fear for your children."

"Yes," Elizabeth whispered to the feeling of connection brought to her by the very stillness.

The old crone leaned back against the wall of her hut. She had tried many times to get in touch with Elizabeth before Edward died, but Elizabeth had forgotten about her. Tonight, the old crone tried to reach Elizabeth again. "Listen carefully, there is a young girl who carries the answers you seek. She has not the power to come to you. For you to know what she knows, you must find her. I am old and will soon die. You have stayed away too long. Perhaps there is still time. But you must not wait."

Elizabeth did not answer.

"She no longer hears me. The tides have changed. I cannot help her." With that, the old crone shuffled her blankets and lay back down. In a short while, she was gently snoring.

Elizabeth listened for a long time. She could not hear the answer. Perhaps the old crone had suddenly died. "No, that cannot be. I need help." She tried again to contact the old crone. Only the sounds of an impending storm blew through the alley. The long night brought no sleep for Elizabeth, or peace. Only a greater sense of urgency and fear for the safety of her two innocent boys.

CHAPTER 22

DRUE LED NICOLA AWAY FROM KEATON and his men. When they had traveled far enough away, he stopped and started removing the hoof coverings and other materials used to keep his and Nicola's riding gear as quiet as possible.

Nicola still felt stunned. "Keaton just ordered my death. Is that what you have planned?" she asked, anger and fear pushing all else aside. "Tell me again where we are going." Surely he would change his plans, after hearing what they both had heard, unless he had the same idea.

"We are going to London," Drue answered.

"London? Why would you do that to me?" Nicola asked, angrily. Keaton had just given the order to find her and get rid of her. Now, Drue was leading her to that very place. "Why?" Nicola persisted.

Drue did not answer; he only held up his hand and shook his head. After he had removed all the leather from both horses, he mounted and rode.

Nicola knew her only choice was to follow. There were too many searching for her. She had no idea where she was or how to get out of the thick forest. In fact, she had no idea what she could do if she did get away from Drue. *What was Father thinking, when he left me to them?*

Silently, the two rode on for several hours. When they entered a small meadow, he stopped. "We can stop here. The horses need to rest and eat. You do, also," he added.

"I am fine, Lord Drue," Nicola answered coldly. *He best not tempt me. I can make this ride much worse.* Though she had to admit, she had no idea what she was to do in London, or how she would stay safe without Drue. The greater question was why he was taking her to London. "I suppose you have a reason for withholding information. You heard Keaton order me killed. There are three of them, and one of me."

"There are three of them, two of us. You will be fine." Drue looked up from the fire he was starting. "I will see you are not harmed." Standing, Drue studied Nicola for a moment. She returned his gaze. "Lady, I would see what you have to share with Henry Tudor. I believe I may know what it is." He stood still, waiting for her to respond.

"You cannot possibly know, Lord Drue," Nicola answered. "My father did not share that information with anyone, including me." Nicola was certain Drue was bluffing, but she would not be so easily fooled.

"He did share his dreams with someone. I have spoken to the crone. She explained to Lord Weldon what he should design, when the dreams became too real. She was his friend and more. But then, you know that, do you not?" Drue stepped closer to Nicola. "You have to trust someone, Nicola," he said. His voice was now quiet and gentle. "There is no one here but me. You have to trust me. I understand what it is that I am asking of you."

Her mind wrestled with the unexpected news, and she tried to fit pieces together that refused to fit. She blurted out, "If you already know, then you do not need me to share anything." Nicola could not see how this was possible, although he was correct in his assertion that the old crone and Lord Weldon were friends. Nicola had seen them together with her own eyes. They did know each other, and well. *But how did Drue know that they were friends? How would the crone know someone like Drue?*

Drue turned away. "We need to be in London before Keaton, so we are going another route. It will be a hard ride for you, and you should rest as much as you can now."

Nicola watched him as he stood with his back to her, as if resisting the urge to look at her. Why that even mattered, or why she would consider his feelings, she did not know. *No time for these things.*

She sat on a nearby stump. *He does know the crone. Is it possible Father shared with the crone what he made? I wish I knew what I should do.*

THE OLD CRONE WOKE UP AGAIN. Sitting up, she smiled. *I wondered when you would reach out to me. Not an easy task for one such as you, child. But help*

you, I can. Closing her eyes, she felt as though she was sleeping while sitting up. Then she began to sway, side to side. As she slid deeper and deeper into her meditation, she began to hum in a soft tone. *You do know what to do, child. Drue can help you, like no other can. You must trust him, and your instincts. Show him what it is you carry. And beware of the storm brewing around the throne. Do not get caught up in that tempest. Keep your mind open, child. Listen for me.*

When the crone opened her eyes, she could tell the time was coming. Soon she would have to make ready for company. *But not right now. I find I need rest more often these long days.* Lying back down and rolling over, she pulled the covers close and slept.

NICOLA WAS WATCHING DRUE, though she was thinking about her father. Suddenly, she felt rather than heard someone talking to her. She was alarmed, instantly listening and looking around, though there was no cause that she could discern for it. The meadow was silent, their little camp was still, and there were no other people around them.

Drue glanced at Nicola. "What bothers you, lady?" he asked, walking toward her.

"I . . . I thought I heard someone talking to me," she said, looking around nervously. "Perhaps I am more tired than I thought," she added sheepishly.

"I suspect it is the old crone. Relax, let her speak to you. She can help you." Drue sat on the ground beside her, rolled his shoulders, stretched his legs, and leaned back against the stump. He did not look at Nicola, but instead stared at the fire. To Nicola, it appeared Drue was more patient with her. She was certain he was a soldier. His physique spoke to years of activity, but his hands were not calloused. She would remain cautious, but she understood that his weapons were simply the tools of his trade—and she had to admit she was slowly becoming more comfortable with him around.

I need help from someone I can trust. Father trusted the crone. Nicola remembered her kind eyes. Hesitantly, Nicola closed her own eyes and tried to clear her mind. Then it came again. Nicola stiffened, but she concentrated on what she was seeing in her mind. She could see the symbols. They appeared to be in a whirlpool, swirling around, yet Nicola could see the images clearly. Once more, the feeling came over her. The message came to her without sound. After several long moments, she opened her eyes. She closed them again, but everything was gone, as if it had never been. Nicola stared at the darkness. Finally, she spoke. "I am supposed to trust you, and show you." She frowned at Drue. He remained silent, waiting. "I am not certain I am comfortable with that advice." Nicola waited, but Drue remained silent. "Please allow me some privacy." So saying, Nicola stood and walked away from the campfire and its light.

Drue sat watching the flames dance, waiting. When Nicola returned, she held in her hands the two objects her father had left her. She started to sit back on the stump, but Drue patted the ground next to him. He had spread a saddle blanket out and patted it again. In the darkness, she could not see his eyes, but she knew they were green, surrounded by thick, dark eyelashes. Even relaxed, there was an air of command about him, as if it mattered little what happened and he would handle everything as it came. She, too, truly had little choice.

Nicola sat down, then handed the two pieces to Drue. As his fingers folded around the jeweled pieces, he softly whispered, "All will go as it should. I will not leave your side, until you have no further use for me. I promise."

Nicola nodded, but again she felt the chill of doubt and fear. She closed her eyes. At least now she would not carry the burden alone.

Drue opened his hand. In it lay the two identical jeweled pieces she had carried for what felt like so long now, set in the brightest gold, with rare stones embedded flat within the surface. Etchings wound around the stones and seemed to float off into the background. Handing the smaller piece back to Nicola, Drue studied the larger piece. She was afraid of him, of the message the pieces might carry, and of the task her father had left her. Softly, he touched her arm. "I need you to help me, lady."

She turned to him. "How can I help you, Lord Drue?"

"I know what likely lays ahead, and it will not be an easy course. You have to help me if we are to succeed." He was not convinced she would have the strength and drive to stay the course. "The images are clear, but I do not know their meaning. I do not know what the different stones mean, nor what the drawings are telling us." Drue watched her closely.

She opened her hand and looked at the piece in her palm. She stood and moved closer to the fire, allowing its light to unveil the treasure in her hand. "I know what the stones stand for, I think."

"Tell me." Drue stood up next to her, studying the symbol he held, studying the girl beside him.

"Black could mean death. White could mean purity. Red is sacrifice." Examining the piece, she shook her head. "What does that tell us?"

Drue frowned as he inspected the piece. "Let us start with the bar itself. Gold?"

"Gold is kingly . . . kingship. Denotes an important piece." Nicola reached deep into her memory, playing her father's talks over and over. "There is brass here, too. Brass is for strength, endurance."

"And the etching along the sides? Do they mean anything? They must." Drue glanced at Nicola, then looked back at the piece he held. His voice was low, the tone encouraging, gently pushing Nicola to try.

"I know an oak leaf means strength. I cannot remember ever seeing a herder's staff before." Nicola looked up at Drue, then at the darkness beyond the fire. She made a slow circle around the flames. "I have to think on it. I am sorry. I just cannot see what this all might be telling us."

"Start with the stones." Drue brought the blanket close to the light and sat down. Nicola sat down beside him. The fire's quivering flames bounced light off Drue's face. He was relaxed but still had an air of confidence about him.

Nicola studied the piece again. Suddenly, it came to her. "Drue! There are crowns etched in the gold. Look, near the left side is a crown. How did I miss that before?" Her voice dropped when she added, "But it's broken. Why?"

"There is another crown on the right side, and it is not broken. It's complete. Do you see that?" Drue added.

"I do." Nicola frowned. "See, the stones below the broken crown are white. Is that not a York rose? Could that be King Edward? It's broken, and the white rose is half black . . . death."

"That must be King Edward," said Drue. "And he just died."

"Drue, every white rose is half black," Nicola noted, her voice revealing her rising anxiety. "There will be more deaths? Look, there is a second crown next to the first one. There in the middle, it is also broken and its white is half black. The smaller white rose next to that crown is also half black. But *death*? To all these people? That's treason! We cannot get caught carrying these." Nicola clutched the symbol against her breast. "We could die because of this!"

"We are not going to die," Drue insisted, as he reached for Nicola's arm. "Tell me what else you see. We must know the entire message." Drue again studied the symbols on the piece he held.

Nicola reluctantly opened her hand and looked again. "The only unbroken crown is the one at the end. The rose beneath it is red on the outside petals, but white superimposed on the red. That last crown is surrounded by oak leaves. The herder's staff finishes the message." Fearfully, Nicola looked at Drue. "Can that be? Four more deaths?"

Drue was listening intently to Nicola. His voice was low when he finally spoke. "If we are right, the York kingship is doomed. The smaller roses must mean all three boys will die as well." He stopped for a second and looked at the symbol predicting such doom. "The only unbroken symbol is surrounded with the oak leaves. It has to be Henry Tudor. Henry must understand he is fulfilling his destiny." Drue's eyes studied a world beyond the fire. "Our mission becomes much more dangerous. We may have little time."

"Perhaps whatever caused Edward's death will also take his children." Nicola's voice faded. "But the other two . . . who else might die now?"

Drue turned to Nicola. "His brother Richard and Richard's son, I am certain. We will have to keep riding. We must find the crone. She will know more. It would be better to travel under the cover of darkness. Can you ride now?"

"Yes," Nicola answered quickly, renewed energy in her voice. Her distrust of Drue was forgotten. They worked together to put the fire out and scatter the ashes.

"I will saddle the horses. Pour water over the rocks near the ashes. It would be better to have cold rocks if someone should come upon this camp." Drue was already working with the horses.

"We will travel very slowly at night," Nicola said, looking around. "Someone following us could catch up easily."

Drue glanced at her, smiling. "Not necessarily. I know where I am going. We must get to the crone." Lifting Nicola upon her horse, he added, "Perhaps by the time we get to London, Keaton and his men will be gone."

"We can only hope," Nicola whispered. Drue looked up at her.

"You will be safe with me, lady." He nodded to her, then walked to his horse.

Once he mounted, they looked around the small camp one last time.

Nicola's eyes moved from Drue to what was left of their campfire, to the forest surrounding them. She could not envision how anything would ever be fine again. Taking a deep breath, she followed Drue.

CHAPTER 23

THE RIDE IN DARKNESS WAS MORE DIFFICULT than Nicola had imagined. Drue shied away from roads or trails, preferring to ride through the thick forested areas. He knew exactly where he was going, leading them as easily as if they were on a road. Nicola had to stay alert to follow his dark form and duck under branches while trying to keep her skirts from being snagged. At one point, pulling up her horse, she tried in vain to loosen her skirt caught by a thick stand of brush. Exasperated, she called to him softly. He heard her and stopped immediately.

"Lady?" His voice barely carried to her through the vegetation.

"I . . . well, I need help," Nicola replied.

"Are you tired? We still have some way to go, if you can," he answered. She could tell he was riding back toward her.

"I am tired, but I can ride further, if we discount the brush that holds me captive," Nicola whispered. She could hear Drue chuckle softly. *At least he is not angry with me. Perhaps this is a good time to tend to personal business.* "Please, allow me privacy when you have freed me from this mess. I will not take long." Nicola was becoming more entangled trying to pull free.

Drue shook his head. "Of course, lady." After dismounting and taking out his knife, he quickly cut her free. Then, before she had time to dismount herself, as was her habit, he lifted her out of the saddle and set her aground. He then busied himself checking their riding gear. When Nicola finished, she returned to find him leaning against her horse. "Better?" he asked. His voice was light.

"Yes, thank you." Nicola nodded.

He helped her mount, then handed her a small water bag. "'Tis filled with wine—drink very little, or I will have to tie you onto your horse while you sleep. I would offer water, if we had any fresh."

Unaccustomed to such a duration in the saddle, she hurt everywhere. It was painful to sit. Refusing to be the cause of any further delays, she kept silent. She squirmed in the saddle and prayed the ride would end before long.

Drue began riding slower and slower. Suddenly he stopped, and Nicola stopped also. Drue dismounted and walked cautiously toward her. "I will be right back. I feel we are being followed." His voice was so low Nicola could scarcely hear him. His manner was focused and intense. Nicola nodded and watched his form slip soundlessly out of sight. She thought briefly about getting down off her horse to stretch her legs, except Drue had never before acted this way—there was the chance they might have to leave quickly. Nervously looking around her, she prayed. Time crept by. Still, Drue did not return. Nicola tried not to think about how she could survive without Drue's help. Much as she had distrusted him, and possibly still did, she now felt he would keep her safe from Keaton. *Will he stay around long enough to keep helping me to the end? If he is caught, surely I will be, also.* Remembering what the symbols seemed to indicate, the thought of possible capture sent chills through her.

After what felt like hours to Nicola, she heard the sounds of someone coming quickly, straight toward Nicola and the horses. Whoever was coming knew exactly where the horses were. Nicola waited expectantly.

When Drue came into view, he motioned to Nicola. "We are being followed, though I doubt they know it. Because they seem uncertain where they are bound, they travel much slower. Still, we should ride. Stay close, lady." His tone was level but urgent.

"Who follows us?" Nicola asked, but Drue was already at his horse, mounting. As he rode ahead, she stayed as close as she could, given the terrain. Drue seldom looked back to check on her. He was more intent on putting distance between the two of them and the riders behind them. As time went on, they began to move even faster. Nicola was exhausted. The effort to keep sight of Drue in the darkness and stay alert to prevent a torn gown or being knocked off by tree limbs was becoming progressively difficult. Even the horses were tired. *Will this ride never end? Surely we cannot keep this up.*

Nicola struggled to remain mounted. She had never felt so tired, yet Drue kept on. *How does he do it?* Barely ducking in time, Nicola dodged another low-hanging branch. This time, instead of sitting back up, she leaned forward and clung to the horse's mane. Slowly, slowly, her head dropped, until it was lying on the horse's neck. She could feel the animal slowing down, but it was useless to resist slumber.

It felt like no time had passed when her horse jerked his head up, waking her. "Lady, stay strong. We are nearly through with this ride. Just a short distance now," Drue said.

"I am sorry, Drue. I will be fine. I swear." Her voice came out tired, faint, as if not her own.

Drue nodded. After patting her horse's neck, he took her reins, got back up onto his saddle, and led them on.

When they broke through the thicket, Nicola was too tired to even care why they might have stopped again. The outline of the mound before them was like so many others they had ridden past. She closed her eyes and waited for him to head out again. She was startled to hear his voice at her knee.

"We are here, lady. You can rest now." He reached up for her. This time, she made no attempt to jump down herself. She let him pull her off the horse and lead her toward the mound. They ducked beneath the huge trunk of a fallen dead tree before it.

Looking around, Nicola gradually remembered everything. She could hear her father laughing with the old crone and smell the concoction they had all shared for their midday meal. *We are here. This is her home–this is where she lives.* Nicola felt a wave wash over her—she was safe for now. "How did you know where to find her?" she asked.

"It does not matter. I found her. That is all that matters now. Come, you can rest for a short while." Drue led her through the door that had opened for them. He stepped away from Nicola and hugged the old woman. She patted his arm and smiled up at him.

"You found your way? And you brought the girl, I see." She turned to Nicola. "You must be tired. Here." She took Nicola's hand and led her to a cot along one wall. "You can lie down here. Sleep. When you are awake, I will have food for you." In the light cast by the flames from the fire pit, Nicola could see the kind eyes she remembered.

Safe. I am safe for now. I can sleep in peace. Nicola lay down on the cot and began to drift.

CHAPTER 24

*T*HE OLD CRONE WATCHED NICOLA for a short moment, then turned to Drue. "Show me what she carries, after you both sleep. They will be here by late tomorrow. You must leave well before they come."

"I cannot sleep—there is not time. I will wake Nicola shortly, and we can talk." Drue started toward Nicola's sleeping form.

"Stop. They come for me, not for you or the lady. They want to know what I see." She paused a moment, looking at Drue, her smile pushing the wrinkles aside. "I have waited to speak with you. We must speak now. You cannot turn from what is your responsibility." The old crone limped across the room and pulled an ancient wooden box from a shelf near the cot. She handed Drue a letter with a broken seal, addressed to her. It was the seal of Drue's father. Carefully, Drue opened the document and read. His father had written to the crone, telling her he had named Drue as successor to the throne should Cicero die without an heir.

The old crone's voice was gentle. "Neither you nor the lady can go farther the way you are. You must protect her. How can you do that if you are not listening to what is around you, Drue? No, you sleep. While you sleep, I will do what I must do." She reached up and patted his shoulder with a bony, wrinkled hand.

Drue grasped the hand and kissed it gently.

"Go, be off with you." She pushed him toward a spot in one corner where she had already piled blankets.

"How did you get this?" Drue asked. "It would not do to have anyone know you are—"

The old crone interrupted. "I felt someone looking for me, and I knew he was not here to harm me. I walked into the forest and met him. He handed me a package with the scroll and a ring from your father." She pulled the ring from a pouch at her waist. "It is a ring special to your father and to me. Now, I give it to you. He knew you had another path to walk, for a time. You have done all he ever asked, and more. You know what you must now do." She set the ring in his hand, and he wrapped his fingers around it. "You must not wear it until you are ready. I will talk with the girl when she is awake. She has never been prepared for what now belongs to her." The crone reached up to touch his face. Drue bent to kiss her cheek. Gently pushing him, she nodded again toward the blankets piled in the corner. "Now, sleep."

"He died while speaking of you, Mother. He died loving you." Drue spoke softly.

"I know. I knew when he died. I shall miss him a great deal. We lived far apart, but he was always here." She touched her breast. "Now," she said, smiling at Drue, "he watches over me from heaven's window. Go to sleep, son."

NICOLA STRUGGLED TO WAKE UP—never had she felt such a fog in her mind. She was certain someone shook her. She rolled over to confirm it, but there was no one near. As she propped herself up, she saw the crone bending over the fire pit. Remembering everything, she closed her eyes but immediately opened them to look for Drue. He was not in the tiny shelter. *He left me?* As she hastily pulled her shoes on, she spoke to the old crone. "Excuse me, my lady. Has Drue gone?"

"No, child. He is checking on the horses." She limped to Nicola and smiled. "You, Nicola, have a gift that—"

Nicola held up her hand. "It feels more like a curse, what you call a gift. People hunt for me, lie to me, try to trick me into saying something I would never say and to admit believing something I would never believe. People would burn me or imprison me. No, I am quite certain you are mistaken." Nicola paused, thinking. "Perhaps my father had this gift. But not me. I was already a babe in her arms when my mother married the man I called

Father, so he could not have given me any gift." By this time, Nicola was leaning toward the old woman.

"Nicola," she began again, quietly but firmly. "You *do* have a gift. Your father was not gifted in the same way. He was extraordinarily creative. He had a keen sense of observation and interpreting what he saw. He could read the signs of a storm, people's bad behavior, and he knew when the trials of living were more than his people could bear. That is why he came to see me when the dreams became so real. I asked him to bring you to me. I knew you were the one. He never questioned me. He brought you to me, but you were not ready. There simply was not time."

Nicola digested this information. "How did Father know you?" Her eyes searched the crone's eyes.

The old lady sat down in a chair. Her voice softened. "When I first came back to England, your father saw me waiting at his gate. People used to wait there."

Nicola cut in. "Begging for alms."

The old woman nodded. "Yes. I stood at the gate too, but I needed a place to live, not alms. I was willing to work at whatever needed to be done. Your father spoke to me. As soon as I answered, he stopped his horse and stepped down to talk with me. We understood each other immediately. I asked to live alone and away from meddling travelers. He led me here, and here I stayed."

Nicola's gaze wandered around the tiny living space, while she tried to accept and understand what she was being told. Finally, closing her eyes, she admitted her terror, adding, "I know not what to do with this gift as you call it. I do not care to foresee events that have not yet transpired." Nicola opened her eyes and continued. "I pray you are wrong. I do not want to live my life alone, hidden away, fearful and hunted. This cannot be what was meant for me."

"Can you feel when danger is near?" the crone asked.

Nicola nodded. "Yes, usually."

"And," the crone continued, "do you not feel when someone you are close to has need of your help? Do you not know when people are speaking to you, but their words are false? You have always known if the child will be a boy or a girl. You know if that child will live. You cannot tell exactly when it began or how or even why you feel these things, but you do. In the beginning, you thought everyone was like you. They are not. With time you will come to trust those feelings. You will also learn when you must share what you know. Remember, Nicola, you do not bring the troubles to anyone; you simply know they are coming. You sometimes know when good tidings are coming as well. It is special to be able to put someone's mind at ease. And you should never doubt what you know."

The crone smiled and gently touched Nicola's face before she stepped away to the fireplace. She set a kettle of vegetables and fish on a small, low table near it. Standing at the door, she whistled. Nicola pulled the symbols from their pouch and clutched them tightly. In the distance, someone whistled back. When the crone turned back to Nicola, she smiled. "I never call out for anyone. I cannot know who might be near. I would not live long if I were found. Sometimes, I simply whistle to the birds. Sometimes they answer." The crone set out bowls, spoons, and chunks of bread. "Nicola, the gift you have is not easy to possess, but you will learn to trust what you feel. One day you will discover a place of peace where you can find solace." She limped to Nicola and placed her hand over Nicola's. "Now, we will eat, and then ask of me what you will."

Uncertain if she wanted to ask all her questions, Nicola hoped Drue would come in soon. He was in the thick of her mission now. He should hear whatever was to be told. And at that moment, Drue ducked through the door.

"Good morning, Lady Weldon. 'Twas a short rest, but I pray it helped." He smiled at her. Sitting on the floor, he patted the spot next to him. Nicola sat next to Drue. The crone filled everyone's bowl, then sat at the tiny table. Nicola was surprised she felt hungry as soon as she took the first bite. It had been a long time since her last meal.

When they had finished, Nicola stood and pulled the extra chair next to the crone, then laid the two symbols out. The crone kept the smaller one and handed the larger one to Nicola. "Nicola, turn the symbol around so the images are right-side up. Start at the left, as if you were reading a story. Tell me what you see."

"I see a crown, etched in the gold," Nicola began. "A king. His crown is broken. Below the crown is a rose formed by white stones edged in black."

"Who does the crown over the white stones represent?" the crone prodded.

"King Edward, the white rose of England?" Nicola softly replied, looking up.

"Yes. The stones are set as white roses but edged in black. Black is . . . ?" Again the crone paused. As of yet, she had not even glanced at the piece lying before her.

"Death," Nicola answered softly. "King Edward dies."

"Then?" The room was silent but for the sputtering of the fire. Drue leaned against the wall, saying nothing, listening.

"There are two smaller white flowers, whose petals are edged in black, but without any crowns. Edward has two sons. They will never be kings. They too will die?"

The old crone simply nodded.

Nicola looked at the piece in her hand again. "There is another broken crown etched into the gold, and beneath it is a rose such as the first, also edged in black. Next to that crown, a smaller white rose with petals edged in black. Again, no crown. Richard will be king, but he too will die, as will his son. There is no crown for Richard's son." She hesitated. "The last crown is etched in gold, overlaid in brass."

"Do you know what that means?" the crone asked softly.

"I know brass is for strength and endurance," Nicola answered. "The flower beneath that crown is red, with white petals at the center. The crown is encircled with oak leaves—also strength?"

The crone spoke. "At the end is a herder's staff, also for endurance, but guidance is included."

Nicola sighed. "The last crown is for Henry Tudor."

"How do you know that, Nicola?" Drue asked. "It could be any of the families that believe they have a legitimate claim to the throne."

"The red rose is what the people are calling Henry," Nicola answered. She glanced at the old crone, who was smiling as she nodded. "But," Nicola continued, frowning, "he cannot mean to become a York. What does the white say?" Nicola looked from Drue to the crone.

"Henry will unite the houses of York and Tudor." The old crone leaned back, her palms flat against the table. "You have done well. Now, you two must see that Henry Tudor gets this, and that he clearly understands what it means. He is not only to be England's king; he is to unite the houses of York and Tudor. A Tudor dynasty will begin with Henry Tudor. Without what you bring, Henry will quit. He already grows weary of his life the way it is. Henry is meant to bring many years of Tudor rule to England. But you must get to him before he removes himself from the path to England's throne. Take care. If you are caught with these things, you will die a traitor's death." She slid the smaller symbol bar back to Nicola. "If you can get to her, take this to Lady Margaret, Henry's mother. She will resist you. Try, but you must never place your cause in jeopardy over her." Turning to Drue, she was silent for a long moment. "You take care, too, my son." There was sadness in her voice.

"You see my capture?" Drue quickly asked, frowning.

"No, only my death in the near future. Better this way. I will be dead when the visitors come."

At that, Drue's eyes clouded. The old crone continued. "You must leave, Drue. Quickly. The visitors will be here soon. It would not go well with you here." She stood slowly, painfully.

"We are going to die!" Nicola burst out. "This is treason. It is treason to predict the death of a king, surely. And all the male heirs? We will certainly be tortured and killed." She could feel the rising panic.

Drue crossed the room. "We are not going to be caught. You will deliver the pieces to Henry Tudor, and to Lady Margaret, if we can get to her. Then, you will no longer have the pieces, and if we are taken into custody, they will not find anything on you. There was nothing at your home. No one even suspects you might have such a thing as this." He handed her the small piece. "Now, we must leave. I will care for you, Lady Nicola. You will be safe."

"They will all die?" Nicola turned to the old crone, who nodded.

She touched Nicola's cheek. "I do not arrange it or ask for it. I only tell you what I see coming. You will do the same. Sometimes, it is better to keep the information to yourself. This is not one of those times." Turning to Drue, she spoke with quiet urgency. "Go, son. Before my visitors come."

Drue leaned down to kiss the woman's cheek again. "I fear we have brought you trouble. Others come looking for you, and we have been followed by the men who were with me."

The old crone shook her head as she held his face and kissed his cheek. "No. Only one of the three following you survives. He is in London. The men on their way now were coming before you. They have been sent by the kingmaker's daughter to find me. You only happened to get to me first." She tenderly touched his cheek one last time. "Now go, before you interrupt my plans." At that she smiled.

"I have loved you, Mother, always." He kissed her again, then brushed past Nicola and stepped outside.

"I know," the old crone murmured, as she watched him leave.

Witnessing the exchange between Drue and the crone, a sense of trust—born not of necessity but of witnessing a moment she recognized intuitively as truth—slowly began to grow within Nicola.

CHAPTER 25

"**T**HANK YOU FOR YOUR HELP." Nicola kissed the crone's misshapen hand. "I still believe this gift is more of a burden." The crone only smiled. "Can I do this?" Nicola asked doubtfully.

"I know you are afraid," the crone answered. "Your eyes reveal your uncertainty. But then . . . how could anyone not dread, at least a little bit, a task so daunting? I am glad—that fear will make you more cautious." The old woman took Nicola's hands in hers. For a long moment, she looked deeply into Nicola's eyes. "Yes . . . the answer is yes—you can and you will do this." With that, she gently pushed Nicola out the door and closed and locked it.

Drue had already brought the horses to the door. He helped Nicola mount and brushed away as many of their tracks as possible. Looking behind her as they rode away, Nicola saw it was as if they had never visited the little shelter. Nothing looked disturbed. In truth, the mound gave no sign of any disturbance, and the shelter was totally hidden. Nicola looked at Drue. He had a grim expression that did not invite interruption. Nicola glanced behind them one last time. Already, the surrounding forest seemed to have reclaimed the mound to protect the old crone. There was nothing to suggest human life resided there. Again she looked at Drue. He rode silently, his look telling Nicola that his mind was somewhere far away.

She called him son, and he called her Mother. No wonder he knew about her.

AS SOON AS THE DOOR WAS CLOSED, the crone prepared the little shelter. Briskly brushing the dirt about the floor left dust on the table and chair. The fire was already dying. She waddled around the area one more time. Then, having folded the extra blankets, she fluffed the pillows on her bed. With a smile of satisfaction, she snuggled beneath her covers and closed her eyes. "My life has seemed endless. I only longed to see my son once more. My last wish. I am finished. Now I long to see you, my love." As she relaxed, she saw a man wearing a black hooded cloak. His face and eyes were evil as if his very soul dared not stay near. The man pushed his mount and as the wind blew his cloak around him, she could see he was well armed. "It would seem I am not finished." She sighed. Then, the images of Drue and Nicola came. "The man I see is danger, Nicola. Stay away. You must leave this country. Go to Tudor." She spoke softly, her eyes still closed.

NICOLA FELT A WHISPER OF WARNING. She looked at Drue, but his mind was still in another place. Nicola did not know how to bring the whisper back. She took a deep breath and tried to clear her mind. The whisper came again softly in her mind; then, like a wisp of smoke, it was gone.

IT WAS NOT LONG UNTIL A TROOP OF MEN pushed through thick vegetation into the tiny clearing. "The same as all the others," the leader grumbled. "We've covered every step of this forest. There is no old witch . . . or whatever one would call her. Another wild chase." He looked around again, carefully, without finding even one sign of life, other than the creatures of the forest.

A large falcon sat on the limb of an enormous dead tree that in some year long gone had fallen against the mound. "If there were anyone living around here, the falcon would not have built a nest. See, above the falcon's head?" He pointed to a huge nest in a tree near the mound.

As if to be certain all the men below knew this was her domain, the falcon swept over them, circling once and landing back near the nest.

"Move on. We need to find the road. We are riding back to London." Complaining about the lack of leadership with Edward dead, he led his troop on through the little clearing and beyond. *I am sick to death of sleeping on the ground. An old forest witch indeed. Who tells Lady Anne Neville these stories?* Making a quick decision, he suddenly turned southward, determined to stay at the first small village he could find for at least two nights.

"We're not going to London, sir?" his second asked.

"London, by way of someplace south. We have searched for this witch for a month now, at Lady Anne's request. Not one person we have questioned can tell us anything. They all look at me as if I have lost my mind. I like Lady Anne well enough. She is kind to everyone, but enough is enough. I must speak with Richard before young Edward takes the throne. It would not do to have anyone say Richard's wife is unwell." The man looked at the skies above them. Only patches could be seen through the thick forest. Those patches were becoming darker, heralding another rain. "We need to find shelter soon—someplace with beds and food. Then we will ride to London."

His second grinned happily. "Hopefully ale and women, and not just beds and food?" the man suggested.

"Hopefully." He nodded, smiling. "Women who would not part a good man from his last shilling."

116

CHAPTER 26

RUE AND NICOLA RODE UNTIL the sun began to drop. The clouds were building again—soon it would rain. He remembered a small cluster of huts in the area and was relieved when he was able to find it. Small sheds, struggling to stand upright, sheltered a few cattle, most with calves. Pigs roamed freely between the huts, grubbing for what few scraps they could find. Pulling his horse up at a hut on the settlement's edge, Drue started to dismount. From behind the hut, a man appeared carrying a bucket of water and several pieces of wood.

"Be you needing help, my lord?" he inquired.

"I hoped to find some shelter tonight for the lady," Drue answered. He knew there would not be an empty bed, but perhaps they could at least get in from the cold for the night. The weather was beginning to turn.

The man looked from Drue to Nicola. He regarded Nicola carefully and gave her a half smile. "I was sorry to hear about your father, Lady Weldon." He turned to Drue. "Would be safer if she stayed in the back of our place. There be men looking for Lady Weldon. Not the king's men, I would say."

Drue frowned. "By what do you determine that?"

The man smiled wide, exposing great gaps between what few teeth he had left. He did not answer Drue; instead he noted, "I fought with Lord Weldon, I did. Come, we have a fire." The man turned and headed toward the center of the settlement. Drue hesitated but urged his horse to follow.

As Nicola sat listening to the exchange, she suddenly trembled. A dark feeling enveloped her. The feeling was so strong she struggled to sit still. "Drue, we must leave," Nicola said, looking squarely at Drue when he turned back. She never looked for the man now disappearing into one of the huts.

Drue turned his horse around and led Nicola away, just as the rain began. The man called out, but neither rider looked back.

Nicola and Drue rode eastward. Drue pushed them as fast as he dared, though both horses were beginning to slow. The rain that pelted them through the trees was cold and unrelenting. After stopping, Drue leaned over and wrapped Nicola in his cloak. To keep moving would help, but they needed shelter, food, and rest. Nicola eventually broke the silence. "I know we gave up shelter, Drue. I just . . ." Her voice faded—she could not explain the strange feeling the man gave her.

"Trust your instincts," was Drue's only response. At last the rain quit, but still Drue led them on. Finally, he stopped. He sat silently studying the area surrounding them. Nicola watched him, fearing they might be lost.

"Trust your instincts," Nicola softly advised.

He smiled briefly. "Indeed, lady." He urged his horse on, leaning down to pat its neck. "Just a little longer."

Nicola was so tired she felt numb. She had been safely wrapped up in her little world with her father for so long that she felt woefully inadequate for the task at hand. She remembered the old crone's confident nod, but the vision of her poor father loomed before her, always. She tried to remember every good time spent with him, in an attempt to chase away the awful image of his beaten, dying body. She tried to forget Allie and her horrible deception. It was useless to do either.

Nicola became aware that her horse had stopped moving. Drue had pulled his horse up and now sat still. As usual, Nicola was unable to tell why. He slipped off his horse and walked to Nicola. As he reached up for her she leaned over toward him. He caught her and set her down. "We need to lead the horses from here. 'Tis not far. Can you make it?"

"Yes," she answered, trying not to lean against him too heavily, but unable to resist given her fatigue. He took her reins and walked with her to his horse. Securing her reins to the holding leather behind his saddle, he grasped her arm from beneath, providing support. Taking the reins of his horse, Drue led everyone through the thicket. Grateful for the strength of his arm, Nicola let him lead her, concentrating on putting one foot before the other. Neither spoke. To Nicola it seemed like they walked forever. She was hardly aware of her surroundings, moving along with the horses and the unusual man she had come to depend upon. It felt as though what little sleep she'd had only heightened the fatigue she felt.

"Here, lady—now you can rest safely." They stepped into a clearing where there were several tents set up. Small fires burned near each tent. A larger fire burned near the middle. Men were standing around or sitting, evidently waiting for someone or something.

Nicola guessed that very little moved in the forest unnoticed by men such as these. Everyone stood up when Drue and Nicola came into the light. "And we thought you were having troubles. Foolish us!" One of the men stepped forward, grinning, and introduced himself to Nicola as Lord Bruce. He was a large man, broad-shouldered and tall. His dark hair was held in place by a leather strap at the nape of his neck. Clean-shaven but for a large dark mustache, his face lit up as Drue walked into the light from the fire. When Drue walked closer, the man turned to Drue. "The lady, she looks exhausted. Take her in here." The man began to lead the way to what Nicola prayed was a tent with a cot.

Drue dropped his reins and left the horses to another man standing nearby. He walked with Nicola to the offered tent. "Lady, you may rest now. We will be here all night. These men are with me. You are safe now." Drue opened the tent flap for her.

"Hmm. I seem to remember being told that before," Nicola noted, remembering Keaton. Drue frowned slightly. Nicola managed a smile. Much too tired to even think about who the men were or where she and Drue might be, she collapsed onto the cot. It was enough that he had taken care of her so far. "Thank you, Drue." Her voice sounded small and weak. When she lay back, Drue covered her with a blanket lying nearby. She could feel herself falling asleep before he had even left the tent.

OUTSIDE THE TENT, DRUE WAS GREETED warmly by Bruce, who grabbed his shoulders and hugged him. Drue returned the gesture, speaking with relief. "You and your men are a welcome sight, my friend. It seems like a year since we last spoke, though it was only several weeks ago. I have much to discuss with you." Drue acknowledged the men gathered around as they stepped up to grip his arm or shoulder. "I pray we are not too easily found, as I am being hunted. Rather, the lady is being hunted." He looked at the men now circled around him. "We will have our fight."

"Good, but first, sit and eat. You must be tired, and your companion looks worse," Bruce said, gesturing toward the tent where Nicola slept. Another man handed Drue a tankard of ale and a hunk of venison. Drue sat on a fallen log and ate, Bruce sitting next to him.

It was not long before the men sitting near the fire began to share what they knew.

"Richard of Gloucester had the Woodville man who kept young Edward killed, and Edward taken to the Tower," someone commented.

"Not so unusual—that is where the princes go before their coronation, is it not?" Drue observed. "It is well known the court is not so fond of the Woodvilles." Drue looked at Bruce. "And so the throne begins to smolder."

"I bet my best sword he is not being kept to await his coronation." Bruce's voice betrayed his disgust over the recent events. "There are darker things afoot."

Drue stood and walked around the fire. The comments coming from the men clearly expressed their unease over England's future. He cleared his throat to speak. "You know, Richard of Gloucester will have a great many men willing to follow him, should he decide to push the issue. He has proven himself an able commander and has held the northern borders secure, without help from either of his brothers. King Edward favored Gloucester and trusted him." He paused for a moment, waiting for comments. There were none. "Gloucester does not pursue women or food. Of course, Edward did not either, early in his reign. That aside, I believe Gloucester would have a tighter hold on the finances of the kingdom. That would perhaps mean taxation might ease."

Bruce stood and looked at his men, then back at Drue. "Drue, are you suggesting we support Richard of Gloucester? You cannot mean that."

"No, Bruce. I have not changed my thinking. I do not support any man for the throne of England but Henry Tudor. However, it is important that each of you search your own minds and come to your own convictions. This will not be settled by what Richard does or does not do, in the next few years. There are four contenders for that crown. One, young Edward, may have been removed, though he will still have support while in the Tower. That leaves three. The man who will wear England's crown will be the man left standing on the battlefield when the fight comes. Be it young Edward or another, that man will be the king of England. Our mission is to be certain Henry is in the thick of that fight."

"Well, I am glad to hear you say so," Bruce replied. "For a minute, you worried me. We are taking on a cause where even distinguished men can easily become cruel in their fight for a crown, Drue. It becomes a matter of great import that every man with us is fully committed."

"Exactly," Drue agreed. "This is not going to be easy. I have met Henry Tudor. He has trained since childhood to fight and lead. He saw, at a young age, how quickly a battle can turn. Henry has been away from England for fourteen years. French is his preferred language. He has witnessed, firsthand, French thinking in regard to how a king should behave. While that does not take away his drive to win the crown his mother believes is his by birthright, it does give weight to those against him. I have listened to the arguments against his claim. No one can deny that he is the best remaining Lancastrian claimant to the throne of England. Still, his claim is not as strong as any of the four current contenders." The camp was silent but for the crackling of the fires. Drue continued, "I have also met Jasper Tudor, Henry's uncle. Jasper is a man I would follow. He believes in Henry, as do I."

"Then it is settled," someone spoke out. "We ride for Henry."

"What about the lady? Who does she support?" Bruce asked. The skepticism in his voice was plain.

"She supports Henry Tudor. I doubt she knows much about the politics of the crown. What she does know is that Henry is the rightful king. She has already lost everything for his cause. She now risks her life to help him." Drue's gaze drifted to the tent where Nicola slept. He turned back to Bruce. "Our job is to find more men willing to fight for Henry Tudor. Tudor badly needs soldiers."

Eventually, men began to wander to their tents, until Drue and Bruce were the only ones still at the fire. "What do you hear about Keaton?" Drue asked.

"The talk is that Keaton and Carnell are the only men left in that party," Bruce replied.

Drue thought of his mother's comment noting only one of the three survives. He had no way of knowing which one of the three men was left standing.

"What about Harding?" Drue asked.

"Harding left Keaton. He is convinced Keaton killed one of his own men, some man named Garrett. Keaton and Carnell are longtime friends, so Harding guessed he had little chance of surviving. Keaton is deadly with his sword. Harding would not have been much of a match, I am thinking." Bruce added wood to the fire and sat back down.

Drue sat staring at the flames. "Might you know where Keaton is now?" he asked.

"No, I have not heard. But then, we've not been near any place that might have news." Bruce watched Drue stare at the fire. "I know that look, Drue. What are your—*our*—plans?"

"I have to deliver Lady Nicola to Henry Tudor and his mother. The mother will be a problem. Last I heard, she had gone to work for Edward and Elizabeth. She is a fanatical supporter of Henry and suspicious of everyone. It is well known that Nicola's father was an Edward man. Not certain how this will work out. I'll tell you when I have had time to think on it." Drue turned to Bruce. "Bruce, how do you know about Harding? Please do not tell me you have taken him in."

"I did briefly think on it. But no, I did not take him. He was on his way to London. He thinks to find a place with young Edward. Personally, I doubt young Edward will have need of men." Bruce stood. "You need to rest, Drue. Come on."

Bruce led the way to an empty tent with two cots.

Harding is in London. Mother said the last man is in London. Drue set the information aside and followed Bruce into the tent. Both men were asleep immediately.

CHAPTER 27

Anxious to see Richard king and herself queen, Anne Neville encouraged her husband to take the crown. In her heart, she believed he was the one man capable of securing the throne and leading England. Rumors of a witch in the forest southeast of London were swirling again. Anne had heard all the stories. Her sister, Isabel, was convinced dowager Queen Elizabeth and her mother were both witches, and that they were responsible for the death of Isabel's son. Isabel's husband, George, was the brother of King Edward and Richard. George had publicly accused his sister-in-law, Queen Elizabeth, of killing Isabel using witchcraft. There was never any proof for his claim or the rumors about the queen's mother, but the ideas lived.

With these thoughts in mind, Anne called for one of Richard's men, the one Richard trusted the most. When the man came to her, Anne suggested it would be in Richard's best interest to get rid of the crone. "First," she instructed the man, "find the symbol maker. He is said to be able to tell the future. Bring him to me. I must know what he sees. If he does not support Richard and his cause, he must be silenced."

"Yes, Lady Anne. I too have heard of this man. He lives in Weldon Castle with his daughter. The man, Lord Weldon, fought by Edward's side. I believe he would be strong for young Edward."

"If Richard is to take the throne, Edward's supporters must be dealt with swiftly." She paused, thinking. "Bring Weldon's daughter, too. If Weldon can truly see the future, his daughter might also. Best to take both."

The man bowed and backed out of the room.

Anne knew Richard had loved and was devoted to Edward. But Edward was dead. Their futures lay in Richard's ability to move forward. Anyone who continued to support Edward was problematic. Lord Weldon could potentially raise men against her husband. *My father believed you must deal with your enemies without giving them a chance to grow stronger. I am my father's daughter.*

Determined to be seen as a fit queen, not as a commoner like Elizabeth, Anne was plagued by paranoia. Schooled well by her father, she understood the king was king, certainly, but the people behind the scenes were the ones who made everything happen. Unlike her poor sister, Isabel, Anne had always been treated very well by her husband. Isabel's husband, George, was domineering, quick to anger, and offered little support. It was his wife's wealth he most liked. Richard, however, genuinely cared for Anne. Those feelings made Richard easy to sway. Anne reminded Richard, repeatedly, how close he was to the crown and the power—he had to know there could never, would never be another chance. The wheels began to turn. Once young Edward was in the Tower, the hard truth was that King Edward's youngest son could not remain free. Both sons had to be taken out of the line for England's throne. And they were.

ANNE AND RICHARD WENT TO VISIT with Elizabeth. Anne spoke first. "We have come to take young Richard to his brother. Prince Edward should have someone with him as he prepares for the coronation."

Elizabeth did not trust Anne any more than she had ever trusted Anne's father. She tried to stall the move, tried to beg Richard to allow the young boy to stay safe within the walls of the Abbey. "Please, Richard. You were my brother not so long ago. You were named Prince Edward's protector. His younger brother has no part in this play. Have mercy, Richard. Let him stay with me, here, in the Abbey." Richard refused to consider any alternative. With a breaking heart, she watched Richard and Anne walk away with King Edward's last son. Outside, storm clouds began to converge, and thunder rumbled in the distance.

CHAPTER 28

Harding left Keaton and Carnell without a second thought. Since Garrett's death, they had made him feel uneasy. And Drue could not have killed Garrett—he was not even there. That left the two men. The plan to roam around looking for Drue felt random.

Harding rode for London. When he entered town, it was midmorning. Recent events had cast a shadow of uncertainty over all of London, but life went on. Stalls along the market street—offering everything from hides to produce, dairy products to breads—were already crowded with customers. Horse-drawn carts slowly made their way through the masses, selling straw, firewood, baskets, and other items. Men roamed through the crowds looking for any chance to take advantage of people who could do little to defend themselves. Robberies, muggings, and even murders were not uncommon. Only the brothels, where women worked at their night trade, were quiet. Most of the patrons had returned home, and the women were sleeping.

Stepping into one of these brothels, Harding hoped to find food. At a corner table, an older man and a woman sat quietly talking. When Harding entered, they both fell silent. Finally, the woman spoke up. "We are not open for business yet. Long nights make for late mornings, you know." She smiled at him amiably.

"I had rather hoped I might get something to eat. I am able to pay and willing to do so." Harding stood waiting. He had stepped away from the door, keeping his back toward the wall.

The woman glanced at her companion and, at his nod, stood.

"I can offer you mutton stew and bread. We have ale. I will bring your food to you. There are no rooms available." With that, she left Harding and her companion watching each other. The man stood and waved Harding to his table.

"Sit here with me. A man should not eat alone, not good for his stomach." The man smiled and indicated a chair to his left, allowing Harding to face the door. Harding sat and, when the woman set food before him, began eating.

"London is a busy place these days. Everyone looks with a narrow eye at everyone else. Times will be rough for a while," the man noted, watching Harding carefully. "How long will you be staying? I can offer you a room, if you stay at least a week. Need the other rooms for quick turnaround." The man lifted his mug, but Harding stayed his arm.

"If I can come in another door. Not this one." Harding nodded toward the front door.

The man frowned. "Are the king's men looking for you? They come in here regularly. I do not want trouble."

"No man looks for me. I am not hiding from any man. I prefer not to announce my presence, though. I want information. Just information." Harding leaned back in his chair, waiting.

The man swirled the ale in his mug. "You can come in through the back. There are two doors in the back. The smaller one will take you directly to the upstairs. Do not come in that door. Some of the men coming here use that door. Would not do to have someone meet you. The door next to it leads to my private quarters. There is an extra room down that hall, at the end. I will see it is ready for you."

"Perfect. I will pay for the week now. If I get my information quickly, you will still make your fee. Thank you." Harding held out his hand and the man shook it, then stood and walked toward the back without another glance. Harding left money on the table and walked through the front door.

Harding spent the rest of that day and the next roaming from inn to inn, through the markets and along the streets, listening, always listening. The brothels were still closed during the day. He never saw Nicola or heard anyone speak of a woman traveling alone. Talk that Richard had had the dowager queen's brother killed and her son, young Edward, held in the Tower was met with mixed opinions. Some felt Edward was being protected until his coronation. Others believed Richard was moving after the throne himself. Those who believed Richard was trying for the crown were not necessarily against such a move. Richard was already known as a fair and honest man, treating those under his command with respect. The general opinion held that Richard would make a good king, though the crown belonged to young Edward.

Harding knew it would not be such an easy task to prove himself worthy of a post at court if there was not a strong contender for the crown. Young Edward was a strong contender, with Richard as his protector. *I doubt Richard would think of trying for Edward's crown. Richard was always very loyal.* Emboldened by how easily he was able to wander about without undue notice, Harding made a daring decision. How better to reach a young king than through his mother?

Rumors about Elizabeth and her mother had circulated for years. Yet, of all the times when Elizabeth was within Abbey walls, no one had ever seen anything to prove the women were involved in witchcraft. While Harding scoffed at the idea of the queen being a witch, he believed in the same things everyone else believed. Special potions, the power of the planets, and, certainly, the possibility of witches were all very real beliefs. All things considered, he viewed the chance of obtaining a court post with young Edward enticing, outweighing the fear of potentially unkind spells by the dowager queen. Besides, if Harding was on the side of her son and she were a witch, she would protect him. He made a trip to Westminster Abbey his next move.

Finding transportation on the Thames River would be easy. However, Harding discovered it might not be quite so easy to reach Elizabeth, as talk on the streets confirmed Elizabeth certainly was not alone and was under careful watch. With her were her children from King Edward, a son from her first husband, and her brother. Harding knew the Abbey had been utilized as a sanctuary by Elizabeth twice before, and certainly the nuns would know her well. The inhabitants of the Abbey gave the area Elizabeth occupied a wide berth, but daily activity around and in the Abbey made it impossible to make any clandestine contact with the dowager queen. Harding wore no man's colors. He decided it would be easier to meet with the dowager queen openly, without any hint at secrecy.

As the small boat carrying Harding followed the curves of the Thames, the Abbey came into view. Harding's plans would have to change quickly. Richard, King Edward's brother, was at the Abbey. Harding could see

Richard's men. He watched as they disallowed anyone stopping on the river, at or near the Abbey. Guards in Richard's colors stood nearer the Abbey, preventing anyone near the Abbey grounds. "Keep on, do not stop here," Harding instructed his boatman.

Despite this obstacle in his path, Harding did take it as a good sign that Richard was there with Elizabeth. Certainly they were working out the details of young Edward's coronation. Harding knew enough about court dealings to know he could not be seen as too eager—and he was not well connected. After traveling a little farther, Harding disembarked and sent the boatman on his way. He proceeded carefully along the bank, before moving as close to the Abbey as he dared. He found a spot where he could watch for Richard's departure. Whenever Richard of Gloucester came out of the Abbey, Harding planned to slip in to see Elizabeth. But Harding was dumbstruck when he saw Gloucester walk out of the Abbey—his wife, Anne, was with him, and the guards were escorting King Edward's youngest son, Richard, to Gloucester's boat. The boy appeared frightened and kept looking over his shoulder, presumably for his mother.

Harding was a soldier. He had seen his share of hostage exchanges. He knew in an instant that Edward's son was not leaving with Gloucester willingly. That would certainly mean his mother had not been willing to give him up. But why?

Harding scrapped his plan to speak with Elizabeth. Much more comfortable taking orders than planning any critical move, he needed to think on what he had just witnessed. *The rumors I've been hearing. They are true! The Duke of Gloucester is trying for the crown. Where will I stand?* With his mind in turmoil, Harding slowly returned to his boarding house. *Did Keaton know this all along? He must have suspected it. Perhaps it was more than a suspicion. What now? This town will be a boiling cauldron before too long. Do I stay with Edward, or stand with Richard?*

Harding had no way to determine with any certainty who would actually take the throne, but he intended to be in the service of whoever it turned out to be. Logic said the throne would soon belong to the Duke of Gloucester. It was a long walk back to his room. Night had blanketed the land with darkness, but London was still awake and moving. Crowds in this part of London gathered at the inns, and women moved through the throngs of men, looking for a night's work. He took the back entrance of the inn as instructed and had nearly reached his room when the owner called out to him.

"Where have you been? Come, join me for a drink." He waved to Harding and walked with him into the crowded room, where food and drink were flowing. "You heard Gloucester took young Prince Richard to the Tower today. Poor lads. Those two boys are finished. No one leaves the Tower. The great Duke of Gloucester is going for the throne. What do you think of that?"

Harding had thought of nothing else since he had watched the frightened young boy ushered onto the waiting boat that would take him to the Tower to join his older brother. "I think the greater question is whether Richard will garner enough support for his bid," Harding replied. "Edward had little trouble gathering a force to fight for his throne. Through all the battles, his brother, Richard, was always at his side. Still, one wonders how men will feel about a contender who imprisoned the dead king's sons—the rightful heirs to the crown." Harding sat down opposite the inn's owner, briefly allowing his eye to run over the crowd of men drinking and busy sizing each other up.

"Honestly, I do not know," the innkeeper replied. "I know Richard was well respected by men who have fought at his side these years. But to stick those poor boys in the Tower, I just . . . I just cannot find a peace with that." The man looked at Harding. Harding was studying his ale.

The innkeeper persisted. "What are your thoughts?"

"Without Edward to hold his council together, I think neither son has any chance. The dowager queen has a large and powerful family. Men talking sound fearful of the Woodvilles running the country. Certainly, it seems very few of those in power care for the Woodvilles." Harding drained his mug. "'Twill be a long summer, I fear. Very long. No matter. I doubt anyone cares what the likes of me think of this mess." Harding stood to leave.

"I beg to differ, man. You carry a sword and firearm and look to be at ease with both," the innkeeper observed. "I think you will be asked to take a side, sooner than later."

Harding did not answer. He simply walked out.

After thinking on the events he had witnessed, he knew he would much rather stand for a man who had been an able commander and fought well, than a young boy whose position came to him through the death of his father. At that moment, Harding made a decision on where he would place his loyalty. It had to be with Richard. He was the only one who stood any chance of keeping the throne.

The next morning, as before, Harding wandered the streets of London, looking and listening. But this time he had another objective. He needed to find someone credible. Someone he could trust. By now, the air of unrest was thick. As always, Harding kept an eye out for Keaton or Carnell. Even if he saw them first, he knew he would be hard-pressed to survive an attack from them. His best move for safety would be to find someone representing Richard and make his intentions known. To that end, he wandered ever closer to Westminster Abbey, spending several days watching the preparations for Richard's coronation.

Clearly, the event was hastened. Equally clear was the fact that not everyone favored Richard, though few felt comfortable enough to say so aloud. The very circumstances of the upcoming ceremony left many an Englishman with a bad taste for the whole affair. All of that mattered little to Harding. He was determined to find a way to gain favor with the king.

CHAPTER 29

Awake early, Nicola lay still for a long time, listening to the sounds of the camp coming alive. In the tumble of voices, she did not hear Drue, but she was no longer afraid he would leave her. She straightened the tent, then stepped out. She knew she must look frightful. She had worn the same clothes for days now. There had not been any chance to comb her hair, or to wash up. Indeed, she knew she looked like a stable maid. There was little she could do about it, and in the grand mix, it seemed to not matter.

When she stepped out of the tent, the camp became quiet.

Bruce came forward. "Please, come and eat. You must be very hungry. Drue is tending to the horses." He led her to a spot near the fire and handed her a hunk of cheese and a piece of dried meat. For a short moment, Nicola glanced around at the men watching her. Nodding to Bruce, she began to eat. It was uncomfortable, but she was too hungry to care. Drue walked up and sat beside her as she was finishing. She tried to smooth her hair again, ducking her head self-consciously.

"Fear not, lady—you look beautiful," Drue told her.

"And you lie, but thank you," Nicola murmured.

Drue looked at her for a moment, before speaking aloud. "I see Bruce has introduced you to his version of food." He smiled at her. "'Tis not too bad, really. When you are ready, we can take our leave."

Nicola rose. She walked away from the camp area and scraped her platter off. When she returned, she saw the men were watching her. Nicola felt she must say something to them. Not certain just what, she glanced at Drue. With a slight nod, he waited.

"I thank you for your hospitality. I hope someday to be able to repay the kindness you have shown." Nicola looked around the camp, then walked to her horse. The soreness from riding so much was beginning to ease the more she rode. She only wished the soreness in her heart would go away.

Drue helped Nicola mount, then turned to shake hands with Bruce. "I will keep in touch, my friend. We should be in London within two days."

"Take care, Drue," Bruce warned. "There will be men only too eager to make points with young Edward or Richard. You must have eyes behind you. And the lady? How does she fit into all this?"

Nicola held her breath while waiting for Drue's answer. Drue answered casually, as he mounted his horse, "She does not. I will let you know if that changes. She is caught up in something else. She is not schooled in the dangers of politics, nor is she involved in the quandary currently surrounding England's throne. An innocent bystander, unfortunately."

Bruce nodded sympathetically. "Go with God, Lady Nicola. Drue is a good man and he will see you to safety." Turning back to his men, he observed, almost as if to himself, "Say what you will, I doubt she is not involved. You would not be babysitting her if it were otherwise. I think it best my men find our way to London. You will need help, sure as the rains fall."

One man agreed, adding, "It is time we moved out anyway. It was beginning to get boring. I've won all the money around here."

"Perhaps we will see each other again soon," Bruce said. He waved to them, as they rode off.

DRUE KEPT A STEADY PACE, Nicola not far behind him. The pounding rain of the last several days had stopped, leaving the ground soaked. They stayed off the roads, and the dampened earth muted the sound of their horses' hoofs. The sun finally broke through the clouds, making the ride much easier.

Drue felt a growing sense of admiration for Nicola. He was keenly aware that Nicola had been thrown into circumstances that would make any man uncomfortable, especially given the dangers of her task. She never complained despite the miserable conditions. She just kept moving forward. He watched her for a moment before he spoke. "I have been thinking about the meaning of the symbols. The time is coming to decide how best to act on that information. For certain, we will have to keep it well hidden. The talk at London will provide me with more information."

"I wish I knew more about these matters," Nicola confessed.

"That does not matter," Drue told her. "I just pray Lady Margaret has not convinced Tudor to continue seeking amnesty. Richard will send Henry to the Tower to be executed, clearing the field of any contenders for the throne of England."

The chatter of children's voices broke into their conversation. Drue immediately slowed, then stopped. Signaling to Nicola, Drue indicated they would give the area a wide berth.

Over the next several hours, Nicola seldom spoke.

"Are you well, lady?" Drue asked.

"Yes, thank you," Nicola replied, but she did not look at him. She just stared ahead.

"I think you are not doing well," Drue pushed her. "It would not do to have you ill. We still have hard times before us. Maybe getting so wet was not good. Do you feel hot?"

"I will never have a family," Nicola blurted out, her voice filled with anguish. She turned her face to him, and he saw that it was filled with deep sadness.

"That is not true, lady. This will not last forever. This will all end. You will have a family."

"No."

"I am in unfamiliar territory here, and I am uncertain as to how to reassure you. But I know you will have a family and a home."

Nicola looked at him, shaking her head. "You don't understand. I have been riding all over this land in the company of men I hardly know, and without any chaperone. No other ladies with me. No man will want me now. No man would believe that I am yet a maid, that I have not been with a man. What woman does what I have done?" Nicola turned her face away, hiding the tears that filled her eyes.

Drue spoke without delay. "I have not considered this, having been so consumed with how to best protect you and help Tudor. Now that you speak it, I see your concern. But you have ridden with men who were chosen by your father. Men chosen to protect you when his castle was being overrun. When you discovered the deception of those men, you escaped, alone, and returned to your home, only to find it deserted. I am escorting you to Henry Tudor, although you cannot say that to anyone." Drue watched Nicola. He knew she was trying to decide if his explanation rang true.

Finally, Nicola turned to Drue again. "Thank you, Lord Drue. What you say is the truth. It is likely I may never find anyone for me, but I know my actions and cause are without blame." She smiled at him. For the first time, Drue saw how her face lit up. He smiled back.

They still rode in silence for great distances, but when either spoke, it felt more comfortable. When they were a day's ride from London, Drue pulled up. "I know a place where we can rest, and you can enjoy the company of a very gracious lady. She is older and has seen more than most men have seen. She will delight in a few days with you. We can use the time to plan."

Nicola looked down at her ragged clothing, torn and filthy. She looked at her shoes, mud soaked and coming apart. Shaking her head, she looked at Drue. "She may not want me in her home. I look a mess. I am so embarrassed."

"There is no need to feel so. You will see. Come, it is not too far now."

A moment later, Drue stopped his horse and Nicola did the same. Drue turned to her, his expression serious. He kept his voice quiet and firm. "Before we go any further, I must correct you, lady," he said. "I *never* lie. Never." He looked at her for a long moment before he turned back and moved them on.

Nicola did not respond, instead riding silently beside Drue. She was well aware how she must look. She was filthy and her clothes were in tatters. A small smile found its way to her face. *I look frightful, but Drue sees beyond all that.*

DUCHESS WRIGHT—ENY TO HER FRIENDS—sipped her evening tea. It was a habit she had picked up from her late husband, Jonas, the

Duke of Wright. He had traveled extensively in his younger days, much to the disapproval of his stern father. However, Duke Wright never let parental or public opinion sway his leanings. When he met and fell in love with a German countess, Enide, he found his need to travel was curtailed. After two years of haggling with both their parents, the couple was finally allowed to wed.

He brought his young bride—and five of her ladies to serve her—home to England. They lived quite happily. Eny had wealth of her own, and the duke was astute enough to see that it did not leave his control. This meant, along with other adjustments, that Eny learned to deal with fewer staff, smaller living arrangements, and fewer of the elaborate jewels that were so popular. She was quite content to live more simply, if it meant she could stay with her husband, whom she loved dearly, and keep her wealth. Miraculously, keep it she did.

Eny championed education for the women in her keeping. She encouraged reading, music, and parties. Her favorite pastime was tending her garden. The castle grounds were beautifully manicured. Flowers, fruit trees, and benches made it a place she loved. When Duke Wright died of what seemed to be simply old age, Eny was devastated, but she never considered returning to Germany. England was now her home.

On this particular evening, she had eaten late, having spent more time than usual listening to several of her ladies reading aloud a play. She had already finished her rounds to check the house. Although there were certainly enough staff to do such a task for her, Duke Wright had taken such pleasure in closing his home for the night, that when he died, she had simply continued his nightly ritual. Now, it had become a part of her evening routine. A way to stay connected to the man she adored and the life they had once lived.

With tea in hand, she entered her study to pick up reading material. The sound of horses crossing the courtyard reached her. Pausing to be certain it was not her imagination, she frowned. Calling to one of her ladies, she returned downstairs. Her captain, Gilbert, met her near the grand entrance. He had been with Duke Wright before he married Eny, and now he was Eny's protector and friend. "My lady, there are travelers outside. They do not wish to disturb you but hoped to rest this night." Eny could hear the mischief in Gilbert's voice.

"And, Gilbert, I believe I may know these travelers?" Eny replied dryly.

"Yes, that you do, my lady. May I show them in?" he asked.

"Please," Eny responded. Her curiosity was more than pricked. Visitors to her home were few since Duke Wright's death. While she missed some of the times at court, she was older and alone. She no longer found the intrigue and politics of court entertaining. Consequently, she had withdrawn to the point that Edward and Elizabeth had left her in peace.

Walking toward the fireplace, where the fire was dying, she had wood added. Turning, she was shocked and pleased to see Drue. He was followed by a bedraggled woman. It was not his style to travel with anyone, especially a woman, but Eny brushed her surprise aside. "Drue! How pleased I am you have found time to come visit an old friend. Please, make yourself comfortable." Turning to the attendant with her, she added, "Please have food and drink brought out for Drue and his companion. Also, ready his room and the third guest room. Those rooms are cold and dark, not at all a place to keep guests." Eny turned her attention on Drue again.

He smiled and kissed her cheek and hand.

"Eny, it has been too long. How are you doing?" He moved around the room. "Still alone, I see. And it all looks the same." His voice was gentle. "Wright would be well pleased."

"In truth, Drue, he is still here with me." She patted her heart. "I am happy enough, for an old woman. My people take good care of me. Now, you must introduce me to your companion."

"Of course." Drue took Nicola's hand. "Eny, this is Lady Nicola Weldon. Nicola, Lady Enide Wright—Eny to her friends. She and her husband are as dear to me as family."

A wisp of sadness passed his eyes, and Eny caught it. "Ah, your mother is gone. I am saddened at that. She was a great woman, Drue. But of course, you know that." Turning to Nicola, she took both Nicola's hands in hers. "You, my dear, must be frozen and starving. Please have a seat. There will be something for you to eat served shortly." Placing a hand on Nicola's shoulder, she indicated a chair closest to the fire with a slight wave of her hand.

NICOLA WAS GLAD ENY AND DRUE conversed together over Duke Wright and times past, allowing Nicola to eat without feeling so awkward. With food and wine in her belly, she at last began to relax. Eny seemed to sense her comfort and pulled her into the conversation. "Drue tells me you are the daughter of Lord Weldon. Weldon fought next to my husband many years ago, maybe twenty or so. He was a most gracious and kind man, yet a formidable commander. I am sorry to hear of his misfortune."

Eny's voice and expression were kind, but Nicola felt as though she were on trial. *She wonders if she can trust me, wonders why I am with Drue and why I look so awful. I do look frightful, dirty, and ragged.* "Duchess, thank you for your kindness and attention. I miss my father, but I know he died with his honor intact." Nicola paused. "I am so sorry I—"

"Please, do not say another word. Tomorrow, after you have had a chance to bathe and change, the world will look much better. And," she added, laughing, "you will look better to the world." Standing, she continued. "Come, child. Drue, you will excuse me for a moment. Your companion has a great need to rest." With that, Eny led Nicola upstairs and into a room prepared for her. They were followed by several ladies. "Water will be brought in, and you can bathe. I have a few gowns from my thinner days," Eny said, smiling, "and I am quite certain they will fit you just fine."

Nicola shook her head and started to speak, but Eny interrupted her. "Now, you are not to say anything. I give these things freely, and certainly have no need for them any longer. Think nothing of it, Nicola. Welcome to Wright Castle and my home. You are welcome to stay as long as you like. Even several months if you wish." Turning to the chambermaids, she ordered the tub and water. Following them out, Eny closed the door, and Nicola stood looking around at what was surely the most elegant room she had ever seen. It was furnished in heavy, ornate wood, with thick rugs and wall tapestries. Two fireplaces kept the room warm, a smaller one on the wall near the foot of the bed and a larger one across the room. There were two chairs, a small table, and a small chest. Nicola felt the bed. It was soft and piled with blankets.

With a knock, Eny returned holding a stack of gowns. Following her, two chambermaids carried in several bed gowns, robes, cloaks, underclothes, stockings, and shoes, which they lay on the bed before leaving. "Here, try these on when you are ready. If they do not fit, we can have them adjusted. I am so happy for someone to wear them. I simply did not have the heart to tear them into pieces for the fabric." Eny plopped her stack onto the bed, while a third chambermaid began to fill the tub with water. "This is Lizzie," Eny said. "She will help you while you are in my home. Please let her know what she can do for you. Lizzie, run and fetch towels for Lady Nicola." She turned to Nicola. "You make yourself comfortable. Ask for what you might need. And sleep well, child. You need it, I would say." After giving Nicola's cheek a quick pat, Eny was off.

For a moment, Nicola stood very still. Everything had happened so quickly. For the first time in days, she would be able to bathe. *Bathe! What a luxury.*

Nicola was scrubbing away when Lizzie returned. Frowning, Lizzie watched Nicola. "Lady, I think I will have fresh water brought in."

Nicola glanced up at the girl, down at the water, then nodded. "Good idea, Lizzie." Lizzie handed Nicola a large towel and a robe. Lizzie called to someone beyond the door, and Nicola soon had a second tub filled with hot water. After a second bath, when she was clean, warm, dry, and dressed in soft bed clothes, Nicola slipped between the plush linens and immediately fell asleep.

DRUE STOOD WATCHING THE FLAMES in the fireplace dodge each other. Harding was the only one left of the men he felt would have posed a threat for Nicola, at least for now. Drue knew Nicola meant to try to find Tudor's mother, Lady Margaret. He also knew it would be difficult to reach the woman. Lady Margaret trusted very few people. Her reaction could well be one of condemnation toward Nicola, if she perceived the information in the symbols had come from visions. One outcry from Margaret and Nicola would be finished, very possibly burned at the stake. He shook his head. Nicola was determined to see Margaret, but Drue believed Nicola should get to Henry first. Even Drue's mother had warned Nicola about jeopardizing the real task at hand—Henry was the one who required the message most. As Nicola and he traveled to track down Tudor, Drue would have an opportunity to gauge the probability of support for Henry from among the men they would meet. Tudor needed men. He also needed the message Nicola carried. A message of hope.

Eny sat quietly watching him. At last she spoke. "How did you come by that girl? I pray you did not take her by force." *It would be out of his character, but one can never tell with a man.*

"It is a long tale, Eny." Drue sat down opposite Eny and stretched out. "The short version is that her father gave her a message she must take to Henry Tudor and his mother."

"You cannot mean to go to Lady Margaret!" Eny replied. "She will chew the girl up and spit her out. She has little trust of women . . . and certainly not women whose fathers are known Yorkists."

Drue closed his eyes. "I know, but I am not certain I can dissuade Nicola. I intend on trying. What do you hear from London? Has a date for young Edward's coronation been set?"

"Humph. There will not be a coronation for Edward, mark my words. Gloucester is too close to the throne now. I fear for young Edward and his brother. If Gloucester takes the throne, he will have to imprison both boys. I think the people will not support such a move. Richard will be forced to make a terrible move. Their poor mother, how her heart must ache. It is just awful." Eny's voice dropped. "I have forbade any of my people to enter London. It is not a safe place for the likes of them or me. King Edward left us alone after Jonas died. He knew how simply we lived, and assumed we were of little use to him. I still pay the taxes asked, and I try to pay those of the people living around me. I must take care though, or someone could get the idea that, where there is some money, there must be more." Eny closed her eyes for a moment. "Drue, I felt your mother die. Is that possible, to feel such a thing?"

"She was very fond of you, so I would say yes." Drue stared into the fire. "She disappeared after she left Father. She just faded into the forest. At least that is what everyone believed. She was miserable around people anyway. Unlike you, Eny." Drue smiled at Eny, then sat quietly. "I feel at peace with Mother's death. I no longer live in fear someone will find and harm her. She is finally safe."

CHAPTER 30

WHEN NICOLA AWOKE, she lay staring at the ceiling. She desperately wished she could forget what her father had asked of her. What did it really matter to ordinary people who was on the throne? Yet, recalling what the old crone told her, Nicola knew in her heart she could not stop now. From the depths of her memory, something her father said to her when she was just a child came back. "It says in the Bible, many runners enter a race, but only one wins. So run your race to win." *I cannot win if I quit.*

Soft knocking on her door interrupted her thoughts. "Yes?" Loath to leave the comfort and warmth of the bed, she waited.

Lizzie's voice was cheerful. "Lady Nicola, would you like to break your fast with Lady Eny and Lord Drue?"

"Oh my goodness, yes. Please come in." Nicola threw the covers from the bed quickly and opened the door. In a short time, Lizzie had Nicola dressed and her hair done. "You're really quite good at this, Lizzie." Nicola slowly smoothed the gown and touched her hair. "Thank you. I feel like a real person again." After all she had been through, Nicola knew she was changing. *Father was right. I must run this race to win.*

Lizzie smiled broadly, well pleased. "Thank you, my lady. Anything I can do for you, just ask."

Eny and Drue stood in the atrium where the stairs met the great entry hall. "Eny, there might be a way for me to . . ." Drue suddenly stopped speaking. Nicola was coming down the stairs. She knew it was because she looked every inch a woman and not the young girl he had first met only weeks earlier. He watched her as she gracefully crossed the room and curtsied to Eny. The gown was a soft green, with a silken overlay of white. Her hair, shining like the richest onyx, was pulled back with a white ribbon and hung down her back in soft curls. He remained silent, unable to take his eyes off Nicola, until Eny spoke.

The change in Drue was not lost on Eny. "Lord Drue, please, I believe we are ready to be served. This way." Eny led everyone to the table. Seated at the head, she sat Drue on her right with Nicola across the table from Drue, to Eny's left. "There now, we can all visit. How did you sleep, my dear?" She smiled at Nicola.

"Very well, thank you. And thank you for the clothes you've loaned me." Nicola smiled.

"My dear, the gowns and other items are not on loan. I gave them to you. As I told you last night, I can no longer wear them. Age brings changes, some unexpected." Turning to Drue, she added, "She looks beautiful, would you not agree?"

"Yes, yes I would."

"Nicola, Drue tells me you are headed to London," Eny began. "I would advise against such a trip at this time. With King Edward gone and his eldest son too young to govern, there will be great unrest." Eny shot a disapproving glance at Drue. "I doubt you could stay at the places Drue might find. You should stay here or perhaps return home, until such time as it is safe."

While Drue seemed quite comfortable with Eny, Nicola did not know her well enough to share her mission with her. Quietly, she replied, "I will certainly consider your kind advice, Lady Eny." She then turned to Drue, effectively ending the conversation. Or so she thought.

"Eny speaks well, Nicola. This is not the best time for you to be in London," Drue said. "We will wait until we know how current events play out." He met Nicola's gaze steadily.

Nicola knew Drue well enough to know he would not like what she was about to say, but he must realize she had no plans to change her course. It was something she thought about every waking hour, it seemed. She had not intended to have this conversation with Drue at this time or in the company of someone she did not know well. When she began to speak, she could not stop herself. "You are neither my father nor my husband. You have no right to tell me what I can and cannot do." Unable to stop the words tumbling from her, she added, "If you are frightened and do not wish to go to London with me, certainly you could remain here with Lady Eny. I made a promise. I intend to keep it."

Drue's eyes flashed with rage. He sprang to his feet. "What? Frightened? That you could ever accuse me of being afraid of *anything* is beyond my comprehension, after everything I have done for you. If a man said such a thing to me, I would run him through." He took a half step toward her but stopped himself. He only glared at her. His hand rested on his sword, as he fought to control his outrage.

Nicola turned to Eny and was pleased to see the shock on Eny's face. *Better they know with whom they deal, from this day forward.* "Perhaps you would be so kind as to allow Lizzie to come with me, lady. It is most unseemly for me to continue anywhere alone, without another woman." *I have the coins from my jewel chest. Lizzie and I will be fine. I swear I will find some way to protect what is left of my reputation and dignity.*

Eny was speechless. After a long pause, she hastily agreed. "Of course, my dear. I release Lizzie from service with me, if Lizzie agrees. I believe she would make a wonderful companion for you." Her voice sort of drifted off, as she looked at Drue, who was still glaring at Nicola.

With a scathing voice, he responded to Nicola. "I think it would be perfect for you and Lizzie to go to London without me. I promised I would not leave your side until you no longer had a need for me. Evidently, you feel that time has come. Go." His voice was cold and sharp.

"Drue!" Eny exclaimed. "You cannot mean that. Why . . . they are both in grave danger, alone in London at any time, but now? Surely you jest."

"Not at all—I agree with the plan. When did you think to leave?" Drue asked, his voice hard.

Nicola refused to be intimidated. "As soon as I have spoken with Lizzie and packed. You will loan Lizzie your horse, will you not?"

"I most decidedly will not!" Drue snapped. "I never loan my horse to anyone, certainly not to a woman!"

The situation was spiraling out of control, and Eny spoke up. "There is no need to borrow Drue's horse, Nicola. I have a very fine stable, and Lizzie can choose whichever one she likes."

Before Nicola had time to think about it and change her mind, she continued. "Perfect. I will go upstairs and talk with Lizzie." Nicola could not get out of the room fast enough, and she stood to leave.

Drue was finished trying to change Nicola's mind, and by now Eny's voice had taken on a soft, pleading tone. "Really, dear, you have no idea what London is like under *ordinary* circumstances. At this time, it simply is not safe for a woman of, well . . . higher station. I am simply trying to dissuade you from what could very well be a life-ending decision."

"I will be just fine, Lady Eny. You have been most kind. A very pleasant change." Drue had not been particularly unkind, but Nicola could not resist the dig. With the words out, she turned and quickly left the room.

"DRUE, YOU MUST STOP HER," Eny said, once Nicola had sped from the room. "I have no idea what the two of you are doing together, but I do know you are a gentleman. Or at least you used to be. So act like one!" she angrily ordered. "Or perhaps her mission truly is not of importance to anyone."

"You are not subtle, Eny," Drue observed dryly.

"No, I am not. I find subtlety does not work well with stubborn men." Then Eny too left the room.

Drue stood staring at an empty room. He knew he should go after Nicola, but she was a grown woman. Sort of. She would soon find out how little she knew of the world. *At what cost would she learn that lesson?* He began pacing, trying to quiet the voice of pride and indignation still running out of control in his mind. Nicola was unlike any woman he had ever known. Never had anyone spoken to him like she just did. She pushed him into unfamiliar territory. He never lost control of his anger unless it was to his advantage. This was to no one's advantage, yet the feeling stuck deep inside his gut as if he had been hit there.

UPSTAIRS, NICOLA SPOKE WITH LIZZIE. "I plan on going to London, and I have asked Lady Eny if you might accompany me. Lady Eny has

144

agreed and has released you from service to her, if you wish. We will be going alone, you and I, if you are willing. I have not been to London in several years, but I think we can make our way."

Lizzie agreed readily. "Do not trouble yourself, Lady Nicola, I lived in London for most of my life. It is my home. I am always ready for an adventure." She smiled at Nicola. "We will be safe, I am certain."

Nicola felt the first tinge of relief. *I think Lord Drue will find he is dealing with someone who will not be treated like a child or a puppet. It is time I stood strong. I must be seen as a proper lady, and I cannot do that while traveling alone with only a man. And I will keep my promise to Father.*

CHAPTER 31

ENY RETURNED TO THE GREAT ROOM where Drue was still pacing. *Just like a man! If he cannot use his blade, he can barely use his mind!* Grasping her skirts around her, she left the room again. This time she headed for the stairs. Without knocking, she opened the door to Nicola's room. Nicola and Lizzie were packing all they could fit into an old bag belonging to Lizzie. "Stop. You will never get everything to fit in that. Just a moment." Eny left them, returning with two heavy robes and two sizable bags that would tie easily behind their saddles. "Here." She gave each lady a beautiful crucifix laden with precious jewels suspended on a thick gold chain. "Keep these safely hidden, but if you need help, use them. Those of us who support the church and the church's work with England's less fortunate all have one." Next, she opened the first bag. "This is how you do it. Pack the underclothes inside the gowns. Wrap the gowns with these robes. Shoes will fit easily along the ends. Personal items, like hairbrushes and such, you can lay along the sides. Let me show you. Lizzie, go bring your clothes." With that, Eny began to pack the clothes she had given Nicola into one bag. It took Eny very little time to pack both bags. Although heavy, they were still manageable.

"You have done this before, lady," Nicola noted.

"Many times. The duke was not always timely in notifying me of his travel arrangements. I learned early on to pack efficiently." Eny stood back and looked at both women. "I do not approve of what you are going to do, but I will not try to stop you. Please send word of your safety. Here, Lizzie, you have not been paid this month yet." Handing Lizzie a small bag with money inside, she added, "I expect you to take good care of Nicola, as if she were my own blood."

Lizzie nodded.

"I do not know if I can ever repay you, Lady Eny, but I will come again if you will allow it." Nicola's voice was soft.

"I demand to see you again." Lady Eny gave Nicola a quick hug. "With or without Drue," she added. Eny sent one of her ladies to have the stable master help the women prepare their horses. Lizzie took Nicola out a separate exit, avoiding Drue.

NICOLA WAS NOT EVEN CERTAIN JUST what she would do when she got to London. Finding Lady Margaret could be a dangerous task, but having Lizzie's happy chatter helped calm Nicola's nerves. The time passed quickly. Shadows were lengthening and the sun was fading. The women were within sight of the lights cast by small fires along some streets of London. Not willing to enter London at night, Lizzie suggested they stop at a hamlet near the outskirts of town. She led Nicola to a home beside the stables.

After dismounting, Lizzie knocked on the front door, and a small boy peeked out. Soon, a middle-aged lady appeared, her face breaking into a wide smile. "Lizzie! Come in!" Nodding toward Nicola, she added, "Bring the lady." Calling to another young man, she instructed, "Teddy, bring their bags in and care for the horses." As she ushered them into the home, Nicola was relieved. There would be no hiding from unwanted attention tonight. The woman asked about Eny and any news Lizzie could share. She never asked where the two were headed, or why they were alone.

"You know her, I can see. I pray we do not endanger her," Nicola whispered when the two were alone.

"We do not endanger her. She used to work for Lady Wright. Her husband was a blacksmith. He settled in this place after they wed. I have visited with her before. We are safe, lady—"

"Please, my name is Nicola." Nicola squeezed Lizzie's hand.

Morning brought with it the sun and clear skies. The day was well on before Nicola awoke. Nicola lay listening to the sounds of life that filtered into the room. Loath to give up the feeling of peace the sounds gave her, she lingered in bed. Finally, after rising and dressing, she left in search of Lizzie and found her helping the lady of the house with her chores, both laughing and talking.

"Nicola, good morning. Come sit and break your fast. We can ride easily this day and be in London before the day is done." Lizzie waved Nicola to a nearby chair. Nicola sat down with the ladies. For the first time in days, she relaxed and joined in casual conversation that stretched into several hours. The visit gave Nicola a moment without anxiety. When she and Lizzie rose to leave, Nicola pressed several coins into the lady's hand. Folding her fingers around them, Nicola kissed the lady's cheek. Lizzie and Nicola rode to London.

"Do you have a special place to stay, Nicola?" asked Lizzie.

"No. I cannot remember where we stayed the last time I was here with Father. It has changed too much." Nicola stared at the city sprawled before her. "This is so much larger than I remember."

Lizzie's eyes shone with excitement as they traveled over London's expanse. "I know where we can stay, but you probably have never seen a house such as this."

"Grander than Eny's?" Nicola asked.

Lizzie glanced at Nicola before she replied, "Different."

The women entered London, with its narrow, dirty streets, early in the evening. Garbage tossed from homes along the side roads splattered as it hit the dirt. People ducked but kept walking. Merchants working at stalls selling wares were shutting down their operations. Nicola had learned, during that morning's conversation, that business had been slow. News of the king's death and rumors over the fate of King Edward's son brought a somber feeling that hung over the whole of London. Different kings usually meant different laws. A new king always meant more taxes for the general populace. On the bright side, preoccupation over the fallout from an unsecured throne was such that little notice was given them as they rode into London, two unescorted women. Lizzie led Nicola deeper into the town, weaving her way through alleys and streets.

London's streets were darkening but for splashes of light here and there, cast by the open doors of the inns. Voices and the clinking of mugs drifted onto the streets. Few men of station ventured to this section of London alone. Women who worked in the inns eked out a living by keeping company with any man willing to pay. Nicola guessed that robberies and murders were most likely largely ignored, and the thought gave her a shudder. Now that King Edward was dead, this section of London was overrun by criminal elements searching for easy targets. Lizzie led Nicola to a stable whose owner she knew.

"Take good care of these animals. See they are not stolen, and you will not have to work for a long time." Lizzie's tone was quiet and sincere. She slipped several coins into his hand.

The aging stable master helped Lizzie from her horse, replying, "The horses will be here when you return, m'lady." The man paused, then added, "Lizzie, 'tis not a safe time for ladies. Not on these streets."

"Thank you, sir," Nicola replied before Lizzie could answer. "We will heed your warning." Nicola gave the man a small smile before Lizzie and she disappeared into the darkness beyond the stables. Both women stood in the shadows and surveyed the street beyond. Men were moving about in tight groups, speaking in harsh whispers. Lizzie led Nicola onto the street. With their luggage in hand, they stayed close to the darker areas, hoping to avoid attention.

Without pausing, Lizzie led Nicola down and across the street, then slipped around the corner to the alley. A fleeting sensation they were being watched passed through Nicola. Staying close to the buildings, Lizzie eventually turned onto a street where the houses on both sides were modest, three stories, and quiet. Stopping at one near the middle, Lizzie announced, "This is it. Lady Kelly runs, er . . . owns it. She is very kind."

Nicola's mind felt scrambled, now that she was finally in London. Preoccupied, she failed to take note of the particulars of the house until they were well inside, waiting for someone to fetch Lady Kelly. Looking past the foyer, Nicola could see a large dining area. Although clean, the floors and rugs were worn and spoke to a life begun long ago. Nicola followed Lizzie's gaze up the stairway to the top. It led to what looked to be an endless hall, with rooms on either side. "Is this some kind of inn? Can we sleep here, Lizzie? There is no one around."

"Of course we can sleep here. It is nearly dark, so I guess the women are busy. We will be able to eat soon. Come with me. I know just where to go." Lizzie started up the stairs.

Nicola hesitated but followed. Both women heard a lady call out from below. "Lizzie, is that really you?" Looking down, they saw a striking older woman standing in the doorway of the foyer, smiling. Her gray hair was neatly piled atop her head. Her eyes were deep green and her face gave evidence of a hard life taken with a sense of humor and purpose. Her clothes, although worn, were made of a rich material, in good repair and clean. The woman started up the stairs. Lizzie, meanwhile, had set her bag down and was hurrying to meet the woman. "Lizzie, you look so grown up and pretty. It has been too many years." She gave Lizzie a long hug. "And you have brought help, I see?"

Lizzie laughed. "No, no—this is my friend, Ana. We are in need of a place to stay for a few days, if you have the room. And we can pay." Lizzie turned to Nicola. "This is Lady Kelly, Kelly to her friends. She has been a kind friend of mine for many years."

Lady Kelly nodded to Nicola. She studied both women, then remarked, her eyes twinkling, "I believe neither of you have plans to work. No matter. Your room is still closed and waiting for you. I will see you both are fed shortly. Put your things away and come down."

When Nicola and Lizzie were alone, Lizzie spoke softly. "I do not think you wish to have it known you are here for other reasons. She will only know you as Ana. I worked for Lady Kelly before Lady Eny took me in. One does what one must."

Thinking back on her father's fate, Nicola replied, just as softly, "Yes, one does." She smiled and impulsively hugged Lizzie. "You are taking good care of me. Come, let us eat and get rest. I think we have much to do tomorrow."

The women ate while Lady Kelly shared how the town had changed. Everyone was on edge, no one spoke about the trouble, and most feared for the lives of King Edward's sons. "Many feel Richard will be a good king. He was a fearless and wise commander. His men respected him." She stopped and looked at her hands. "For most of us, it usually means more taxes when we get a new king. They say he will surely have to fight for his crown. Fighting is expensive." Kelly shrugged. "We will survive. We always have."

Lizzie then lightened the conversation asking about the style of dress currently favored, the different people around, and the growth of London itself. Nicola spoke very little. Kelly never asked any questions. Eventually, Kelly walked with Nicola and Lizzie to the stairwell. "Lizzie, I am so pleased to see you again and pleased to meet you, Ana. A friend of Lizzie is a good reference. If you have need of anything, please come for me. Good night."

Lying in bed, Nicola listened to the foot traffic as men came and left. She understood what kind of inn Lady Kelly managed and how Lizzie had survived before Lady Eny. In the dark, thinking on what lay ahead, Nicola had to admit it was the best place for Lizzie and her to stay. *Surely the likes of Keaton and his men would never pay for the services of a woman. He probably has all the women he could handle.* With a pang, she thought of Drue. Did he have women too? *Probably, he is a man.* Trying to forget his kindness and the emotion in his eyes when he had remarked on her beauty in spite of her appearance, Nicola forced herself to recall the indignation she had felt at her confrontation with him. His anger at her had been painful for her to feel. She did need his protection, but the promise she made would be kept.

By morning, Nicola had a simple plan to find Lady Margaret. To that end, first she and Lizzie would simply wander around London listening to the talk. Lady Margaret and her husband were high in King Edward's court. Sooner or later, someone would surely mention Lady Margaret or Lord Stanley. Easy enough.

With a stab of guilt, Nicola felt she should tell Lizzie something. Lizzie had already proven to be great help. Afraid she might somehow put Lizzie in danger, she chose her words very carefully. "Lizzie, I have a job to do. I wish to speak with people, but I must be careful to not let anyone know what exactly I am doing. I believed in King Edward, and I am saddened by what may happen with his sons. I know nothing about Richard, Duke of Gloucester. When my father was alive, he fought for Edward, and had nothing against Richard. But if there is truth to the rumors, I fear England's people will be fighting against each other." Nicola wanted to add she might know help could be coming. Instead, she paused to see what Lizzie might say.

"I say, we go out and just see what we can see. The markets are a great place to hear gossip. Not that you want to listen to gossip, but sometimes . . ." Lizzie looked at Nicola with a happy, innocent expression. "Well?"

Nicola smiled. "Lead on, lady."

The activity in the markets of London was overwhelming. There were dozens of stalls set up selling goods. Vendors called out to men and women walking from booth to booth. There were cloths of such color, it took her breath away. There were spices, ribbons, fruits, breads, cheeses, even hats . . . beautiful hats. Nicola was so caught up in the sights and sounds that she forgot why she was there. As her gaze took in all the activity around her, she saw him. Harding stood with his back to her, at the door of an inn. He was deep in a heated discussion with someone she could not see. Stopping in her tracks, Nicola grabbed Lizzie's arm and whispered, "I have to hide. That man will kill me if he sees me!"

Lizzie looked in the direction Nicola indicated. Pulling Nicola with her, Lizzie ducked into the closest alley. Arm in arm, they ran to the end of the alley and along another one, where Nicola stopped, pulling Lizzie with her, to slip beneath a stairway that led to the second floor of a larger inn.

"I have to think for a moment." Nicola looked around, her heart pounding.

Lizzie peeked around the large pillar supporting the stairs. "Oh no, he's coming this way."

Across from them, the buildings had no cover. Next to them, the alley was blocked with barrels and carts. Lizzie looked at Nicola, fear on her face.

"I refuse to go down like this," Nicola hissed. Pulling Lizzie behind her, she flattened them both into the corner of the inn, beneath the stairs. Deep within the shadows they stood, waiting. "When he comes in view, hold your breath," Nicola whispered, listening for the steps.

Someone called to Harding, and a person approached him. Walking toward the two ladies, the men were deep in conversation when they reached the stairs. "Come up. We can talk privately there," the second man suggested.

"My room is just down this alley, through the second door. Although . . . we have to walk past the kitchen and down the hall. Too many ears. Better I follow you." Nicola could hear the men go up the stairs and into the inn. She waited until she could no longer hear them talking before she slowly stepped out of the shadow enough to look up the stairs. There was no one. Taking a deep breath, she leaned against the wall.

"We should be going," Lizzie commented in a shaky voice. "Maybe Lady Kelly will have something new to talk about."

"Come." Nicola took Lizzie's hand as she led the way down the alley.

AS HIS COMPANION OPENED THE DOOR, Harding paused. "Wait one moment," he instructed the man. "I think I have seen someone whose presence could be a problem for us." Harding began slowly descending. *I know I saw two people beneath the stairwell. Smaller forms . . . women. Why would they be hiding?* He stopped at the bottom and looked beneath the stairway ramp. The space was empty. Surveying the alley, he saw two women casually walking away. They were nearly out of view when one turned to face the street. *It is Lady Nicola—I am certain of it. But who walks with her and where are they bound?* Harding stood just inside the shadows and counted. *They entered seven doors down. Easy enough now.*

SAFELY IN THEIR ROOM BEHIND A LOCKED DOOR, Nicola felt herself calming down.

"Why did we hold our breath?" Lizzie asked as she shook her hair loose and dropped into a chair.

"I find it is sometimes hard not to gasp when I am startled or scared. If I hold my breath, it keeps me from making any noise." Nicola slumped onto the chair opposite Lizzie.

"I need to remember that. It is useful advice!" Lizzie leaned her head back and stared at the ceiling.

"I have not been at this for very long, but I am learning." Nicola smiled. Neither spoke for some time, each lost in her own world. It began to dawn on Nicola that she would need to enlist the help of dowager Queen Elizabeth, if Tudor were to unite the houses of York and Tudor. There must be a union between Henry Tudor and one of King Edward's daughters.

Lizzie broke the silence. "Did you hear what you needed to hear?" Her voice was hopeful. "Can we go back home now, or at least to someplace where that man is not?"

"I did find out something. I fear our next outing will be a little more challenging. I think I must find a way to talk to the dowager queen, Elizabeth. It should be safe. After all, she is in sanctuary at Westminster Abbey and it is assumed Richard is getting ready for his coronation. I'm certain, like kings before him, he plans to go on Progress. He would want his people to know their new king. On Progress he will travel around parts of England, with most of his court. That should give us some time."

When Lizzie didn't respond, Nicola looked at her. Lizzie was staring, open-mouthed.

"Truly, you jest. Are you quite mad?" Lizzie asked, her face showing her disbelief.

"I do not jest. I have no idea where Westminster Abbey is, but it's an abbey. No one will harm us there. Do you know where it is?" Nicola asked.

"I do. By the river. But not on our side." Lizzie waited, frowning.

"We cannot take a boat. We would be far too exposed," Nicola noted. "How does one get across? Surely there are bridges."

"Yes, there are. We can take the bridge used by most people. But it is not close to the Abbey. We would need to walk a long way. But I already see that nothing discourages you." Lizzie smiled. "I doubt that man would walk there. He does not look like the kind of man who ever goes to chapel, let alone to an abbey."

Nicola laughed. "It is settled then. Let us find a meal, then rest. Tomorrow promises to be better than today. I enjoyed today . . . well most of today." *Truth be told, I enjoyed all of today. I can do what I must, and do it easier without Drue trying to stop me at every turn.* Nicola's heart gave a tug at the lie. She ignored it.

OVER TWO WEEKS ON, AND DRUE was still with Eny. He spent most of the time riding around the grounds and studying maps. At night, he walked the floor. His anger had dissipated and, in its place, grew an uneasy feeling for Nicola he fought to push away. The knowledge that she could be the one to move Henry Tudor toward the battle, a battle Tudor must win, amused and angered him by turns. Helpless to change the course of destiny, that was what his mother always told him. Nicola was a piece of Henry Tudor's destiny, on a grand scale.

Eventually, Eny had had enough. After breaking fast with him, Eny set her goblet down and straightened in her chair. Firmly she stated, "Drue, you either go after the lady to help her with whatever she needs, or you do whatever else it is you should be doing. What you are doing now is of no use to anyone."

Drue sat back in his chair. He looked at Eny and slowly smiled. "My dilemma is they are both one and the same. The lady is difficult to understand, Eny. But she grows stronger by the day, I can see that. She is not a little girl any longer."

"Ah. You are in unfamiliar territory, I see. Well, do *something*. You are driving me quite mad. At my age, I cannot afford to go mad—I do not have that much time left." So saying, she stood and left Drue alone in the room.

He lingered, watching the shadows stretch across the floor. When he stood, it was with resolve. *Why do I think so much? This is a time for those of us who support Tudor to be moving.* "Eny!" he called, his voice echoing through the empty room. "Eny, come tell me goodbye. I am leaving."

Eny found him walking down the hall toward his room. "Well! You look like a man with a purpose. Finally! Just promise me you will return with Lizzie and Nicola. Bring them back safely." With that, she kissed his cheek, and he was off.

CHAPTER 32

*T*HERE WAS NO SIGN OF EITHER KEATON or Carnell. Harding was getting tired of looking over his shoulder. Perhaps they had decided to ride north. So far, there had been no sign of Drue, either. Drue was too well known to be able to slip around unnoticed. For once, Harding was glad he himself was still relatively unknown, free to wander.

That afternoon, Harding visited with his proprietor. The man put him in touch with a group of men that lingered around the inn most of the morning and were determined to see Richard take the throne. Richard had set a date for his coronation and preparations were already underway.

Harding met with the men for their evening meal. By the time the men had dispersed, it was agreed to bring Harding with them, when next they were called upon to ride for Richard. Harding moved on to his next project. Now that he had found the girl, he intended to find out where she stayed. He could ill afford to leave her alive when things were finally moving in his direction.

Early the next morning, Harding walked to the door he had seen the women pass through, then rounded the building to enter from the front. Stunned, he stared. Kelly's place was well known. The only men who spent time with her ladies were men with money. The entrance was inconspicuous, and the building was nothing of note. All part of the plan to keep discreet the activities of the men who frequented the establishment. *Lady Nicola works in a brothel?* Harding could not believe his luck.

Kelly's patrons paid in advance. Harding devised a plan to prevent him losing what little cash he possessed. Taking her at Kelly's would be the best plan. It would be of little consequence when one of the ladies died during the night, especially now, with Richard's focus on morality. *Perfect!* For the next several nights, Harding visited Kelly's without paying. Knowing full well

Kelly would not want undue attention on her business, Harding wasted no time informing Kelly his employer was King Richard. Harding gambled that Kelly would accept his thinly veiled threat. She did.

Meanwhile, with calculated persistence, he made his way into group after group of Richard's men. When he was called, he would be ready. All Richard's soldiers, especially those of any importance, would know him. He wandered the streets of London every day. As yet there was still no sign of Keaton or Carnell. The thought of his old boss gave him a bad feeling. He could only hope they were north.

Harding met with another man, by far the most senior of the men he knew. The soldier was close to Richard. He alone had command of fifty handpicked men specifically assigned to be certain no one outside Richard's circle could approach Richard. Fearful of drawing suspicion over his trips to Kelly's, Harding stayed late talking to the man, then went to bed.

Loud pounding on the door woke him up. He immediately grabbed his weapons and stood to one side. "Yes?" With his firearm ready, he called again, "Who goes there?"

The man spoke so rapidly Harding missed his name. But the message he carried, Harding heard well. "Come, man. We leave now. Richard is making known throughout England he takes the throne this day. There will be men guarding the gates and doors, and anywhere else some rat might try to slip in. You said you were ready to fight for Richard, so come now." Harding heard the man run back down the hall. After dressing quickly, gathering every weapon he possessed, he was soon dashing around the side of the building just in time to catch the reins thrown to him.

Alongside over one hundred of Richard's men, Harding rode out toward Westminster, in the early morning hours of June 25. The year was 1483. That same day, Richard formally claimed the throne as King Richard III.

If any of the hastily assembled noblemen objected, none spoke of it. Instead, they accepted Richard's claim that his brother's children with Elizabeth Woodville were illegitimate, since Edward was precontracted to another, a Lady Eleanor Butler, when he wed Elizabeth. Therefore, neither young prince Edward nor his little brother could take the throne. From that afternoon forward, the court was in a frenzy, openly preparing for Richard and Anne's coronation. It would be an extravagant affair—a coronation England would remember.

Meanwhile, disturbing news came that thousands of northern troops were marching on London in protest of Richard. Many had erroneously assumed the north would support Richard. The oncoming march caused a melee with Richard's troops in London. A paralyzing cloud of helplessness hung over all of London. In the short span of three months, England had lost King Edward, witnessed his son young Edward usurped, and was now under the rule of King Edward's brother, the new claimant King Richard III. King Edward's youngest son was already ensconced in the Tower with his older brother. Richard was rising, and Harding was determined to rise with him, making himself available and willing to squelch any challenge to Richard's claim.

Harding was given command of a small contingent of men. Only ten, but they were allowed full access to the court and Richard's guard. Harding had nurtured a reputation as a fanatic in Richard's defense. Richard would need just that kind of support.

CHAPTER 33

ONLY DAYS EARLIER, Nicola stepped onto the streets of London awash with despair and fear over what the future might hold. She and Lizzie saw no sign of Harding. The walk to the London Bridge was a short distance from their inn, but Westminster Abbey was much farther west of the bridge. "Nicola, we can pay a boatman to take us closer to the Abbey. Boats are docked along the river. We simply blend in with the crowd and hop off when the greatest number of passengers do so."

Knowing Lizzie was not in favor of them walking very far unescorted, Nicola slipped coins to Lizzie for them both, and Lizzie led the way to the busiest boatman they could find. By the second stop, Nicola could see most passengers were going to the Strand, an upscale area of London. They also heard King Richard's coronation was to take place at Westminster Abbey. Pulling Lizzie along with her, Nicola moved into the line of people stepping off the boat.

"Nicola," Lizzie spoke carefully as they casually walked along the street, "are you quite certain you would like to go to Westminster Abbey? Surely it will be guarded and difficult for the two of us to enter. I fear anyone speaking with us will remember us. We are unescorted and . . . there are simply too many reasons not to go. And I hope you do not plan on wading through the middle of preparations for a coronation!"

"The coronation is set to take place in a week or so, so I think we will be fine. It is important that we do what we must do as soon as possible," Nicola replied softly. She smiled at Lizzie, hoping to encourage her friend. It did not seem to work very well.

The crowd slowly thinned. The closer they came to the great Abbey, the fewer people were about.

Nicola was somewhat prepared for what she was walking into. Rumors regarding Elizabeth's mother and her "spells" made it such that few visitors came to see the dowager queen. When Nicola reached the convent with Lizzie at her side, she rang the bell at the convent entrance. She asked the nun who greeted them if they might speak with Elizabeth, and the nun looked very surprised. Nicola assumed that it was because she and Lizzie did not look like the typical individuals who would ask for an audience with the dowager queen. Nicola was grateful for the heavy gold crucifixes hung on golden ropes around their necks. Eny had told them once that most of the church's richest patrons wore just such a cross, and she could see the nun recognized the crosses.

Nicola spoke before the nun could question her further. "I come for Lady Eny Wright. My lady believes any mother who has had her sons taken from her, as Queen Elizabeth has, is in great pain. Lady Eny wishes to tell the queen she will remain in our prayers, and I am to offer what comfort I can, in the short time I will be with her." Nicola knew Eny to have a reputation as a very devout woman, and she hoped this would serve as their entry.

With a nod, the nun swung open the gate. Lizzie and Nicola entered the courtyard and followed the nun to the cells occupied by Elizabeth and her children. Elizabeth was sitting on a low bed, holding her youngest child, a small girl who was weeping, her tiny frame trembling as she sobbed.

"Lady," the nun called softly, "you have visitors." When Elizabeth looked up, the nun stepped away and left them alone.

Elizabeth spoke softly to the child before she lay the little girl down and stood. The room was a large cell, with several beds, a table with remnants of foodstuffs, and a few chairs. Several windows allowed sunlight to fill the room. Two chests were pushed against the walls, one with its lid opened, revealing clothing. Before she thought, Nicola noted sadly, "I too have lost everything. But I had no children." Elizabeth had been crying, it was plain. Her older daughters stood nearby, listening and waiting. The air in the room was thick with fear and suspicion.

"Who are you, and why are you here?" Elizabeth asked calmly.

"My father designed several jeweled pieces for you, Your Majesty." Nicola saw the shadow of sadness in Elizabeth's eyes. "I come with a message, but it is for you alone. Is there a spot where we might speak freely?"

Elizabeth studied Nicola for a moment, her gaze reserved. Nicola was not surprised—at this point, she had lost a husband to death and her two young sons to a betrayal. No doubt she felt there was little left anyone could do to her now. "Yes, I can take us to a private place," Elizabeth said, waving Lizzie inside the cell to join the girls and stepping out to join Nicola. Elizabeth took Nicola down a back hall that opened to an alley between the massive walls surrounding it and the Abbey. It was deserted. The brisk breeze that blew through would certainly cover anything spoken.

Nicola took a deep breath and began. "My father knew a woman who could help him understand the designs he made. I am not certain how to say this. I know your heart must be saddened beyond what I could ever imagine." Nicola paused. The pain in Elizabeth's eyes moved Nicola to gently touch her arm. "My own father was killed and our home overrun by men wearing colors unknown to me. I do not understand all of this, but I promised to bring this message to you. From the old woman."

Elizabeth was listening intently. Her sadness was apparent. "I know who it is you speak of. Through the years, I have received messages from her. My mother and I shared the gift of an awareness of things to come. But my mother is dead. My husband is dead. My sons have been taken from me. I no longer have any sense of what might be. I am alone." Elizabeth paused. "I have never before shared so much with anyone. I have no desire to burn as a witch, yet I desperately need help. What is your message for me?" she asked softly.

"Your bloodline, and that of your husband, will go forward, but not through the men. You have a daughter who will be the queen of England, uniting the houses of York and Tudor. But you must put the pieces in play." Nicola did not know any other way to put it. At that moment, she knew she could be accused of treason, since she foretold Richard's reign would end without an heir.

The two women stood looking at each other. Elizabeth spoke first. "I know my sons are lost. Richard would never feel secure on the throne if he let them go. I have heard of a plan to try to free them, but I know in my heart it will not happen. If I could only see them once . . ." She could not finish, and she turned away briefly before facing Nicola again. "When did you get this message?"

"Only days ago," Nicola replied.

For a long moment, the queen was silent, studying Nicola, then watching the clouds above slowly drift away. "Somehow, I must find a way to work with Lady Margaret for the sake of my husband and sons. There could be no other way to unite the houses of York and Tudor, but through Henry and my daughter, Elizabeth." Queen Elizabeth reached out and touched Nicola's face. "I thank you, and your friend. You both took a great chance. Go now. I have heard you well."

The queen and Nicola returned to Lizzie and the children. Nicola and Lizzie departed the same way they had entered and were surprised to find the area empty. As they neared the entrance, an older nun stepped from one of the doors nearby. "You are leaving so soon?"

"It does not take long for one to express their deepest condolences, and to share a moment of sorrow. Thank you for letting us in." Nicola gave the nun several coins.

The woman gratefully accepted them. "Yes," she noted. "It never takes much time to offer comfort to anyone. Take care in these uncertain times. It is not safe about. God bless you both."

Nicola and Lizzie walked in silence for a long time. "Are you all right, Nicola?"

"Yes, I think so," Nicola answered, glancing at Lizzie. "But we must find Lady Margaret. She worked in the service of Elizabeth, but surely is not working for Lady Anne. We should plan on leaving tomorrow. That means we must find where Sir Thomas Stanley lives."

"Why?" Lizzie asked.

"Lady Margaret would be with her husband, of course." Nicola smiled, and Lizzie moaned.

Edward's youngest son was taken from his mother, Elizabeth, on the sixteenth of June. A fiery sermon by theologian Dr. Shaa on June 22 claimed the children of Edward and Elizabeth were illegitimate because of Edward's supposed arrangement with another lady before he married

Elizabeth. Within four days of the sermon by Dr. Shaa, Richard formally claimed the throne as King Richard III; the citizenry of London scarcely had time to breathe. Their hopes for the best did little to lighten the weight of impending harder times that now hovered over everyone.

On July 6, 1483, the coronation of the new king was already underway. London was crowded with representatives from all of England. In spite of concerns over their futures, on this day Westminster shook with the sounds of trumpeters and minstrels, some from as far away as Rome. Hordes of people crowded into a brilliantly decorated hall. The entertainers and the abundance of kitchen staff gave the whole affair an aura of pageantry. The meal, a feast of forty-six different dishes, included beef, mutton, roast crane, peacock, oranges, and an assortment of fine wines, as well as ale, for those of lower rank. It was a lavish show of grandeur. Richard was the new king.

An undercurrent of distaste for the removal of King Edward's son persisted. If King Richard's throne was to be secure, the two young boys could never be allowed to leave the Tower. Their only crime was having been born the sons of King Edward IV.

When the celebration was over, Richard held an audience with the summoned nobles, instructing them to keep order and not extort his subjects. Lastly, he summoned his closest captains and guards. They were to accompany him on a Progress to be certain all of his subjects saw their newly appointed king. They would know he was different. He would refuse to accept the usual gifts and monies offered a sovereign during Progress, insisting instead on returning the offerings with a gracious suggestion they could certainly be put to good use. The next morning, with Queen Anne at his side, King Richard began his Progress.

Queen Anne's thoughts never strayed far from the two young boys imprisoned in the tower. How could the reign of her husband be secure as long as the two boys lived? But the murder of two innocent young boys made her shudder. Instead, she tried to focus on being a good queen, hoping to garner support for Richard. As the two rode along the countryside, Anne glanced at her husband. Who could have ever foretold this turn of events? Richard turned to her and smiled. He reached for her hand and gently squeezed it. Anne knew she was blessed. They had a son, Richard was king, and he loved her. He would never put Anne through what Edward had dragged Elizabeth through, with all his women. Anne's family was not touched by the blight of gossip. Anne resolved to be a kinder, gentler queen. England would grow to love her. Sitting straighter on her horse, Anne felt the first real surge of power flow through her.

CHAPTER 34

WHILE KING RICHARD RODE ON PROGRESS, Drue rode into London. He could see that scores of other men, some alone like himself, others in small groups, were entering London too. None were attached to any regiment or following any particular leader—most came in response to the king's orders summoning the nobility. Henry Tudor stood in the wings, waiting for the right time to challenge him for the throne, and King Richard was shoring up his forces. Few noblemen had the heart for a conflict on English soil, especially for a man many felt was a usurper, although none would dare say it. At this point, it mattered little. King Richard sent for the men, and his subjects complied. Still, the thread was already beginning to unravel. There was a steady undercurrent of rebellion in the north and in pockets to the south. It promised to be a long, hot summer. Drue liked long, hot summers.

After Drue reached a particular stable in London, as was his habit at any stable, he walked the length of the building. It always paid to know where the exits were and what might be out the back alley. He noticed two horses at the far end penned side by side, deep in the shadows. The horses belonged to Nicola and Lizzie. Well aware he was being watched, Drue gave no indication he had even seen the horses. A man stood by silently. Finally, Drue called out. When no one answered, he turned back and called out again, louder.

The stable man spoke as he walked toward Drue. "I only have one stall left. Your horse does not look like the kind you would leave in the open." The man looked squarely at Drue. "I keep only the best in this area." He pointed toward the back stall, where Nicola's and Lizzie's horses stood.

Drue's eyebrows shot up. Then a slow smile spread. "Tell me, where then does Bruce keep his horse? Or does he own other stables?" The man stepped forward and offered his hand, as Drue continued. "I wonder if you might know where Bruce is staying, or does he still sleep in your loft?"

At this, the man laughed. "Aye, he does still sleep in the loft." The man looked upward. Drue followed the man's gaze. Bruce stood with his hands on his hips, laughing down at Drue.

"You are losing your touch, my friend. It took you longer." At that, Bruce climbed down to join Drue and the stable hand.

"Not so much, Bruce. That is your tack hanging on the wall and your boots hanging on the stakes. Which would explain why that stall is empty. Even your own horse cannot tolerate those boots!" At that, the stable hand laughed loudly.

For his part, Bruce growled under his breath. "Come, let us eat and talk of days gone by. When we were young and we both knew everything."

Drue tossed a few coins at the stable hand, then left with his arm around Bruce's shoulders. Once out of earshot, he asked, "Have you been here long enough to see anything interesting?"

"Seen some things. Heard more. Come with me. I know a quiet place." Bruce led Drue away from the main streets, toward one of the docks clinging to the bank of the Thames. They caught a boat headed east, away from Westminster Abbey. Drue watched the buildings, parks, and people alongside the river as they drifted by. The peaceful roll of the river was deceiving—London was certainly the furthest from peaceful.

The boat continued on, rounded the curve past the Strand, and came to a stop near London Bridge and the Tower. Once on land, Bruce led his friend along streets now in the shadows of a setting sun. Eventually, Bruce turned into a small alley and entered a building. Both men took stairs up three flights before Bruce stopped to knock at a heavy door secured with steel bars. It opened without a sound. Several of Bruce's men, who sat around eating, stood when Bruce and Drue entered. A fireplace was burning low, and a large pot of chicken stew hung next to a skewered pig on the spit over the fire. There were beds, a long table surrounded by chairs, and a smaller table laden with breads, butter, cheeses, wine, and various fruits. He spoke briefly to the men and helped himself to the food, Bruce joining him in two empty chairs at the table's end. The men resumed eating amid friendly banter, but Drue couldn't bring himself to relax.

Bruce, speaking in a low voice, shared the information he had. "Let us first talk of what I have heard. Unrest is widespread. Talk in the streets is growing bolder. Richard has a reputation for being an upright man, not taken with the women like his brother was. In fact, he had his brother's mistress in public stockade, to make a statement. Poor lady. Rumor has it he will not accept the usual gifts of monies that the lords give the king during Progress. Insists there is to be no more extortion of his subjects." Bruce paused. "Do not know how that will work out."

"No talk of another king?" asked Drue.

"Not much, but Henry Tudor's name is heard. Most do not care to be found guilty of treason. Ugly way to die," Bruce replied. Talk lagged while both ate.

Drue broke the silence. "What have you seen?"

"First, I have one more tale for you. Your friend, Harding, was given command of a small contingent of men. He has full access to Richard and travels with him on Progress." Bruce shook his head. "Richard has no idea what he got with Harding."

"What he got," Drue noted, "was a very skilled swordsman. And he is not my friend."

One of Bruce's men interrupted. "Harding is not on Progress with the king. I saw him this morning. He and his men rode into town at night, looking none too pleased. Do not know if it is true, but the talk is Richard may cut his Progress short because of increased problems in the north, and likely more in the south." The man stood and stretched. "I know not the reason, but Harding is here in town. So is the lady you brought with you when we last saw you, Lord Drue. She and another lady are staying at Kelly's."

"What?" Drue asked, turning to the speaker. Kelly ran one of the busiest brothels in London. The building itself looked common, but it was clean and each room was furnished in the best. Her clientele were men who paid well for the girls and the privacy Kelly provided. "Are you certain?" Drue was now standing, looking at the man. "You know it was Lady Weldon?"

"Yes, I am certain. Saw her myself and recognized her. She did not see me, but I've been following her since she and the other lady with her came into town. A lady such as her should not be alone in London without an escort. They have gone in and out of Kelly's every day. Harding made several trips there, too."

A second man spoke up, "I too saw her at Kelly's. And Harding. He was leaving late at night, and he will surely be back. He spends a great deal of time there. I doubt he knows the lady is there, but of more concern, she does not know he is around." After pausing for a moment, the man added, "She is not working, Lord Drue. She is only lodging there. I do know Kelly is not fond of Harding. He has a habit of not paying. He claims he is one of the king's men and not to be challenged."

"That will not get him far, if King Richard finds out where Harding spends his spare time. The king is bound to change the reputation of London's royalty. Harding could well be left without a post, and quickly," Bruce noted. "We can only hope."

Drue was already walking toward the door. "I have to get Lady Nicola out of there, before Harding sees her. He would have her arrested for treason."

"Can we help you?" Bruce asked.

"Not yet. I will contact you." Drue left. He moved through the crowded streets as fast as he could without drawing undue attention, while keeping an eye out for Harding. The walk from Bruce's rooms to Kelly's only provided additional time for his anger to fester. *She was worried about her reputation riding alone with me. What does she think being seen at Kelly's place will do to her reputation? She does not yet know who I am, but she will, soon enough.*

KELLY ARRANGED FOR NICOLA AND LIZZIE to eat alone with her. They had just finished eating their evening meal when Drue strode into the foyer. Lizzie saw him first. Leaning toward Nicola, she whispered, "Lord Drue just came in. He looks very angry."

"Here?" Nicola turned to see him looking around the room. She quickly turned away. She tried to think what to do. *Maybe nothing. After all, he chose not to accompany me.*

Kelly, ever watchful for customers entering, was already walking into the foyer. She stopped Drue and spoke to him. Nicola started to stand, but it seemed of little use. She and Lizzie would have to walk through the foyer to get to the stairs.

To Nicola's horror, Kelly brought Drue to her. At that moment, one of Bruce's men entered the foyer and quickly stepped to Drue's side. "Lord Drue, Harding is on his way here with several men. He will surely see the lady." The man nodded toward Nicola.

Nicola stood immediately. "Harding is here? I must leave. Is there another way out?"

"No time for that," Drue said brusquely, grabbing Nicola's arm. "We're going upstairs. Which room, Kelly?"

"Third floor, room ten!" Kelly called after them. Drue was already pulling Nicola toward the stairs, moving quickly. With the thought of Harding looming so close, Nicola had no trouble keeping up, nearly pushing Drue aside to get to the top.

MEANWHILE, BRUCE'S MAN PICKED UP a bucket of ashes and began to clean the fireplace. He conveniently spilled some and smeared it on his hand and face. Kelly hated asking Lizzie for the one thing that she thought would actually work to distract Harding and placate him. But she needed to get Harding out of the foyer and into a room, allowing Drue and Lizzie's friend time to escape.

"Do you think you can, one more time?" Kelly asked hesitantly. To Kelly's immense relief, Lizzie happily nodded.

"Of course. I really did love it, you know." She moved into the foyer just as Harding and two other men walked through the door.

ON THIS NIGHT, CATCHING NICOLA was at the bottom of a very dismal list for Harding. Richard had released Harding and his men after the king's commander shared information that Harding rode for a man named

Keaton, a known Edward supporter. Harding's services and those of the men with him were no longer required in protection of the king. Harding was lucky to escape without being arrested. Instead, Harding and his men would be sent to the far south, to settle the unrest brewing. Harding's chance to be a member of King Richard's court was gone, unless he could crush the unrest and somehow prove himself loyal. That would not be likely, given the fact that Harding knew nothing about leading anyone or commanding anything. He was a fighter, a soldier. Nothing more. The men with him were fallout from Richard's displeasure. None were in a giving frame of mind, and none were too pleased to be with Harding.

Lizzie smiled seductively at him. Nodding his approval, he spoke to the men with him. "This looks like a quiet place. You two check out another business. I will catch up with you." Harding walked toward Lizzie, looking her over carefully. "Are you new here?" he asked casually. *She looks about the same size and build as the one I saw with Lady Nicola.* Perhaps all was not lost. There might be a chance he could reclaim his place with Richard, but only if he could find Nicola.

The girl smiled back. "To London, no. I was born and raised right here in London, though not in this house, of course. I am new to Kelly's." She met Harding near the stair landing. "If you are interested, m'lord, I can walk with you upstairs. It is early—we will not be disturbed."

Harding reached for her hand. "I am interested. Show me." While they walked, Harding studied her carefully, taking note of her soft features. Together, they slowly moved up the stairs, stopping at the nearest open door. The number three was painted on the door.

ON THE THIRD FLOOR, Drue opened the door of room ten, shoved Nicola inside, followed her in, and locked the door. Nicola had never seen this side of him. He was beyond angry, and in some ways, it impressed her. Nicola was proud of what she and Lizzie had done so far, without anyone's help. Yet she had to admit she felt safer with Drue around, even though he had changed. She sat on the bed, then remembering how the beds were meant to be used, quickly stood up. As quietly as possible, she crossed the room and sat on a chair.

Drue turned to watch her. "I would have never thought to see you in a brothel. But I have to admit," he began, "it is the perfect place for someone like you to hide, and men tend to talk when they are pleased, and even more so when they want to impress a woman." His eyes narrowed as he walked toward her.

Watching Drue approach, Nicola prepared herself for a fight. "If what you are suggesting is that . . . the answer is a firm no. But I will not quit in what I set out to do. Not ever." She had not intended to speak out, but the words in her head flew out of her mouth. Lowering her voice, she added, "I have already accomplished much. I—"

Drue held up his hand, and she stopped speaking, clasping her hands to stop the trembling. "What are you doing here?"

Momentarily confused, Nicola, so ready to battle over her father's request, was at first not sure what he meant. "I am doing what my father asked me to do." Drue frowned, and she could see he was not interested in that answer. Something else was on his mind. "You mean *here* here?"

Drue did not answer. He simply stood before her, glaring, his fists clenched.

"Lady Kelly has allowed us to stay here. I am afraid of Harding. So far, Lizzie and I have avoided him. He was rumored to be with the king, but he came back too soon." She paused before adding, "We have been able to get information I felt I needed. It is really easy." She could see Drue becoming angrier. Unable to understand, she babbled on, "By walking around, you can hear all manner of talk, especially at the markets. Lizzie was raised here, so she knows where we can go and not be noticed." Nicola stood up, facing Drue. "What is wrong with you? I know you would rather I had stayed at Lady Eny's home, but I could not do what I promised to do, if I chose to stay. I do not understand why you are so angry."

"Perhaps I am angry with myself. I need to get you and Lizzie out of here."

"Where is Lizzie?" Nicola asked, suddenly aware she had no idea where Lizzie had gone.

"I don't know, exactly." Drue hesitated. "She may be helping Lady Kelly to get Harding out of our way."

Nicola's mouth was suddenly dry. Drue lowered his voice. "I am going downstairs to find Lizzie. Kelly will know where she is. Do not open the door for anyone. You are in grave danger while Harding is here. I will return for you."

Nicola briefly thought of asking him to stay. Instead, she asked, "What if he sees you?"

Drue only glanced back at her as he unlocked the door and disappeared from sight.

WHEN LIZZIE AND HARDING were inside the room, Harding locked the door, casually removed his scabbard, leaning it against the bed, and turned to face her. "Tell me where Lady Weldon is." Now his voice was cold, threatening. As he spoke, he walked toward her.

Lizzie backed up against the wall. "Who? I know no one by the name you speak of." She was trapped, without the possibility of help. She knew plenty about men, and Harding was dangerous.

He grasped Lizzie by the throat. "Lady Weldon. I want her. If you do not tell me, I intend to accuse you of treason." At that statement, Lizzie began to tremble. "Prisoners found guilty of treason are hanged until they pass out." Lizzie gasped. "Then they are tied down, and a man with a blade red with heat removes their bowels while they are still alive."

Lizzie suddenly felt faint. Harding released his hold on her throat and grasped her arms, to keep her upright.

"Please," she begged. Tears flooded her face. "Please tell me what she looks like. I do not know the ladies who work here, but I have not heard of the one you want."

"I work for King Richard," Harding lied.

Desperate, and knowing King Richard's stand on morality, she gambled he would not want the king's men to find him in a brothel. "His men come in here on occasion. They kick open the doors of rooms, searching. The men are taken and the women are placed in stockades." Lizzie could barely speak.

"When do they come?"

When he asked the question, Lizzie realized he was reluctant to be found in a room with a whore. Praying she could keep him talking until he decided to leave or someone came to help, she replied, "Not every night. We do not know when—they just appear." Harding's hold on her was still too tight for her to move. Instead, she kept talking. "Please let me go."

"Do you know who I am?" Harding asked, pulling her closer.

"You must not tell me. When the king's men come, they ask who has been here. I cannot tell what I do not know, if they should ask." She knew she had to buy time. "I never know the names of any of the men who come here."

Suddenly, the door was kicked open. "They're here!" Lizzie screamed. Taken by surprise, Harding lost his grip of her. She sprinted across the room, away from him.

Harding was stunned to see Drue's figure in the doorway. Lizzie ran from the room without looking back.

NICOLA NEARLY JUMPED OUT OF HER SKIN at the sudden banging on the door. "Nicola?" Lizzie's voice came in a tremor. "It's me. Please open quickly. Please!"

Nicola opened the door and pulled Lizzie inside before locking it again. Lizzie began to weep, and Nicola sat with her on the bed and held her. Slowly, Lizzie settled. "He threatened to have me tried for treason, Nicola. If Drue had not come, I think I would have died."

"Who threatened you?" Nicola asked. Harding would not know Lizzie.

"The man who came with the others," Lizzie replied. "Harding."

Nicola jumped up. "He must know I am here! But how?"

"He has seen us, somewhere. He intends to find you. He says he would accuse me of treason." Lizzie continued, "I do not want to stay here. We have to leave."

"You spoke to him?" Nicola asked, aghast.

"Of course we spoke. I took him to a room," Lizzie explained, still watching the door. "Please, let us leave."

"I should not have brought you here with me. I have put you in grave danger." Nicola's heart ached. Her anger at Drue had brought her only friend into Nicola's ring of danger.

"I am your friend, Nicola. You owe me no apology." Looking back at the door, Lizzie continued, "Please, let us just leave now."

"We have to stay here until Drue returns," Nicola replied. "The danger is over. We are safe now."

REALIZING IT WAS DRUE AT THE DOOR, Harding dove for his sword. Drue, expecting the move, flicked the weapon away with his own and stepped backward to close the door behind him. "You are afraid to fight me? You coward!" Harding goaded, while trying to move toward the sword now lying nearly under the bed.

"You know better," Drue replied. "You would have an innocent lady charged with treason to secure your place with the king. Who's the coward, Harding?" Drue, using the point of his weapon, forced Harding back until he fell against the bed. "I intend to see you sleep until the lady can leave here. Then, whatever tale you tell will be useless, without the lady herself. You see, it has already been determined her father was innocent of the charges against him."

Harding frowned, trying to think. Drue drove his point on. "Someone already talked to the king. He knows the whole incident makes it appear he is running scared. Not a good thing for a new king. I do not intend to fight you, Harding. I would only keep you quiet for a while." With his sword at Harding's throat, Drue poured something from a small flask into a glass, then handed it to Harding. "Add wine and drink. You will not become ill, only sleepy." Drue's eyes never left Harding's.

Harding knew he had no choice. His future looked bleak at best. If Richard's men found him, he would likely be sent to the Tower. At King

Richard's first stop, a small crowd of people had come to see the new king, including one man who identified Harding as having spoken out publicly against Richard, causing a near riot at the time. Then the tale of Nicola's escort from Weldon Castle was told. Things went poorly for Harding after that. Even the men assigned to Harding fell under a cloud of suspicion. Harding and his men slipped away during the night. For all he knew, King Richard's men were already looking for him. Harding slowly poured half a glass of wine out, then drank it down. It took effect quickly. He sank back. Setting the glass down, he smiled at Drue. "Maybe I can sleep this night, for a change." He lay back. Drue waited a short while, then lifted Harding's legs up onto the bed.

FOR THE LADIES WAITING IN ROOM TEN, it seemed hours before a soft knock and Drue's voice sounded at the door. When Nicola opened it, she wanted to hug him.

"We have to wait for a while before we can leave. Richard's men are walking the streets." He pulled a chair close to the locked door and sat down. "Nicola, tell me what you have done while in fair London."

For a moment, Nicola hesitated. She glanced at Lizzie, then shared her visit with the dowager queen. "You actually went to her?" Drue asked, frowning. "Though it is abundantly clear you can achieve much on your own, it is just as clear you have no idea what the aftermath would entail, should you be caught. Who saw you?"

"No one of any significance. Of more importance, I believe she will follow my suggestion, to unite the houses of York and Tudor. We need to get to Lady Margaret. She will further the unity of the two houses." Nicola wanted to add how much safer she felt now, with him around, but refused to let him think she could not take care of herself. When she had finished, Nicola could see Drue was no longer angry. "Why is Harding back?" she asked. "Is the king's Progress over already?"

"I am not certain, but for whatever reason, he is back. We must leave this place and this area of town," Drue answered. "Lizzie, are you all right?"

Nicola turned to Lizzie and sat back down beside her. "Lizzie, you took Harding to a room? Alone?"

"That's the way it is done, Nicola. Never again! But nothing happened between us." Lizzie proceeded to share what occurred while she was with Harding. "He said he works for King Richard, but I could tell he was afraid when I told him they had been coming around."

"When were they last here?" Drue asked.

"No one has been around. I just knew I needed to keep him talking. When I saw how uncomfortable he was with the idea they might find him here, I kept talking." Lizzie looked from Drue to Nicola. "We'd best move, before one of Harding's men *do* come for him."

For her part, Nicola was digesting the fact that Lizzie had been brave enough to take Harding to a room, alone. Involuntarily, she shuddered as Lizzie turned to look at her.

"Nicola, what did you mean, unite the houses of York and Tudor?"

Before Nicola could answer, Drue stood, holding his hand up to silence them and opening the door to check the hall. Motioning for Nicola and Lizzie to follow, he walked carefully down the hall and stairs. When they reached the ground floor, Kelly was waiting. "Go! Swiftly, to the back," she told them. "When you leave, walk on the right and duck below windows." Giving Nicola a quick hug, she kissed Lizzie's cheek and nodded to Drue. Drue led them away, passing through the foyer and along a hall to the back door. They came to an alley leading to the street.

Cautiously, Drue slipped to the corner, surveying the street beyond. He waved them toward him and, when they reached him, he spoke rapidly. "Meet me at the stables. Move as quickly as you can without drawing attention. Wait inside. I have something to do." Not giving them time to respond, he turned and slipped away.

Looking at Nicola, Lizzie wrapped her cloak more tightly around her shoulders. "This way. Pray whatever he has to do does not take too long." They walked along the street, talking casually yet moving as fast as they dared. When they reached the stable, the stable master was not there. The women headed toward the back stall, where their horses were being kept. They sat down on the floor and waited.

DRUE RETURNED TO KELLY'S ESTABLISHMENT. After entering through the same back door that took him out, he stood silently, waiting and listening, to be certain no one was about. The foyer was still vacant, and it was too early in the evening for the type of clientele that frequented the place. Silently, Drue moved up the stairs to the second floor, stopping at room three. He carefully let himself inside. When he had surprised Harding earlier, it had been easier than he thought it would be to make him drink the wine—wine with a twist. Unfortunately, Drue had used only the half-empty flask left over from Garrett. Now, he used a full flask. Harding was just coming around. Carefully, Drue poured more of the potion down Harding's throat. When Drue was certain Harding had ingested the potion, he slipped the second small flask back into his pocket. Harding would no longer be a problem. He emptied Harding's pockets. Like a shadow, Drue stole downstairs into Kelly's empty room, setting a purse filled with coins on the back of her dressing table.

Leaving through the back door once again, Drue headed deeper into London's underbelly. At this hour, someone might recognize him, but he needed Bruce and his men. Careful to stay within the darker shadows that lingered beyond the lights from inns and brothels, he searched. Just as he thought to turn back, he caught sight of Bruce. Bruce and his men were leaving an inn across the street. Drue whistled, and Bruce looked toward the sound. It was too dark to see anything, but another whistle told Bruce what direction Drue was taking. Retracing his steps, Drue headed for the stable. Bruce and his men walked in the same direction.

THE MEN WHO FREQUENTED KELLY'S establishment paid the women directly, so Kelly never checked on the rooms until late morning, giving the men a chance to leave unnoticed when they were through. Harding was bad-tempered in the mornings, so Kelly left him alone.

In the early morning hours, five men entered Kelly's foyer. She heard the bell of the front door. It was barely light outside. She threw a robe on, picked up a candle, and walked to the foyer. "'Tis scarcely morn, sirs, and none of my ladies are free," she told them. "I do have something to eat, if you are hungry." She knew they were not after food. Two of them were the same men who had come with Harding the evening prior. She had not seen or heard from Harding since he had taken Lizzie up the stairs.

"We did not come for food. Lord Harding was here last night. We came for him," one man informed her gruffly. "He's kept us waiting long enough."

"We need to get out of here, before Richard's men come looking for us," another added apprehensively.

"Shut up!" the first man ordered. Looking back at Kelly, who pretended to be starting the fire, he asked, "When did he leave?"

"I do not know," Kelly answered. "I do not make it my business to keep my patrons under watch. Nearly all pay before they go upstairs. Your friend never pays. He says he works for the king and is not to be questioned. So I do not question him."

The men looked at each other without answering. The silence dragged on. "Do you want to eat?" Kelly offered.

"No, and it would be better for you if you have not seen us," the first man answered. Kelly nodded and turned back to the fireplace. She heard the men leave. The flame was catching hold well, before she turned back around. The foyer was empty.

Kelly quietly took the stairs to Harding's room. Opening the door, she saw what she expected. *He is still asleep.* She walked to the bed and gently shook him. Gasping, she pulled her hand back. Harding was not sleeping—he was dead. *Another one. These are bad times. I must get rid of this body.* Kelly could ill afford having the king's men snooping around looking for Harding—finding his body here would kill what business she had.

Kelly left the relative safety of her building and walked the streets of London. She searched for one man in particular—one who always handled her problems discreetly. The streets were moderately busy, beginning the day's business. Walking without making eye contact with anyone, Kelly made her way into the poorest area of London. She reached a run-down shack where the man she knew frequently slept and knocked on the door and asked for him. She then waited for him to step out. The odors of humanity were strong, made worse by the heavy air and absence of even a slight breeze.

When they had found a quiet corner, she explained the situation. "I would have need of the services of someone who can remove a problem for me. This morning. Second floor, room three." Kelly let her eyes casually glance his way, then move beyond. He was now very serious. He did not answer immediately, and Kelly walked a short distance past him.

Then he started to cross the street. "Done." Looking in both directions, he added, "It will cost you."

"Agreed," Kelly replied as she walked on past the building. She slowly wandered London's streets, stopping to buy a few items, killing time. She entered an alley and moved between buildings to emerge along the streets again.

When Kelly entered the front door to her building, she was relieved to find the ladies were still asleep and all was silent. Ignoring the impulse to return to Harding's room, she started bread baking and porridge cooking for breakfast. After some time, she walked up the stairs and gently opened the door. The bed was already stripped and empty. The window remained locked from the inside. Taking a deep breath, she left the room. Downstairs, everything was as she had left it.

Relieved, she entered her own room. It was undisturbed, but for the first time, she noticed a large pouch filled with coins tucked to the back of her dressing table. The man she hired to remove Harding's body had never entered any other rooms before, and he certainly had never left money. If he found any money on Harding, he would have kept it without telling anyone. Had Harding's men returned? She told them Harding never paid, but she knew they were not close to Harding and would never have paid his debt. The fact remained that, in daylight, someone had come into her quarters, perhaps the very men who were said to work for King Richard. Had they found Harding's body? This could turn very ugly for her.

CHAPTER 35

Lady Margaret sat alone in her room, staring at a plate of uneaten food. Tonight the old doctor who helped her would come again. He would have news about the two young sons of the late King Edward. With both boys locked up in the Tower, life for them looked bleak indeed. However, never one to leave anything to chance, she had to act quickly. When one of her ladies told her the doctor was in the garden, she rose hastily to meet him. "Tell me, what is the news?"

"Lady." The man bowed swiftly. "The two boys are still locked in the Tower and the coronation has taken place, but rumor has it that some of the York supporters will attempt to rescue the princes."

Frowning, Lady Margaret asked anxiously, "Is that possible?" Events were moving closer and closer for her son. Henry Tudor would be king, she was certain. But if the princes were rescued . . . "Can the Tower be breached?"

"It never has been, but it has never been tried. More likely, the princes would be rescued with help from inside." He waited for further instructions. Lady Margaret simply nodded before leaving him standing alone in the darkness.

Back in her rooms, Margaret began to pace. *This cannot happen. If they are freed, surely there will be many of Edward's men willing to follow them.* Still pacing, she tried to think how she could turn this in Henry's favor. The princes must be killed in the rescue attempt. *Anyone trying to rescue them would be hanged, including guards within the Tower itself. There must be someone I can enlist for Henry's cause. Someone inside the Tower. Someone who would never talk but would do what needed to be done.* In the early morning light, Lady Margaret waited in her garden. Lord Stanley had been called to court, along with most of King Richard's lords, in anticipation of the king's return. If the princes were to be freed, it must happen soon, before King Richard returned. If it happened successfully on this coming night, Richard could be prevented entry by King Edward's followers. That would not help Henry. The rescue attempt could not take place without warning. Pacing back and forth, Lady Margaret waited.

The sound of a rider entering the yard echoed off the walls. Margaret held her breath. *Dare I believe the man is coming?*

"Lady?" the man called as he leapt from his horse.

"Here, sir," Lady Margaret answered.

"Tonight, they plan to free the princes. What is your command, lady?" The man stood waiting. He worked for Lord Braggio. Always had. When Braggio sent him to Lady Margaret, he never hesitated.

"This cannot be allowed success, sir. If the guard is warned, the followers will be executed," Lady Margaret replied. "That would stand as a warning to any other of Edward's men."

"Does that not put the princes' lives in danger, lady?" Braggio's man asked. His fears were coming to fruition.

Lady Margaret did not answer. She looked at the man for a long moment, then turned away.

THE MAN STOOD WATCHING HER LEAVE. *Surely she does not wish harm to those innocent boys. Boys who have no defense.* As he rode away, he turned once to look back at Lord Stanley's estate. *If Lord Braggio is correct, the guards in the Tower have already been alerted to the planned rescue. No one knows who is behind the plan or who alerted the guard, but I was given strict instructions not to share that piece of information with Lady Margaret.*

Upon returning to camp, he reported to Braggio. Braggio commented, "Lady Margaret is known as a pious, devout woman. Not so devout, it would seem. We all want Tudor, but at what price? Make ready to leave, quietly." The man nodded and backed away, as it was clear Braggio was already lost in his own world. Men were laughing and talking outside. "I know how each of my men would react, what they would think," Braggio muttered. "If my prince is to come, he'd best come soon."

The man took his leave, entirely unnoticed.

WHEN DRUE REACHED THE STABLES, Bruce was waiting. He told Drue where the ladies were and, before joining them, the two men talked. Bruce spoke to his men, now gathered around, then left. Drue ordered the stable hand to saddle the remaining three horses. He handed the man a small bag of gold coins and nodded. The man knew what was expected. "I have not seen you, your friend, or the ladies. God go with you, m'lord." Drue clapped the man on his shoulder. He called softly for Nicola before entering the stable.

"Thank heaven it is you, Lord Drue," Nicola whispered. "I feel that my luck could well run out at any moment. I want no part of London any longer."

Drue did not reply. He led the horses out. With the help of the stable master, all three were saddled and ready in short order. With Nicola and Lizzie mounted, Drue led them out.

"Where are we going, Lord Drue?" Lizzie asked. "I am happy to stay with Lady Weldon, if you allow."

Nicola turned toward Lizzie, frowning, but Drue replied before Nicola could speak. "We are going to Lady Wright. From there, we can decide how best to get to Tudor's mother, Lady Margaret."

With Drue in the lead, Nicola and Lizzie followed. Though she spoke very softly, Drue could hear Nicola ask Lizzie to go with her.

"Lizzie, you are my friend. Remember that. Later, we should speak in private. You should know more about what we are undertaking."

Drue smiled. The stillness around them gave way for voices to carry with little effort. Nicola had a great deal to learn. Much as he swore he never would, Drue knew he had become very fond of her. *There is still the matter of Kelly's. That will not happen again.* Thinking of Kelly, he knew a conversation with Bruce was due. It would be a long year or two. Under normal circumstances, it would be the kind of year he would enjoy. With Nicola in the mix, the ordeal took on a greater weight. *You picked a bad time to leave, Mother. I could use your advice now.* Slowing his horse, Drue turned to the ladies. "Are you both able to ride to Eny's without stopping? We are safe there. I do not know what may happen tomorrow, nor do I know where King Richard is right now."

Both women readily agreed to keep riding. After that, Drue spoke little, concentrating on the land around them. He listened to the low voices of Nicola and Lizzie. The ride was steady but unhurried. There was a calm sense of relief hovering around them. Drue was well aware it would not often be that way again.

CHAPTER 36

B RUCE AND HIS MEN RODE INTO CAMP as Braggio's men were settling down to eat. While Bruce's men joined them for a quick meal, Bruce and Braggio stepped into Braggio's tent where they could talk in private. "Drue's answer is no, thank heaven," Bruce informed Braggio. "He is firm on that matter. He said we are not in the business of killing the innocents for the throne of England."

Braggio agreed heartily. "Yes, and the attempted rescue will go down poorly, I fear. There will be trouble for the men involved and the princes. We cannot be party to any of it. Henry Tudor will have to fight hard for his claim, and a win for Tudor is not assured. If it is discovered that Henry's supporters were involved in the killing of those two young boys, it would certainly crush support for Henry. Richard prepares as we speak. Tudor cannot have his move for the crown tainted by even a hint that his side played any part in that mess." Braggio stood at the tent entrance, staring at the darkness beyond. "This fight, when it happens, will be a bad one. Richard easily outmans Tudor. Together, you and I do not have a hundred men. I wonder if anyone has heard from Jasper or Henry. How many men can Jasper come up with?"

"I am certain Lady Margaret has heard. I have not," Bruce replied. Nicola's intention to visit Lady Margaret was on his mind. "Do you know Lady Weldon? She plans on talking with Lady Margaret."

"Who is Lady Weldon?" Braggio asked, frowning.

Bruce described Nicola. Braggio began laughing. "Ah, I do know her. She rode alone when I saw her. Swore she lost her companion to the sweat and released her guard because they were afraid of the illness. She said she hid out in the forest for days, for fear she would pass the illness on. Good story, bad liar." Braggio chuckled.

"There have been deaths from the sweats," Bruce reminded Braggio. "How could you know she was lying?"

Braggio smiled at his friend. "To begin with, she was much too clean. Nor did she look the part of one who is fearful of much, though I have a suspicion she does well to cover her feelings. The lady will know fear well if she meddles with Lady Margaret."

"I see. You should know, she has picked up traveling companions. One, a young lady named Lizzie. Lizzie worked for Lady Wright," said Bruce. "Oh . . . and Drue."

"Drue? How did that happen?" asked Braggio. "And how is Lady Weldon involved in all this?"

"That I cannot answer, but Drue is helping her, and I know she works to get Tudor on the throne." Bruce caught the spark in Braggio's eyes. "Lord Drue is not courting the lady. At least not as of today."

"The fight coming to us will decide if Tudor takes the crown. If we survive, we will not stay." Braggio smiled, his voice wistful. "Perhaps we might go home."

"We have been gone so long I cannot remember what home is like." Bruce stretched out on one of the cots. "Home . . . do we still have one?"

Braggio looked at his friend. "Of course we do," he replied quietly. "We always have that. I remember every detail of my home." Braggio's mind wandered to the dark-eyed lady who lied with such confidence, unaware he did not believe a word she said. Late into the night, Braggio still lay awake. He had never before thought about home, except as a place he had loved and left. He never thought of home as a place he could return to and make his own. *Perhaps it is time I took a wife.* Would the lady he met riding alone and unafraid be happy with a war-hardened soldier?

WHEN DRUE AND THE LADIES RODE into the courtyard of Wright Castle, Eny was watching from her bedroom window. The hour was very late. With the castle long since settled down for the night, quiet peace blanketed the area. Eny met them in her grand hall, where a fire was already blazing.

Drue followed Lizzie and Nicola inside, watching Nicola. Nicola hugged Eny tightly. Eny returned the affection. "I feared for your safety, Nicola. Thank heaven you are back. You both look exhausted, but none the worse." Turning to Lizzie, she kissed her cheek. "You took good care of Nicola, I see, Lizzie."

Drue stood near the fire, watching the women. Eny stepped closer to him. "Lady Eny." Drue kissed Eny's hand. "This was an experience I do not wish to repeat. Neither lady takes the time to consider dangers before they act." He shook his head. "I hope we might stay a few days with you, while I decide how best to proceed. Nicola will not be going without me again." He paused a minute, watching Nicola, before adding, "If you can still spare her, Lizzie is the perfect companion for Lady Nicola."

Eny laughed softly. *Foolish man. He still thinks he can tell Nicola what to do.* "Of course, you may stay as long as you wish. And Lizzie is free to decide what she wants to do. I do not own her. I think Nicola certainly needs her assistance more than I do." Eny spoke out to Lizzie. "Lizzie, are you willing to stay on with Nicola?"

"Oh yes," Lizzie replied.

"It's settled then. We shall all sleep. Lizzie, I have moved you in with Nicola. When we rise in the morning—or afternoon—you can decide how best to move forward. Safely, God willing." Nodding toward the stairs, Eny led the way to the sleeping quarters upstairs.

Once inside their room, Nicola sank down onto one of the chairs near the fireplace. Lizzie plopped opposite her. When they finally lay down, sleep found them quickly.

After breaking fast together the following morning, Eny took Lizzie with her, leaving Nicola alone with Drue. Nicola walked around the room, studying the art and tapestries hung around the room. Drue watched her a short while before speaking. "Come, lady—sit. You and I have much to discuss." He sat, feeling relaxed and in control.

Nicola had stopped walking, and now faced Drue with a determined look in her eye. "I plan to speak with Lady Margaret. I am certain you or Eny must know where Lord Stanley lives. When can you take me, since you insist upon going?"

Taken aback, Drue stared at Nicola. "Lady, you do not understand the gravity of what will take place in the near future." The mild expression on her face told him she did not know what he spoke of. "Nicola, you know there is a movement afoot to rescue the princes from the Tower."

"I would expect that." Nicola's voice was indignant. "It makes perfect sense. If Edward's heirs are to succeed him, they must be rescued. And I think Prince Edward's succession is something King Richard would never allow. I cannot even think about what he might order."

"You should also be aware that escape from the Tower is nearly impossible. The princes must have reliable help from inside. If it fails, which is most likely, all involved will be put to death." Drue paused. He watched Nicola's face cloud. "I am certain you are aware that the punishment for a traitor is to be hung until nearly dead, then taken down, and disemboweled while still alive, or quartered. Although with the number of men involved, in the interest of time, I doubt that will happen. No matter, because I am certain the young princes will not survive."

"How awful!" Nicola covered her mouth with her hand. "That could be me."

"It could, but it will not," Drue answered quietly. "I must have a promise from you. You will not take off on your own again, unless it is part of a carefully executed plan. Am I clear?" Now his voice was stern. He knew women were more likely to give up their head or be burned than executed by the method used on men found guilty of treason. He had no intention of allowing Nicola to be taken prisoner.

Nicola was pensive for a moment. "I will promise on one condition. You must swear you will help me complete the mission my father gave me. If you try to stop me, the promise I make will no longer be binding."

Drue sat quiet, studying Nicola. "We have an agreement," he finally answered.

Nicola nodded. "I am confident that you can add some measure of logic to all that has happened. Will we know if the rescue is successful?" she asked.

"All of England will know the outcome." Drue stood. "Nicola, come walk with me."

A small smile warmed Nicola's face. "I would like that, Lord Drue." Together, they strode through Eny's vast gardens. Nicola had not relaxed in so long she was afraid to allow the feeling to linger. Yet, with Drue near, it felt comfortable. "Lord Drue, I question whether I should tell Lizzie what it is I do. I am afraid what happened with Harding may not be the only time I will place her, or you, in danger." Nicola looked up at Drue. "I have no right to do that to anyone."

Drue walked along for a short while, thinking how to answer. He stopped alongside a small pond. "See the ducks swimming? The mother takes every duckling with her into the water. She knows the dangers, even as she slips off the bank, but still she leads on. Many of her babies will perish before the summer fades. She never hesitates next season, still mating and moving forward, to raise more. When she is gone, the cycle will continue. Life does that." He looked at Nicola. "I think Lizzie should know as much as you can tell her, but only after she agrees to stay with us until the end of this. To tell her and then have her decide to leave would place both of you at a great risk, if she should be taken, for whatever reason."

Nicola's gaze wandered, settling on the ducks. Nicola turned to Drue. "Drue, what do the ducklings have to do with Lizzie and I?"

Drue grinned. "Nothing, really, except no matter what we do, life keeps on. The seasons keep changing, the sun rises, and so it goes. I believe you must do what in your heart you believe is best for Lizzie, keeping in mind what it means to us." When Nicola's brow shot up, he added, softly, "It is *us*, Nicola. No longer is it just you. Bruce is also with you, as are others."

"Does Bruce know—"

"No, he does not." Leading her back toward a waiting meal, he reminded Nicola, "We are to talk in the afternoon, you and I. I know you want to talk with Lady Margaret. I will try, but you should know, she will not be as easy as the dowager queen." They walked on a short way. "I have some things I must think on, before you and I make any move. This afternoon would be a good time. You must think carefully on what I decide."

"You decide?" Nicola asked, stopping.

"Yes, I decide. I know what you want to do. I will do all in my power to get you where you want to be, but you agreed I will decide how and when we move. I will share my plans with you, but although we discuss them, that does not necessarily mean I will change my mind." Drue walked with his hands clasped behind his back—it was a manner of strolling that often soothed him, when his mind was running wild.

Nicola followed. "I will cross one stream at a time, as my father always advised," she told Drue. "And, for the first time since that awful day, thinking of him does not cause such a deep, tremendous pain. *He is still with me, but it no longer hurts.* I realize I no longer feel like crying with every thought of him."

"Ah, that I understand," Drue told her, returning the smile. "I wonder, lady, if we might be better served to take your message to Henry Tudor first. It takes time and money to raise an army. King Richard will have little trouble with either. I cannot imagine where Henry Tudor will find a following large enough to take on King Richard, or how he will fund it."

Nicola stopped walking. "I believe Lady Margaret might be able to help. She is rumored to be the richest woman in England. The sooner she knows the situation, the quicker she can raise funds. And what about Lord Stanley? He has money and men."

"Yes, Stanley does, but he will never commit for either Henry or King Richard, until he is certain the side he backs is going to prevail." Drue stopped as well and turned to look at Nicola. "He is not one we can count on helping. If he does, it will be when the battle is nearly done."

Nicola frowned at Drue. "We? You are not going to fight, are you?" Nicola had never seen anything resembling a battle until the men overtook Weldon Castle. And that takeover at her home happened so quickly it was impossible to tell if her father's men had even had time to fight. "You cannot think to leave and fight, Drue." Nicola was only too aware of the flutter in her chest. *Hmm, that cannot happen. Not now. I must remember to keep a tight rein on my heart. I know what an assassin does, and I should not think we have need of each other but for the promise I made to Father.*

"You fear for my safety, lady?" Drue asked, smiling.

"Certainly not," Nicola answered haughtily. "I fear you are thinking of breaking our agreement." Nicola could not give any validation to the feelings she now was certain she felt for Lord Drue.

In an instant Drue's face became expressionless. He turned on his heel and began to walk back to the castle.

Left standing, Nicola was startled. "Drue?" She could not catch him unless she ran. She started to, then stopped herself. *How undignified! I will not run after him, or anyone else.* Gathering her skirts around her, she gracefully continued along the walkway.

CHAPTER 37

AS THE GUESTS AT WRIGHT CASTLE gathered for the evening meal, the air was chilly between Drue and Nicola. Nicola refused to discuss it, and Lizzie knew better than to try. And so the meal began in an awkward silence. Just as Eny thought she'd had enough drama, her server announced they had company. The page entered announcing the arrival of Lord Braggio and Lord Bruce. Both men walked in smiling, but those smiles faded when they saw Drue. Exchanging knowing looks, they instead walked to Eny, who stood to receive them.

"How pleased I am to see you both. It has become a little chilly here." She nodded toward her table. "And your men? They must be hungry also. Please, bring them in. These old walls could use a little laughter again." With that, she ordered additional tables and food be provided.

Drue stood and greeted his friends. Pointedly, he ignored Nicola.

His behavior was difficult for Nicola to understand, but seeing Bruce and Braggio walk in together gave her something else to think about. When the men reached their table, Eny introduced everyone. Nicola could feel her face get hot when Braggio kissed her hand. "Please forgive me the lie, Lord Braggio. I had no desire to be detained."

Braggio laughed loudly. "You, Lady Weldon, are a poor liar. Beautiful, but poor," he answered, laughing again. Nicola smiled back at him, wishing he would keep walking. She could feel all eyes upon her. As Braggio walked past Nicola, she watched as he caught sight of Lizzie, who looked back at him with great blue eyes surrounded by thick black lashes. She was smiling, her face dimpled, and her golden hair tumbled in curls down her back. Braggio returned the smile, still gazing at her, before walking on. Twice he turned back to look at Lizzie.

Nicola wanted nothing more than to leave the table. At least with the new guests, there was no need to speak to or look at Drue. She could not understand why he was so cold, or why she cared what he thought. Unable to eat, she sat still, miserable in her own world. Eny finally took pity on her and, standing, asked Nicola to join her in her study. Gratefully, Nicola accepted.

When the ladies were seated before a soothing fire, glasses in hand, Eny asked, "Just what is going on, Nicola?" She leaned in to add, "Men are never easy, but Drue is a special breed, you know. He has lived his whole life doing whatever he chose. That has all changed now."

"Then it is not just my imagination. He is upset," Nicola replied.

"I may be old, but I am not out of touch with everyone. At least not yet. You both are upset. Please share. It helps to talk with someone, you know. Lizzie is wonderful, but she is not aware of some things." Eny leaned back and waited.

"I do not know what is wrong," Nicola replied softly. "We were talking when he suddenly turned cold." Nicola paused. "Truthfully, Eny, I was so upset that he will get pulled into the fighting over the crown, I cannot remember just what I said." As she spoke, Nicola suddenly understood exactly what happened. "He asked if I was worried about his safety. I denied it and made it clear I was only worried he might break our agreement." *I could not dare tell him what my heart feels.*

"What agreement, dear?"

"That he would help me. I did not mean to sound so selfish. I just could not let him see what is going on in my head," Nicola finished lamely.

"You mean in your heart," Eny corrected her gently.

"Yes, that is where everything is getting so mixed. Eny, I cannot let him go on thinking so poorly of me. I must clear this up." Before Eny could respond, Nicola was out the door. She flew down the stairs and burst into the great room.

Intimidated by the room filled with men, she stopped dead in her tracks. Lizzie sat at the head table, where she had been all night. At her side, Braggio sat, clearly not aware of anyone else in the room. Drue was not to be found. Neither was Bruce. Taking a deep breath, Nicola approached the table. "Lizzie, do you know where Drue is?"

Bruce answered immediately, "Why yes, lady. He is with Bruce and some of the others, at the sleeping quarters for the men." Braggio was standing by this time. "I will go for him," he said.

"No, I will go myself. Where is this building?" Nicola had regained her composure. "Just tell me where."

Braggio frowned. "It is dark and—"

Before he could finish, Nicola stated firmly, "If you cannot tell me where it is, I will find it myself. Thank you." She turned to leave.

Braggio spoke quickly. "It is along the east wall. Near the stables, lady." With that, he turned back to Lizzie.

Nicola left the great room and stood in the dark, empty courtyard. *Now, just which way is east?* Closing her eyes, she tried to think where the sun first came up. She had no idea. *But the stables! I remember them. Just as we came into the courtyard.* She headed in that direction. As she got closer, she could hear talking and laughing. She was startled when a man stepped from the shadows. He stood still, as if planted in the spot.

"Lady, can I be of service to you?" He made no motion to stop her, but Nicola had the feeling he would if she did not speak with him.

"Yes, please," she replied. "I would speak with Lord Drue." As the man bowed slightly and turned toward the door, Nicola stepped closer. "I must go with you, sir. I do not believe he would like to speak with me, but he cannot run in front of so many men." Nicola smiled.

"No, my lady, he cannot." The man laughed softly. "However, there is no need for you to enter a place such as this. I will—"

Nicola interrupted. "No, I insist, please." The man looked at her for a moment, then chuckled and opened the door for her. Inside, two burning fireplaces along with candles on several long tables lit the room. The tables were loaded with mugs and food and surrounded with men on benches.

The room went silent when she entered. The man at the door called out loudly, "Your Grace, you have a guest!" All eyes were on Nicola. Drue slowly turned to the door. Surprised to see Nicola, he stood and shook his head as he stepped away from the table. Fearful he would ask her to leave, she immediately moved toward him as she spoke, "Lord Drue, I must speak with you. This cannot wait for morning." Then to her embarrassment, she nearly tripped over a small stool. Everyone jumped. Drue met her, and with his hand on her elbow, led her toward the door as hurriedly as he could.

As they left the building, his grip on her tightened. She had no doubt he was angry that she dared to come after him like that. When they were a sufficient distance from the building, he stopped. Before he could get a word out, Nicola spoke. Her voice was serious, level, and firm. "This is the worst time to speak of this, but I must tell you, Drue. I lied. I am terrified for your safety. I have no right to say these things to you, but what little I have seen of life tells me I must say what I feel when I can. I . . . I have feelings for you. I have no right to say such a thing to you, but you must know." Unable to stop, Nicola bumbled on, "I do not expect any reciprocation, but you should know what is in my heart. Please, you must not get hurt or die. Please, Drue." To her horror, she began to cry. "Please forgive me," she murmured, and tried to get free of his grip. All she had said and done left her with nothing but the need to get free.

Drue did not let her go. She could almost feel his anger leave him, like an exhale. He folded her into his arms and kissed the top of her head gently. "And you, lady . . . please forgive me." Then, lifting her face up, he kissed her cheek, then her lips. Nicola returned the kiss. "You are right, this is a poor time to speak of this, but life never moves to our demands. You are a very unusual lady. A great lady. Make no mistake." His voice was soft, and he held her face in both hands. "This will be a long, rough time for us. And you must know, I *will* fight, Nicola. That is what I am. One day, all this will be behind us, and the time will be ours. You have my heart, Nicola." He smiled at her, then nodded toward the castle. As he took her arm, under his breath, he added, "Much to my surprise."

They had not taken two steps when a great cry came from the front wall, followed by a loud crack. Drue ran, pulling Nicola with him, and they ducked behind a small retaining wall running alongside the guardhouse. "Secure the gates! It's a siege gun!" Drue yelled as he scrambled to stand. "That was a warning shot." Men inside the guardhouse came pouring out, immediately taking control of the courtyard at Drue's initial cry. Another explosion resounded outside the walls, and a second projectile slammed into the ground inside the courtyard. Men were running this way and that, securing the animals, herding the few women and children living within the courtyard itself into the castle proper while other men climbed up the steps onto the walls. Nicola still lay where Drue had thrown them both down. Drue was already in the courtyard, yelling orders and directing the men. Nicola sat up slowly, then crawled back against the guardhouse walls and stared aghast at the mayhem before her.

The voices of both Bruce and Braggio had joined Drue's, shouting orders. Eventually, the activity slowed, then stopped. The courtyard and castle were filled with an eerie silence. A loud call could be heard coming from outside the walls. "You, in Wright Castle! In the name of King Richard, we demand that you open the gates!"

Nicola could hear Braggio's voice boom out, "Who orders in King Richard's name? Who orders fire on this castle and the widow living within its walls?"

The voice called out, "Lord Harding, the king's Commander of Guard."

Braggio replied, his indignant voice heard throughout the courtyard, "I ask again, who orders the attack on this castle? I know about Lord Harding. I know it is impossible for Harding to have come here this night. I ask again, who orders this attack?"

There was a long moment of silence, before the voice answered, "Open the gates or be overrun!"

Braggio and Bruce were now standing alongside Drue. "This is not the work of King Richard, Your Grace. He is a very competent commander. He would never think to engage us this way. Nor at this time. He has no need for Wright Castle. 'Tis a rogue band."

Drue agreed. "Richard would already be inside, so poorly are we prepared. The shot was an ill-played warning. If they were sure of the outcome, the shot would have come during light, and hit something, even the wall. Instead, they waited until darkness, to avoid hitting anyone, if possible, thereby allowing them to plead intent to do no harm. The question becomes, who or what do they come for?" In his mind's eye, Drue scanned every possibility. It was connected, he believed, to either Eny or Nicola. Eny was known both to Richard and all of young Edward's supporters. The most useful thing Eny could provide would be money. Nicola would be of no use to anyone unless someone had actually seen what she carried. He was certain that was not possible. Perhaps this attack was a distraction, or a desperate ploy to buy time. *But for whom?* If this ploy failed, what would the invaders do to save face? Drue made a decision. "Come with me. We must speak with Eny." Drue then turned to look for Nicola.

He found her against the guardhouse wall where he left her. She stood when she saw him. "Come, we have to move now. I will explain later." Grasping her hand, he ran with her to the castle itself, followed by Bruce and Braggio. Inside, they entered a room deep within the keep. Eny and Lizzie were waiting there, and several men were already standing around the parameter.

Drue began without a preamble. "This is a hunting expedition. I think they are not even sure what might be of use in this place. We must do all we can to show it was a useless venture, without gain."

Bruce looked around the room until he found Drue. "I am certain, my lord, you have a plan. To take this place and those in it would indeed be a coup for the fools running this attack." He paused before adding, "I know your strategy must include some way to get the people inside these walls out unnoticed. Am I correct?"

All eyes turned to Drue. "You are, my friend," he replied. "Eny, I cannot remember exactly where Lord Wright's escape is located. Have you ever used it?"

"It is beneath the stairwell, from the kitchen side. Lord Wright used it at least monthly; I have not been as diligent. I do not know if it is even passable."

"You soon will," Drue answered. He turned to speak to one of the men standing against the wall, when he was interrupted by Eny.

"You must take everyone, Drue. If even one soul not in my colors is left, we all are doomed." Eny knew what she asked of Drue. She knew it would not sit well with him.

"That leaves you totally alone and unprotected, and that is not acceptable," Drue answered firmly.

Braggio stepped forward. "Alone, yes. Unprotected, no. Even the mudworms outside have a backside." Braggio looked intently at Drue.

"True enough," Drue agreed, looking at Braggio, thinking hard, trying to remember every detail of an attack such as this one that he and Braggio had defended successfully against. "That is a good idea, Braggio. Now, listen carefully, ladies." Drue gave clear directions to the three women, ordering the few women and children who lived inside the castle walls to leave, led by two of the soldiers. As Eny and Lizzie left to gather everyone, Drue pulled Nicola aside. "All the lives with you will depend upon you. Take them deeper into the forested area, beyond the castle. They should travel as quietly and as far as possible. Eny will know when you come to a safe area. Wait for us there." He gave her a quick kiss. "My own princess . . ."

"Princess? I do not think so. I am but a well-educated puppet that must now become an untrained soldier. God help us," Nicola whispered to him. When Nicola reached the kitchen, Eny and Lizzie were busy handing water bladders and foodstuffs to anyone who could help with the carrying. Eny sent two ladies for blankets.

"If you are not back when we leave, we go without you," Nicola called after the ladies.

Drue entered the kitchen. "You must leave now," he ordered. For a long moment, his eyes held Nicola's eyes. Then, bowing to her, he turned and left.

Eny and Lizzie pulled the doors to the pantry open. At Eny's direction, they pushed against a wall of heavy shelves. The wall gave way, revealing a narrow opening beyond. "Oil lamps!" ordered Eny.

Before sending them on, Nicola cautioned the young ones, "If you cry or make any noise, the bad men will come for you. We must leave as quietly as possible so they do not know we are going or where we've gone." With one soldier leading the way, everyone began filing into the darkness.

Eny stepped back. "Take care, ladies, of the little ones and yourselves."

"Eny, you must come. Drue said—" Nicola started, but Eny interrupted her.

"No, Nicola. You must be certain all are safe. If I go too, it tells the men who seek to capture this place there are people missing. That cannot happen. I stay, as will several of my ladies. Now go, before the devil is knocking on my door. Go!"

Lizzie kissed Eny, then followed the rest into the tunnel. Nicola could think of nothing to say. "I could never repay what you have done for me." Nicola hugged Eny, then she too disappeared from view as the second soldier followed. With all inside the tunnel, Eny and the ladies with her closed the door, cleared any evidence there might have been activity in the pantry, then quietly headed up the stairs to Eny's study. Eny stopped and returned to speak with Drue. He was already outside again. Eny followed him.

Drue and Braggio, leading a group of men, crawled up to the back of the castle wall. With ropes tied to support pillars, they dropped the weighted ends over the wall. One by one, the men shimmied down the ropes. Then, armed with stakes, gunpowder, and cords, they circled the attackers. The cords were strung and tied behind the invading camp, clay tankards of gunpowder were set around and across the road leading away, and sharpened stakes were driven into the damp earth. Next, men with arrows made for use with fire were positioned to allow a clear shot at the gunpowder tankards.

In the tunnel, Nicola and Lizzie kept the little line of women and children moving. Most infants were accustomed to sleeping tied to their mothers' backs or bellies, while the women worked. Tied in this manner now, they did what they always did . . . they slept. The toddlers were caught up in the excitement and urgency felt by the adults and moved steadily along. Light from the man out in front barely reached walkers in the rear. They moved, each touching the one in front. So it went. Just when Nicola felt she would suffocate from a smothering feeling, the line stopped. Straining to look around the line, Nicola could see the flickering light ahead. "Why do we stop?" she asked. Lizzie, holding a small child who could not yet walk, simply shrugged. Nicola began the slow struggle to squeeze past each body. Some of the children began to whimper. Nicola spoke softly, patting them as she passed. At the front, she quietly whispered, "Why are you not moving?"

The soldier remained quiet but indicated the space before him. It was solid. The wall blocked further advance. Nicola looked from the soldier to the bricked wall before them. "Is this possible? Why would it end? Lady Wright said Lord Wright used it at least once a month." Nicola reached out and touched the cold stones. "I want to see the top." She pointed upward. The soldier held the light higher. It was clear, the tunnel simply ended. It had never been completed. "We must have missed a turn. But how? We are surrounded by wall."

The second soldier studied the walls on both sides as he slowly made his way from the back toward the front. He knelt and felt the ground as it changed from floor to side to top, continuing along the tunnel. Nicola stood looking around, fighting to control the panic that threatened to consume her. "How does this not fall on us?" she whispered to the first soldier.

"There are timbers, lady." He held the light higher. Frowning, he stared, then moved the light slowly, back and forth. He began to search overhead. Backtracking, he moved the light to expose the surface above their heads. Nicola followed. At length, he stopped. Looking at Nicola, he pointed toward the area above him. Nicola squeezed next to him. She could see timbers above the soldier. "Look," he whispered. With the light, he exposed where the tunnel made a sharp turn.

"How did we miss this? I walked right by." Nicola looked upward again.

"You were meant to miss it. Look at the walls, lady. The overhead is lower, there is a small wall, and the turn is so sharp one is led to believe the tunnel leads the way we moved. Quickly—we have lost time." The soldier moved the group along the side tunnel, one by one. The tight space felt oppressive. Nicola could sense the unrest building. "Not far, now," the soldier spoke softly to those nearest. Nicola was already moving everyone in the new direction. With the first hint of cooler air, everyone tried to move faster. "No, we cannot run," the soldier said calmly. "We must not shake the structure and timbers overhead. They will not stand. Move steadily, quickly, but always carefully."

At last, Nicola could feel the air move around her, and she saw the night become visible ahead. As dark as it was outside, it was bright to the line of people. Once everyone was outside, Nicola said, "We are not yet safe. We must walk deeper into the forest. No talking, little ones. I know you are all tired, but everyone who walks without speaking or crying will get a present when we stop for the night. Help each other stay quiet. Stay together. One of the soldiers will walk in the back with Lady Lizzie—I will be up front with the other soldier. Keep watch over those in front and behind you."

Nicola looked at the tiny faces around her, then at the mothers. "We will stop soon. The men left behind are doing all they can to be sure your homes are protected. We must do our part and keep their children safe." With a sinking heart, Nicola remembered Eny was supposed to tell her where it would be safe to stop. But Eny was not with them. In the tunnel, her every thought had been to get everyone out safely. *Now what am I supposed to do?* She looked around the forest surrounding them, then back at the people.

The soldier in front stepped closer to her. "Lady? Where do we go now?" he whispered.

Nicola looked up at him and took a deep breath. "I am not certain. Eny was to tell us where it would be safe to stop."

"Eny? That will not work well." He looked around. "We must put out the torches. Too easy to be seen." The one he held was already smothered.

Grateful the skies were clear, Nicola prayed what little moonlight that splashed through the trees would be enough. "I will be right back. I want to be certain we still have everyone." Nicola made her way back to where Lizzie walked, then grasped her hand. "Is everyone well, Lizzie?"

"Yes," Lizzie replied. "And, in my heart, I pray it ends well tonight."

Nicola could hear the worry in her voice. "You think of Lord Braggio?"

"Yes," Lizzie answered. "He will take good care of me, I think. It will be easy for me to take good care of him," Lizzie added.

"You know Lord Braggio is helping us. You will see much more of him." Nicola lowered her voice. "Words cannot express the feeling in my heart for all you have done for me. I will never forget."

Lizzie squeezed Nicola's hand. "I am having a grand adventure with you, Lady Nicola. Lord Braggio will be gift enough for me, if you can see a way I might stay with him when this is over."

"Indeed I will. I swear to you."

The soldier stood where she left him, not certain what they should do next. Nicola addressed him. "Drue said to go deep into the forest, so I would say we keep moving away from the castle." Nicola looked around again. "We are moving away, are we not?"

"I am not sure, my lady." He looked around again. "The door and tunnel we took moved us one way, but the turn angled us another way." He continued to look at the forest and skies above. "Yet . . ." His voice trailed off.

Nicola frowned. "We then made another sharp turn, leading along the way we came. We are nearly in front of the castle!" Nicola whispered harshly.

She looked at the soldier. "This could be a disaster. If we are found, everything is lost. This is awful."

The man nodded. "His Grace could not have known about the turn in the tunnel," the man replied, his voice low.

Nicola heard the sounds of horses moving around, but she was not sure how far away the animals were. Desperate, she knew what she had to do. "Bring the other torch to me, quickly," she said. She roughed her hair and dirtied her clothes, face, and hands. Pulling at her gown, she tore one sleeve, then handed her shoes to the soldier as he came up carrying the torch. He stared at her, frowning. Grasping the light, she spoke softly. "I have a plan. This worked once before—God may help it work again. Move everyone back. Do not show yourselves." Nicola could not explain the feeling that had come over her. "We will be fine. We were not meant to be harmed this night." Time to play her part again. Her hair clung to her in wet ringlets and straggling strands. Oppressive hot air from the trek through the hidden tunnel, coupled with the excitement and terror of possible capture, had flushed her face—she felt hot and clammy. Staying as close to the flame as she dared, she began walking toward the marauders' camp.

It was a tattered, scratched, and dirty lady who staggered into the circle of light. Some men were standing around; others were mounted. All activity stopped.

Silence greeted her. Praying she looked the part, she gasped, "Help us. Have you come to help us? The sickness. People are dying. Please help." Mounted men began pulling their horses backward, some bumping into those behind them. Those afoot were rapidly moving away.

"My lord, come quickly!" one man yelled. He backed his horse farther away.

"Stay, lady. Come no closer," another commanded, before turning to the man who had approached him. "It is the sickness. It is in the castle!"

"Tell me from where you come, lady," the second man demanded.

Nicola looked at him as if she could not understand, then answered, haltingly, "I . . . I lived in the castle beyond. We have been put out. The sickness is claiming everyone. Please help me. Help us." In the distance, one of the small children began to cry. The men looked at each other with fear.

"The sickness that struck London last year?" the man asked, frowning.

"We are not so fortunate," Nicola replied. "Those people died quickly. We do not." Taking a chance, Nicola took another step toward the man. "It lingers—except for the children, they die sooner. Please help."

"Stop!" the man ordered firmly. "God forgive me, but I cannot help. I cannot afford to lose even one man." At his words, Nicola collapsed, crying. The men around her moved away even farther.

"We are leaving this place tonight. Move!" he shouted at his men. The men scrambled around behind him and in short order the camp was being broken up. The leader rode closer to Nicola, still lying where she fell. "Here, the water is good." He dropped a water bag near her.

"I cannot swallow," Nicola replied, her voice breaking. Shaking her head, looking around at the forest, she added, "We are doomed." She spoke with a sense of finality.

DRUE AND SEVERAL MEN were now close enough to see the invaders with the light from the fire blazing in the center of their camp. Drue's men continued to push sharpened stakes into the ground along the road. The logic behind this tactic was that horses would step on the stakes, throw their riders, and fall into other animals in their push to escape. When he saw someone who looked like Nicola step into the light, he grasped the arm of the man closest to him. "Pull the stakes. Move it!" Drue ordered. The men rushed to pull the stakes from the road and move out of sight. When Nicola was taken, as she surely would be, he would not risk her injury from a falling horse. The order to pull the stakes snowballed into a general undoing of all the measures he had directed to save Wright Castle. With his heart in his throat, he watched helplessly as Nicola took center stage, and even more helplessly when he watched her collapse to the ground. By this time, both Bruce and Braggio were lying next to him. But something was changing— the men attacking the castle were retreating. Spellbound, they watched and heard everything.

When the camp was clear and the sounds of the horses had long faded, he finally stood. Speechless, he looked at his two friends. Then, he was at her side. Helping her stand, he held her closely. "Do not ever do that again," he said, his arms tightening around her. "Ever. Having said that, what an unbelievable idea."

Both Bruce and Braggio were standing, looking on in awe. "Everyone is safe," Nicola replied, tears escaping her eyes. "It was awful."

"Shush," Drue gently ordered. "It is over." *For now*, his mind said. Several of Braggio's men returned, saying they had come upon the women and children and were in the process of taking them back. Drue stopped them. "I want to be certain they are in fact leaving."

"He leaves, Lord Drue. We have two men following to be sure," one man replied.

"Still, we wait," Drue insisted. He knew any chance of surviving another incident with that attacker would be nonexistent.

The man bowed and left, passing on the new orders. Braggio walked up to Nicola, who was by this time standing on her own. Grinning, he said, "You were so much more believable this time, Lady Nicola. Great story. I must add, this time you look the part." He bowed low to her and walked away, laughing.

"Eny's people are safe. She can sleep well tonight," Nicola noted softly.

Drue's expression changed. "Nicola, they fired another siege gun after you left. Eny was standing in the courtyard."

"No!" Nicola cried. "No, all this and . . . no, please no." She could only stare at Drue.

He held her shoulders firmly. "I am sorry, Nicola. This fight has only begun." His heart was heavy. With Eny's death, Drue had lost the last semblance of family in England. Nicola leaned against him heavily. Looking down at her, Drue realized he was wrong. Nicola was still alive.

CHAPTER 38

The men began gathering the women and children. There were cries of joy as the women saw their men coming for them. Nicola realized what little chance they would have had trying to make a stand. Few of the men with families were soldiers. They were farmers, groomsmen, groundskeepers, and household staff. The only seasoned fighting men were those who followed Bruce and Braggio.

As the little huddle of women and children made their way to Drue and his men, Nicola found the soldier who had led them and spoke to him. "What are you called, sir?"

"Jon," the soldier replied. "Jon at your service, my lady."

"Jon, I . . ." She looked around. "We owe you much."

"No, my lady—I owe you and these people." He glanced back at the straggling group behind him. "You are an example of why it is we fight. You have given this cause a face. I will not soon forget that." He bowed to Nicola.

Nicola started to leave, then turned back. "Please, Jon, remind me . . . when this is over, I would learn how to use a weapon." Nicola turned away, calling to the small group of Eny's people. "Come, everyone. We want our gifts." At this, the children moved closer. "To the castle." Trying to smile, she waved everyone ahead.

Drue stood aside, watching her. He could hardly recognize the young girl he had met in the cave behind the falls in this woman standing strong, helping everyone. The vision of her staggering before the invading band still made his hair stand on end. The outcome could have been unimaginable if the man had thought to challenge her. Still, it worked. As Nicola led the last of Eny's men along with their wives and children toward the castle, Drue called to the young soldier, Jon. When the man approached, Drue asked, "Do you know who I am?"

"Yes, I have been told."

Drue spoke quickly. "I am naming you as my personal attendant and a member of the court of Vieneto. You are not to speak of this to anyone while we are on English soil."

The man stared at Drue. "How do you know I am not English, Your Grace?"

"You are never to use that title in speaking to me, until I decide it is acceptable. It would endanger our purpose here, and the Lady Weldon." Drue lowered his voice. "Your speech and knowledge of other languages gave you away." Drue smiled. "You will always be with me, unless I order otherwise. You did well this night." Drue turned away and stepped in stride with Nicola.

"What gifts, lady?" he asked. He strongly suspected she had no idea. Perhaps she would surprise him yet again.

Nicola didn't answer. Instead, she asked, "Where is Eny now?"

"In her chambers. I will take you." Once they were inside the courtyard, Drue led Nicola away from the group. They slipped through Eny's private entrance and took the stairs to her rooms, in silence. When Drue opened the door, the smell of blood and death was heavy. Nicola seemed not to notice. She walked to the bed where Eny lay, misshapen and bloody. Drue wished he had not taken Nicola to see Eny as she lay broken—there had been no time to prepare her body. No matter. Tonight made it clear: This campaign would have more of the same. Better that Nicola would see just what she had committed to.

Nicola knelt at Eny's bed. Gently, she reached out and placed her hand over Eny's hand. Cold, stiff, and still bloody. The ball from the gun had struck her in the face, smashing her face into her skull, and her own blood had gushed over her. "She died quickly?" Nicola turned to Drue, and he nodded. "We must bury her quickly. Who can care for her people? What happens now?"

Drue waited a moment before answering. "There are papers in her private table telling what is to become of her estate. That will help. I have already called a priest to assist. He will see the papers reach King Richard.

The lands belong to the king, as Eny had no children or family. Her ladies will prepare her for burial. It has all begun." He walked to Nicola and helped her up. "Come. You need to clean up and come to the great room. The men who follow me will be helping you. There is much to do, and the events of today show we have little time."

They had started to walk, but Nicola stopped abruptly. "Drue, does what I am supposed to do even matter? Who cares what some symbols claim? Maybe I play no part in this game." She looked at him with such pathos that he knew his answer would have to sustain her now and often, in the days to come.

"Lady Nicola," he started, "all of England is in turmoil, and the people will feel the effect of the coming years. There will be expectations made of them, for which they will have no choice but to comply. You are the only one who can give hope for peace within England's shores. The hope you give will be to Tudor and his followers. We can only pray for the princes in the Tower—they will not survive what is coming."

"How can anyone murder those boys? They are children, Drue. I do not understand."

"And yet," Drue answered quietly, "you must realize that King Richard will not be secure on his throne as long as they live. Even imprisoned in the Tower, they represent the legacy of King Edward."

"And Tudor?" Nicola asked. "Does anyone support him or his cause?"

"Some, though not as many as he will need," Drue answered.

"Perhaps the symbols are nothing more than a man's dreams." Even as she spoke, Nicola knew the symbols were more. Much more. Drue did not answer.

IN THE GREAT ROOM, food was being laid out for everyone. The mood was solemn but for the children, for whom it had been an exciting adventure. As of yet, Nicola and Drue had not been seen, but the children kept a close watch. They had been very good, so surely there would be gifts.

As Drue and Nicola started down the stairs, Nicola suddenly remembered her promise. "Wait, I must take gifts for the children. I cannot go in empty-handed."

Drue stopped. "Gifts, lady?" His eyes widened as Nicola related her ploy to keep the little ones quiet. He looked around. "How did you plan to fulfill your promise?"

"Tell me again what will happen to Wright Castle?"

"It becomes the property of the realm," Drue replied, eyeing Nicola.

"King Richard? This becomes his property? Are you certain?" Nicola asked excitedly.

"Positive," Drue replied. "What are you thinking, lady?" he asked.

"I think we relieve King Richard of some of the useless items in this castle," Nicola said, smiling. Drue had to smile too.

"I will meet you in Eny's study, with help. Take care when choosing what you give away. We do not want anyone accused of thievery," Drue cautioned her as he left.

In Eny's quarters, Nicola found stacks of soft, thick blankets, pillows, and small rugs. The men came upstairs, gathered all they could carry, and followed Nicola to the great room. When she entered, childish chatter ceased. "Come," she told them. "These are for you." At her invitation, there was a rush as the children crowded around the men carrying the bounty. When all was said and done, every infant and child had a blanket, pillow, and rug.

DRUE WATCHED NICOLA PASSING OUT the luxurious gifts and wondered how she would handle what was sure to come. Better than he once believed. Staying in Wright Castle was beginning to bother him. He needed to push Nicola to leave soon. Drue knew Nicola still believed she must see Lady Margaret. After the events of this night, Drue was even less in favor of such a plan. Nicola believed Lady Margaret would be able to gather support for Henry Tudor. Drue knew that without Tudor's active pursuit of the crown, Richard would stay as king, with or without Lady Margaret.

When all had eaten their fill, the families had filed out, and the staff had cleaned, Drue walked Nicola to the room she shared with Lizzie. At her door, he paused. He thought of kissing her again, but instead lifted her hand to his lips. "You did well on this day." He could see the sadness in her eyes. "Eny is with Lord Wright, Nicola. Where she longed to be." As he released her hand, he lifted her face. "Rest, Lady Nicola Weldon." His voice was gentle. Without waiting for her reply, he turned and was gone.

NICOLA CLOSED HER DOOR BEHIND HER and walked to the window. The courtyard was quiet and peaceful. *I long to gaze upon our courtyard, Father, with the peace of night undisturbed.* With effort, she turned from the window and began to remove the torn, soiled gown. Standing before a small mirror hanging between the beds, tears filled her eyes and trickled down her face. Her hair was matted, her face and hands streaked with dirt and smoke. *I do not feel like Lady Nicola Weldon. I feel like a part of me is dying. There comes a change in the winds, and I fear it will be more than I can bear.* The pot of water left near the fire was barely enough for her to wipe the dirt and grime off her face, hands, and feet.

She pulled a bed gown over her head. As it slid down, covering her body, she whispered, "I know you are gone now, but is there a way you can tell me what is coming next?" But the old crone didn't answer. Not waiting up for Lizzie, Nicola crawled between the bed coverings and eventually felt herself drifting away.

CHAPTER 39

DRUE HAD JUST SETTLED IN BED when the sounds of men running echoed below. Never a good sign! He was up immediately, dressed and moving down the stairs, two at a time. He entered the great room just as one of his men, Jon, started for the door. "The rescue attempt was not successful, Your Grace. It is believed the princes are dead."

"How is the mood in London?" Drue asked.

"Frightened mostly. Richard is not back in town yet, but apparently the Tower guard were warned of the rescue attempt. The men involved have already been executed. England's throne is not easy to take and harder to keep. Everyone fears for the lives of the princes." He watched Drue closely. "What are we to do now, Your Grace?"

Drue cleared his throat and looked at the man pointedly. "First, I believe you were told you are never again to call me that while we are in England. It could cost the life of every man who stands with me. I will not allow that to happen. Am I clear?"

Jon stood back a step. He looked at Drue nervously. "I beg your pardon, Lord Drue." There was a moment of silence.

"It is past. Now, we concentrate on what we do next. Tell Lords Braggio and Bruce I will meet with everyone in the morning, before Lady Nicola or Lady Lizzie are up and about. Early."

"Yes, my lord." Jon backed away and left the room.

Drue knew his reputation as the best at what he did was well deserved. Men would follow wherever he led them. Not all were aware of his profession, but all knew he was a strong commander . . . with a very short fuse on occasion. Alone in the great room, Drue stood staring into the dying embers in the fireplace. If Tudor were to stand any chance of winning, he would need men.

Unfortunately, Henry Tudor was an outsider to most of England. Gathering men would take time, a thing he had little of.

Drue turned and climbed the stairs. Before he took on this cause for his father, Drue had merely followed his father's orders, modifying those he disagreed with and pressing forward. But this . . . this was different. He'd come to believe in young Tudor. The lineage might not be perfect, but it was there. Drue hated that the young princes had to be sacrificed.

In his mind, Drue could clearly see the symbols Nicola carried. *It never really mattered what anyone chose to do–the move had been made. Who could have ever imagined that, out of the five possible heirs to Edward's throne, only two remained, and they are not meant to live?* Shaking his head, he lay down on the bed and tried to sleep.

Drue dreamed. He was falling, and no matter what he grasped on to, he kept falling. Below him, a great battle raged. Men lay dead and dying. Drue plunged ever faster toward the struggle below. He could hear the sounds of weapons clashing, the sounds of a terrible violence. Hard pounding on his door woke him up. Drue sat up in bed. Drenched in sweat, he struggled to bring his mind back from where it had plummeted. The knocking was persistent. "Drue, wake up." Lord Braggio's voice pushed through the fog in Drue's mind. "The news is urgent."

"Come in!" Drue called. Braggio opened the door as Drue was pulling a shirt over his head. "What is it with this night?" He finished dressing, then poured a goblet of wine for Braggio and one for himself. "Now, talk."

"Tudor has quit. He has instructed his mother to stop trying to garner support for his cause, and his uncle to find a country where he can live in peace without running and hiding." Braggio paused, watching Drue's reaction. "He has refused to return to England. He makes ready to denounce any claims of his right to the throne."

Drue walked to the window and looked out upon a dark, silent courtyard. "I cannot find blame in him. For years, he has been forced to leave England to stay alive. Henry Tudor's life would be as a king in his mother's country— the same country that would pay to have him killed."

"Only as long as another wears the crown," Braggio noted.

"True." Drue turned to Braggio. "When did you first know he wanted to quit, and who told you?"

"Just before I came for you," Braggio answered. "Jasper sent a messenger to speak with you. That man is below."

"A messenger from Jasper is here? Tudor must have decided this days ago. We have little time to change anything. I wonder who else knows of this." Drue crossed the room and headed downstairs.

When Drue entered the great room, he saw Bruce and several men talking to another man unknown to Drue. The man looked exhausted and dirty, and he had just started to eat but began to stand. "Sit," Drue ordered. "We can talk while you eat. Tell me what you have been sent to say."

The man sat back down and resumed hungrily shoving the food into his mouth. Drue waited until he had stopped eating and sat staring at his plate. "I was instructed to tell you that Henry Tudor has decided he will deny his rights to the throne." The man turned to look at Drue as he continued. "Jasper Tudor begs you to do what you can to stay the course, while he tries to soothe Tudor. Your Grace, we have men. Not as many as Richard, but we do have men. We can get many more. There are those who have no place in the king's army, convicts who have served their time and know nothing but fighting. But they would fight for Tudor."

Drue glanced at Braggio and Bruce. Both were still staring at the young man. The man would be heading back to Jasper Tudor. No one outside the room would have heard the man speaking. "Where did you anchor your boat?" Drue asked, ignoring the title the man used to address him.

"I am from England, Your Grace. I know the east coast well. We found a small inlet deep enough to move up. The boat is tied there and hidden well."

"When you have rested, take a fresh horse and return to your boat. Tell Lord Jasper I am on my way." Drue started to turn away, but turned back. "Your boat, can it withstand storms?"

The man shrugged. "Not big ones, but we do well enough. I will make it back. Jasper Tudor will be waiting, Your Grace." The man looked around for the kitchen lad to refill his bowl.

Drue spoke to the young man. "I know you are tired, but time is important. When you have eaten, take the message back to Lord Jasper. You have done well."

"Thank you, Your Grace. There are those ready to follow, when you decide the time is right." He added, "I am not too tired. The horse does most of the work." He grinned at Drue. Drue smiled, nodding in agreement.

Motioning to Braggio and Bruce, Drue left for Eny's study. Inside the room, Drue stood at the window again, thinking. He would need to leave, immediately, and change Henry Tudor's mind. Tudor would no longer wish to abandon his quest for the throne of England when Drue played his trump—Nicola and her symbols. The challenge would be convincing her that the right strategy would be to forgo going to Lady Margaret.

Bruce and Braggio followed Drue into the study and waited. Finally, the three of them sat at the study table to review the map Braggio had brought with him. "The quickest way to Tudor is from this port," Braggio said, pointing to a port at St. Malo, in Brittany.

"That is too close to Normandy," Drue noted. "If, by chance, it were known we were bound to Brittany, or to be more accurate, to Tudor, it could spell trouble for Duke Francis, in Brittany. Better to land further along the southernmost border. We will have to rely on Jasper to get us to Henry." Looking at the two men whom he trusted the most, he waited for comments.

Bruce and Braggio both agreed. "It will mean more land travel, but we can do it," Bruce said.

"Are we agreed, then?" Drue asked. Both men nodded.

"How, if I may be so bold as to ask, are we going to convince Tudor?" Braggio asked.

Drue smiled. "We are not. Lady Nicola is." Both men stared at Drue. He waited a moment before adding, "She has the best argument. She has the only argument, actually. Henry is tired of living in Brittany. He has been there more than ten years and is sick of the whole mess. Nicola can change that." Bruce and Braggio exchanged looks. Drue added before he left the room, "I will go alert Lady Nicola and Lizzie of our departure. We should be ready to ride soon." He never looked back.

NICOLA AWOKE TO LIZZIE SITTING ON THE EDGE of her bed, waking her. She was giddy. "Lord Braggio has expressed his fondness for me." She was all smiles. "I enjoy his company as well. He is a little old, but I think that is better for me. He has probably been to all the whorehouses he might need. Now he is ready to belong to just one lady." Her face clouded. "Do you think I am a whore, Nicola? I told him I have been, but he just laughed." Lizzie shrugged. "I was honest with him. What do you think?"

I think I should not be distracted. I still have things to do. Nicola smiled at Lizzie. "We need to sleep. It has been a long, long day." She turned over in bed. "And I think he will take very good care of you. He does not care what you were, only what you are now. You two will be very happy, Lizzie."

"Thank you, Nicola." Through the darkness, Lizzie spoke softly. "Thank you for everything." Nicola closed her eyes, willing herself to drift off to sleep.

WHAT FELT LIKE ONLY SEVERAL HOURS LATER, Lizzie was awakened by the sound of someone knocking on the door. Lizzie immediately sat up. "Who knocks?" she asked. Drue entered the room as Lizzie hurriedly threw a robe over her bed gown. "Lord Drue," Lizzie said, tumbling out of bed.

"Wake, Nicola. Pack what you care to take with you. We are not coming back," Drue told her. As he turned to leave, he added, "Your horses will be ready soon." Lizzie looked from Drue to the still-sleeping form of Nicola and back at Drue. He was already walking out the door.

Lizzie gently shook Nicola. "Lady, please wake up. We are leaving tonight."

"What?" Nicola rolled over. "Did you say we are leaving?" Nicola pushed the blankets aside and stumbled to the window. "It is still dark outside, Lizzie. Why are we leaving during the night?"

"Lord Drue came here. He ordered us to pack. He says we leave soon." Now fully awake, Lizzie was already dressing. She pulled from a chest the two bags Eny had given them.

Nicola began to dress. "Did he say why? What is happening?" Lizzie shrugged, already focused on packing clothing and other items into one of the bags. Nicola began packing her own bag, trying to think what she needed the most. "I am quite certain we are not returning, after all that has happened here," Nicola noted.

Lizzie nodded. "Yes. We leave tonight and will not return. We need to take heavy clothing, too. Brushes, shoes, night clothes . . . what else?"

Nicola was filling her bag. "I don't know. We have few clothes. I think we pack everything. All of England is warmer now, but the rains come soon."

"England is always cold. Well, almost always, and it always rains. But when the sun favors England with its warmth, the land is covered with grasses green as emeralds. And flowers, so many flowers. The trees are filled with leaves. 'Tis a beautiful country, this England." Lizzie smiled at Nicola. "Surely he will take us to someplace safe."

Nicola did not answer.

WHEN BOTH BAGS WERE PACKED and she was dressed, Nicola went in search of Drue. She found him in Eny's study. Without preamble, Nicola asked, "Lord Drue, what is happening?" She knew leaving at night usually meant they were no longer safe. The whole of Wright Castle was bustling. There was a general air of something afoot.

Drue was studying maps as usual and looked up as Nicola entered. "We leave because we have a long ride ahead of us, and I do not wish to be delayed by people who would take Wright Castle." Drue straightened up to watch Nicola.

"Take Wright Castle? Would anyone try such a thing again? Who even knows poor Eny is dead?"

Drue looked into Nicola's eyes. "I am quite certain whoever led the poorly run invasion will make it his business to inform King Richard of all that took place. With his own interpretation, of course. The greatest prize will be the castle." He stopped talking, glancing down at the map again, as if he only wanted to end the conversation and return to the map before him.

"Who travels with us, Drue?" Nicola persisted.

"Everyone," he replied, frowning.

"Everyone?" Nicola asked.

"No, not everyone here," he patiently corrected. "Only everyone who does not belong here. Braggio, Bruce, their men, you, and Lizzie. Why do you ask, lady?"

"I need to pack food for us all."

"No, only pack what you and Lizzie might need. The men going with us are accustomed to moving. They will know what to take." He smiled.

"In that case, Lord Drue, we are ready," Nicola told him, returning his smile.

Suddenly he was serious. "You do have what your father gave you?"

"Of course," Nicola answered. "It would do little good to leave something like that lying around. They are always with me."

Drue nodded in satisfaction, and she left him alone, studying his maps.

Standing in the courtyard of Wright Castle, Nicola felt a sharp pang. Poor Eny. Lizzie had already brought their bags down and stood watching the men. *No doubt looking for Lord Braggio.*

"Lizzie, has the priest taken care of everything for Eny? I wish we were not in such a hurry to get to Lord Stanley and Lady Margaret. I would have liked to stay for her service."

Lizzie leaned closer to Nicola. "They have already buried Eny. The story will be that she died with the sickness and could not be allowed to lie in state or wait for a service. The priest and Drue spoke at length last evening, after the families left. Father Lind suggested it be done this way. The people will know where she is buried. There are several other recent graves near. It will be better that way."

"Other graves?" Nicola looked at Lizzie.

"Lord Braggio knew there must be more graves than just Eny's if the sickness did indeed strike Wright Castle."

"So much to protect these poor people. I pray they will be treated well." Nicola looked around again.

Braggio and his men rode up. Bruce followed, leading Nicola's horse and the one Lizzie had chosen from Eny's stable. Jon stood near and began tying the ladies' bags securely to the two animals. He bowed to Nicola. "May I?" He laced his fingers together to help her to mount.

Nicola stepped up and was easily lifted upon the horse. Jon then helped Lizzie before mounting his own horse. When Drue came out to the court-yard, he saw the ladies mounted and waiting. Smiling, he said, "You are good for your word, lady. We will be riding in the dark for several hours yet, but the road is well traveled." Turning to Braggio, Drue asked, "Have the lead men left already?"

"Yes," Braggio answered.

Looking over the group, Drue nodded. Walking to Nicola, he spoke to her quietly. "You and Lizzie are to ride in the center, in case there are unwelcome travelers. It will not be like our other rides. This should be much faster." Before Nicola could respond, he returned to the front and mounted. With Drue leading, everyone moved out.

CHAPTER 40

Λs the sun began to rise, Drue had his party well on their way. However, with the rising sun it became clear to Nicola they were not headed toward London. Not certain just where Lord Stanley's land was located, Nicola rode another hour before she began to question the direction. Shadows demonstrated they were headed south. Riding up through the men surrounding Lizzie and her, she was soon at Drue's side. Braggio let her move in closer.

"Lord Drue, just where does Lord Stanley live?" Nicola asked, frowning and looking up at the sky and then surveying the land around them.

Drue glanced at Nicola, then replied, "He lives in Derby, north of London. His title is Thomas Stanley, Earl of Derby. Why do you ask?"

"No reason," Nicola answered. "I must have gotten turned around."

Drue knew the time had come when he would be forced to tell Nicola exactly where they were going. He also knew she would not take the news well. He had already made arrangements with Bruce, should it become necessary to restrain her. He prayed it would not come to that, but Drue would do whatever it took to get to Tudor before he gave up on his and England's future.

For a moment after he explained, Nicola was stunned, surprise and disappointment creasing her smooth face. "You are not taking me to Lady Margaret?"

"No, I am not," he answered simply, then waited for the explosion he was sure would come.

It did.

Nicola responded instantly. "Then, I strongly suggest you turn around at once and take me to Lady Margaret! I think I made it very clear we were to travel to her as soon as possible." As she spoke, she had pulled her horse up. She sat glaring at Drue.

When Drue stopped, everyone else stopped. While he was acutely aware that nearly everyone would hear what he and Nicola said, he had also decided it was time Nicola understood he would help her, but they would move at his direction. "Lady Nicola," Drue began. His voice was measured, quiet, and firm. "You are not going to Lady Margaret, at least not in the foreseeable future. You, Lizzie, the men with you, and I are riding to meet a boat that will take us to Brittany. When we stop, you and I can discuss just what will happen in Brittany."

"Pardon me. I think not!" Nicola exclaimed. "You will turn around now, or I go alone! I have before," she reminded him smugly, "and will gladly do so again, if need be." Making good on her statement, she quickly turned her horse around. At a slight nod from Drue to the men behind her, Nicola was quickly surrounded tightly by the men. It was obvious she would not be allowed to go anywhere but where Drue directed. "Lizzie!" Nicola called.

Lizzie looked around her, then weakly announced, "I cannot turn the horse; there is no room." Braggio was smiling broadly.

"You cannot make me go with you!" Nicola declared, turning in her saddle to glare at him.

"You can go with me and behave." Drue's voice reflected his intention. "Or you can fight me and you will go restrained. Either way, you will go. How you ride is up to you."

By this time, Nicola was so angry she could barely speak. "You would kidnap me?" she asked incredulously. Drue did not answer. "Why are you doing this to me?" Nicola asked. "Why?"

"Because," Drue answered quietly, "you made a promise. I intend to give you every opportunity to keep that promise." Nicola stared at Drue. Drue continued, "Remember, you must not sacrifice the mission for Tudor on Lady Margaret."

As soon as he spoke, Nicola gasped. The old crone had advised the same. Her eyes filled with tears. She could not speak, only nod. Slowly, she turned her horse around. Drue moved everyone out once more without looking back.

Nicola rode in silence for several hours. Drue glanced her way only once. The sounds of talking around her gradually resumed, but Nicola was uninterested in listening to the conversations. Lizzie finally quit watching her. All that had happened washed through Nicola's mind again. It seemed the longer she carried the symbols, the more people she dragged along with her. Of all of them, Drue was the only one who could see her through to keep her promise. It would not do to have Drue decide he was no longer going to help. Uncertain what to say or if she even wanted to say anything, Nicola wondered, once more, why her father had given her such a mission, with so many decisions she had to make, alone. Again, there was no answer.

As they continued to ride, Nicola approached Lizzie. "I am so sorry I've pulled you into all this," she told her. "I've no idea what comes next, but I want you to know, you are dear to me. Whatever I can do to keep you out of harm's way, I promise I will do."

"Nicola, I am not troubled," Lizzie replied. "You have trusted me with your life. And introduced me to someone I know I love. I am doing well." Lizzie smiled. Then in a serious tone, she added, "I am worried about you, Nicola. I do not know what this is all about, but to have all these men with you tells me you could be in trouble. Are you?"

Nicola thought for a moment before answering, "Not if I am not caught."

Nicola knew she must clear the air with Drue before they reached wherever it was he led them. She worked her way to the front again. And as before, Braggio moved aside to allow Nicola access to Drue.

Trying to decide what to say kept her silent a long time. Drue glanced at her when she rode up, but he did not speak. Taking a deep breath, Nicola began, "Lord Drue. I feel I must clear the air between us. I . . ." Nicola could not finish. She started to turn back.

"You what?" Drue looked at her. His voice stopped her.

Nicola tried again. "I am not certain what to say, only that we should not waste time being—"

"Waste time, lady?" Drue watched her struggle. "I think the lady has had little practice apologizing!" Nicola caught him smiling at her, and she could feel her face get hot. "Lady Nicola. If you think I am angry with you, you are mistaken. I am not," Drue told her.

"Good." Nicola quickly turned her horse and rode back toward Lizzie. She could hear both Drue and Braggio laugh. *This is not some trick. You will see I can finish this.* Nicola could not, however, imagine how life would turn.

Nicola had not complained, but as the hours rolled on, they were all beginning to fade. At midafternoon, when Drue let everyone stop to eat, Lizzie whispered, "Oh, thank goodness. I can barely stay upright. And I cannot drink anything. If I do, I have to ask him to stop so I can . . . well, you understand." She leaned against her horse.

Nicola nodded. "I do understand, but do not be fooled, Lizzie—they stop sometimes too. It is just so much easier for a man. Come, walk with me. It feels better if you move around a little. It is quite peaceful here. One could almost believe the world is right."

"I care little how it looks around here. I have another issue. Perhaps we can take turns, then?" Lizzie suggested. "We have to do something—I am very thirsty."

Nicola had to laugh. "That is a good plan. Have a drink from my water bag. Then walk with me. Take advantage of this pause." Even a short stop made a great difference. Men were still eating when Drue had everyone moving again. Nicola and Lizzie were ready. Braggio helped both of them back onto their horses. "Thank you, Lord Braggio," Nicola murmured.

He smiled. "Of course, lady. You give me a chance to see Lizzie, too. Any time, please just call for me." He winked at Lizzie, who blushed.

When Drue finally stopped, they had been riding for twelve hours. A lone tent was set up for Lizzie and Nicola. Drue had not spoken to Nicola since she tried to smooth things over. As he made it clear he was not angry, she refused to think about it any longer. What she could not forget was the feel of his lips on hers. *I wish he had never kissed me. When this is finished, when I have kept my promise, I will have nothing. My home is no longer mine; it belongs to a king, whoever wins that title. I have no one left alive to live with. Drue will undoubtedly go back to assassinating people or whatever it is he does, and will soon forget about me.*

"Lady, are you well?" Lizzie asked.

Pulled from her reverie by Lizzie's gentle touch on her arm, Nicola realized Lizzie had been talking to her. "I am so sorry, Lizzie. There have been so many changes in our lives I find myself wondering what I will do after this is over. Even if you did not have a man who cares for you, you would do well. You are so independent, whereas I have never had to do anything on my own until now. I am ashamed of how poorly prepared I am."

"Listen to yourself!" Lizzie fired back. "You know so much more than you realize. You are just too comfortable letting everyone make decisions for you. Stand up for yourself, Nicola! You have earned the right to speak and be heard."

At first, Nicola was startled. Then she started laughing. When she began to laugh, Lizzie did also. "Look at us, Lizzie. We must be exhausted." It felt good to laugh. "You are such a good friend. And you are right. No more. If I think something, I will say it."

"Well, I do not advise you to go to extremes," Lizzie cautioned, "but do start letting people know you are here."

The men with Bruce and Braggio were accustomed to traveling fast and taking advantage of every stop to rest. Food was set out. When everyone had eaten, the area was cleared and men were spreading their saddle blankets around and lying down to sleep.

Inside the tent, Nicola found sleep evading her. *Lizzie is right. Everyone has an opinion about what I should be doing. Maybe it is time I decide how best I can keep my promise and restore Father's reputation.* "Lizzie, are you awake?" Nicola whispered.

"Yes, I cannot sleep. I think I am too tired. Is that possible?" Lizzie murmured.

Nicola laughed softly. "Come. Let's walk. It is so peaceful at night." Nicola stood, pulling a blanket around herself.

"I think that sounds better than lying here staring at the top of this silly tent." Lizzie pulled at her blanket and both slipped outside. Standing still for a moment, Lizzie whispered, "Which way?"

Looking over the campsite, Nicola could see that no one was awake. The fire was dying and men lay around it. Theirs was the only tent. Nicola nudged Lizzie, then crept around the back of their tent and into the surrounding forest. They picked their way through the brush and trees, until only the silhouette of the tent was visible. Nicola stopped to listen to the comforting sounds of night. Neither spoke. An owl hooted nearby while crickets signaled to each other. They could hear the horses occasionally stomp. Nicola sat down and leaned back against a tree. Lizzie followed suit. For several moments, they simply sat, leaning against each other and the tree.

Suddenly, all night sounds around them stopped. Nicola sat up, alert, and listened. Lizzie leaned closer and whispered, "Why is it suddenly so still?"

Nicola shrugged and shook her head. Before she could answer, they heard the snap of a twig, then another and another. The sounds, coming from behind and farther on either side, were moving steadily toward the camp of sleeping men. "We have to warn someone." Lizzie started to stand, but Nicola held her still.

"We cannot call—we need to get closer," she whispered. Slowly, the ladies crept closer, until Nicola could see the shape of several men. Just as she stood, a cry went out. At once Drue's men were up—just as intruders burst into the camp. The ladies moved backward.

The night exploded in complete pandemonium. There were shouts, cries of the wounded, the clank of weapons and gunfire. To both ladies, it seemed darkness surely made such a fight nearly impossible for either side. Lizzie and Nicola scrambled deeper into the surrounding trees, crawled under brush, and waited. The chaos seemed to last for an eternity. Lizzie was trembling and silently weeping. Nicola held her, as both waited for the end. Gradually, the sounds of combat died away. At last, Nicola heard Drue call out.

"Nicola, where are you?" Alarm was clear in his voice. "Nicola!" He called again.

Nicola stood up, pulling Lizzie with her. "Here I am! With Lizzie!" She pushed through the underbrush and stepped into the opening. Bodies were still lying where they had fallen. Men were being bound and shoved together. Horrified by what she saw, Nicola stood frozen. Drue reached the ladies first, followed by Braggio. Braggio held a now hysterical Lizzie.

Drue grasped Nicola's shoulders. "You're not hurt?" His eyes scanned her. He pulled her close. For a moment, neither spoke.

"I think I bring trouble to you. I prayed you would be unharmed, Drue. Maybe you should leave me, and keep yourself and your men safe." Tears cascaded down her face, and she ducked her head into his chest.

Drue lifted her face and brushed her lips with his. "Never say that to me again." He held her a minute longer. "There are things that must be done now. Take Lizzie and return to your tent. Do not come out until I come for you. It will not sound pleasant, but it is necessary. Such is the warning of this night. You must stay inside until I come for you, understand?"

"Yes," Nicola replied, nodding.

"Go now, lady." Drue released her and turned back toward camp. Nicola walked to where Braggio stood calming Lizzie. Taking Lizzie's hand, she walked them to their tent, not looking at anything or anyone. Inside the tent, they tied the flap closed and huddled onto one cot.

"This is not a place I want to stay. I want to return to London," Lizzie whispered.

Nicola did not answer. She wondered, again, how her father had ever imagined she could finish what he had started. She reached down and felt the small bag of symbols.

There were few sounds from outside, men calling to each other and an occasional moan. Waiting, Nicola felt like the world her father had left to her was crashing down.

"What is happening, Nicola?" Lizzie whispered. "Why were we attacked? Who are those men?"

"Only Drue can make sense of what this night brought to us," Nicola replied. "I understand little of what has been and less of what might come."

When Drue finally came for her, she had fallen asleep.

"Lady Nicola," she heard him say, as he gently shook her. "Nicola, I need you to come with me and look at these men. Tell me if you think they are the same men who took your home and murdered your father." He helped her stand. "It will be unpleasant for you, but we must know who commands these men. Can you do this?"

"Of course I can," Nicola assured him. The memory of what her father looked like when the men who took the castle were finished with him was embedded in her mind. Wrapped in her blanket, Nicola followed Drue outside. The bodies of the dead men were laid out side by side. Jon, carrying a torch to push back the darkness, met Drue and Nicola. At the first body, Nicola recoiled. The man's head was barely attached to his body and one arm was gone. Nicola looked down the row. Although it was still night, darkness could not hide the silhouettes of bodies. Looking back at the corpse before her, Nicola shook her head. Jon shined the light on another, Nicola shook her head, and so it went. They were nearly finished, when Nicola stopped in her tracks. She stared at the lifeless body before her. "This one. He was with the men who overtook my home. He stood guard at my chamber door." Looking at the man's body, Nicola hesitated. "But there is a difference."

"What difference, lady?" asked Bruce, who had walked up just as Nicola spoke.

"These men all wear the same colors. But they are not the colors of the men who took Father's life." She pointed at the dead man. "He is the same man, but now wears different colors."

Drue frowned. "You are positive?" He looked at Bruce, then Nicola. "Come look at the rest. Do you recognize any others?" Drue turned to Bruce. "I know whose badge they all wear."

Bruce agreed. "The badge is Burgundy. Burgundy is on the move, I see."

Jon and Nicola continued along the line. Again, she stopped. All three men with her stood waiting. "I do not remember ever seeing this man, but he is wearing the colors of the invaders of my home."

"Lord Lareau's colors." Bruce looked at Drue. "Burgundy's badge."

"Ah, Lareau is now serving the Duchess of Burgundy. I suspected as much." Drue smiled bitterly. "I wondered how long before she jumped into the ring. Ah, Burgundy. They would have the monies to gather a sizable retinue for King Richard if she supports him. I think she still is strong for her brother's sons. I doubt she believes the princes have disappeared." Drue shook his head. "If she can be convinced to join King Richard, Henry Tudor will have a real fight on his hands, provided we can persuade him to stay in the fray."

Nicola was moving along the line with Jon at her side. "I don't recognize any others," she said.

Drue stood waiting for her. "You should rest if you can. We leave as soon as this is cleaned up."

"Cleaned up?" Nicola stopped walking. She stood looking at Drue, frowning.

"Yes. We cannot leave anything behind that might be found and tie us to what took place."

Drue gently nudged Nicola along to her tent. "These men are not supporting King Richard. However, they are very strong supporters of King Edward's sons. They have circulated the rumor that the sons are alive, living in Burgundy."

"Could that be true?" Nicola asked.

"No. The princes were moved even before the infamous rescue attempt. Their cell was empty, but they did not leave the Tower, sadly for them." Drue held Nicola's face and spoke softly. "You are safe for now. That is the greatest job we have right now: keeping you safe."

"And I thank you for doing so. Lizzie and I will be ready whenever you are." Nicola started to duck into her tent, but Drue held her back. He kissed her gently. "Good night," Nicola whispered.

"Not just yet, Lady Nicola." Drue's voice became firm. "Why were you out of your tent? Alone?"

Nicola paused before answering. "First, I could not sleep. Second, I was not alone. Lizzie was with me. We walked into the forest to be able to talk without waking you or the others." She frowned at Drue. "Why does it matter? If I had been asleep, I might have been dead. I am not a child, Drue. I know you have a hard time believing me, but I am a grown woman."

"I am well aware, Nicola. I am also aware that you act before you think. Everything you do touches the lives of each of these men. They are here to protect you, but you must do your part." He stopped for a second. "Just to be clear, we knew those men were coming. Do you think men actually sleep fully armed if they do not expect a fight? I did not lose even one man. The men who came tonight came looking for you."

Nicola stepped back. "I am sorry, Drue. You are right, I did not think. I will be more careful. But I do think I could understand more of what happens around me if you share more with me."

Drue nodded. "'Tis a fair bargain. If I will share more, you will behave more?"

"Behave! Did you say behave?" Nicola asked indignantly.

Drue did not answer. Instead, he held her face and kissed her again. She made a feeble effort to pull away. "Behave," he reiterated. Before she could respond, he turned and walked away.

Nicola entered the tent to find Lizzie sitting up in bed, hugging her knees. "Are we not a little strange?" she observed. "We have fallen in love with men who live to fight and will probably be gone most of the time. Does not seem so smart."

"Well, I am not in love," Nicola retorted. Lizzie just laughed before she lay back down.

GENTLY SHAKING LIZZIE, Braggio whispered, "Wake up, lady. We are ready to move out. Wake Nicola. We leave immediately." When Lizzie rolled over, Braggio kissed her. She sat up, but before she could speak, he put his finger over her mouth. "I know I take an advantage not given to me, but I am grateful you are still among the living." At his words, Lizzie smiled. At that, Braggio was gone.

"Nicola, wake up." Lizzie touched Nicola's shoulder, speaking softly. "We are leaving."

"Already?" Nicola sat up, but sank back onto the cot. "I do not think I can. I am exhausted."

"Quick, Nicola, here comes Drue!" Lizzie exclaimed.

In an instant, Nicola was up and braiding her hair. Drue stuck his head in. "Ladies, it is time!" He looked pleased to see both were up.

Nicola followed Lizzie out of the tent. It was still quite dark outside, but a quick survey of the campsite gave no indication there had been any trouble during the night. It was as if the whole event had been a dream.

"Do you see? Everything is just as it was. How did they do that?" Lizzie asked softly.

"I do not know, but I am happy they did. Perhaps I am still believed to be dead. I pray Drue is wrong. No one is looking for me. I hope." Nicola's eyes scanned the camp again.

Drue made one last walk through the camp and surrounding area before walking to where the ladies sat on their horses, surrounded by Braggio and Bruce's men. Touching Nicola's foot, he spoke. "We were very lucky, both you two and the rest of us. None of our men were badly injured. However, it is clear we must reach our destination today. This will be another hard ride, Nicola. I intend that you both are kept in the middle of these men. We will ride with as few stops as possible, but if you or Lizzie need to stop, just let someone know." He did not wait for an answer. Soon, the party was on the move once more.

CHAPTER 41

MARGARET, DUCHESS OF BURGUNDY, wandered through the grounds of her home. With her walked her chief barrister and the captain of her guard. Margaret had lived long enough to know the strife that was headed for England with her brother's untimely death. Reading the letter clutched in her hand again, she sighed. Her sister-in-law, the dowager Queen Elizabeth, was still in sanctuary at Westminster Abbey. This latest communication from her was filled with horrible, but not unexpected, news. Elizabeth's two sons had not been seen since the failed attempt to rescue them. Elizabeth was grief-stricken. From a king with four heirs, to a new king with one heir, in only months. Now, the duchess would be forced to declare for her brother Richard. She had always thought highly of Richard and knew her other brother, King Edward, had also. However, she was hard-pressed to deny it certainly looked like Richard had ordered their own nephews murdered. She could not speak it aloud—it was too painful.

Instead, she turned to the men at her side. "This was to be a simple undertaking—to find out if Weldon actually had information telling of his support for Tudor. Instead, we found nothing, killed Weldon, and, it would appear, killed both his daughter and our informant." The duchess looked at the sky slowly turning rose with the setting sun. "This is not helpful when we are pushing our supporters in England to turn out against Tudor."

The barrister nodded in agreement. After a moment, he added, "You are aware that the rumor of dowager Queen Elizabeth's move to promise her eldest daughter's hand to Tudor, thereby uniting the houses of York and Tudor, is much more than a rumor. It is believed to be true."

"I know, I have been told. There is a better rumor, you should hear. It is widely believed Elizabeth found a way to smuggle young Richard out, and replace him with a boy who looked very much like Prince Richard. That might allow us time to move forward to save the York dynasty by providing another choice for the crown."

They walked along in silence for several moments. "Prince Richard is very young," the captain noted. "King Richard is a York king. Why would we want to displace him? Already Tudor has openly stated he intends to deny any claims to England's crown."

The duchess explained, "King Richard will most likely not keep his crown for so long. I would imagine Tudor is moving, as we speak—would you not do so?"

"I would," the captain quickly replied. "In essence, the impostor would be the best answer to a replacement for Tudor?"

"Exactly. To be used if necessary." The duchess continued, "There is one troubling issue. If it comes to pass that Princess Elizabeth does marry a Tudor, namely Henry, we would be taking away the crown from her also. Not a big issue, but an issue nonetheless." Quickening her pace, the duchess added, "Keep your eyes and ears open, sirs. I must know every tale, true or not. We will make a stand against Tudor." With a slight smile, she walked rapidly through the great doors leading into her courtyard.

A messenger stood waiting for her. "You have news for me?" she asked expectantly.

"Yes, my lady. Lord Lareau's men were sent to spy on a camp three nights ago. The camp was believed to be that of Drue Vieneto, Duke of Padronale. Those men never returned, nor has there been any sign of them. Lord Lareau's message tells you they disappeared."

The man stood waiting for his next instructions, and the duchess stared at him. "Do you expect me to believe that? The Duke of Padronale would never be caught on English soil, unaccompanied by at least his guard. And you say every one of Lareau's men are gone? Lord Lareau uses disappearance as an easy explanation, it would seem. The Lady Weldon disappeared, our informant disappeared, his men disappeared. Honestly, does he take me for a fool?"

She began to move past the man, but he persisted. "My lady, I am to take further instructions to Lord Lareau. What message would you have me deliver?"

"When I called him back to Burgundy, I expected he would bring his men, also." Her patience having been tried enough, she began to walk away.

"Duchess," the messenger called after her, "there is something else I am to tell you."

Irritated, she paused, without turning around to face him. "And that would be?"

"Lord Lareau believes one of the princes was an impostor. Somehow, Elizabeth was able to keep young Richard and send another in his place. That would mean young Richard is still alive, but we do not know where he is being kept." He stopped talking when Margaret turned toward him. He then added, "Lareau also believes Lady Weldon is still alive. We have not been able to find her. What are your orders for Lord Lareau?"

The duchess looked off into the distance. With more people claiming young Richard had escaped, the tale grew stronger. "Come to me this evening, after we have eaten. I will have an answer for you. Meanwhile, you should rest. You will be returning on this night. Until this evening." Nodding, the duchess walked away, toward her quarters. *There could be truth to the tale of young Richard's being alive. Elizabeth might consent to her daughter's marriage to Tudor to assure the throne stays in Edward's bloodline. However, if young Richard is alive, he will surely take the throne from Tudor. Edward's daughter is of little consequence in such an event, unless she has a son.*

The duchess paused to watch her grandchildren playing on the grounds, thankful they were far from the unrest shaking England. Turning back to the hall, she continued walking. The messages from Lord Lareau brought to mind an additional problem. *The matter of Lord Weldon's daughter is another issue. If the girl is still alive, we must find her, put an end to her, and stop any support for Tudor.* Closing the door to her chambers, she shook her head. *The Duke of Padronale in England. Ridiculous!*

Inside her chambers, the duchess called a special meeting of her three top advisors. They would do whatever she thought best, no matter what advice they might offer. But she always listened.

When the men arrived at her study, there were papers scattered about her writing table. She stood at a window, holding a glass of wine. "Lords, we may have a solution to Henry Tudor's quest for the crown of England. It seems very likely that young Richard, my nephew, was not with his brother in the Tower. Our job now becomes finding him. I cannot risk writing to Elizabeth. But I think we have enough supporters on English soil to find out where he is, if he indeed lives. Someone special should speak with Elizabeth, face-to-face." At this, she turned to the men. "And, lords, I want the daughter of the man who was rumored to have foreseen the end of the York dynasty found. I want her to disappear by our hand. Once she is gone, the people will soon forget about the false prophecy." She paused before asking, "Is this all clear?"

One of the lords stepped up. Bowing, he asked, "Is it true the Duke of Padronale is in England?"

Margaret slowly shook her head. "I do not believe so. I have spoken with our ambassador to King Vieneto of Padronale. He not only had an audience with the duke, but he and many others also dined with him. I think someone is trying to create trouble between the duke and me." Then looking at the men, she answered firmly, "No, I do not believe the duke can be in two places at the same time." The duchess started for the door, but turned to speak one last time. "I would trust that the next time we all meet, we will have completed our plan." Then, she gracefully left the room.

Once inside her private sleeping quarters, she requested the presence of Fantasma Diablo, the Ghost Devil. He was a quiet older man who found pleasure in music and poetry, and he served as the henchman for the Duchess of Burgundy. She never asked how or when. She only gave the command, and the person she considered an obstacle was gone. When her husband died and his captain was killed in battle, Diablo came to the duchess offering his unique services. He now worked independent of the captain over her guard, her chief barrister, or anyone else. Tonight, she needed to see his familiar calm face and hear his low voice. She felt certain he must sound menacing to the one about to die, but to her, he sounded in charge, in control, and sure of himself, though he still left her feeling unsettled. When he came in, he bowed deeply, as was his habit.

"You sent for me, duchess?" Standing just inside the door, he waited patiently.

"Yes. I hear rumors that my nephew, young Richard, is still alive and hidden away. I have also heard whisperings that the Lady Weldon still lives.

Confirm both for me. If Richard is indeed alive, please bring him here, to Burgundy . . . to me. If Lady Weldon is alive, bring her here to speak with me. Unharmed." Looking at Diablo, she spoke firmly, "I want neither harmed."

"The Lady Weldon brings danger with her," Diablo noted. "She would be better served to die in obscurity."

"Perhaps," the duchess acknowledged. "But I want to hear myself if she knows something so far-reaching. You see, it is possible she is innocent and knows nothing of her father's doings. Lareau found no evidence supporting the accusations of Lord Weldon's treason."

"My lady." Diablo bowed and left the room. As always, the duchess was relieved when he left her presence. The fact that he was in her service helped, but it could not dissolve that feeling of danger he evoked in her. Time would tell.

CHAPTER 42

DRUE BROODED AS HE LED EVERYONE on through the darkness. The peril of this undertaking continued to grow. Drue knew Lareau—while he might take orders from the duchess, Lareau's first loyalty was always himself. Lareau still had a chance to salvage something from a very large mess. Given the fact that Nicola's father died without providing any evidence of treason against King Edward, Lareau had to find Nicola and force her to talk with him. Nicola was in danger, Tudor was nearly giving up, and the men with him would need a strong hand to lead them. *Ah, brother, your choice to stay home was wise, it seems.*

He faced Bruce, who rode next to him. "Bruce, tell Lady Nicola I would speak with her. Time to make certain she does not even breathe without letting one of us know."

Bruce nodded and turned back to retrieve Nicola and bring her up front.

NICOLA SAW BRUCE RIDING TOWARD HER. She guessed Drue had a message for her. "Lord Drue would like a moment to speak with you," Bruce told her. She rode ahead without answering Bruce. *I care not for the habit he has taken up. He sends someone else to request my presence as if he thinks he has great rank. I think I should not come at his bidding. I must keep my heart and feelings in rein.*

"Surely Lord Drue could have asked me himself?" she said to Bruce, who rode directly behind her, as if she were a child being escorted. Smiling sweetly, she turned to look at Bruce. He frowned and shook his head.

"That would not be wise, lady. He feels great responsibility for the safety of everyone, and would not leave the front for fear any signs of danger might be missed."

Nicola raised her brow. "Honestly, Bruce? It is dark as cold coals. What could he possibly see?" Bruce moved as if to take more drastic measures bringing her to the front.

"If that is what he wants, he shall have it." So saying, she moved to the outside of the formation of men and made her way to the front. Riding up to Drue, she spoke briskly. "You wish to speak with me, Lord Drue."

Drue looked at her for a moment before he answered. "Yes. You and I must have a clear understanding of the events ahead of us." He paused to glance at the men behind him. "I remind you again, what you do and say will have great implications for the men with me."

"Then it would seem the burden is yours," Nicola noted.

"You were told, lady, to behave, and I meant what I told you." Drue's voice was quiet. It had a certain edge to it Nicola had never heard before. She sat up straighter.

"You feel I have behaved badly, Lord Drue," Nicola replied. "Please do explain."

"I think you do not recognize the danger in what you are trying to do. So saying, I intend to do all in my power to protect you and allow you to complete what you have begun. The information I have received indicates that Queen Anne has several different companies of men actively searching for you. She is convinced you are a witch. If you are caught, you will most certainly be burned at the stake. Do you understand?" Drue looked at Nicola.

She jerked back so suddenly she feared she might fall from her horse.

Drue looked at her with concern. "I do not tell you these things to frighten you, but to make you aware of how precarious and fragile your life is at this time." Drue waited quietly, as what he told her registered.

"Why did my father ask me to do this?" she asked. The reality of the risk her father had subjected her to was becoming more and more evident.

"I cannot say, lady. I did not know your father. I do know how the policies of nations can become tangled. I also know England has serious funding issues. It is always easier for a ruling house to blame the previous ruler for the conditions the people are forced to endure. In this case, King Richard can ill afford to blame King Edward for anything. King Edward was well favored. However, the Woodville family is not well thought of. Anne lost her sister to what she believes was a curse from Elizabeth. Anne is determined to find and execute anyone even remotely touched by such a rumor, thereby improving Richard's standing." Drue stopped talking for a moment. He then quietly observed, "You are not safe here in England, lady."

As the implication of what he said became clear, Nicola pulled her horse up sharply. "What are your plans?" Nicola asked, frowning. "I cannot just leave all this undone, Drue. I have thought on this a great deal and will not leave England without speaking with Lady Margaret. If I leave with you for Brittany, I will never speak with Lady Margaret. I am not leaving England. I would rather die!"

"That may be your choice, but I cannot let it come to pass," Drue answered quietly. "Keep moving, Nicola. We still have a long way to go."

"No! We settle this here and now!" Nicola's voice rose. "I have been pushed too far. I will not go where you are leading me. You are taking me out of England, without even trying to get to Lady Margaret, are you not?" She held the horse firmly. The troop came to a stop, all eyes on Drue and Nicola.

Nicola watched as the expression on Drue's face hardened, like a wall being put up. He called back to one of the men behind him. "Jon! We have little time to reach the ship waiting for us, and the lady is having trouble with her horse." With that, he kicked his horse and rode ahead. In the blink of an eye, Jon rode up to Nicola and slipped the reins from her before she could stop him. Then, with Jon leading Nicola's horse, everyone followed.

Nicola had to hang on to the saddle to stay on her horse. Her temper boiled. *If he keeps doing such things, I will not have to reckon with my feelings for him . . . they will die of their own accord.*

Drue was too far ahead to hear anything she wanted to yell at him. Nicola was forced to endure the ride until Drue stopped. At last, Drue cooled enough to halt everyone for a break. There was a stream nearby to water the horses. He dismounted, then strode to Nicola. "Lady." He stretched his arms to assist her.

Just the sight of him stirred Nicola's temper again. "How many other ladies have you kidnapped, Lord Drue?" she snapped, her voice dripping with disdain as she dismounted without his assistance. It was surprisingly easier than she thought.

"You are the first who would not follow gladly, lady." Turning, he began to walk away. Both Braggio and Bruce laughed, as did several other men who were near.

"When this is over, I will never speak to you again," Nicola stated, glaring at Drue.

"Oh, you *will* speak to me, and often," Drue replied calmly without looking at her, as he continued to work with his saddle. "In truth, *before* this is over, you will *bow* to me."

Aghast, Nicola turned to stare at Drue. "Bow? I will bow to you? Never! Do you hear me? Never!" she yelled, whirling around and storming to where Jon stood watering her horse.

Nicola caught Lizzie exchanging a worried glance with Braggio. He winked and smiled at Lizzie. Shaking his head, he indicated Lizzie was not to intervene with the trouble between Drue and Nicola.

"Nicola," Lizzie said, approaching her and attempting to take her arm. "Come, let's walk."

Nicola stopped her, shaking her off. "I believe Lord Drue is quite full of himself. He will be impossible to deal with now."

"Full of myself, Lady Weldon?" he commented. Drue had apparently stepped behind her without her noticing. "I think you describe your own demeanor." Not waiting for Nicola to reply, he added, "Does Jon need to lead your horse again, lady?"

Nicola could feel her face burn. She did not dare look at anyone, but she knew they all looked at her. "Indeed not!" she snapped.

"Good," Drue replied. "I am quite sure Jon appreciates that. Right, Jon?"

Jon nodded. "Yes, my lord." Nicola groaned inwardly.

The remainder of the ride was quiet. Even Lizzie, who rode just ahead of Nicola, seemed afraid to speak and was doing her best to stay out of it. She seemed content to have Braggio so close. Whenever she glanced his way, he always smiled at her. She never asked where they were all bound, and Nicola guessed their destination didn't concern her much. Other than Wright Castle, Lizzie had not traveled beyond London.

As the sun rose above, the morning mist cleared. It was beautiful, and even in her turmoil, Nicola could appreciate it. A lake spread out before them. The blue water was calm but for waves gently rippling toward the land. A large vessel was anchored off the shoreline. There were few houses and no one was about.

Unable to contain herself, Lizzie turned to the man closest to her. "Just look at all that water! What lake is this?"

The man frowned at her. "'Tis not a lake, lady. 'Tis the English Channel." When Lizzie only looked puzzled, he added, "The ocean. 'Tis the ocean." When Nicola heard the man answer Lizzie, she held her horse up.

"The ocean?" Lizzie sounded incredulous, and suddenly a little fearful. "That is the ocean? We are going on the ocean?"

"Yes, on board that ship." The man pointed toward the vessel. Nicola turned toward the ship, stunned.

Lizzie slowed momentarily to allow Nicola to catch up. Nicola was staring at the sea and the boat. "Nicola, what are we doing now?" Lizzie's voice quivered with what sounded like excitement, but Nicola could also hear the terror in Lizzie's voice.

True to his word, it was abundantly clear Drue had no intentions of allowing her to search for Lady Margaret. Her protest would be useless now. "I believe Lord Drue takes us to Henry Tudor." She turned to her friend. "It will be safe, Lizzie. There are no storms. The ship is large. We are safe."

Nicola glanced at the ocean and ship. She remembered well the terrible waves and wind, and the ships that smashed against the rocks beneath her home with every storm. *The sea is always angry.* Swallowing hard and taking a breath, she forced a smile. *How am I going to do this? I never thought about Tudor's physical location, only that I needed to reach him.* With confidence she did not feel, she stated, "Lizzie, we are going to be fine. Do you think Lord Braggio would ever place you in the face of danger?" Although Lizzie shook her head, she continued to stare at the water.

WHEN DRUE HAD TIME TO LOOK at Nicola and Lizzie, he could see the anxiety on their faces and in the way they both sat frozen, staring at the expanse of water before them. Granted, Lizzie had never seen either the ocean or a ship, but he was not certain why Nicola would look so afraid. Surely she had been aboard a ship? He trotted his horse over to them, dismounted, and again reached to help Nicola down. This time, she allowed his assistance. Braggio had already helped Lizzie down. Drue looked out to sea. "Some storms are expected to roll in soon. We must cross now, to be safe. If we wait, we may not be able to cross over for days." Reaching for Nicola's arm, he added, "Come. Welcome aboard the *Guardiano*."

When Nicola looked at him, her face no longer bore signs of the anger she felt earlier, only fear and uncertainty. "That means?"

Drue smiled. "*Guardiano* means guardian, protector. It is a good name for this boat. It can keep you safe while you travel."

"Yes. Well, I think I would not like to be out there during a storm." She looked out to sea again. "Best we get on our way." Nervously, she glanced at the water again.

"You have seen storms from your home, no doubt. The Channel is not an open ocean. Storms are not fun, but we have land not far away on either side of us." He waited a moment for what he said to sink in. Nicola did not seem convinced, but she was not fighting him. This was the perfect time. "Nicola, Tudor has decided to quit. He is sending word to those who are trying to raise men and weapons for him, including his mother, to stop. I have been able to convince Jasper to wait until they hear from me. You must find a way to convince Tudor to continue. He cannot stop now." Drue saw the frown on her brow, but she did not answer. She merely turned to lead her horse toward the ship, leaving Drue behind.

As the horses and people were being loaded, one of the men escorted Nicola and Lizzie to a small room with two beds. He left two buckets near the beds. "In case you get sick," he informed them, ducking back out the door and closing it behind him. Nicola and Lizzie looked at each other.

"Sick? We are going to get sick?" Lizzie moaned. "How long do you think this vessel will take to get wherever we're going?"

"I wish I knew," Nicola answered. She slumped onto the bed. It was hard. *Of course. Nothing about my life is soft. Father, I fear you have asked too much of me.*

"I think I want to go outside. Please come with me, Nicola." Lizzie's voice sounded small and frightened. Nicola cared little for the prospect of seeing Drue, but her friend's face told the story. Lizzie was beginning to panic.

"Of course. We can look this ship over. It seems so large . . . I am quite certain it must be safe." One look at Lizzie told Nicola she was not convinced. "Lizzie, again, Lord Braggio would never place you in danger. You know he adores you. Do you really believe he would do anything to hurt you?" Nicola smiled and wrapped a shawl from her travel bag around her shoulders as she handed one to Lizzie. Nicola opened the door, and she and Lizzie stepped out. Men were finishing loading the rest of the horses, and then the ramp was raised. From somewhere behind them, a man was shouting orders—the sails began to unfurl and the boat moved slowly away from the shore. Standing at the ship's side, both ladies watched as England began to shrink.

"I have seen enough, Nicola. I would rather be in our room."

As the ship moved farther away from shore, it began to softly rise and fall with the waves. Both ladies grabbed the buckets. It had started.

CHAPTER 43

$\mathcal{T}$HE DUCHESS OF BURGUNDY WANDERED the halls of her home and out into the lavish gardens surrounding it. Rays from the afternoon sun glinted off the polished tiles around the fountain as water cascaded into the lower basin. The peaceful sound felt out of place given the storm brewing. *Could Prince Richard be alive? My heart tells me no. No matter. If King Richard loses the fight with Tudor that is sure to come, I will make my move.* Sighing, she briefly closed her eyes before quickly looking around to be certain no one saw and took it as a sign of weakness. To remain strong and stay the course, there could be none of that. Prince Richard could be alive . . . at least as far as anyone knew. She heard footsteps coming rapidly toward her. Turning slowly, she waited. The man she most trusted had information. Hoping against reason, she prayed he had found out where young Richard was hiding. Poor Richard. She would see he was well protected and cared for. "You found Richard?" She smiled expectantly.

"No, Your Grace. But I have word of a ship that has sailed from England," the man answered.

"And?" she asked. Perhaps that ship bore her nephew.

"It does not fly an English flag. It flies the unmistakable flag of Padronale," he replied. "We do not know of any person in England from Padronale. Should we intercept the ship?"

For a long moment, the duchess remained silent, thinking. "No, not yet. England has few ties with Padronale. Could it have been a Papal flag?"

"No. It was Padronale, I am told."

The duchess could think of no reason for Padronale men to be in England, but who could tell? Spain and Italy certainly would be interested in English ties, with so much trouble from France. *Could young Richard have found safety in*

Padronale? No, Elizabeth knows no person from Padronale that could help. Doubtful. The Duke of Vieneto is accounted for and not in England. "I do not believe a ship from Padronale means anything to us, if the story is true. Stay the course. We must find young Richard." She walked on, her mind always searching for any way to keep the York family, her family, on the throne. *If only I could talk with Elizabeth. I will write again, with caution lest my letter is intercepted. There must be a way for her to tell me if Richard is still alive.*

"My Lady Grandmother," as the mother of the duchess and King Richard was called, sat under a great canopy watching her grandchildren play. When the duchess approached, her mother spoke. "This is a good place for the children. Out of the tangles of political strife." The old lady waved her hand toward a nearby chair. "You look troubled. Can I help?"

"I wish you could, Mother. I have word that young Richard may still be alive. If King Richard loses the crown, we must do all we can to move young Richard into play." The duchess looked at her mother. She caught the old woman frowning before looking beyond the children, beyond anything, shaking her head slowly. A shadow of sadness washed over her face. "You do not agree with me, My Lady Grandmother?"

"Margaret, Charles was my son, Edward was my son. King Richard is my son. I pray the rumors claiming that the princes in the Tower are no longer alive are just that . . . rumors. But the fact remains, brothers kill brothers, families are destroyed, and still we push onward. When do we say enough is enough?"

"I cannot believe you would say such things!" the duchess challenged her mother. "You mourned deeper than even Elizabeth when Edward died. You would give up the throne so easily? To a Tudor? One who, by anyone's defense, has little or no authentic claim to the throne."

The old woman sighed. "Daughter, I have lost a husband, two sons, and a son-in-law to fighting over a throne. It seems I may have lost two grandsons now. I may yet lose my only surviving son. I am so ill from losing those I love." She paused for a moment, then continued softly, "I suppose I believe I have given more than any mother or wife should have to give. I have given nearly all I hold dear." She turned her head slowly to look at her daughter. The Duchess of Burgundy could only turn away. "I see how it is. As always, you have already begun. God willing Richard wins and you can cease planning your next war. Be at peace with life, for once." The old woman rose slowly and with her hand firmly on her walking stick, she left the duchess alone.

CHAPTER 44

DRUE STOOD AT THE BOW OF THE SHIP that would signal
Tudor's quitting or his reawakening. While he could easily understand
that sinking feeling Tudor must be dealing with, he could not understand giving up with so much at stake. To give up now when so many were coming to aid
his cause felt wrong. Drue knew better than anyone, except perhaps Tudor's
uncle, Jasper, what a long shot the fight would be, but to not even attempt it?
Drue shook his head. Below deck, in the first mate's quarters, probably in the
middle of vomiting up the contents of her stomach, was the one who might be
able to turn young Tudor around. Time to put his dice on the table.

"Jon, check on Lady Nicola for me—I wish to visit with her. I believe she
is probably indisposed, being an unseasoned sea traveler." Drue smiled. "If
Lady Lizzie is willing, escort her to visit with Braggio, and I will visit with
Lady Nicola. And please notify Lord Braggio he will soon have female company. Be a gentleman." Drue chuckled. "Life does go on."

At the knock on their door, the ladies exchanged worried looks. The
buckets provided had been well used. Neither felt like seeing anyone. "I will
go this time," Nicola offered. "There is nothing left in my stomach anyway."

"Nor in mine," moaned Lizzie, as she leaned over to retch again. Nicola
staggered to the door, trying to stay upright in the swaying ship.

Jon stood outside, looking like he would rather have been anyplace else.
"I am sorry to bother you, lady, but Lord Drue wishes to speak privately with
you." Jon glanced at poor Lizzie. "Lord Braggio awaits your visit, lady. If it
is at all possible."

"Like this? You jest," Lizzie replied, glaring at Jon.

"I will go to Lord Drue. Lizzie, you stay here and continue." Nicola
waved weakly to Lizzie, who had a death grip on the bucket. *What is it with*

men? Surely my father never behaved like this with my mother. After stepping to a deep basin with water sloshing around in the bottom, Nicola tried to freshen up. Looking in the mirror hanging above the basin, she cringed. She threw the towel down and turned to Jon. "This is not how I wish to be seen, but then, I doubt Lord Drue cares much about what I wish."

Jon escorted Nicola to Drue's cabin, opening the door for Nicola. Drue looked up, surprised, then stern. "Did I not give clear instructions?" he asked Jon, standing as both entered.

Before Jon could answer, Nicola spoke out. "Yes, I am certain you did, but I refused to let Lizzie leave. She still has her head in a bucket, unable to stop vomiting. My appearance gives little proof, but I am doing better than Lizzie."

Drue had to struggle not to laugh. "I see. Jon, ask Lord Braggio to see to Lady Lizzie."

"Oh no! She would be so humiliated," Nicola exclaimed. "Please, you cannot."

"Lady Nicola," Drue replied, "Lord Braggio is the closest to a physician we have on board. He will be able to assist her."

Jon nodded and was off.

Drue walked around the writing table and indicated a chair to Nicola. "You and I must have a conversation, Nicola." He watched her for a moment. "Are you feeling well enough to step outside? It helps the nausea to be able to see the horizon."

"Yes, I am quite well, thank you. I would like to go outside. Our room is a bit stuffy." Nicola stood and took Drue's offered arm. Outside, the breeze felt fresh. Nicola tipped her head back slightly and took a deep breath. Drue studied the outline of her face and neck. When Nicola realized he was watching her, she quickly released his arm. At that moment, the boat rolled slightly, and Nicola fell into Drue. "Maybe I am not as steady as I feel," she admitted, feeling herself blush.

"I can tell you have never sailed before. But you are doing remarkably well. Look, the sea gradually becomes lost in the distance where the sky brushes the waters." He stood looking at the waves and clouds.

Nicola was surprised, but she did feel better standing on the deck, looking at the horizon. She lost herself in the sounds of the waves and voices of the men working the sails. Slowly, she relaxed. Still, she held on to Drue's arm—he seemed in no hurry for her to let go. Instead, he led her around the deck, careful to stay clear of ropes, barrels, and other obstacles. Nicola was relieved to have the nausea at bay.

"Lady Nicola," Drue began, "I know well you feel bound to speak with Lady Margaret. I cannot permit you to do that at this time. King Richard's wife, Anne, has make it her mission to find and destroy anyone she feels might threaten Richard's reign." Drue paused. Nicola had stopped walking and stood staring out to sea. A teardrop clung to her eyelashes, and she blinked it away.

"I will not let anyone harm you, Nicola," Drue stated. "Not Queen Anne, not King Richard, not anyone."

Nicola turned to him. She was teary-eyed, but still in control. "You speak gallantly, Lord Drue. I do not know from where you came, but we both know how kings and queens have a way of removing obstacles. I am an obstacle." She turned to look at the ocean again, hoping he would not see her tears. He simply handed her a cloth from his cape and stood waiting for her to gain her composure.

"Someday, I will tell you where I come from, and I will tell you about my country. Now, we must plan on how you can get to Tudor, and what you must do to convince him he cannot quit."

"Does it matter so much if he does? Maybe he was meant to be someone other than the king of England. Maybe his fate is where he is now." There was a hint of wistfulness to Nicola's voice.

Drue turned her around to face him. "Do you not believe your father or the old crone? Do you believe your father was mistaken?" he asked. "Do you really not believe what is to be?" Nicola tried to turn away, but he held her fast. "Answer me, Nicola. You must search your soul and find peace with what you have promised to do. If you cannot do this, I need to know now. Not when I have men lined up, ready to die for Tudor." Nicola turned her head away, but Drue held her chin and gently turned her back to face him. "Think, Nicola. Tell me what it is to be." His voice was quiet but pressing.

Nicola suddenly felt weak. She swayed, and Drue caught her. Still, he stood and waited. At last, she looked at him, searching his face for any signs of pity or disdain. There was nothing of that, only patience. "I am frightened, Drue. I fear I will not be able to make Tudor believe in what I say. So many people depend on me. Can I do this?" she asked.

Drue grasped both her shoulders and answered her, his voice intense with emotion. "Yes! You can. Your father and my mother both knew you would be the one to turn Tudor's wavering into a powerful stand. You, Nicola. Only you."

He wrapped his arms around her and held her. "You are so much stronger than you think, Lady Nicola Weldon." The wind was slowly picking up, and he wrapped his cape around her. "It looks to storm. This could well be a long night." When Nicola rolled her eyes, he laughed. "Best you take care of poor Lizzie." Holding her face with both hands, he kissed her forehead softly. Then, with his arm around her, he walked her toward Braggio and Lizzie, who were now standing on the deck across from them.

Drue's nearness was comforting, but unnerving. Nicola's thoughts turned to the old crone. *Can you help me? Please talk to me.* There would be no reply. As Drue and Nicola made their way toward Lizzie and Lord Braggio, Nicola felt a strange urgency. As if something needed her attention. The feeling passed.

BRAGGIO KNOCKED SOFTLY on Lizzie's door as soon as Jon had delivered Drue's message to him. "Lady, it is me, Braggio."

Lizzie made it to the door, opened it, and tottered back to the bed, in time to grab the bucket again.

"I am so ashamed, Lord Braggio. I know I must look frightful." Lizzie's voice was weak.

"On the contrary, lady. You are still beautiful, to me. I knew you might be ill. Perhaps I might be of service. Come with me." He helped her to stand. Too ill to argue, she let Braggio lead her onto the deck. They crossed to the side, opposite where Braggio could see Drue and Nicola. "First, Lizzie, look to the horizon. It helps the feeling of sickness." He stood with his arm around her. As the queasiness left her, Lizzie had to smile at him. "Are you better?"

He smiled when she nodded. They remained just so for a long time.

"Lord Braggio, may I ask you something?" Lizzie's expression became serious.

"Of course, anything," Braggio replied. He stood silent, waiting.

Lizzie began to examine her hands, as she leaned against the boat side. "I have overheard several of the men, at different times, refer to Lord Drue as 'His Grace.' Why is that?" She faced him, frowning. "Is he not who he says he is?"

For a moment, Braggio studied Lizzie, trying to decide if he could share Drue's secret with her. "I need to tell you something." Braggio's voice was serious. "You cannot share this with Lady Nicola. You absolutely must not tell anyone. You risk Drue's intense anger." Braggio paused. Lizzie's eyes had widened. "I would lose you, there is no doubt. We would be separated, period. I will not risk that. I must know you *will not* repeat what I say to you. In good time, it will come out, but not by any of us."

"I do not understand." Lizzie looked worried. She hesitated, but agreed. "I have never kept anything from her. But if you say I must, I will."

"Do not worry, lady. 'Tis not bad. But it is not our story to tell. Lord Drue is actually Prince Drue. His father was—and now his brother is—a king. Their kingdom lies near the Papal States. Drue has chosen not to make his title and birthright public. There is a story to this, but we have not the time. Suffice it to say, he has ordered us not to call him by any other term that might give away his real title. When you hear men do so, they are making a mistake, and I am guessing you'll see them corrected."

Lizzie was stunned. She started to speak, but stopped. Braggio brushed her hair aside and pointed to the distant horizon. "Beyond are both our destinies, yours and mine. Beyond the waters in lands you know not. It is a land of beauty. Her people are beautiful. The times are not." He turned to Lizzie. "So, Lizzie, how do you feel?"

"I am not certain, but now it is not my stomach that tumbles."

Braggio laughed softly, then became serious. "I have something to give you. It is not much, but I give it to you, to pledge my love for you, and my intention to take you as my wife when we are finished with this job we have undertaken." At that, Braggio slipped a gold band set with two rubies onto

Lizzie's finger. Before Lizzie could speak, Braggio kissed her soft lips. When he straightened, they both saw Drue and Nicola walking toward them.

"Lord Braggio." Drue's voice interrupted any further talk. "Lady Lizzie, how do you fare now?"

Lizzie nearly curtsied, but a slight frown from Braggio stopped her. "I am much better, but I fear I may not be able to stand here until we reach land. I intend to try, though." She smiled.

Nicola was standing near Drue and laughed. "You will not keep that vigil alone, Lizzie. I will be standing right here with you. How watching the horizon can help so quickly, I do not understand, but it matters not . . . it works." For a long time, the couples stood talking and watching the waters begin to ripple. Nicola watched as the waves grew larger. "It was just so quiet, and now, not so much. Strange."

Drue and Braggio exchanged glances. The sea would not be calm through a long night. When Drue was notified the meal was ready, he called to Jon. "Find Lord Bruce and ask him to join us in my cabin. I am told we have food." Jon nodded and left his post.

As the men walked ahead, talking, Nicola leaned toward Lizzie. "How can we eat?" She shuddered, adding, "I can barely keep water down, and I have no desire to try anything else."

Shyly, Lizzie showed Nicola her hand. The ring was beautiful. The two rubies caught the glint of a fading sun. Nicola looked at the ring, then at Lizzie. She could tell Lizzie was happy, beyond anything Lizzie could explain. "It is beautiful, Lizzie. You must wear it always." She hugged her friend.

Lizzie started to speak, but Drue and Bruce stood by waiting to enter Drue's quarters. So instead she smiled at Braggio.

CHAPTER 45

*T*HE THAMES RIVER flowed steadily from Thames Head into the North Sea, where its waters hastened on to mingle with the sea that received it. A busy thoroughfare, it moved goods and humanity. But the Thames River had a dark side. Refuse from settlements and cities along its shore was being dumped into its waters, to be carried along by the current. Heavier objects might sink into the thick silt at river's bottom or be dragged along until they came to one of the bends in the river, where they would sit swirling, gathering more debris until in due course, they were covered, never to be seen again.

Most of England recognized that the Thames provided travelers a fast, if odorous, waterway linking seashore docks to London and beyond. Night travel, however, was usually very light. Only those whose urgent business was better left to the darkness were on the water at night.

Searching for an oarsman was such a man. The man was Fantasma Diablo. Diablo was dressed in dark clothing. A sword, short-bladed knife, a garrote, and several vials of toxin completed his arsenal, the tools of his trade. All were carefully hidden beneath the hooded cloak that shadowed his face.

A lone oarsman lounged against one of many simple huts that served river travelers in need of a boat. The huts were used by the men working during the day and left unattended at night. The oarsman's boat, tied to a nearby dock, bobbed as the undercurrent nudged water against the bank. The man was slightly older, with thinning hair and worn-down front teeth from years of holding fishing lines and boat cords between them. His work, fishing augmented by river transports, was slowly but surely building a comfortable living, as evidenced by the thigh-high fine-grade leather boots he wore. They were his latest purchase, making a statement and keeping his feet dry at the same time. His boots protected him from the occasional sprays of water and the muddy, wet banks.

He quickly recognized the stealthy movements of the figure coming his way. It would be someone who did not want questions and, hopefully, could pay well. Unable to see the customer's face, he simply agreed to the transport, stepped from the dock into his small craft, and, without looking back, headed toward the requested destination.

The stop his passenger requested had no dock. Diablo glanced around. Sliding around in the slick mud, the oarsman held fast to his boat's tie rope with his teeth and the side of the boat with one hand, while waiting for his pay. Diablo rummaged in his pockets and reached toward the man. Forced to lean toward Diablo, the man was sorely off-balance, and Diablo suddenly shoved him aside. The man, unable to regain his footing, fell backward. Unable to swim, he was swiftly carried into the middle of the river, into faster currents. He went under. Diablo watched for a long moment, then, satisfied the man was gone, climbed up the bank and left. The unsecured boat was already drifting downstream. Diablo's entry into London went unnoticed.

Now to find out where young Prince Richard and Lady Weldon pass the time. Diablo had already decided Lady Weldon would never come see the duchess. Weldon could prove much too dangerous to the duchess's plans. And accidents happen.

With King Richard on the move, it would seem the first order of business should be finding the king's young nephew, Prince Richard. Diablo began casually walking the back streets of London. Though the hour was late, men still wandered about between the inns and brothels. As of yet, Diablo had heard nothing to indicate either prince had survived the attempted rescue.

Just as dawn broke, he found himself in front of Kelly's business. For a moment, Diablo hesitated, his mind sliding back into another life. Looking around, he took a deep breath, then stepped inside. Knowing patrons of such a business leave at all hours, he expected the door would be open. Kelly met him in the foyer.

"'Tis been a while, my lord," Kelly noted, smiling. "You're too late for the ladies, so I would be guessing you are looking for information. Might you be hungry?" Without waiting for an answer, Kelly turned and led the way to her kitchen. Diablo followed her and sat down.

"You have not changed, lady," he noted, watching her hips sway as she busied herself at the fire. Kelly was younger than Diablo, but they were both beyond their prime. Still, Kelly's business required she keep herself as presentable as her age allowed. She did not answer, but she glanced back at Diablo and smiled. Diablo smiled back. Both her eyes and her smile spoke of a time past, when life was kinder. "Have you missed me?" His voice was soft, nostalgic.

Kelly turned to face Diablo. "Always. I am sure you know that. But . . . life moves on." She set a bowl of mutton stew and a wooden platter of fresh bread down before him. "Ale or wine?"

"Good wine?" he asked.

"Of course," she replied, walking to a small door near the cabinets, where she stepped inside a tiny pantry. Kelly knew how Diablo made his living. No matter how friendly he seemed now, she knew only too well that he could easily become her worst nightmare. She sat down opposite him. "How did we both get so far off course, Diablo? How could it be some grand plan for me to house whores, and you to kill? How did the man I used to know and love become the man now before me?"

"Time dealt harshly with us, Kelly," Diablo replied. "I did what I had to do." Diablo picked up his spoon. He watched her as he ate. Neither spoke. At last, he set his wine goblet down and asked, "Of what do you think? I can tell your mind is wandering far from here." He watched her closely, noting how she studied her hands before looking him in the eye to answer.

"You must understand how seeing you always makes my mind slip back to a different time," Kelly replied. She shook her head. "It matters not. How can I help you this time?"

"Can you honestly think I care not for those days? Or remember not what our lives were then?" Diablo stood up and walked to Kelly. She remained sitting, watching him. He oozed danger, and he would never change. Diablo pulled her up and held her closely. She still smelled the same . . . sweet lilacs. His eyes closed for a second. He spoke softly, "I remember well and I love you still." He held her for a long moment.

Suddenly, he stepped away. "I have come looking for information," he announced abruptly.

The moment crashed to an end. Kelly sank back down. Taking a deep breath, she asked, "What information?" He walked around the room, looked out the windows, and returned. Standing at the foyer door, he glanced around.

"There is no one here, Diablo," she told him. "King Richard has made it quite clear he is a man of character. He does not like what people like me do for a living. The few ladies I have are already in bed, from last night's work. The gentlemen they serviced are already gone. They leave in the dark, the less likely to be seen."

"I have heard young Richard still lives," Diablo told her.

Surprised, Kelly straightened up. "King Edward's youngest?" She frowned. Looking toward the window, she tried to remember if she had ever heard anything that might give credence to what Diablo was telling her. She turned to him. "I have heard nothing like that. Surely if he is, King Richard would be looking for him. He does not seem to be doing that." Her eyes narrowed, as the thought that he might be trying to lead her down a dangerous path crossed her mind.

"I need someone to get a message to the dowager Queen Elizabeth. Can you get to her?" Diablo asked.

Kelly shook her head. "Not likely. King Richard has met with Elizabeth and promised her safety. She and the youngest girls. They are all gone, to some place in the country. The two older ones are now ladies with Queen Anne's staff."

Diablo stepped close to Kelly again, but not to hold her. "You would not lie to me, would you, Kelly?" He spoke softly, but this time there was an edge to his voice.

Kelly sat very still. He had never used that voice with her, but she had been with him when he spoke to another man in that same voice. The man had died. "I have never lied to you, Diablo. Why would I start now? Ask around. The king's men like to eat at the Oarsman Inn." Kelly remained motionless, looking straight at Diablo.

"Have you had a young girl come to you for work?" Diablo finally asked.

"Of course. I always have girls come looking for work. Every week they come. Times are hard since King Edward died."

"She would be alone," Diablo added.

"Most are," Kelly replied.

"She had no family. Her father is dead," Diablo continued. "He was killed, maybe a year ago."

"What is her father's name?" Kelly asked. "I do not know of the father of any of my ladies having been killed."

"Her father was Lord Weldon," Diablo replied. "She may have had a companion or maybe was alone."

"Diablo," Kelly answered dryly, "all of my ladies are alone or with a companion. I seldom know why they show up here. Only that they need to make a living somehow."

"Take care, Kelly. I have a good memory," Diablo warned, his voice low. Then he turned and exited. Kelly sat still for a long time, fearing he would come back. When he did not, she hurried to her room. She pulled a bag down from the top of her armoire and began to pack. Taking only what she could stuff into the bag, she departed through the back door.

DIABLO WANDERED THE STREETS OF LONDON, listening, always listening. Just as Kelly had told him, the Oarsman was filled with men wearing King Richard's colors. He was seated at a table alone, but not far from a table of Richard's men. The table was laden with food and cheap ale. Men sat around laughing and drinking. Diablo knew he would have one chance to gather information. It would be far too dangerous to be seen by more than one group of the king's men, asking the same questions. However, with ale in their bellies, men always talked, and it would be worth trying. He was a patient man; he would wait.

CAPTAIN ODE, ONE OF RICHARD'S commanders, sat off to the side, quietly watching his men as they got to know each other. He watched as a stranger entered and was seated at a table alone. *Somewhere I have seen this man.* None of the Ode's men gave the stranger any notice. Captain Ode spoke out loud enough for his words to carry over the noise. "Someone reach out to our friend. 'Tis not good to travel alone."

The men looked around, and one younger soldier made the offer. "Come, there is room here," he said. "Plenty of food and ale. Here." He patted the chair next to him. With interest, Captain Ode watched as the lone man grinned in a friendly manner, lifted his mug of ale, and made his way over to their table. Captain Ode studied Diablo. *This man looks to be someone who could hold his own in a battle, but he also looks and acts like one who does not fight in the light of day, but in alleys under cover of darkness.*

Most of the men had resumed talking among themselves once the stranger was seated. As the innkeeper set his stew down, Captain Ode asked, "Where are you bound?"

"To Gloucester," Diablo answered, looking around and shrugging. "Much has changed since I was here last." At that comment, several of the men sitting around stopped talking and watched the stranger.

"And when would that be, when you last were here in London?" one man asked.

"Many years ago. When Princess Margaret of York wed the Duke of Burgundy," Diablo replied.

Suddenly, Ode remembered. "You were the captain of his guard," he noted. Everyone knew Burgundy was expected to side with King Richard. The Duchess of Burgundy would have men and money for Richard's cause. However, thinking on the relationship between the duchess and Richard, Captain Ode doubted help would come from Burgundy. The duchess was said to be distraught over the rumors of the death of her nephews.

"Yes," Diablo replied. "I was. But London is not the London I remember."

"How so?" another soldier asked.

"It is much larger. There is a different feel to the streets. The Thames runs dark now." Diablo looked at the soldier. "It is different now. I suppose we all are," he added.

Captain Ode stood and walked to where Diablo sat. "Come, let us walk, you and I. I too see the change and would remember a quieter time." He stood waiting. Diablo got up and handed one of the women several coins. Nodding to her, he followed the captain outside.

For a moment, neither man spoke. "For what do you search?" Captain Ode asked quietly.

"The duchess sends a message to the dowager Queen Elizabeth," Diablo answered without looking at the captain. "But I find she is no longer in sanctuary. A good thing for her, I feel."

"And the message was?" Ode asked. He knew this could be the telling of the stranger's real purpose. He waited for an answer.

Diablo answered easily. "The duchess has lost a husband, two brothers, and now, it would seem, two nephews. She prays for peace in England. She has lost enough." Diablo glanced at the captain as they walked on.

The captain listened without comment. *Not a real commitment to King Richard, yet a reasonable request. Knowing the duchess as I do, I doubt the message. I think he looks for some proof the princes are both dead.* "I wish you luck. I think you seek information about the princes. If you are able to find an answer for the duchess, you will have discovered more than others have, including even the king." With that, the captain crossed the street and returned to the inn.

As Diablo watched the captain walk away, he rolled Ode's comments around in his mind. Perhaps the captain was aware that one of the princes may have escaped. Still, he had made no move to keep Diablo.

Diablo wandered aimlessly for several hours. There was no gossip regarding the fate of the princes. With good cause, people were too afraid to speak. Finally, making a decision, he walked to the stables. His next stop would be Cheyneygates. Elizabeth and her daughters reportedly lived there, surrounded by servants, unable to leave. A house imprisonment.

CHAPTER 46

WITH A VENGEANCE, the vision exploded. Abruptly, Nicola sat up in bed, staring into nothing, trying to make sense of what she had just dreamed. The images were gone. She was alone with Lizzie in the cabin. She looked around, shivering, and pulled the blankets closer. Waves crashing against the hull rocked the ship. Even their tiny cabin was lit by flashes of lightning—the thunder was deafening. Rain pounded the vessel. The storm had been raging for several hours now. Falling back onto the bed, she closed her eyes.

Slowly, the images appeared again. This time, she lay still, letting them move through her mind. Again, they faded. *Drue! I need to talk to Drue.* Nicola checked on Lizzie and found her finally sleeping. Pulling the blanket over her bed clothes, Nicola pulled the cabin door open. The raging wind blew the door against the wall, nearly knocking her to the floor. She hurried outside and, pulling with all her strength, she struggled against the gale to close the door. Cold rain stung as it pelted her face. The combination of the wind and rolling ship knocked her against the wall. She clung on and tried to move toward Drue's quarters.

She saw Jon also fighting his way to get somewhere, but from the opposite direction so that he faced her. When he reached her, his features were tight with concern. "Lady Nicola! What are you doing? You could be washed overboard."

"I must speak with Lord Drue," Nicola yelled over the wind that whipped all around them. Jon nodded, and with his arm around her, they both staggered along the cabin wall and the ship's side, toward Drue's cabin. Jon knocked at Drue's door.

Braggio opened the door. At the sight of Jon and Nicola, Drue stood and crossed the room to the door. Jon nodded and stepped back outside. "What are you doing outside in this?" Drue demanded with a frown.

"I must speak with you, Drue," Nicola told him.

Drue looked around his quarters. There was little space to provide privacy. His bed was along one wall, the working table in the middle of the room, and latched cabinets along another wall.

Braggio and Bruce exchanged glances. Braggio spoke up, as both men made their way to the door. "We will be in the galley, if you have need of our services."

Nicola was shivering, her teeth chattering so hard she could not speak. Drue pulled the soaked blanket from her and wrapped her in a second dry one. He held her closely, rubbing her arms, and waited. Slowly, as she warmed, Nicola stopped shaking. "I saw things, Drue," she told him. "I saw things." She reached for his arm. "You have to help me understand!"

Drue led her to the small bed. Sitting next to her, he held her closer. "What did you see, Nicola?" he asked quietly. "We can figure it out. Tell me what you saw."

After taking a deep breath, Nicola described her dreams. "I saw two men. They rode hard, Drue." Nicola closed her eyes, trying to remember. "They did not wear colors."

"Can you tell me anything about where they were? What did it look like around them?"

"I feel they were in the land we sail for. I have never seen that land, but I felt it. I . . . I cannot explain what I felt." She gazed up at Drue.

Drue looked into her eyes. "I think the men fleeing could be Tudor and his uncle, Jasper. If they are caught, the Tudors will be killed."

Drue glanced at the maps on his desk. "Nicola, relax, close your eyes, and let your mind tell you. What do you see around them? Any landmarks, anything at all?"

Nicola frowned at him. "I can't recall the images at will. I cannot do that. They just come to me. I do not even know when they might come." *Could the old crone make images appear?* She stood and walked across the room. Slowly, she began walking alongside the wall, brushing her hand against its smooth surface to keep from falling.

Closing her eyes, she tried to bring the images back. She had nearly given up, when the two men raced across her mind's plane of sight. She straightened and stopped walking, her body tense. "There are trees around them; the ground around looks very damp, with the kind of reeds and grasses you'd see near a bog or swamp. The winds are blowing and it is beginning to rain. The men have horses that are starting to slow. I can see the animals galloping, but they do not move beyond my sight." Nicola started to sway, side to side. "Now they stop, and they are arguing. One man, the older one, is trying to get the younger man to continue, but . . ." Nicola became silent.

"But what?" Drue asked. "What do you see?"

Nicola turned to him. "Nothing. It is gone now." She shuddered. "Are we too late?"

"No," Drue replied, "but we must make it to land as soon as possible. Damnation! The storm has blown us off track." He strode to the desk and leaned over, studying the map. "Last notice, we were headed this direction." Nicola stood watching him. She knew she must look a wild mess, her hair scattered about her head in ringlets, but she didn't care. She felt calm now, but distant, almost numb.

"Where are you, Nicola?" Drue said, crossing the room to her.

She started, then shrugged. "Trying to think of a way to get an audience with this Henry Tudor." She changed the subject. "I am very tired. I think I should rest."

Drue gave her a small smile. "You remind me of my mother, the way your mood is always shifting. Of course I will take you back." After grabbing a thick robe made from hide, he covered her with it, and they stepped into the relentless storm.

Surprisingly, Lizzie was still asleep when Nicola came in. Drue shut the door gently on his way out. She lay the hide that had covered her over a chair to dry. Having replaced her wet gown, she slid between the bed coverings and slept fitfully.

When she awoke, the ship was no longer rocking. She slipped off the bed and crossed the room. Opening the door, she could see the sun. Lizzie walked to the door and stood looking over her shoulder. "Sun! There is a sun, after all," Lizzie exclaimed, laughing. Lizzie pulled Nicola close and hugged her. "We made it, Nicola. I truly thought we would die."

Nicola agreed. "This was not pleasant, but it is over, at least for now."

"What do we do next?" Lizzie asked as she began to dress. Lifting the hide, she eyed Nicola. "You were out in that storm? And you did not take me?"

"Hmm, you might have helped, for certain. I had to question our captain. If we were to begin sinking, just what would they do? No one talked to us about that." Nicola shared the first thing that came to her mind. When the words were out, she wished she had not put more fear in poor Lizzie's mind.

"And?" Lizzie asked. Her face showed the panic Nicola's comment brought.

"He was busy with his maps. I think he is worried we were blown away from the planned landing site, wherever that was. I hope we can quickly return to England. Have you ever been to this Brittany?" Nicola hoped to get Lizzie's mind off her night jaunt.

"No, I have not, but I once met a man from this country, or maybe it was Burgundy. Anyway, it sounded much like England. I think they are more inclined to pursue literature and music. I am so thankful Eny taught us to read. I want to be what Lord Braggio would need." She turned to Nicola. "I hear the court of France is grand. I love the French dresses one sees sometimes in the shops of London. Those do not stay in the shops long. I could never buy one, but they are beautiful," Lizzie noted wistfully.

What little she had once shared with Lizzie made no sense now. She felt she must tell Lizzie more. Lizzie should know why they were aboard a ship bound for another country. "Lizzie, I must tell you something. I have not been totally honest with you. Not because I sought to hide things from you, but because I want to protect you." Nicola paused, watching Lizzie's reaction.

Lizzie smiled. "I know what you shared with me before is certainly not the story now. I have not asked questions. I trust you, Nicola. But you must know, from what I have heard from Lords Bruce and Braggio, I think we are trying to help someone named Henry Tudor, the man who would be king. I would never say such a thing publicly, with a king sitting on England's throne . . . a king whose name is not Henry Tudor." Lizzie shrugged. "Men sometimes speak when they think a woman is not listening or interested in what they might say. Of course, I listen to every word Lord Braggio says."

She smiled. "When he is deep in conversation with Bruce, he oftentimes is not aware I have come near."

Relieved, Nicola sighed. "Yes, I am supposed to take a message from my father, who was murdered, to a certain Henry Tudor. We are sailing to a place where this Henry Tudor is now living. I am to bring the message my father left with me." Nicola shook her head, discouraged. "Lizzie, how am I going to get a chance to speak with Tudor alone? Truly, it is keeping me awake at night. Why would he ever deign to talk with me? I am not a person of importance. I am certain he never knew my father." Nicola sank down on her cot.

"Oh, I think you are someone of great importance," Lizzie informed her. Nicola laughed. "Why would you say that?"

Lizzie smiled. "Because you are my friend." She hugged Nicola. Moving to sit on the other cot, Lizzie looked at Nicola seriously. "I don't think it will be difficult for you to talk with him."

"But alone?" asked Nicola.

"He will be alone, I am certain. He has a reputation for liking the ladies. You are a lady. What other requirement is needed?" Lizzie smiled at her friend.

Nicola tipped her head. She had not thought of such an approach. "Are you certain?"

"Absolutely," Lizzie replied.

"You are right. That is a great idea." Nicola was excited. "I can deliver my father's message, only to him. Then leave. Simple. Perfect!"

"Well, except for one thing," Lizzie noted.

"What one thing?" Nicola frowned.

"Lord Drue will not like that idea at all," Lizzie warned. "He will hate it, in fact."

"That matters little. I need not have his approval to do what I need to do," Nicola stated, grasping at independence as it continued to slip away.

"We shall see. Come. Let us find Lord Drue and Lord Braggio," Lizzie bubbled. The two women tidied up themselves and the room as much as they could. After latching the door open to allow the air and sun inside, they headed for Drue's quarters. Smiling at the men they passed, they spread the feeling of imminent success around. The mood of the ship lifted.

"Whoever said it was bad luck to have women aboard?" Nicola over-heard Jon asking Bruce.

"Someone who left behind an irritating wife, I would suppose," came Bruce's reply. Nicola couldn't help but chuckle.

Lizzie boldly knocked on the door and was happy to see Braggio answer. He grinned, opened the door wide, and waved them both in. Bowing, he pulled up two more chairs and pushed a tray of cheeses and sliced meat toward them. Nicola and Lizzie took one look at each other and broke into smiles. Lizzie gently pushed the tray back. "I think it would be too early to start last evening's activities," she noted. "Although our buckets were emptied, I noticed."

Drue was glad to see Nicola seemed none the worse for her bout with the storm. "I suggest the dried bread. It works to settle your stomach. You will have to eat something later." He moved a tray with slices of hard rolls across the table. While Nicola was tempted to send it back also, she picked up a small one, and began to eat. Lizzie watched her for a minute, then picked up a piece and nibbled at it.

"Do you think we might get to land sometime today?" Nicola asked.

Drue nodded. "Yes. We should make the shore late this evening." Drue looked to Braggio, who nodded.

"Well, I have an idea how I can get an audience with Tudor," Nicola said.

Drue glanced at Braggio. "You do?" He waited for Nicola to go on.

"It seems he may like to entertain ladies frequently. I could go to him, and he would see me. Then, when we are alone, I could give him Father's message, and leave. I think he would have much to think on, so it would be easy to slip away." She smiled at Drue and Braggio.

Both men were staring at her. The room went still, until Drue's voice shattered the silence between them.

"You will absolutely *not* try that. I forbid it."

Shocked at his tone and hurt at the immediate rejection to what she felt was a great plan, Nicola raised her chin. "You, Lord Drue, will not tell me what I can and cannot do," she said, looking directly at him.

"Do not push me, Nicola." Drue's voice took on a dangerous tone.

"I will do as I please," Nicola told him. "You do not command me." She found she could not stop herself.

Lizzie looked from one to another. "Lady Nicola . . ." she started. Drue gave Braggio a withering look before glaring at Lizzie. Ignoring Drue, Lizzie turned to Nicola. "You never speak to . . . anyone that way. You are a lady," Lizzie told Nicola. "He is . . . You simply cannot talk to him that way."

"He is *what?*" Before anyone could stop her, Nicola blundered on. "By that measure, he"—Nicola nodded toward Drue—"should behave as a lord, but he does not. He is quite full of himself at this moment."

Lizzie's brows popped up, her face registering the discomfort she felt. She tried to speak, but Drue suddenly stood. "What did you just say? I am full of myself? You should be grateful I do not confine you to your room." His voice was like steel. "You will not speak to me again until I allow it."

Nicola glared at Drue. "I may not be allowed to speak to you, but that does not change the fact that I made a promise to a father I watched dying. I intend to keep that promise! Someone tell Drue that for me."

Before Drue could respond, Braggio interrupted, taking Lizzie gently by the arm. "Lizzie, come with me. Let us allow Nicola and Drue some time to sort this out."

"Confine me to my room?" Nicola continued, after Lizzie and Braggio had gone. She stood up angrily. "You cannot do that!"

"I can and I will, if need be. I am captain of this ship, lady," Drue informed a stunned Nicola. "There will be no more talk of you seeing Tudor as one of his lady guests. Am I quite clear on that?" Drue had walked toward Nicola and stood towering over her.

Nicola was seething. "I alone would be the one burned for heresy if Tudor felt so inclined. He could easily turn me over to whatever authorities there are in a land I know nothing about. How can you not see that?" She stopped only long enough to take a breath, then charged on. "Why does it matter how I get to him? Is it not my purpose to convince him to continue seeking his rightful place as king of England?" As she spoke, she could see Drue's eyes narrowing.

"You heard my command, Lady Weldon. There will be no more talk of that plan, lest you want me to throw you overboard—if you weren't quite so important, I might! Do you understand me?" Drue's voice was low and hard. "I will talk to Jasper. He can be certain you see Tudor alone."

Nicola fumed. "No! You will not talk to Jasper Tudor, nor anyone else! Only Henry Tudor will know what it is I carry. I am finished talking." She was standing toe to toe with Drue, but that only emphasized his height. Nicola abruptly turned away. "And I did speak to you . . . without your permission!" she added smugly as she started for the door. But at that moment came an urgent knocking.

"Yes?" Drue snapped, his eyes still on Nicola.

One of Bruce's men opened the door. Nicola imagined it was obvious to him that neither she nor Drue were very happy. He interrupted anyway, speaking rapidly. "We are being fired on. They fly the flag of Burgundy."

Drue immediately responded. Moving toward the door, he grasped Nicola's arm and forced her along. Outside his quarters, he ordered the messenger to escort Nicola to her cabin. To Nicola, he gave a curt nod. "You will stay in your room, both you and Lizzie. I do not care to allow anyone to know we have women on board. When it is safe, someone will come for you."

He started to walk away, when Nicola grabbed his arm. "Drue, do not get hurt. We . . . we need to finish our disagreement," she blurted. Fights never ended well for one party.

Drue stood for a second, looking at her. "Everyone will be safe, Nicola. Now go, before they see you." His voice had not softened. He turned and ran toward the cannon line. Men were bolting to stations, barrels were already being rolled closer to mid-deck, and others formed a relay to move cannonballs closer. Still other men were manning the sails while Bruce yelled instructions. To Nicola, as she was hurried along to her cabin, it was mildly comforting that each man appeared to have been in this state before. Win or die.

CHAPTER 47

Lord Lareau was pacing on the deck of his ship. The whole incursion into England had gone badly. Lord Weldon died, the daughter and his spy, useless as she was, died. To cap it all off, King Edward died. *Everyone dies in that cursed place. And I . . . I am forced to return with nothing to show!* Just then, the man sitting in the crow's nest called down.

"*Ship. Due east,*" he cried, pointing.

Scanning the horizon, Lareau found the ship in little time. She was too far away to tell if she was armed. "Get closer," he ordered. Studying the ship, he tried to decide if he would simply pass her by, or . . . *Much too small to be a cargo ship. Could not be carrying anything of any value, unaccompanied by escort. Simply crossing the Channel?* He watched the vessel moving through the waters. *There was a bad storm last night, so perhaps blown off course? Maybe, but why not get back on track?* As Lareau followed the ship, he noticed how swiftly it moved. Her speed told him she could not be carrying anything weighing much. He admired the structure. *Clean lines, small enough to slip in and out of ports easily. Just the kind of ship I need. While the duchess will never openly agree with the action, she certainly approves of any disarray caused by a little harassment of ships trying to cross the Channel. That ship is not English. Strange.* He ordered a warning shot. "Let us see how they respond."

He watched as the shot fell short, just as intended.

"They are just close enough, Lord Lareau," said his captain, who now stood beside him. "Would you like to take the ship?"

Lareau smiled at his captain. He was one of the best fighting men Lareau had ever known. However, his preferred stage was on dry land. He knew nothing of strategy fighting ship to ship. Neither did Lareau, but that ship looked to be easy prey. "Ah yes, I want the ship. Take her, but do not damage her."

The captain frowned. "I believe we must move closer, if we are to take her as is."

Lareau thought for a moment. "Fire another shot. This time, beyond her. I want them to know we can easily hit them if we so desire."

The captain stood behind one of the cannons, made quick adjustments in his head, then gave the order. The man manning the gun looked back at the captain. "Sir?" he questioned, looking back out at the target.

"You think that I am wrong?" the captain asked. When the man nodded, the captain noted, "Good. I do not want to hit her. Lord Lareau wants the ship intact. He likes how she moves." The man shrugged, adjusted the cannon, and fired it. The shot fell short only by several feet.

"Over her—I said *over*!" Lareau bellowed.

BRAGGIO WAS DIRECTING THE BOAT'S steersman. Maneuvering back slightly, he tried to not give the aggressor a side target. The firing ship was slower than Drue's ship, a fact Drue knew they must have not counted on. Most of the ships like his were for pleasure transport, and certainly not battling. Clearly, the *Guardiano* was neither a battleship nor a transport vessel. Since his ship was manned with a moderate number, Drue wondered why anyone would even fire on her. Looking at the ship, one could not have told that Drue actually did sail a ship built for battle. Not in a battle as a member of a flotilla, but more as a hit-and-run vessel. Built for speed, heavily armed, though well disguised and small enough to be more easily maneuverable, the *Guardiano* was perfectly built. Although Drue had utilized her in battles before, he had not foreseen trouble on this particular trip.

Braggio held the ship steady. Bruce leaned to Drue, pointing at the flag. Drue could see the captain of the aggressor scanning Drue's ship—her guns were well hidden behind ornately carved panels. Any indication of armament had been carefully disguised. She simply looked like any pleasure boat. Traveling alone between England and Europe's western coast would not be so unusual. "They must know we're not armed and that we do not carry valuable cargo, yet they fire on us. Why? Simply because they fly a Burgundy flag?" Drue asked, watching the captain.

"They want the ship. They think they can outfit it and make a neat trickster," Bruce said, as he stood waiting for the order to go after the assailant.

"Not a bad idea, now that I think on it," Drue noted dryly. "I think we could easily make them back down. But when that captain sees what we can do, he will be determined to take us, or die trying. Remember, he sails for Burgundy."

"We fly under the flag of Padronale. Would they still try us?" Bruce wondered aloud.

"I am certain word of what this vessel can do will get back to those he knows. Soon, we'll have every ship working for the highest bidder looking for us—believe me, the whole world will know the story." Drue sighed. "No, we do not have a choice." Drue looked at his friend. "Let's get this over with."

He looked back at his men standing by waiting for the next order. "I hate to do this, but we must engage, if they continue their aggression. They are not a match for what will come."

Close enough to pick out the captain of the other ship, he cursed the timing of this confrontation. He watched only the man seeming to give the orders. "I know that man. I know him well. He is a mercenary by the name of Lareau. Usually works for France, but he's wearing the colors of the Duchess of Burgundy. Flying under the Burgundy flag. France must know of Burgundy's move. I agree, Bruce. He wants my ship." For a second, he looked at Bruce, thinking. "Bring Nicola here."

Bruce frowned. "Are you certain?"

"Yes. I want to know if she can identify them. If I am correct, that is the man who killed her father," Drue replied.

Nɪᴄᴏʟᴀ ᴀɴᴅ Lɪᴢᴢɪᴇ sᴀᴛ ᴏɴ ᴛʜᴇ ʙᴇᴅ, listening to the sound of men running around, then the two shots. Now, it was deadly quiet. When Bruce knocked, it startled both ladies. "Yes?" Nicola called.

"'Tis I, lady. Lord Drue wishes to see you." Bruce opened the door. "Best to come quickly. Before the fighting starts." At those words, Nicola stood. She looked back at Lizzie, then pulled a shawl over her shoulders and followed Bruce.

Drue stood at the boat's side, watching the other ship. When Nicola joined him, he pointed to the ship. "Lady, I would like you to look at the man commanding that ship. Have you ever seen him before?"

Nicola studied the ship moving ever closer. It took but seconds for her to find Lareau. She stood back with a gasp, her fists reflexively clenched. She found herself trembling. "Look again. I must be certain," Drue gently commanded.

"I do not need a second look; it is a man called Lareau. He is the one who overtook my home and had my father tortured." Seeing the man again, even from a distance, filled Nicola with fear. "Can he get to me?" she asked.

ABOARD THE AGGRESSOR SHIP, Lareau carefully took note of every detail of the other ship again. Suddenly, he stared. He saw the lady come to the captain. "It is her! I am positive! She lives! Now there is a prize worth the fight. Take the ship, but do no harm to that lady. I want her alive."

DRUE STUDIED THE SHIP AGAIN and what he saw next clearly indicated grave danger for Nicola. There was Lareau, suddenly smiling—no, leering—at them, then gesturing wildly to his men, shouting orders that Drue wished he could hear. Unfortunately, he knew what this meant. "He has spotted Lady Nicola. It was a mistake to bring her up here! Lareau has gone mad. He is yelling and moving about like one who has lost his mind. His directives and motivation are clear to me, even from here."

Drue turned to Nicola. "Best you get back to your room, and quickly.

I think he no longer wants my ship, but much more than that. Bruce, take Lady Nicola back to her quarters." His voice was grim.

NICOLA WAS ALREADY RUNNING BACK to her cabin. Inside, she locked the door and ran to Lizzie. "It is him. The man who killed my father. He is the one firing at us. If he takes this ship, he will surely kill me, or have me tried as a traitor in England. Oh, Lizzie . . ." Nicola sank to the floor, numb and terrified all at once. The sight of Lareau brought back the image of her dying father, and, with that image, a great stab of fear. The odors in Lord Weldon's cell, the cold feeling of hopelessness and pain, it all came rushing back. Leaning over, she vomited into the bucket.

Lizzie knelt next to her friend and held her. "Pray, Nicola. We must pray Drue and the men aboard this ship can save us. Pray."

"I THINK WE HAVE TO SINK THEM," Bruce said. Drue nodded in agreement, watching as Bruce stepped away to speak with Braggio. There would be a battle. The command was given by Bruce, who was now standing on the bridge. Every man aboard the *Guardiano* was quiet, waiting for the first order to fire.

Drue walked up to stand between Braggio and Bruce. He spoke to the crew. "We fight to win, gentlemen. Not by a breath, but decisively. That ship wants Lady Nicola. So do I. I intend to make her my wife and your princess. Fight for Nicola. Fight for me."

The power carried in his simple command fired every man up. At his announcement, the cry went up. "For His Grace! For His Grace!"

Drue knew, by assessing the shots fired at him, that his own ship had a greater firing distance advantage. While he kept that in mind, the *Guardiano* moved farther away, then swung around, opened the gun ports, and fired.

The first shot fell onto the deck of Lareau's ship. Immediately, another shot hit the ship's mast. It fell down, crushing anyone unlucky enough to be stuck beneath it.

Lareau's ship fired again, hitting the farther side of the *Guardiano* and smashing the railing, sending splinters flying into men. Another cannonball fell short of the *Guardiano*. The wind had pulled the ships apart, reducing the force of the cannonball.

LAREAU ORDERED HIS CAPTAIN TO RAM the other ship, but his captain shook his head. "My lord, the mast is gone. We cannot move toward her fast enough to do any damage."

"You heard me—ram that ship! I want that lady! Just get us close enough to board her. Now get to it!" Lareau felt as if he had gone half mad with the taste of what Nicola as prisoner would do for him. It was useless to resist his need to acquire her.

Lareau watched as his captain raced toward the steersman. As he reached him, the steersman fell, his chest pierced by a flying piece of wood. The captain grabbed the wheel and tried to change directions. The maneuver was slow without sails to help, and the process made Lareau's blood boil. Finally turned in the proper direction, Lareau's ship was headed directly toward the other.

DRUE'S MEN FIRED TWO CANNONBALLS in quick succession, hitting the bow of Lareau's ship. Drue ordered the sights adjusted to the water level. Three cannons exploded, projecting the balls just below where the water met the hull. Lareau's ship gave a great shudder, then began to sink. Drue's last order was a success—he knew there could be no rescue for the men now crying out for help, trying to swim toward the *Guardiano*. No one could be left to tell the story of his ship and his cargo. At last, the shouts and cries died away.

When there were no longer men floating, and only debris, Drue left his post. He spent two more hours looking after the men on his ship, talking to the wounded. Finally, he stood watch over the dead for a long time. His losses were few, only five, but with every man who had perished, Drue felt like he had lost part of his soul. He was accustomed to working alone. The only life he usually directed was his own. This was different. He glanced toward Nicola's quarters. He had not the stomach to take up their argument, or even to talk to her.

Braggio approached him, and the sight of his friend was a balm. They had been together many times before, but when Drue became an assassin for his father, their lives had changed. Drue knew that to keep his father and his kingdom safe amid the turmoil surrounding them, he had to do whatever was necessary. There were only two Vieneto sons. One would be king, the other would be the crown's executioner. For the first time since he had knelt before his father and received that commission, he grew weary of all it took from him. Braggio had been in many battles, had seen men killed, and knew well the cost of victory, even for the victorious.

"You will make a good king," Braggio told him, putting his arm across Drue's shoulders. "Better than your brother. Men will follow you."

Drue did not acknowledge the comment.

"Come, my friend," he told Bruce. "The skies look to be calm. We sail for Brittany. We sail for Tudor. We reach land this night."

Together, they walked to Drue's quarters.

The battle and night wind had again changed their speed and direction. When the sun rose above the horizon, Drue felt they were near land. He opened his door. The sun exposed a distant shoreline. Not certain where exactly they were, he walked the ship's length, studying the shore. After speaking with his steersman, he had a better idea. Inside his quarters, a review of the map told him. Sending for Bruce and Braggio, he began planning. He hoped Nicola could remember more of what she'd seen in her vision—they might be able to find Tudor quickly. Tudor had tried once before to meet Richard in battle, only to be turned back because of weather. That retreat came after years of running and narrowly escaping with his life. Small wonder the man wanted to quit. Drue knew at this point that Nicola was their best hope, their only chance. She had to find a way to convince the young would-be king to stay in the fray. Could she do it?

NICOLA AND LIZZIE SAT HUDDLED TOGETHER on one bed. When the sounds of the fighting died away, they waited for someone to come to them. No one came. Eventually, the ladies fell asleep. Awakened by the sounds of activity outside their door, Nicola tried to freshen up. After combing and braiding her long hair, she changed her gown and pulled a robe over her shoulders. Opening the door, she was surprised to see the clouds were gone—the sun was bright and the sails billowed. In fact, there was little sign that any conflict had occurred, and none of the men working wore Lord Lareau's colors.

Walking toward Drue's quarters, Nicola was acutely aware of the wide berth every man now gave her. An uneasy feeling gripped her. She was nearly at Drue's door when she heard the first whisper. "They swore she is a witch." Nicola's heart lurched, her step faltered. Taking a breath, she took another step. She could hear indistinguishable whispers all around.

Nicola knew a response from her was necessary. *I must do this now if I would have them fight for a man I believe could be king. I have to try.* She stood still and looked around for someone with the authority to call the men together. Drue would not do. He was clearly the leader, but a man apart from the crew. It would have to be one of the men. She spotted an older man called Elric working the ropes. She knew the rest of the crew looked up to him, and he seemed to know everyone's duties. With determination, she walked to him.

"Elric," Nicola spoke to him, touching his shoulder.

He startled when she spoke to him. "My lady?" he responded, straightening up as he frowned at her.

"I hear the whispers from these men and know I am not wanted aboard this vessel. I also know condemned men are allowed to speak. I ask for that same privilege." Her voice was soft. "I am accused of something of which I am innocent and would like to address the men. I request the opportunity to speak in my own defense, as there are none here to do this for me, it would seem."

For a moment, the man stood staring at her. He knew full well that this lady was a favorite of Drue's, but he also knew the whisperings of the crew. The man who should have been standing in his place, taking the lady's order, would be Lord Braggio or Lord Bruce. "Of course, as usual, they are not around when I need them," he muttered. He nodded briefly to Nicola and turned to call out to the men.

Before he could, Nicola added, "In particular, I would speak to those among the men who are the most certain of my accusations."

Again, the man nodded. "I will call all men not needed at their station to ensure those who are speaking against you are present."

Anxious to hear what the lady might say, the men began to crowd around. Nicola looked at the eyes staring back at her. Some were just curious, some frightened, and others defiant. Calmly, she began. "On what grounds do you believe I am a witch? Why would you say that?"

"We heard what the men yelled last night. A dying man always tells the truth. They say you used magic to escape them. Your home was surrounded. The gates closed and carefully guarded, yet you were suddenly no longer there," one man boldly claimed.

"Ah, those dying men must have had a great deal of time to say all this," Nicola answered. Elric, who stood near her watching the proceedings, smiled.

The crewman who had just spoken mumbled, then admitted, "I heard about you before. From a man who was with that Lord Lareau."

Nicola pointedly looked at the sea of faces staring up at her. Her gaze settled on the man who had spoken out against her. "First, my home was *not* surrounded. That would be impossible. My father's home was built at the top of a ridge, surrounded by three walls. The fourth side met the cliff's edge, then dropped into the ocean, as anyone could tell looking at the structure. Three walls were surrounded, true enough. I cannot speak to the gates, as I did not use them when I left." She paused. The outspoken man looked around, sneering smugly.

Nicola continued, "I am certain you all are aware that every castle has secret passages allowing its inhabitants easy movement in and out of the structure. Father maintained a secret passage—a way to leave the castle unnoticed." Nicola stopped for a moment, thinking how best to describe the cliff trail. "The edge of the cliff was overgrown with brush. Everyone knew not to walk too close to the brush. However, few knew that the brush hid a trail leading down the face of the cliffside, descending to a place where the land's edge softened. At this place there is a pool, fed by water spilling from the rocks above it. The pool flows into the ocean. Behind this waterfall, a passage leads toward the heart of England. I knew the trail, as did several of Father's men. No one else knew. On the night we were attacked, Father's groomsman helped me. On Father's horse, I simply rode down the trail, which Father's horse knew well. I did not magically disappear."

The men relaxed. Some were even laughing at the crewman who had started the rumors. Nicola added, smiling, "Do you honestly think I would spend my days bending over a bucket filled with vomit, if I were capable to doing otherwise? I am now and will forever be indebted to each of you. We are mere humans, you and I, trying to stay afloat in an angry sea of political upheaval. Do not be afraid of me. Be fearful for me. The task I was given would be better handed to a man. My father did not have a son, only me."

When she had finished speaking, one man spoke up. "To Lady Nicola! We stand with you, lady!" The cry went up among the men. Nicola allowed herself a quiet sigh of relief. She turned to thank Elric for gathering her audience. He only nodded and went back to his business with the ropes.

One hill climbed, now to take the next. Nicola took a deep breath, then strode resolutely toward Drue's quarters.

BRUCE HAD STOOD UNNOTICED and witnessed the exchange between Nicola and the men. He nodded in satisfaction. *She handles herself well. The girl has grown into a woman. Drue should know of this.* Bruce slipped into Drue's quarters. When he finished relaying the event, Drue stood and walked around his table and began to pace slowly. He looked conflicted, and Bruce spoke again. "I think Lady Nicola will change Tudor's mind. If anyone can do that, it would be her. His uncle is too close to him—Henry will disagree with Jasper even if he thinks he is right. Jasper also feels the despair of so many defeats, narrow escapes, and long absences, and likely conveys that despair to Henry. Nicola feels none of those things. She has a calm way about her, Drue. She is the best one for this job."

Drue studied his friend. "Maybe. I pray you are right, Bruce." The idea Nicola had presented to get to Tudor alone still rankled Drue. He could not allow her to proceed with such a plan. Just thinking about it made him angry again. "Where is she now?"

Bruce opened the door and watched Nicola headed his way, her head down, her step firm and with purpose. Bruce smiled. "She is coming here as we speak. Good luck to you, Drue. Keep hold of your temper, my friend." Laughing, Bruce slipped out the door and was gone.

Hold my temper! I think not! Drue thought. He returned to his table and sat down, waiting for the confrontation he knew was coming. She would have to stand before him, listen to his command, and not argue, for once. He intended for her not to be comfortable. Not this time.

Drue bade her come in, and she stepped into his quarters. The look on her face told him she understood he was still quite displeased. "Lord Drue," she began, "I can see you have not changed your mind. I respect your opinion greatly; however, it is still my promise, and I intend to see it kept. If that means I slip into Tudor's room under false pretenses, so be it. I will have my time with him."

Drue stood, his anger charging every fiber of his being. *What is it with this damnable woman? I would be better served to tell her just who she is dealing with, and have it over with. She will do as I say, whether she likes it or not.* "You, lady, will *not* go to Tudor, until I decide how, where, and when. You will not present yourself as a possible liaison for his pleasure. You will remain on board this vessel, in our camp, or anywhere else I determine is best for you, until I, not you, plan a meeting between you and Tudor."

Nicola waited a moment before answering. She closed her eyes and replied, "I hear clearly what you are saying. You are reminding me that you love me." She waited another moment before opening her eyes.

Before he could respond, Nicola turned and left the room.

Drue stared after her. He had to admit, he could not dispute her assessment of his anger. *Mother, are you mixing all this together? Better you left me alone with my work. I have little time or use for any lady, especially one like her.* He looked back at the closed door. *I beg you to stay near her until she can speak with Tudor.* Drue walked around his table, sat back down, and ran his hand over the maps and notes. Shaking his head, he spoke to the empty room. "I need to get back on solid ground. I was not meant for life at sea." Drue leaned back in his chair. Staring at the ceiling, he forced himself to think about Tudor. Instead, his thoughts wandered to his family, such as it was.

Drue knew his mother had loved his father. She had never spoken one word against him. Yet, she had left his father's house and all it offered, and slowly moved farther and farther away, until she was once again on English soil. The one place, she always said, where she felt at peace and at home. That peace came with a terrible price. His mother was forced to leave behind a young son, too young to understand the workings of royal politics, religion, and a young woman's heart.

Drue's father had made certain his sons—Drue and his older half-brother, Cicero—both knew their father loved them, though the road each would take would be worlds apart. When Drue's training was complete, he realized he had a certain talent. That talent found its way into his father's strategies, schemes to play a quiet part in world politics and shape events to protect his kingdom and his people. Many times, those strategies called for the talents of a very potent and lethal assassin. It was well known that the king's monarchy was in protective hands as long as Drue stayed alive. Drue believed in his soul that he was following his destiny. But now, in this moment, Drue felt the first stirrings of a strange restlessness and dissatisfaction.

CHAPTER 48

Nicola returned to her quarters. "Lizzie, I have made a terrible mistake." Lizzie looked up, concern furrowing her brows. "I told Drue I know he loves me. He has said as much before, but I told him so, just now." Nicola sank down onto her cot. "What am I thinking? This cannot be spoken of at this time. There are too many things that depend upon my success with Tudor." Looking up at Lizzie, she felt near to crying. "How could I have done such a thing? A lady should not display such emotion."

"Why did you say it?" Lizzie asked, watching Nicola's face.

"I do not know." Nicola shrugged. "The words just came into my mind. I do not know from where. He was angry with me because I shared with him my plan to get to Tudor alone."

Lizzie sighed. "How did you get to the part of his feelings about you?"

"It just came to my mind, and out of my mouth," Nicola admitted glumly. "The worst is," she added quietly, "he will not want to be around me now. And I have feelings for him." Nicola looked at Lizzie. "Feelings that have no place in my life at this time. I must set them aside." With an air of determination, Nicola sat up. "I will avoid him, and set my feelings aside."

"Certainly," Lizzie replied drily. "You can do that with no trouble at all."

Drue came out onto the deck, looking to find Bruce. "Bruce!" he called to his friend when he spotted him. Bruce looked surprised to see Drue headed his way, walking the deck as if he had just received orders to march. Drue did have a mission in mind. Taking the hint, Bruce met Drue mid-ship.

"Yes, Your Grace," Bruce greeted him and, before Drue could object, added, "That is what you are, and to pretend otherwise is not going well, after the battle you helped all these men win. You are who you are, Drue."

Drue looked at Bruce and glanced around at the men closer to them. As he looked their way, they immediately found anything at all to look busy with. The effect was almost comical.

Drue nodded an unspoken acknowledgment of sorts—he would have to mull that one over. But for now, he had other things on his mind. "Please bring Lady Nicola to my quarters. Then, order food, for you, Braggio, Lady Lizzie, and Lady Nicola. For me as well. Meanwhile, I would know for certain when we will reach land. I believe it will be soon." With that, he retraced his steps. Inside his quarters, he poured a glass of wine and waited.

At the knock on their door, Lizzie opened it, much to Nicola's disappointment. Smiling at Bruce, she opened the door wider. "Please, Lord Bruce." She gestured toward the room.

Bruce nodded to Lizzie before addressing Nicola. "You are summoned to the captain's quarters, lady." He stood to the side, waiting expectantly.

Nicola could feel a knot forming in her stomach. *He is not going to let this go, I see. Pray I can keep my tears at bay, as well as my temper.* "Of course, Lord Bruce." Shaking her head to Lizzie, she followed Bruce out the door.

"Do not give in to him," Lizzie whispered as Nicola passed her. Nicola's eyes shot back to Lizzie. Lizzie was serious.

"Give in?" Nicola mouthed, frowning. Lizzie nodded, before closing the door.

The walk to Drue's quarters felt like it took forever, though Nicola desperately wished it would take even longer. At Drue's door, Bruce knocked before opening the door for Nicola. Nicola took a deep breath, then stepped into the beginning of a new world.

Drue stood and nodded to Bruce as he closed the door, leaving Drue and Nicola alone. "I know it is not customary for a lady to be alone in a man's room. Surely this is not the first time we have been alone. However, given the circumstances of our journey from the beginning, I feel this is the only arrangement that will allow both you and me privacy. We have some very serious things to discuss." With that, Drue nodded toward a chair across from his table.

Nicola sat down without speaking. She was so nervous she had to grip her hands together to keep them still in her lap. "Lady, first let me say, I am not angry with you. At least not as long as I do not think on your plan to get Tudor alone. Having said that, we will not discuss that plan again. Ever." He stopped speaking and watched Nicola.

Taking a second to gather her thoughts, Nicola responded, "Agreed, but only provided you are able to come up with another way I can get to Henry Tudor alone without drawing attention to myself. I care little for the possibility that anyone might accuse me of witchcraft. I also care little for the method in which England punishes witches." Looking at Drue directly, she waited for his response.

Drue's tone remained firm. "You did not understand me, I see. I will not entertain any other response from you but total agreement. We will not speak of that plan again ever again. Whether or not I am able to come up with some way to get you and Tudor alone matters not. That plan is dead and gone. Period."

His demeanor was different than Nicola had ever seen it. He appeared more commanding somehow. Nicola looked past him, at the maps on his wall and at the room. Eventually, her eyes returned to Drue. He sat perfectly still, waiting. "I agree, Lord Drue. The plan was not to your liking, but"—and she could not help but smile—"it was a good plan. I can move quickly when the need arises." Her smile widened at the frown in Drue's face.

"Your humor is ill-placed," he answered. In spite of himself, he smiled too. The air between them felt softer to Nicola. She knew it felt the same for Drue.

"There is something else you should know, Nicola. I would expect your behavior toward me not to change once you discover what it is. This may not be an easy task at first, but I have faith you can handle it." Again Drue smiled. Then, he became serious. "Lady, I am not who you think me to be."

"You intend to say you are not an assassin?" Nicola interrupted. "Lord Drue, you forget, I have seen you work. You are very good at what you do, as you said."

"I am an assassin, Nicola. But I am also one of two sons of King Vieneto. His is a small kingdom north of the Papal States. I am next in line for the throne, after my older brother, King Cicero. I am usually addressed as 'Your Grace' or 'Your Highness.'" Drue stopped speaking and watched Nicola. She imagined that her surprise was written all over her face. Drue spoke again. "I was sent by my father to assist Henry Tudor. The men on this boat are the only ones who know who I am. England would have executed me had anyone known my true identity. As you certainly must be aware, countries stir up politics in other countries every day. The attack on your father's home is one example."

Nicola did not know how to respond. She sat staring at him. Her mind exploded with all the problems this news posed for her. *This is a mess! What might he decide to do with Henry Tudor? What will become of Lizzie and me when this trip is over? How could he have kept something like that from me?* "Why are you telling me this now?" Again, the question just came to her mind and out of her mouth.

"It was time," he replied simply. Nicola sat still, as if made from stone. She no longer trembled; she no longer was frightened or angry. Only stunned beyond reason.

"There is something else," Drue started.

"There is more?" Nicola asked weakly.

At this, Drue laughed. "Yes, there is more. I never planned on having to deal with another person, especially a woman, in all this." Drue's voice softened. "I never planned on falling in love with you. I never planned on falling in love with anyone. But I have, and I intend to see it through. I intend to marry you. So, Nicola Weldon, you had best get used to doing as I ask."

Nicola could think of nothing to say. She stood as if to leave, but sat back down. "Am I dismissed?" She looked at Drue, uncertain how she should act.

Drue grinned. "Never, until we both are dead and gone. But you may leave if you wish. You and Lizzie are to join us for the evening meal. I like to eat late. I will send for you when it is time." He stood when Nicola stood. Drue rounded his table and stopped before Nicola. Lifting her face, he gently kissed her lips. "You have my heart, Nicola. You will always have my heart. I will always adore and protect you."

Nicola was beyond any coherent thought. Too much information in too little time. She let him lead her to the door. When it opened, Jon stood outside and, at Drue's direction, walked Nicola to her quarters.

Lizzie was waiting anxiously. "What happened? Are you all right?" Lizzie asked.

Nicola still felt as if she were lost in a maze, unsure of the way to escape. "I am not sure. He is a prince, Lizzie. I have yelled at him, scolded him, and told him what I expected of him." Nicola looked at Lizzie, panic welling in her chest. "I have been treating him as if he were one of my father's men! I even told him he was full of himself, more than once. What happens now?" When Lizzie said nothing, it suddenly dawned on Nicola that Lizzie did not seem at all surprised. "And you, Lizzie, are you not stunned?"

"Actually, no," Lizzie replied. "Lord Braggio told me about His Grace before, but made me swear I would not tell anyone, especially you, until it was revealed to you by Drue himself. All of his men have been sworn to secrecy." Lizzie looked at Nicola quizzically. "Is he still angry at you?"

"No, he is not." Nicola blushed. "We should be ready to have the evening meal with him. He said he likes to eat late, and will send for us." Nicola quickly busied herself looking through the few belongings they had in their travel bags.

"We have nothing to wear," Lizzie moaned. "We dare not attend his meal dressed as scrub ladies. What will we do?"

Nicola stood up and spoke firmly. "Nothing has changed with us, only with him. It was his idea to bundle us off on this horrible trip. He is quite aware we have nothing different to wear. You will fix my hair, I will fix yours, and we will be ready."

Lizzie glanced at Nicola's dress, then at hers. She began to laugh. "You are right, Nicola. Only he has changed. He is headed for a great surprise. I have no knowledge of how the women from his country dress, but too bad. Here we are."

Nicola smiled, but it brought another more serious matter to light. "I must speak to him, before we go any further." Lizzie held up a hand to stop her, but Nicola was already at the door. "I shall return shortly, I am certain."

DRUE SPOKE WITH HIS MEN. Restrictions were removed. He was again the prince of Padronale in name. Drue roamed around the deck, stood at the side of the ship, and stared out to sea.

"You seem troubled, my friend," Bruce spoke quietly.

"Yes, perhaps," Drue replied.

"If it is any comfort to you, you are still and always will be the one man I am sworn to die for—sworn before your father, your brother, and all the court. I remember your face, when you first learned your father was dying, leaving Cicero the new king and you next in line for the throne, after Cicero."

"It was an honor I cared little to accept. I loved my father and I love my brother, but my chosen life suits me well. There was never any reason to change."

"Well, now, there is, and I think you find it uncomfortable," Bruce said, smiling. "Every man gets bitten, eventually. It will be a grand experience."

"Humph." Drue turned to Bruce. "And you? Why are you protected from such a grand experience?" Bruce just laughed, and Drue made to walk back to his quarters. The time to find Tudor and turn around his thinking again overshadowed all else. Drue's thoughts wrestled with what his next move could be. The fight had held him up and the storm had blown them off course—and for certain King Richard would be trying all manner of schemes to capture Henry and return him to England, while working to raise an army. Drue needed to get to Tudor before he left Brittany, before he sought sanctuary within another country. Where could he go? Certainly not France—France and England had a long history of adversity, and the French king was already making noise to indicate he was considering "selling" Henry for money and men. Spain? Perhaps. Spain always hung on the horizon, posing a quiet but constant threat to England.

Drue's thoughts were interrupted by knocking.

"Yes?" he asked. "Who's there?"

Jon opened the door. "Lady Nicola wishes to see you, Your Grace." Jon opened the door and Nicola stepped inside. She stood at the door and flinched when it shut. Drue looked at her. She stood so hesitant and unsure of herself—a Nicola he had never before seen. Still, he was silent, waiting for her to speak.

"I will not be joining you this evening," Nicola began.

"And why is that?" Drue asked.

"I am not . . . I do not . . ." she stuttered. "I know not how to act around you," she finished lamely.

Drue did not speak. Nicola tried again. "I think my place has changed. I do not belong here. I think I must not . . . What I was prepared to say is suddenly too painful to accept."

Drue remained silent.

"Please," she implored, "do not just sit there and stare at me. Say something."

"You are uncomfortable around me now?" Drue asked. A small smile broke the severity of his expression.

"How am I supposed to act now?" Her anxiety appeared to be replaced with irritation.

Drue stood and walked around his table. His hands were behind his back, and he strode around the room for a moment, not looking at her. "First of all," Drue began, looking at Nicola, "you are not to scold me again, in the company of anyone. You are not to order me about. You will learn to hold your tongue when you are angry. You do say the strangest things when you are angry." He paused, pleased to see his words were having the desired effect. She was nearly boiling over now. Her face was flushed and her hands were clenched into fists. "Most importantly, you must never strike me." He stopped speaking. Nicola took one step toward him.

"Forgive my interruption. I will *not* be dining with you this evening!" Nicola's voice was flat as she tried to step around him. He stopped her.

Holding both her shoulders, he bent to look directly into her eyes. "You will continue to love me and must trust me." His voice had softened. He held her firmly. Nicola was astounded at his order. She could feel her resolve slipping. "You do belong here, or wherever I happen to be."

"Love you? I love you?" she whispered. Her eyes were wide, her face displaying the shock she felt. Slowly, she regained her composure. "And you?"

"And I will continue to adore you, to love you, and to protect you." He smiled.

Nicola shook her head. "This cannot be. You know that. You are in line for a throne—I am . . . nothing. You need a woman of power. Someone who can sit by you and support you. I am not that woman."

Drue continued to hold her. "You are that woman. You will sit by me. You already support me. You are who I love. We need not speak like this again. I have no need to explain myself, nor do you. We did not choose the hour, but it has come. This thing we do, we will finish it together. Then we can look to tomorrow. My Nicola." Drue released her shoulders, only to pull her closely and embrace her. "Are we agreed?"

Nicola looked up at him. "Yes, we are agreed." She smiled, but her smile quickly disappeared. "What do I call you?"

"You may call me by name whenever we are alone, or among our friends. In the company of guests and others, a formal title would be more appropriate." He smiled down on her. "Do not worry. It will all come in good time." He released her. "You *will* be dining with me this evening." He laughed softly at her expression.

Nicola started to leave, but Drue took her arm. "You must ask to take your leave."

"Are you quite serious?" Nicola asked suspiciously. "I think you may be trifling with me."

"Oh I am quite serious. But you may leave, lady." Drue smiled at her again as he sat back down at his table. Nicola bowed slightly, then left. *I think I could get used to this,* Drue thought to himself.

NICOLA OPENED THE DOOR to her quarters. Lizzie sat in the lone chair, waiting. Two gowns were lying on her bed, clean though well worn. Nicola sat on her bed and looked at Lizzie. Lizzie jumped up. "So tell me what happened," she bubbled. "I am quite happy . . . to be dining with Braggio."

"I am not sure I can do this. I would much rather have a quiet meal with you. He is a prince, first in line for the throne. His brother is now the king." Nicola's face was filled with dismay. "Lizzie, have you thought on what will happen to us after we finish with Tudor? You will most likely wed Lord Braggio. I suppose you will stay wherever he calls home. What am I to do?"

"Drue may be a strange one, but he loves you." Lizzie sighed with what sounded like relief. "I think he has cared for you for a long time. Now that his secret is out, I feel so much better."

"You feel better?" Nicola asked, surprised.

"Think, Nicola—we have escaped capture, weathered a storm, and survived a sea battle. Now we only must find Tudor. You realize we are nearing the end of our quest." Lizzie smiled.

"Yes, now we must only find Tudor." Nicola could not begin to imagine how. Or what exactly she would say to him. "We should clean up the best we can and change. I would not like to keep His Grace waiting. 'His Grace' sounds so far removed from what I thought him to be." *I cannot think to continue with Drue. His family will surely be against me. I am not of royalty. In fact, I am a destitute orphan.* Her mind turned to her old home, but she pushed those thoughts aside.

When Nicola and Lizzie had changed clothes, cleaned their shoes, and styled their hair, Jon escorted them to Drue's quarters. Inside, Drue, Bruce, and Braggio were enjoying a glass of wine. The men stood when the ladies entered. Both ladies curtsied to Drue.

When all had eaten and the dishes were taken away and fresh wine was set down, Drue began speaking. "Thank you both, Lady Nicola and Lady Lizzie, for joining us. We will leave ship in the morning. There is a small castle near our docking site that has been readied for us. Bruce, who is the lord of that castle, has graciously agreed to allow us shelter as long as we have need of it. Our first business is to find out exactly where Tudor stays. The message I received tells me Henry is set on stepping aside. Jasper has done a superb job preventing Henry from sending formal, written notice of that nature to any kingdom, including England. His mother, of course, is adamant he stay in the hunt for England's throne. Admittedly, he and Jasper can only hang on so long. In truth, Henry knows little of real life in his home country, England. It speaks well of his determination, to have stayed on this course for so many years."

Drue went on. "We will have work ahead of us. Braggio, I am sending you in first, to feel out the general mood of the people nearest our landing point. Lizzie, you will accompany him. Bruce, you and your men should make ready for a possible battle, if we are forced to leave before we have finished. I know you have several men who are the best spies known. Use them." Turning to Nicola, he continued, "Lady Nicola, you and I will work on finding the Tudors. I would expect everyone to be ready to disembark at first light." A long discussion followed while the men reviewed how each would complete their task.

Finally, Nicola spoke up. "How specifically might Lizzie and I help?"

Bruce spoke first. "There is nothing either of you can do to assist me or my men." He looked to Braggio.

"We will pose as husband and wife, Lizzie," Braggio informed her. "As a couple, traveling, we might pick up any loose talk from the tavern." Braggio glanced at Drue. "We will plan on returning to the castle in two days at the most."

Drue stood to walk around the room. "By then, Nicola and I will have devised a plan to get to Henry Tudor—that is, as soon as we locate him. Lord Braggio, you will, of course, be on the lookout for any possible additions to our troops. Henry will need all the help we can give him when he faces King Richard. Richard is a superb tactician. He will be fighting to maintain his rule. The fight will be hard." Drue crossed the room and stood near Nicola, who looked to be deep in thought.

NICOLA WAITED UNTIL ALL HAD GONE. "I must speak with you, Drue." She chose to use the same informality she had always used with him.

To say what needed to be said, Nicola knew she must be as comfortable as possible. She could not hesitate, for fear he would know that what she was about to say was not what she felt in her heart. Drue closed the door and led her to one of the large chairs beside the round table that had just held their meal. He sat, but Nicola refused the offered chair.

"Drue, I have had some time to think on what you have shared with me," Nicola began. "I thank you for the trust you have placed in me, but I must share with you how I feel about this tangle I find around me." Drue frowned, his expression intense, and Nicola went on. "I know little of the goings-on in any court. I do know that a man of your rank is expected to marry someone who will increase his country's standing in the political arena . . . someone who is of royal birth, to protect any sons he might have. Someone highly educated and financially sound, as he must be."

The frown on Drue's face deepened.

"Drue," Nicola continued softly, gently, "you know I am none of these things. I could not, in all good conscience, allow you to proceed with your feelings. This thing we share, however wonderful, is not to be." Nicola's voice broke, and her eyes filled with tears. "Your love for me will be all I ever need, the rest of my life. My feelings for you are deep and always will be, but I cannot allow this to continue. I ask only that you stay with me until I can keep my promise to my father. Then I release you from any obligation you may have or think you have. I will be gone from your life, and you will be free."

Drue stood up, his face flushed, lending fire to his eyes. "You think you can discard me so easily? You think you can use me to get to Tudor, then brush me aside?" He stood before her. Her face was turned up to him, her eyes bright with tears, but he saw nothing. "You, Lady Weldon, may leave, now!"

Taken aback by his behavior and tone, Nicola could not reply. She tried to reach for his arm, but he stepped backward and turned away. Nicola was left staring at his back. Struggling to prevent calling his name, she whirled and fled. She could barely make it to her quarters before breaking down. Thankful Lizzie was not in the room to witness the aftermath of her heart breaking, Nicola changed into her sleeping gown and slipped beneath the bedding. Under the cover of darkness, she wept. When Lizzie finally came in,

Nicola lay facing the wall, empty of tears. Lizzie moved about quietly, settling into bed herself.

Her heart was torn. *I must return to England, as soon as possible. I do not belong in the country we sail for. I pray we find Tudor quickly so I can leave this behind.*

CHAPTER 49

Henry Tudor read yet another of his mother's letters—as always, it begged him to stand strong. "You were meant to be king, Henry," his mother, Lady Margaret, wrote. "That is God's wish."

Henry had heard the same lines so many times that they rang hollow. If God wanted that for him, why was he forced to flee for his life over and over? Why did he spend every waking moment looking over his shoulder for another surprise attack? Jasper always agreed with Henry's mother. But Henry could tell Jasper was also beginning to waver. They were both tired. Tired of running, hiding, suspecting every move anyone near them made, and trying to keep up with the constant barrage of tricks that were being used to convince France and Brittany to give him up. Henry Tudor had no home. He belonged to no country. There were none willing to stand for him. All these years had only served as training. *But training for what?* he asked himself. He could fight, he believed he could inspire men to stand with him, but even that would fade if he did not believe it himself. Now, they were to break camp again, head out in the early morning, farther from the coast and farther from France . . . and England. Henry threw his mother's letter into the fire and watched it burn. "I am sick of it, Jasper. Sick of it all."

Jasper clasped Henry's shoulder. "I know, I know. If taking a throne were easy, there would be no long-ruling kings. It is not for the faint-hearted." Jasper watched his nephew stare at the burning papers. "But we go on, Henry. We must go on."

"How long?" Henry turned to Jasper. "How long can I go on? How can anyone expect me to stay this course?"

Jasper looked into Henry's eyes. "If you quit, all the men in England who stand for you are lost. All the men who are uncertain about you will change sides. England will be in chaos again. You must not quit, Henry. You must keep fighting, although this may not seem like a fight to you. At this time, you are not on a battlefield, with men behind you, waiting for your command. But it is a fight, just the same. How you handle this will tell many how great a king you will be. And you will be a great king, Henry Tudor. Mark my words."

Henry shook his head, but eventually grudgingly nodded. "I think I could do the right thing if I only got the chance. But, Uncle, I tire of this life. I am losing the fire to keep running and no longer feel the fight within." He clasped Jasper's shoulder. "I am sorry, Uncle. I know you have given up your life for me."

"All the more reason why you should not quit now . . . not when Margaret is actively seeking men to fight for you. Not when the climb to the throne has suddenly become much shorter. In only two years, the claimants to the throne of England have gone from five to one. Only one stands in your way. We can do this, Henry. I know we can. We must!"

"I hear what you are saying, Uncle. And we shall see," said Henry, taking his leave. He headed to his sleeping room, where a woman awaited him and would serve as distraction. *Hopefully the whore is gentle tonight. I need gentle.*

Jasper watched his nephew walk away.

AS SOON AS NICOLA LEFT, Drue stormed from his quarters. *She thinks to set me aside? I am the one who sets aside any woman I do not want. She is the daughter of a man accused of treason–she has no home, no fortune, and no title. But she would set me aside!* He strode angrily along the ship's side, from bow to stern, over and over. Unaware of activity around him, he paced, seething. Each time he passed her quarters, his anger grew. Yet, try as he might, he could not deny that he loved Nicola. The inability to ignore that feeling only intensified his desire to command and chasten her, to demonstrate his station. He might banish her from his mind, but he could not banish his feelings from his heart. Slowly, a plan began to form. *She will soon find it is not so easy to return to England.*

THE GOSSAMER RAYS OF THE MORNING sun were just visible when the vision struck. Nicola had finally fallen into a fitful sleep when the image seemed to explode into her head. She could smell the smoke and feel the heat. Instantly alert, she bolted from the bed and ran to the door. Her eyes quickly scanned the ship. All was still and quiet. *It was a dream. I had a dream.* "It was so real," she whispered.

Slowly, she returned to bed and lay down. A strange feeling enveloped her. Closing her eyes, she tried to relax and waited. The same image came again. This time, she could see an older man trying to drag someone from a burning structure. The building came crashing down, and Nicola flinched. The older man was trying to lift what appeared to be a younger man onto a horse. The flames, smoke, and noise made the horses fight to pull away. Swirling, the scene shifted, and Nicola could see a group of men riding through a thickly forested area. The man at the front pointed to a broad column of smoke rising to meet gathering clouds in the distance. Nicola had no idea who the riders were, but she was certain the older and younger man were Jasper and Henry Tudor.

Nicola dressed hastily and ran to Drue's quarters. Pounding on his door, she waited. Braggio answered the door and glanced toward Drue, who was standing bent over his table studying several maps.

Drue spoke before Nicola could. "I have not sent for you and have no time to see you." Braggio's face registered surprise, though he kept silent. Drue continued to study his maps.

Nicola pushed past Braggio. "You may be lord of all you survey some other time. Now, you must make all haste to find Henry Tudor, as he may perish in a fire." To Nicola's own surprise, her voice was firm and level. She looked into Drue's eyes without flinching. The time had come to accept who she was—her father's daughter.

At her words, Drue's demeanor changed. "What did you see, and when?" he asked, standing erect again.

Nicola closed her eyes and willed the images back, praying they would come. They came. She began to describe what she was seeing. Drue asked questions, and she answered the best she could.

"The riders? What about the riders?" Drue asked.

"There are four or five. They, too, see the fire." Opening her eyes, she added, "They are close to him, but we are closer." She turned to leave, glancing back at Drue. "If you wish to come, you had best move quickly, Your Grace." With a short nod, she was gone.

Braggio stood at the door of Drue's cabin and called out, "Horses, Jon, unload the horses! We ride immediately."

Drue was already buckling his weapons on. He started out the door, then paused. "Perhaps not immediately." Drue stopped Jon. Looking at Braggio and Jon, he said, "It will draw too much attention if we all go now. Our plan has changed. Tell Bruce to ready his men, but stay inside the castle walls, out of sight. Send Lizzie with Bruce and his men. Braggio, you come with me. We must not be seen until necessary. You can get back to Bruce if we need help."

Drue knew how to get Nicola to Tudor. She would not like it, but it would work. He called back to Braggio. "Tell Jon to bring extra shoes and a cloak." Without explaining, he stepped out onto the deck.

A quick survey told him his plans were already moving ahead. As always, Bruce and Braggio knew him well, and they did not question his logic. As Drue walked down the gangplank, he caught sight of Nicola. Already seated on her father's horse, wrapped in a worn cloak, her hair flying about her head, she was beautiful. One of the most beautiful women he had ever seen. She was no longer the frightened girl they had rescued on the cliff road. The time had not been so long, but what she had lived through had matured her.

He smiled to himself, then remembered their last talk. He knew his pride still prevented him from hearing what she had tried to tell him last night, but no matter—there was no space for that variety of softness. He already had a plan in mind for the day when Tudor no longer needed their support. He would see her humbled and shamed. She would find she still needed him when she was abandoned on foreign soil. He would be certain the land would not be friendly to England. It caused him a slight pang of guilt, his plans for Nicola, but that would be something he would have to bury.

NICOLA SAT ON HER FATHER'S HORSE and waited. "If they do not come soon, I will ride out alone. I have not come this far and gone through all I have suffered, to let Tudor slip through my hands." Feeling she was being watched, Nicola faced Lizzie and spoke softly. "I cannot tell you, with so many ears around us, what I learned last night. Only know that I will see to it you are not affected by all that happened. You are my only friend, Lizzie. My only friend."

Lizzie nodded. "And you are my only friend, too, Nicola. I pray we are both safe and strong once your promise has been kept." Wistfully, she added, "And though he will never take your place in my heart, I do have Braggio. I never believed a man would love me, knowing me. But Lord Braggio loves me. He will protect and care for me, I feel sure of it." Lizzie looked at Nicola, her face clouding. "Nicola, your eyes are bright with tears," she said.

"It's nothing. I am sure you are right, Lizzie. About Braggio." Nicola couldn't help but keep the sadness from her voice, though she wanted to express joy for her friend.

Their conversation stopped short when Drue rode up and addressed Lizzie. "Lady Lizzie, you are to remain with Bruce and his men, in the castle."

Lizzie looked at Braggio, her eyes imploring him to intercede on her behalf. "I do not like leaving Nicola alone. But if I must . . ." Braggio barely moved his head to acknowledge her, and Nicola was relieved that Lizzie would be kept from potential danger. Lizzie squeezed Nicola's hand and rode back to where Bruce and his men were readying to ride.

Drue turned to Nicola. "Where do you believe him to be, lady?" His tone was even and respectful, but it had lost the warmth Nicola had come to expect. Her heart ached.

Quietly, she replied, "I do not know this place, but I can tell you what it looks like. There is a settlement around them. The huts are not as small or as poorly made as those you would see in England. There are pens for the livestock, and crop fields." Closing her eyes, Nicola continued, "Beyond the settlement, there is a range of mountains. I can hear water rushing near, too loud for a small stream. The trees are very large . . . they must be very old." Frowning, she opened her eyes. "So much is burning. Everyone is very frightened."

Drue replied, "Makes it more difficult to find Tudor. Few will be willing to speak to you."

"The settlement looks as though there must have been families." Nicola shook her head sadly.

Drue asked, "Braggio, where are we to go? How long will it take us to get to him?"

"If he even survives his wounds," Nicola added softly to herself, frustrated with how slowly everything was moving along.

Braggio thought for a moment, then pointed ahead. "They are staying in the village of the millers. Nicola's description fits the place." Braggio nudged his horse, and the four rode out.

Jon, Braggio, Nicola, and Drue all rode in silence for an hour. Nicola suddenly pulled up. Everyone stopped with her. Nicola searched the skies. There had to be smoke; they were getting closer. Her anxiety to get to Tudor before the mysterious riders found him increased.

The others in the group searched the skies as well, and Drue suddenly stood up in his stirrups and pointed to their left. "Smoke, there! It is still dark; it has not risen so high yet. We are getting closer. Nicola, you move to the back. I would not risk your injury if we are forced to fight."

Drue, Jon, and Braggio rode on. Nicola let them pass to take up her position in the rear. The faint sounds of men shouting caught her attention, coming from their left. Drue and his party rode toward the sounds.

Nicola was unprepared for what they came upon.

There, in a trampled area, scattered about, lay the butchered bodies of children, men, and women, many clutching infants. It appeared as if everyone had taken flight in a desperate though unsuccessful attempt to escape. The victims had been chased down. In the distance, the sounds of shouting grew.

Nicola sat speechless, her heart shrunken inside her chest. Tears fell from her eyes and a soft moan escaped her. Drue had turned to stop her approach, but was too late. He rode up and dismounted. Standing next to her, he spoke, but she could not even process what it was he said. He reached up and pulled her down, holding her as she trembled. Glancing at the plume of smoke, now darker and thicker, he led her to his horse. Drue mounted, then reached for Nicola. Holding her closely, he turned his horse in the direction of the smoke. Jon was already leading Nicola's horse, just ahead of them. Nicola was aware of little around her, but the comfort of Drue's arms around her brought on quiet. And so they rode, watching the plumes of smoke grow more ominous, the closer they came.

Braggio was now riding in the front. He held his hand up. Everyone stopped. Glancing back at Drue, Braggio nodded toward another clearing before them. The few men remaining were still fighting a fire that was growing. Neither Henry nor Jasper were anywhere to be seen.

Without hesitation, Drue got off his horse and slid Nicola to the ground. "I know not who did this, nor why, but I do know, without the mills and buildings, these people can never survive. Most of the livestock has likely been butchered along with their families. We will offer what help we can." Drue spoke softly to Nicola. "You will be safe here. Stay within the cover of the surrounding brush. I will come for you when we have done all we can." He kissed her forehead. Nicola watched him walk away. When he looked back at her twice, she could see in his eyes his reluctance to leave her.

"Drue, take care. The riders are close now. They will fight you," Nicola called after him.

Drue turned to look at her. "I do not die this day, Nicola." Turning, he departed, followed by the men with him. Jon had hidden and secured the horses, but the smell of smoke so close made them nervous. Thinking to quiet them, Nicola left her cover and stood with them, speaking softly. Slowly, they settled. Focused on the smoke and what little she could see of Drue and the men, Nicola failed to notice the men coming upon her until it was too late—she heard their voices just as they spied the horses. Stooping low, Nicola slipped around behind the horses and moved away. The men rode closer to the horses, then began to look for the riders. It took little time for them to find Drue and his men.

At a whistle from Braggio, Drue quickly stepped behind a broken wagon. Yelling to the men with him, Drue watched as the large, fully armed leader of the intruders rode into the middle of the settlement and called out, "Drue, step forward! It is you I am looking for!"

When the men were out of sight, Nicola began moving the horses around the village to allow Drue and his men a quicker escape.

Holding her breath, Nicola watched as one of the millers ran out toward the mounted men. "Leave, sir. We burn the sickness here." The man was ragged, his body was smudged with soot, and he was barefoot. Several other millers leaned out from around pillars and doors. The smell of burned flesh rose with the smoke. They all appeared ill and weak. The leader looked around. The men with him were already backing slowly away.

Nicola's stomach turned when she realized the intruder would certainly notice the horses had been moved. She waited, fearing what the man's reaction might be. She heard him yell that he had been tricked as the riders thundered back into the burning village.

Nicola could see a cart in the center with several bodies being unloaded and tossed into a burning building. Though she knew this would add credence to the tale of sickness; the sight was horrifying. Praying the ploy would work, Nicola watched the riders begin to pull back once more. She held her breath while the leader looked around the compound. Relief washed over her when the riders left.

From the shadows, Nicola called. Drue and his men followed. Everyone mounted. He leaned down to the miller nearest to him. "I cannot linger here—I bring danger to those of you remaining. I will return when it is safe for you and for me." The man he spoke to nodded, saying, "God keep you. God keep you all!" Turning his horse, Drue led Nicola and his men opposite from where the intruder and his men had ridden.

Nicola shifted into the space between Drue and his men in order to alert him of her intuition. "Tudor is close—I can feel it," she called.

Drue pulled his horse up. "Where? What direction?"

"Ahead, he is ahead. It is a small hut. He and his uncle are alone," Nicola replied.

"We lead that madman to Tudor if we continue," Braggio noted.

"We do. We will stop the madman, as you call him," Drue replied. He rode ahead, calling for Nicola to follow. When he had taken her deeper into the woods, he stopped. "Here, you stay here, deep within this tangle. Do not come out, lady." His voice was stern, but Nicola did not care. She only prayed Drue and his men would survive.

DRUE AND BRAGGIO RODE A SHORT DISTANCE ahead before ordering his men to scatter. They faded into the forest alongside the narrow trail. Silence fell. Not even the horses could be heard. Shortly, the sound of approaching riders disturbed the quiet. The leader was even with Drue, when Drue's arrow struck him. He died as he fell off his horse. The next closest man died the same way. The remaining three tried to turn around. In the confusion, another man fell victim to a well-placed arrow. The excited horses ran into the two remaining men trying to escape. A fourth man fell, followed by the last.

"Jon," Drue called, "return to the village. Tell them where these men are. The bodies should be burned, quickly. Let them have the coins and anything else of value. The weapons must be hidden well. If anyone looks for these men and finds weapons in the village, the village will be destroyed. We will take what we can. Ride on to Bruce. Bring him back with you. Make haste, Jon. Follow our trail."

Drue rode back to Nicola. "Now, lady, where do we ride?" Darkness would soon be on them. He did not know this land as well as England. They would have to find Tudor before dark.

Nicola crawled from beneath the brush, whistled for her horse, and mounted. Without wavering, she led them to a small clearing with a tiny hut at its edge. Drue stopped her before she entered the clearing and could be seen. He moved them back into the forest. Everyone dismounted. Drue brought a package to Nicola. "Change into these. It has to be perfect. No mistake. Understand?"

Nicola frowned, but nodded. Drue pulled his cloak off. He and Braggio held it up, providing a screen for Nicola. When she opened the package, she was surprised to find a long cloak and a long shirt and shoes, all well worn. "Are you certain, Drue?"

"Everything depends upon you, Nicola. Do what you have to do. You must look the part." Drue closed his eyes. *This will never work, but it had better work. It has to work. We will not get a second chance.* Drue stared straight ahead.

The sounds of Nicola struggling with the clothing indicated she was trying, for certain.

Eventually, she walked around and stood in front of them. The long shirt hid her blouse and fell down to her knees, exposing her skirt torn and dirty from hiding under brush.

"This is a good plan—it must work." Drue's voice was doubtful. "You do not look like someone bringing a message of this importance. The hair is a problem, your face is too clean, and you walk much too spryly." Drue walked around her, inspecting her. Then, with a handful of the dark earth around them, he smudged her face, rubbed her hands, and clumped her hair. He shook his head. "You will not fool anyone." His voice was heavy with discouragement.

"I should be old, not just dirty. He will not likely be mean to an old woman. Gloves . . . does anyone have gloves?" Nicola asked. "And the shoes are too big. I need something to stuff into them." Nicola looked at the two men staring at her.

Braggio pulled a scarf from under his tunic, tore in into strips, and handed it over. Nicola stuffed the shoes tightly. Pulling Jon's cloak over her head, she stood looking at both men. Slowly, Braggio grabbed a pair of gloves from his cloak. They were worn, and certainly too large, but Nicola stuffed them with strips of cloth and pulled them on tight. Looking around, she found a tree limb. Holding on to the limb and walking in a way that looked pained, she did indeed look like an ancient.

She started to walk away, but turned to Drue. Her soft voice was edged with sadness. "Surely now, Your Grace, you can see I am not worthy of someone of your station. I have no title, no home, no family—I stand in your presence with everything in this world that I own. When we are finished, I will fade away from your sight and mind. I thank you from the bottom of my heart for all you have done for me and will treasure your memory, held safe within my heart."

Before he could recover enough to speak, she walked into the clearing, toward the hut—the one place he could not follow her. Even as she limped away to see Henry Tudor, Drue knew one day he would go for Nicola.

At that moment, Bruce and Jon rode up, and Jon handed an urgent letter to Drue from Cicero.

NICOLA WAS NEARLY AT THE DOOR when a voice from within the hut demanded, "Declare yourself!"

Nicola replied, her voice weak and low, "I come to see Henry Tudor. I must speak with him. Henry Tudor, King of England, speak to me, before my time is gone. I bring a message to you." At her words, the door opened. An older man stood looking her over. Nicola knew he must be Jasper.

"I am Tudor," he said, standing boldly in the doorway.

"Aye, but you, Jasper Tudor, are not the king I seek," Nicola answered quietly.

The man hesitated, carefully looked around the glen, then glanced behind him before opening the door wider. Nicola slowly and painfully made her way to the door and entered the dimly lit hut. Henry sat on a bed against the wall. He was disheveled, looking ill and thin. Nicola hobbled to him and bowed. "Your Majesty," she said.

Henry looked at Jasper questioningly. Nicola spoke. "I come with a message for Your Highness."

"Another trick of my mother. Tell her to stop—I am done," Henry replied bitterly. His voice, his manner, and indeed his whole person spoke of defeat.

Nicola answered, "I do not know your mother. I come with a message for you alone."

"What you have to say to me, you can say to my uncle," Henry stated flatly. "He is the one still pushing me to the brink."

"No. It is for you alone. What you decide to do with what I bring to you is your business. But I will speak only to you." Nicola stood her ground. There was a long moment of silence.

At last, Henry turned to Jasper. "Leave us, Uncle. I believe I can handle an old woman."

"That is not wise, Henry," Jasper disagreed. "You should not be alone with this woman. We do not know who she is or what she wants."

Nicola turned to Jasper. Slowly, carefully, she stated, "I bring a message from the symbol maker. He was tortured and killed for treason, by supporters of King Edward. Before he died, he sent me to you."

Henry frowned. "Who is the symbol maker?" He looked at Jasper.

"Lord Weldon. He is the man killed by King Edward's sister's men. The man who led the attack on his castle has since left England. I believe it seemed unnecessary for him to stay once King Richard took the throne." Jasper glanced at Nicola. She only nodded.

"How do you know this?" Henry asked Jasper.

"I still have friends in Wales," Jasper replied.

Turning back to Henry, Nicola commented, dryly, "If you take much longer, Your Majesty, I will be dead, too. I have already lived long and seen many things. This is my final task."

Again, Henry looked at Jasper. "Leave us, Uncle, please." Jasper looked at Nicola, then nodded and left the hut, closing the door behind him.

Nicola limped closer to Henry. She reached deep within the pocket of her skirt before finally pulled out the packet with the symbols inside. It was difficult for her to open it, working as she was with oversized gloves, but eventually, she unwrapped them and handed the larger one to Henry. He held it, turned it over in his hand, and looked up at Nicola. "What? What is this? What does it mean?"

Nicola limped over closer to the fireplace. She picked up a candle lying on the floor nearby, lit it, returned to Henry, and held the light closer. "Tell me what you see."

Henry turned the piece over again and studied it. He shook his head and looked back at Nicola.

"Read it like you would read a book. Tell me what you see first." She waited, praying that what the old crone had asked of her would make sense to Henry.

"I see a crown, a broken crown." He looked up at Nicola. At her nod, he continued, "There is a white rose, with black bottom petals."

"Yes, keep reading," Nicola instructed.

Henry studied the piece again. "There are two smaller white roses with black bottom petals next to the larger one. Next is another crown, also broken, another white rose with black bottom petals, and next to that is another smaller white rose with the same black petals." He stopped and looked at Nicola. "What does this mean?"

"The broken crowns are for kings who lost their kingdom. The white roses? Do you know what they stand for?"

"The York flower?" Henry's face brightened as he looked back at the symbol, and then again at Nicola.

Nicola continued, "And what does black signify?"

"Death?" Henry replied.

"Yes, keep reading."

"This says Richard will die, as did his only son? Where did you get this?" Henry asked. "Is this some kind of witchcraft?"

"Keep reading, and I will tell you," Nicola replied.

"The last crown is not broken. Beneath it is a full red rose with a white center. There is no black. At the end there is a shepherd's staff, there is brass, and the crown is encircled with oak leaves." He looked up at Nicola. "Tell me, please."

Nicola repeated the symbol meanings to him. "The black tells of the deaths of King Edward, his two sons, King Richard, and his son. None will survive." Nicola paused. "The only unbroken crown is the last one. The herder's staff and oak leaves are for strength. The brass tells of strength and endurance. The red rose is you, Henry Tudor."

"How do you know?" Henry challenged.

"That is what you are called in England. You are England's red rose."

"Then what does the white mean?" Henry asked. "The red rose has white with it."

"You will unite the houses of York and Tudor, and bring peace to England. You, Henry Tudor." Nicola had to control her voice to keep it old. She wanted to speak more loudly, but dared not. "I hear talk that you want to quit. You know you cannot do that. You will be king of England, Henry, you. You are the only surviving rose and unbroken crown. You cannot quit." Nicola waited. Henry was limping around the hut now.

"I must know how you know these things," he insisted. "You must tell me." He walked toward her. Nicola was afraid he would grab her. To lose the disguise now would compromise all she was telling him. She raised her hand, and he stopped walking.

"You must sit still. I cannot keep up with you, nor try to keep looking up. Please, sit. I will tell you all I know." Henry did as she asked. Nicola carefully crafted her tale, leaving out her identity and any mention of the old crone.

"Can we believe a man who made symbols from dreams?" Henry asked, cautiously.

Nicola nodded. "Did not Joan of Arc have visions? What Lord Weldon created from his dreams was not his plan. He never judged the right or wrong of what would happen. Only what would happen. He had these dreams long before the first death . . . King Edward. Each event has come to pass."

At last, Nicola walked to the door. "It is time for me to leave," she said. Turning back toward Henry, she added, "You must promise me you will see this through. You will be a great king, Henry Tudor. Only you can take this and make it your own. You alone will unite the houses of York and Tudor; you alone bring the promise of peace within England's shores." She waited.

Henry suddenly stood, resolutely. "I promise, old woman. I promise. The fight with Richard will be a hard fight, but fight I will. God care for you, woman." Nicola could see his face was animated, his limp less pronounced— his determination filled the small space. He appeared ready. She watched as he looked down at the symbol in his hand. When his fist closed around it and he slipped it into a leather pouch tied around his waist, Nicola knew she had won.

"You will keep this promise?" Nicola asked.

"Yes. And I will keep Weldon's symbol close"—he patted the pouch— "next to my rosary. It will remind me of this destiny you speak of."

Nicola just nodded, opened the door of the hut, and began to limp away. Henry stood at the door and called to Jasper. "Come, Jasper," Nicola heard him call. "We have much to plan." Determination and confidence rang out in his voice. "We fight for England and her crown. They will be mine."

TWO HORSES STOOD JUST BEYOND the clearing, within coverage of the forest, watching the hut. The riders watched as she spoke with Jasper and then entered the hut. She eventually stepped out again. When Henry called to Jasper, one rider spoke softly. "It is done. Henry will fight. Nicola did well." The confidence of Henry's voice told the story.

After leaving instructions for Bruce, who had ridden to meet them, and Braggio, Drue and Jon turned their horses toward Padronale and Cicero.

NICOLA LIMPED INTO THE FOREST until she was unable to see the Tudor hut, and then leaned against a tree and slid to the ground. Having carried the weight of the promise she made to her father for so long, Nicola now felt an overwhelming sense of freedom. She closed her eyes and prayed, thanking God for protecting her and allowing her to complete her task. She then spoke to her father. "It is done, Father. I finished." She spoke softly in the stillness of the forest, to a dead father. "I am free." She looked around. The world looked new and alive. After replacing her shoes, she stood and began to work her way back to the little camp, and to Drue. *Perhaps he will let me see him once more. One more time, and I will be at peace. His vow to me was kept. He is released from my service. My prince.* She smiled to herself.

When Nicola stepped into the tiny clearing, she found Braggio and Bruce awaiting her return. She was warmly welcomed. Braggio stepped up. "You look successful, lady. As we always believed you would be." He took her hand and, bowing, kissed it.

Nicola smiled. "Yes. Henry has promised to fight. He stood strong and resolute as I limped and wobbled away." The men laughed.

Bruce spoke with sincerity. "We are proud to have you with us, lady. And proud to have been of some small service to you." He laughed, adding, "Although I must be honest—I did doubt you could convince Henry to continue. In fact, I doubted you would stay the course. I apologize for my misjudgment, lady."

"No apology is needed, Lord Bruce. I too doubted I could stay the course." Again there was laughter.

Nicola's heart hurt to see that Drue was not in the small gathering. He and Jon were both gone. But she had already said her goodbyes to Drue,

when she left for the hut. There was that hard fact. She refused to acknowledge the ache in her heart. Not now, not on this day. This day was hers. No
one mentioned him, and she did not ask.

Braggio suggested they move out immediately to the safety of Bruce's
castle in Normandy. It would be a long and hard ride from Brittany to the
western shores of Normandy. In only moments, they had left the clearing
empty and undisturbed.

CHAPTER 50

DOWAGER QUEEN ELIZABETH STOOD at the window, watching her young daughters play outside. They laughed, chasing each other around the courtyard, blissfully unaware of the turmoil around them. A slight breeze brought with it the scent of flowers blooming below the window. The scent stirred a familiar pain in her heart, a wrenching grief so severe at times she felt she could not go on. Her whole world had changed in a flash. Her eyes filled with tears. In one year, she had lost a husband to an unexplained illness. Then a brother was executed, and her sons disappeared in the bowels of the Tower. Young Edward was certainly slain, but she prayed the rumors telling of Richard's escape were true. Her older daughters were in the service of her sister-in-law, now the sitting queen, Anne.

Though it was difficult to accept, Elizabeth had no illusions about Richard taking over his brother's throne. She was well schooled in the ugly politics of taking and losing the crown. Her thoughts turned to the young woman who had visited with her in the Abbey. If her and Edward's eldest daughter did indeed wed Henry Tudor, at least the York line would continue. Her daughter could be the queen of England. Only Richard and his son stood in the way. But there was nothing she could do about it today.

Tomorrow will bring whatever it brings. Then we shall see.

Suddenly, the laughter outside stopped. Elizabeth looked through the window for her daughters. They were both staring at a gate on the far side of the yard. Elizabeth could see a man on horseback entering. He rode alone, but his manner was not social. Calling to one of the women working for her, she ordered both girls be brought into the safety of the house. There were few men around to assist her, but she was quite used to scrambling for safety. Once her daughters were inside, she gave them a reassuring embrace and had them escorted to another section of the house. Returning to the room upstairs and resuming her post at the window, she watched as the man rode the short distance toward the house, carefully looking over the area as he did. When he was at the front door, he dismounted. For the first time, she could clearly see whose colors he wore.

Elizabeth had always been close to her husband's sister, the Duchess of Burgundy. With another brother of the duchess now sitting on the throne, Elizabeth wondered where she stood with the duchess. This man wore Burgundy's colors. He was no doubt a messenger from the duchess. Eager for word from the duchess, she set aside her misgivings and hastened to the door.

The man walked up to the door and called out as he knocked, "Queen Elizabeth. I have a message from your sister-in-law, the Duchess of Burgundy."

Elizabeth opened the door. A feeling of disturbed surprise made her hesitate when she faced him. Dressed like a seasoned soldier, he appeared neither friendly nor threatening. For reasons she could not explain, the man made her very uncomfortable. His weapons were for use, not show. She knew well how a fighter dressed and walked. She had loved one, married him, and watched as he brought a hard-won peace to England. With her world turned upside down, her sons presumed murdered, and her brother-in-law's promise of safety and an end to the conflict between them thin at best, she knew she had no choice but to speak to the stranger, a messenger from the sister of the sitting king. "Please." She waved him inside. After leading him to a large, comfortable room, she sat down near the fireplace.

The man sat down opposite her and took a moment to gather his thoughts. "The Duchess of Burgundy wishes you to know she is desperately saddened by the rumors of the death of both your sons. She too has lost a great deal in the never-ending battle to save thrones." When Elizabeth did not respond, he continued, "The duchess has been told young Richard may still be alive. She offers her assistance, if you should need it, to bring him home."

Elizabeth smiled carefully. "My York sister is most kind. If I have need of her help, I know I can call upon her. However, one must remember, even if Richard were still alive, he would be much too young to take the crown. There is no one strong enough to stand as his regent." At this point,

Elizabeth stood. "Do you have anything to show me to prove that you represent the duchess?"

"Of course—I am not surprised you would choose to ask for proof of my relationship with the duchess." He bowed. "I do." He slipped his hand into the small pocket at his waist and pulled out a ring. "This ring was a gift from you to the duchess. With the ring also comes a note." Handing both to Elizabeth, he stood watching her while she read the note.

Elizabeth,

The man before you, Diablo, serves me. I trust him with my life, as did my husband, the duke. Diablo is more than capable of keeping me safe. I trust if you ever fear for life or limb, you will not hesitate to request Diablo's assistance. Stand strong, Elizabeth. The victory goes not to the weak.

Margaret

Elizabeth carefully folded the letter before laying it upon the flames of the fireplace. *If I say I too believe he lives, King Richard will surely turn over every rock looking for him, and my little ones could be taken from me too. I do not believe King Richard will be able to keep the throne. If I say I don't believe it, any possible chance I might have to raise arms against King Richard is gone. If Henry Tudor cannot defeat King Richard, Edward's line ends. Elizabeth will lose her chance to be the queen. Do I tell Margaret the truth? Can I trust this man? I am between two bad choices.* She was silent a long moment. Diablo stood waiting. At last, she met his eyes, her own filled with tears. "So much has been stolen from me. Please tell the duchess I appreciate her concern and offer. I shall keep her informed of the welfare of my daughters and myself." She looked around her. "This is much better than the Abbey. I cannot complain. If you are this way again, please know you have a place to stop."

Diablo bowed again, then followed one of Elizabeth's ladies to the door. Elizabeth stood at a window and watched him ride away. *If you live, please stay safe, Richard. I am still trying. Pray I receive information about you soon.* In her heart, Elizabeth knew it was likely young Richard was also lost to her. She could not admit it. Not yet. She turned to her daughters and their ladies-in-waiting. "Come, ladies—the sun is much too warm to waste." With that, she swept them out the door into the courtyard.

DIABLO TOOK HIS LEAVE WITH MIXED FEELINGS. The lady who was the late Edward's queen was still quite beautiful though age and stress had left their mark. But, more importantly, he felt unsatisfied with her coy dance around the unspoken question from the duchess, and he needed to think on how he might get Elizabeth to be frank with him.

Meanwhile, there was the little matter of Weldon's missing daughter. As morning slipped into afternoon, he rode into a smaller community with a livery stable, lean-to church, and an inn near several stalls displaying various goods. Sitting along both sides at the far end were a few huts. Behind the buildings, small herds of cattle and sheep grazed in a field. Diablo needed a place to rest and think. Stopping at the stable, he tossed the stable hand several coins, telling him, "Feed and water my horse." The man nodded and took the reins from Diablo.

Inside the inn, Diablo paused to allow his eyes to adjust to the darkened room and moved to an empty table. There were few patrons, and he knew even before he was served his meal that the whole town would know a stranger was at the inn. He could smell the beef stew as it was brought to him. Fresh bread and weak ale completed the meal. As he ate, he glanced around. The room was already slowly filling with an assortment of men. So far, they were all farmers and other laborers. One man in particular watched him carefully. The man was short and squat—his outward appearance uncommon in a place where physical labor filled nearly every waking hour. *This is a man to watch.*

When the proprietor came to refill his mug, Diablo casually noted, "There are no women here, but the food is excellent. My compliments to you, sir."

"Oh, we have women. We protect our women," the man replied.

Diablo looked at him. "I did not come looking for women, only one woman. She ran away. The marriage arranged was not to her liking. The intended husband has tired of waiting and wed another. Her father would like his only daughter home with him again. She is the only woman I am interested in finding."

The man frowned. "She ran away alone?"

"Her father believes so, but I do not. However, I am not concerned with any help she might have received. My only concern is to find her and bring her home."

When the man did not reply, Diablo slid several coins across the table with an empty bread plate. The man picked up the platter and coins. "We have not had anyone new in our village here, but . . ." He stopped speaking. Instead, he walked to the table next to the fireplace used for cooking. After bringing back another bowl of stew and fresh bread, he set both down.

Without looking up, Diablo replaced the bread with several more coins. The man picked the plate up again. "No one has come here, but I hear of a young lady who disappeared months ago. Her father's castle was overrun, and it was assumed she died."

"How would that interest me?" Diablo asked as he continued to eat.

"She did not die. She lives, but I do not know where she is now. They say she is traveling in the company of several men. Would not last, were she alone." The man, looking uncomfortable, turned to walk away. "Your money is good, but that is all I have."

"Wait." Diablo kept his voice quiet yet firm. The man stopped walking and returned to Diablo's table. "Where was her father's castle and what was his name? Who travels with her?"

"Weldon. His name was Weldon. I hear the castle is to the west of London, along the coast someplace. Near Wales. I do not know who is with her."

Diablo had no more questions. He knew well where the castle was located. He was with the duchess when she had given the order for its raid. King Edward had died shortly after, and the duchess had called Lord Lareau back. It was from Lareau that the story of Lady Weldon's "vanishing" first began to circulate. That story had spread like a wildfire, until it reached the ears of Queen Anne. After weeks that turned into months of searching, the conclusion everyone drew was that Lady Weldon had died. Perhaps she'd fallen off the cliff behind the courtyard. Who knew? The duchess never believed Lady Weldon was dead. In fact, she was certain the girl still lived. Now, Diablo intended to find her. When he did, she would not make it alive to the home of the Duchess of Burgundy.

CHAPTER 51

G RATEFUL FOR THE TIME IT WOULD take to reach their destination, Nicola prayed she would have some relief from the gnawing pain of a heavy heart. She had done what her father asked of her and was at peace with a promise kept. She had released Drue from her services. Yet . . . there was no peace, only an ache. What was left for her? Why go to Bruce's castle? Her life was essentially over. The sudden crash of thunder matched the turbulence inside her. As the rain began to fall, Nicola lifted her face to the heavens. The rain mixed with her tears. The ride was long, wet, and cold. Nicola felt nothing. For the first time in her life, she felt empty. Somehow, through the fog of her mind, Braggio's voice brought her back. "I am sorry, Lord Braggio," she shouted to him. "I did not hear you."

"You were far away, lady," Braggio yelled over the rumbling thunder and pounding rain. "You must be weary. Are you able to keep riding?"

"Yes!" Nicola yelled back, nodding.

Braggio shook his head and turned away from Nicola. It was not his place to question his prince, but at some point, someone would have to set Drue down. *He cannot spend the rest of his life as a henchman for the Vieneto family. Drue has already given up too much. If he is not careful, he will lose this lady. 'Twill be a shame.* Braggio looked back at Nicola. She rode staring straight ahead. Braggio exchanged a knowing look with Bruce.

The rain became unbearable. Braggio stopped the troop and camp was set up. They were now in Normandy, technically under English rule, but close to France. There had never been a disagreement between Normandy, France, and Padronale, and it would be unlikely anyone would know Nicola's identity. However, Braggio knew the tables could easily turn if there existed even a small chance someone knew Nicola rode with them. The two men with Nicola were guarding Prince Vieneto's chosen, though neither Drue nor Nicola seemed to remember that.

Braggio sat with Nicola as they ate their evening meal. Nicola ate very little. They still had a long ride ahead. Braggio hoped the distraction of the ride would help Nicola. *How is it I am left with this problem, Drue? You are aggressive, decisive, and brave in every battle I have ever fought beside you. In this battle, you leave much to be desired.*

DRUE LED JON OUT OF THE CLEARING as soon as Nicola had moved beyond his sight. Now it was time to go home. He longed to see his brother and his wife, Lila.

It was taking longer than Drue expected to reach his homeland. As the time and miles passed, neither man spoke. The ride gave Drue ample opportunity to convince himself his part for Tudor was done, although he knew it was doubtful Tudor could ever amass an army to match King Richard's. Drue reasoned that he had agreed to protect Nicola and had done so, whether she wanted it or not. He had fulfilled his obligations. His conscience argued that he still owed Tudor help. Over time, Drue had become an expert at ignoring his conscience. His conscience, however, refused to go away quietly this time. The gnawing truth refused to change. He pushed it aside.

Drue had not been home since his father's death. As he rode across the border of his own country, his mood lifted. The rolling hills were green and trees were gently swaying with a slight breeze. The sun was warm. There was no sign of fog, rain, or mist. Just a sleepy sinking sun, a slowly rising moon, and soft shadows. *Funny, I have never noticed before how good it feels to be warm. I have grown so used to dark clouds, fog, mist, the cold damp feel . . . all of it.* Riding into the capital on familiar streets, he felt himself relax. It was darkening, and the city was beginning to settle down. The smells and sounds were comforting. "This is very different, is it not?" Drue asked, finally breaking the silence between Jon and him.

Jon appeared to be still taking in all he saw and felt. "My father brought me here once, when I was very young. It is more beautiful than I remember. Certainly warmer than England even this time of year, and it feels . . . right?"

Drue smiled. Looking around, he agreed, "It does feel right."

His thoughts returned to Nicola. Her last conversation with him eased the insult of her rejection of him. With a calmer temperament, he knew she had never intended to anger him. She simply could not see herself as he saw her. At least not yet. Uncertain of how she had managed to become such a part of him, his mind wandered in unfamiliar territory. He'd never had room for emotion, before Nicola.

She would have fulfilled her promise to her father by now. He needed to know what Nicola was able to do with Henry Tudor, and was anxious to hear from Braggio or Bruce. He would need to get a message to Braggio. There was still work to be done. And just like that, the knot that had formed in his gut over Nicola was gone.

Drue and Jon were challenged as he entered the family castle courtyard, but then an older guard recognized him and greeted him warmly. There were many new faces, all staring at him. He ignored them. *I look threatening, I suppose. Not royal enough.* The guard handed the horses off to a stable hand before escorting Jon and Drue inside the castle proper. He instructed one of the chamber guards to escort Drue to the king's council and Jon to the barracks, with notice that Jon served His Grace, Prince Vieneto.

"Council this late?" Drue questioned.

The older man nodded. "The king has news of Tudor and England's new king." He paused, then softly added, "And other things."

Drue approached the council door, where another attendant hesitated before allowing him entrance. "The king never sees anyone in the afternoon. He is in council in the until the late evening. You will have to wait until tomorrow, my lord. Please tell me who you are and who you represent."

Drue had no intentions of waiting. "I will see His Majesty today. Now, in fact. If you cannot take me to him, I will simply take myself."

The man stammered before motioning to Drue. "Yes, my lord. This way."

When the door to the council opened, King Cicero looked up, irritated. Seeing Drue, he jumped from his chair and met Drue halfway. The brothers clasped each other for a long moment. The king's council whispered among themselves, surprised to see the king's brother return. Drue had the distinct feeling this council meeting had not been going well. Something was amiss.

"Drue! Drue, so long it has been, brother." Turning to the council, Cicero told them, "Leave us. I wish to visit with my brother." He looked back at Drue, his eyes bright, though lines of distress were etched on his face.

Drue felt cautiously happy. His instincts were usually right. He bowed to his brother. "I do not wish to interrupt your business, brother. I could use a change of clothes and probably a bath . . . I think mother would agree."

Cicero smiled. "You!" Cicero called to a younger attendant. "Take Prince Drue to his rooms. Get water and whatever else he needs. Then we shall meet in my chambers. Go now, and hurry, before I change your job from attendant to floor sweep." The lad jumped and immediately led Drue out of the council. As they left, Cicero called, "And order food and wine."

"I know the way to my rooms, lad. Have water brought in." Drue stopped walking and turned to face the boy. "And by what name are you called?"

"Vincent, Your Majesty. I am called Vincent."

"How long have you been at court, Vincent?" Drue asked.

"I just came today," Vincent replied.

"Good, you and I are both new today. We will get along well, I am sure. Now, water, son—I need hot water."

Vincent bowed and dashed off to get water. Drue walked down the hall to his own chambers, where he tossed his bag onto the bed, laid his weapons on a nearby table, and crossed the room to look out onto the dark courtyard. The trees and well-trimmed shrubs gave the appearance of a garden of misshapen gnomes. *Mother's touch is still alive and well.* He walked around lighting the candles and starting a fire. A knock on the door announced the arrival of water . . . a plenitude of hot water.

While Drue bathed, Vincent laid clean clothes out neatly, stacked towels, and waited.

When Drue was dressed, Vincent took him to Cicero's chambers. Drue stopped him as he made to leave. "Vincent, I expect to see you in the morning. Stay with me until I next leave this court." Drue indicated the door.

Vincent paused, then opened the door and followed Drue into Cicero's chambers, taking his post behind Drue's chair.

Drue was surprised to see that Cicero's wife, Lila, was absent. Drue bowed to his brother, seated near a blazing fireplace. "Brother, I received your message. You are not ill?"

Cicero shook his head, sighing. "Not me, but my queen dies." Cicero's eyes grew misty.

In the silence, Drue watched his brother. He knew Cicero loved Lila deeply. He moved to Cicero's side, dropped to one knee, and put his hand on Cicero's shoulder. Cicero looked up at Drue. "She dies, and we have no heir. She has had three sons. All died before they reached one year. Her fourth pregnancy, another boy, died before it was born. She has never recovered. Just gets weaker." Cicero shook his head. "I do not understand. She is fading away before my eyes, Drue, like a wisp of smoke." Cicero's voice cracked. He leaned forward, his head in his hands. "Will you come see her? She still knows whenever I am near. I cannot watch it alone any longer, Drue. I need you here."

Drue saw the despair in Cicero's eyes. "I am here, Cicero. Now, take me to Lila. We will go together." Drue helped Cicero stand. Together they left the king's chambers.

Her ladies were standing outside the queen's chamber when the king and his brother approached her chamber doors, their faces somber. Without speaking, Cicero entered. The small anteroom was furnished with a writing table and chair, several lounging chairs, and three thickly padded stools. All were upholstered with rich velvet in striking colors. Flowers sat on the table along with several wineglasses. Beyond, in Lila's bedchamber, a bed filled one wall. It faced three grand windows, the shutters closed for the night. Lila lay back on overstuffed pillows. Drue was shocked at her appearance. When he last saw her, she was laughing, dancing, and teasing Cicero. She was so alive. Now, lying here, she was as if already dead. Her emaciated frame barely made a dent in the layers of soft covers. Her once-thick black hair that had shone with the light was faded and stringy, and her face was as pale as the fine linen pillowcases her head rested on.

She did not open her eyes, but smiled. "You are here, my love." Her voice was so weak Drue could barely hear her. Cicero moved to the bed and sat down beside her. "You brought company?" she asked, when she opened her eyes. "Ah, my long-lost brother-in-law. How wonderful to see you, Drue." Her smile faded as she closed her eyes. Cicero picked up her hand and softly kissed it. He could not speak, such was his sorrow. He gently brushed a strand of hair, plastered to her face with perspiration, to the side.

Lila again opened her eyes and spoke to Drue. "Dear Drue. You must say goodbye to me. Then leave us. I would spend a quiet moment with my husband."

Drue leaned over the bed and kissed her forehead. "I will always cherish the times we spent together, sweet Lila. You brought a ray of sunlight to this house. Go in peace."

Drue withdrew from Lila's chambers, his heart heavy. He wandered throughout the castle, eventually winding up in the palace gardens. His thoughts took him to Nicola. *What if that were Nicola? I cannot allow Nicola's nor my pride to deprive us of happy, blessed memories. Someday, that may be all one of us has left.*

CICERO GENTLY LAY DOWN BESIDE Lila. "Cicero, I cannot remain here like this any longer. I feel a great peace, though I regret not giving you a child. You made me feel as if the world were mine. You are my world, Cicero. I have loved you since any memory lives in my mind." She stopped speaking.

"You take with you my heart and soul, Lila. The very life of me." He lay holding her. He could feel her breathing becoming weaker and shallower, until there was no more. Cicero wept. When at last he stood, he pulled the blankets close to her. Leaning over her, he kissed her once again. At the door, he stopped to speak to the attendant. She too was weeping. "I know Father Peter was here this morning with her. Please tell him it is over. This will proceed just as she wished. Where is my brother?"

The lady shook her head. "I do not know, Your Majesty."

He will be in the gardens, surely, Cicero noted. He remembered well how many times Drue had wandered those gardens after his mother left for

England. It had been an awful time for Drue, but also for Cicero, whose own mother had died the day Cicero was born. Drue's mother had been the only mother figure Cicero had ever known. Their father let her leave, but never loved another. Cicero understood very well—Lila truly did have his heart, even in death. Cicero stepped into the gardens. Every plant, every bench, each fountain, and every sculpture reminded him of his wife. His eyes filled with tears again. *Who will weep for us, brother?*

CHAPTER 52

*T*HE LIGHTS COMING FROM BRUCE'S CASTLE were a welcome sight. Bruce was proud to welcome everyone to his home. After handing his horse off, he helped Nicola from hers.

Braggio headed straight to the great room where Lizzie anxiously waited for him. Braggio crossed the room and bowed to Lizzie, then kissed her hand. He smiled, placed her hand on his arm, and walked with her to sit near the fire, while the staff brought food and drink for everyone.

After all had eaten their fill and Bruce's men had left for the barracks, Bruce, Nicola, Lizzie, and Braggio lingered near the fireplace. When Nicola had finally stopped shivering, Braggio asked her to tell them how things went with Tudor. Nicola shared Henry's reservations and his initial feelings of defeat, and his eventual acquiescence to what she asked of him. She described how he seemed to come alive as they talked. "I feel certain he will not quit now. It helps that he will soon know there are men willing to join him in this quest." Nicola looked at Bruce, then Braggio. "You do have a substantial number of men to bring to Henry's cause?"

Bruce and Braggio exchanged glances. Bruce spoke first. "We will bring all we can, but you must know, few of our men are from England. We will take those who have loyalty to us, but we will need far greater numbers, I fear. King Richard will easily amass a great body of soldiers." Bruce turned to stare into the fire. "It will be a fight, for certain."

"A fight whose outcome is uncertain," Braggio added quietly. He looked down at Lizzie, then turned to Nicola. "When do you expect His Grace?"

Nicola turned her face away and stared hard at the fire. "I do not expect him to come. I have released him from service to me. His mission was to get me to Henry Tudor. He did that. I can ask no more of him. In truth, I do not know where he went after I left to see Tudor. I do know Jasper Tudor is trying to gather what support he can."

Again, Bruce and Braggio exchanged looks. Braggio felt badly for Nicola, but worse for Bruce, himself, and their men. "He will be back. He was committed to Henry's cause even before he knew you, lady. He is trying to muster troops from his homeland." The last sentence was a bold lie, but Braggio spoke before he could stop himself. Braggio knew Drue had been called back by his brother. Heaven only knew when Drue would return, but Braggio prayed it would be soon. Indeed, Bruce and Braggio had a great deal to work out. Braggio's eyes found Lizzie's. Her face and eyes reflected her concern, but she smiled at him sweetly. *If I die because of the action I must take, I will die a peaceful man. I found a lady who loves me, as I do her.*

Nicola stifled a yawn, and Bruce quickly apologized. "Lady, you must be weary. Lizzie can show you to your room. You both will be quite comfortable there. Sleep late. There is little we can do tomorrow. I have sent word asking what we are expected to do next."

Braggio offered to escort the ladies to their chamber. At the door, Nicola stepped inside, but Lizzie stayed outside for a moment with Braggio. Braggio lifted her hand to his lips, then leaned down and kissed her. "I love you, lady. Never forget that."

Lizzie murmured, "I love you, also. Though I cannot help but fear what all the tomorrows might bring; in my heart, I know we will be together soon. Please take care."

"And you, Lizzie. Watch after your lady. She carries the burden of a love she believes is lost."

"Is it?" came Lizzie's simple reply. "Is it lost?"

"No, but neither you nor I can say so. It is up to His Grace to make it known. You must not speak of it. Bad enough he does not speak of it," Braggio grumbled.

ONCE INSIDE THE ROOM, Lizzie sat down next to Nicola. "Nicola, you cannot think to give up on Drue. Why do you talk so? He would not have Braggio and Lord Bruce fight Richard without him." Lizzie hugged her friend. "This has been a hard day for you. You will feel better tomorrow."

Nicola shook her head. "No, Lizzie. Tomorrow will only be like today. I have nothing to bring to Drue. Royals do not take a lady without a dowery, family . . . or station. I have nothing. I do not even have a home, Lizzie. Drue needs a lady who will add to his place, not someone like me." She leaned her head on Lizzie's shoulder. "I do not even know where I can reside. I have been so intent on helping Tudor I never thought about what would happen after. Maybe I can work for Kelly." When Lizzie pulled away to look at her, Nicola added, "As a cook, or I can clean. Something like that, only."

"One hill at a time, Lady Wright always said. Our first hill is to get back to England. Right now, we need to sleep." Lizzie kissed Nicola's head. "You will love the bed. It is so soft. You will fall asleep quickly." True enough, Lizzie fell asleep as soon as she lay down. But Nicola lay awake. She had come to depend on Drue—his very presence made her feel safe. She never thought about falling in love with him or anyone else. Yet she had. She knew she could never belong to Drue. There would be no political advantage to a union with someone like her. *It matters little what I feel. He is an assassin. He removes problems for his brother. What would my life be like with him? Better to be an honest woman, cleaning or cooking.*

Even as the thought formed in her mind, she knew she was lying. She would love him for a long, long time.

DIABLO STOOD AT THE WINDOW, cursing. Three days earlier, a storm had brought with it a vicious downpour. It had yet to let up. Now, here he stood wasting precious time cooped up in the place he hoped he would find Lady Weldon.

The storm had just begun when Diablo rode into the Weldon courtyard, and Diablo was allowed to stay. The man now occupying Weldon Castle, one Earl of Blackgrove, clearly knew nothing about Lord Weldon or his daughter. He had taken over the property without approval from King Richard, or anyone else, simply moving his men and himself into an abandoned castle. The earl did his best to needle Diablo into telling him how and why he wound up at Weldon Castle. It was clear to Diablo that the earl feared he might be losing the castle.

The earl had assigned one of his men, Lincoln, to attend Diablo. Lincoln was a nuisance to Diablo, and Diablo assumed the assignment was not one of hospitality or coincidence.

BLACKGROVE WAS PACING IN HIS STUDY. Lincoln, one of his most trusted men, stood waiting patiently. No matter how many times the earl had asked, the answer was always the same. Their visitor was not talking. He seemed even more anxious to leave than Blackgrove was to be rid of him. "There must be some reason he came here. This is not on the way to any place—this is only a destination. Who would send a man such as that to this place?" Blackgrove turned to Lincoln again. "Who and why?"

"King Richard?" Lincoln offered. "He works to gather support to keep his crown. There are still rumblings in both the north and south. They are saying young Prince Richard is still alive." Lincoln frowned. "Is that possible? How would Prince Edward disappear in the Tower, but Richard escape to live?"

"The 'Richard' in the tower is rumored to have been an imposter," Blackgrove replied. "Are you not thinking? If I were the dowager Queen Elizabeth, I would not have allowed the only son I had left to go to the Tower."

"The question is, where did she send young Richard?" Lincoln replied. "Not that I care."

Blackgrove slumped down into his chair. "If this cursed weather ever clears, that man will be gone, and I can rest easy."

DIABLO, ALWAYS ON THE LOOKOUT for someone he could use, decided against his better judgment to try Lincoln. He began to drop tidbits of information. If they made it to Blackgrove, Diablo would know by the questions Blackgrove would ask. If the information remained between Diablo and Lincoln, Lincoln might be trusted. So far, nothing had come back.

One evening, as Diablo watched the endless rain pelt the windows, he casually mentioned that he had heard the castle might be haunted. Lincoln's raised eyebrows indicated this was news to him. As he readied for the evening meal, Diablo added, "It's probably the ghost of Weldon's daughter. But then she would have to be dead to have a ghost, and she is not." He did not comment further.

Within a few days of getting nowhere with Lincoln, Diablo had made up his mind that Lincoln was baggage he did not care to keep. Diablo had arranged a meeting with one of the duchess's men and that meeting had waited long enough. Obviously, the earl knew nothing about anything. Diablo decided to leave in the morning, no matter the rain.

AFTER ONLY A FEW DAYS, most of the earl's men knew Diablo. They also recognized him for what he was and left him alone. Lincoln was the only one who always sat nearby. On one night in particular, Lincoln was called to Blackgrove's table.

"I received your message. What news do you bring to me?" Blackgrove spoke as he ate, without looking up.

Lincoln was immediately uncomfortable. He had not sent a message to the earl. He looked in Diablo's direction, but Diablo was eating without looking at anyone. Blackgrove's captain of the guard was watching Lincoln closely, though. Lincoln made as if he were removing the plates, when he answered quietly. "The man is growing restless. I believe he thinks to leave this evening or tomorrow. Am I supposed to let him go?" Blackgrove was surprised by the information, but pleased, hoping Diablo would be on his way.

"By all means, let the man leave. Just tell me exactly when he rides out. Have your horse readied. I may have another job for you. I will give you further instructions once he goes up to his quarters." Then, slipping several coins to Lincoln, Blackgrove continued to talk with those at his table.

Lincoln clasped the coins in his hand, filled his own plate from the bowl hanging over the fire pit, and sat next to Diablo, as usual. Neither spoke.

When Diablo was out of sight and headed up to his room, Blackgrove called Lincoln to his table again. "You will follow him when he departs. I would know what he might know about Weldon's daughter. I do not intend to lose this place. I pay the taxes—I will stay here. If what I hear about Lord Weldon is true, I think King Richard might be very happy for any information about the traitor's daughter. It is possible I could earn a move to his court."

DIABLO RODE OUT IN THE MORNING, moving beyond sight of the castle and its inhabitants. Turning off the road, he took the forest route to a village. Eventually the rain broke and the sun was mid-sky when Diablo reached his destination. Stopping at the only inn, he gave a young lad several coins to take his horse to the stables. Stepping into the darkened public house, he took an empty table near the door. His messenger from the duchess joined him. Diablo was not surprised to find out Tudor was mounting an offense against King Richard. It was rumored Tudor was not having an easy time getting men to fight with him. Additionally, the duchess ordered the hunt for Lady Weldon to cease. Diablo was not pleased, but he kept it to himself. Finding young Richard became crucial. No matter who kept the crown, it belonged to King Edward's surviving son. If young Richard were really alive, King Richard must not find him. Diablo listened to the man speaking, without comment. When the man had given his message to Diablo, he asked to be released to return to Burgundy. Diablo agreed. Diablo preferred to keep working alone.

LINCOLN WATCHED AS DIABLO stopped at the inn. Lingering in the shadows, he waited and watched. He saw a man wearing unusual colors enter the inn. Eventually, he saw the soldier leave. Shortly after he left, Lincoln watched as Diablo also left. As Diablo rode out of town, Lincoln followed. It was clear the soldier did not belong to Richard's army. Diablo was dabbling in treason.

Caught up in the potential rise of his own status, Lincoln let himself get careless. He knew he was following too closely but worried that if he didn't, he would lose him.

Diablo must have heard him and slipped aside because, stepping out from a small clump of brush as Lincoln rode past, Diablo knocked him from his horse. Lincoln fell, but quickly jumped to his feet. Seeing Diablo armed and ready for the kill, he knew he would likely not leave the scene alive. He had one chance. He had to convince Diablo he was no threat to him, and could actually help him.

Diablo, unfortunately, recognized the panic in Lincoln's voice—Lincoln knew he wasn't gathering his thoughts well. Diablo stayed silent while Lincoln babbled on. "I can ride with you. I know this land well. Lady Weldon is alive; I can help you find her. Better I go with you. You will never find her by yourself. I can—"

Diablo shook his head. Lincoln begged for his life. Again, Diablo shook his head. As Lincoln pulled his sword, Diablo swung his own. Lincoln's head rolled.

DIABLO LEFT THE DECAPITATED LINCOLN without looking back, but he couldn't shake the feeling that he was being watched. He didn't have time to try to discover if that was the case, however. He was already on the next task, which was to meet a messenger arriving from Brittany.

Only hours later, Diablo stood off to the side of the dock, watching ships unload. No one of note disembarked. He could see nothing out of the ordinary in the merchandise unloaded, the men leaving the ships, or the mix of sailors standing around trying to find work on any of the vessels.

Diablo had already walked away when the crew of a smaller ship disembarked. The first mate stopped to speak with a man carrying a pack with his personal belongings, looking for work. He quietly conveyed a message to the man. "Tudor will fight. He needs men."

The man nodded as he replied, "Diablo knows where Lady Weldon lives. He is going to find her." The man walked away as the first mate returned to his ship. Hidden in the shadows cast by the upper deck, the first mate scrutinized the men milling around the dock. Unable to find Diablo, the first mate entered the captain's quarters.

Diablo walked along the docks until he reached a larger vessel. Every passenger had disembarked. His contact from the duchess was not on board. As usual, in his line of work, he was on his own again. He was getting restless. Another frustrating day. Every time he thought he might get information regarding the Lady Weldon, he came up empty-handed. *Maybe she is dead.* Whispers hinting Prince Richard still lived surrounded him, and Diablo knew he would be forced to keep looking for proof. This was a strange time. The air itself oozed with unrest. People were hesitant to talk to a stranger especially about matters of the court.

There was one person he believed knew more than was shared. It was time to call on dowager Queen Elizabeth again. This time, he would not leave so easily. If he lived, young Richard needed safety. The duchess could provide that for the boy until Richard was older; the dowager queen could not. Diablo needed to find Prince Richard. The search for Lady Weldon would have to wait.

CHAPTER 53

Drue heard his brother walking toward him. Cicero's slight limp made it look as if he were swaggering. Drue smiled to himself. When they were both young, Cicero had tried to help Drue learn to walk in that manner.

Cicero spoke as he neared him. "Drue, we will have her mass tomorrow. Today, she will lie in state in the royal galleria. It was always her favorite place." Cicero stood next to Drue. Drue put his arm on Cicero's shoulder. For a long moment, they stood just that way. Then Cicero asked, "Did you ever get to see our mother?" There was longing in his voice.

"I did. Every chance I could take." Drue softened at the memory of his mother. The old crone had lived such a strange life, but she lived it well. "I was with her shortly before she died. She died of living so many years." Drue took a deep breath. "How can I help you, brother?"

"I have always believed poor England needs someone like Tudor. I have met and spoken with both Henry and his uncle, Jasper—who's been the only constant in Henry's life. He has done a good job with Henry. Henry knows how to command, how to fight, how to rule, and how to be humble when he should be. But he grows tired of hiding and waiting. If he does not take the throne soon, it will not matter."

Drue nodded. "I agree with you. I believe, though, he may have been convinced to stay the course."

Drue then told Cicero about Nicola's promise to her father. Cicero listened intently.

"She was able to talk Henry into fighting? A woman? How I would like to meet such a woman," Cicero commented. Drue turned to Cicero sharply. Only when he looked at his brother did he realize Cicero teased him. "Oh, I have spies, too. Does not every king have spies? I know about you and Lady Weldon."

"There is nothing to know," Drue stated firmly.

"Brother, it would have made Lila so happy. She always worried about you. Sweet Lila." Cicero's voice was sad. "Where is this lady now?"

"Last I knew, she was in Bruce's castle, waiting out the weather there, to return to England."

"And you are just going to let her go? What is wrong with you, Drue?"

"Nothing. Nothing is wrong with me. She released me from my obligation to her," he told Cicero dryly. "I think she is done with me. It is done." Drue knew he lied.

Cicero shook his head. "I will not ask any more." They walked a little further. "Drue, will it be possible to find more men for Tudor? If he is going to fight, he'll need men. Richard is on a mission to bring both north and south to his side. You know he has taken both of King Edward's daughters into his court, as ladies-in-waiting for his wife, Queen Anne. If he is successful in gaining the backing of those factions, he will have an unbeatable advantage. Numbers mean more than one can imagine."

"I know. I have already begun to recruit support for him in England. None of the countries around us will join in the fight. It is too risky. If the side they support does not win, it thickens the soup, until one cannot swallow. It is not a good place to be in, and they know it too well. I fear I will find few men willing to go with me to England."

Cicero stopped walking. "You plan on going back to England?" he asked in disbelief.

Drue stood still and looked at his brother. "Would you have me do less?"

"I do not know what to say, brother. I thought you might stay here with me. I will be alone now, with Lila gone. If something happens to me, you are next in line for the throne. I cannot think of you not being here, just in case." Cicero watched his younger half-brother. "Drue, what if something happens to you? I must think on this. I am not certain what I feel or think."

"First let us get through the next days. Then we can talk again about my leaving with your blessing." Drue clasped Cicero's shoulder. His brother nodded without speaking. They wandered back through the gardens to the galleria. Preparations were already underway for Lila's service.

THE SUN FINALLY BROKE THROUGH over Bruce's castle. Braggio came to Nicola and Lizzie's room carrying a tray of cheeses, bread, and wine. After knocking gently, he smiled at Lizzie when she opened the door. "We sail for England today, ladies. I plan to leave shortly after breaking fast." He paused a moment. "I am certain you would prefer to have more time, but it is my plan to get across the Channel before another storm comes in. It is that time of year when storms love to sweep down on us. Neither of you do very well in storms." His eyes twinkled.

"We will be ready to go whenever you are ready for us, Lord Braggio," Lizzie replied. After taking the platter from him, she closed the door and set their food on a small table.

Nicola pushed her blankets away and sat up. She stood and stretched. "I wish we did not have to get on board that ship again. I hate sailing."

Lizzie sat down on Nicola's bed. "What are we going to do when we get to England, Nicola?"

Nicola smiled. "I do not know, but I know we will be fine. We can work at some inn, in a smaller place. Better to not stay in London. There are too many of Richard's men around town. We can decide when we get there. When the fighting is over, Lord Braggio and you will return to his country, wherever that is. You will be his wife. Until then, we will be fine, you will see." *If only Drue were around.* It mattered little now. He was gone. Lizzie's question was a greater worry. Nicola had no money, no family, no place to live. *Oh, Father, I wish you would tell me what to do. I kept my promise. What now?* The uninvited memory of Drue's promise stung. *He said he would continue to love me and protect me.* A small voice reminded her she had in fact dismissed Drue. Nicola began dressing.

Knowing they would soon be aboard a ship, she ate little. Stuffing several rolls into her travel bag, she looked around the room one last time. The pouch she always wore at her waist was much smaller now. It only held one symbol, one small symbol. Nicola made a quick decision. If something happened to her, she could ill afford to have the symbol on her person. It could place both Lizzie and her in serious danger. She slipped the remaining symbol into a pocket in her cloak.

"I think we are ready, Lizzie." Nicola watched Lizzie tuck the last of her unruly curls under her hood. "We have many adventures, you and I." Nicola forced a wide smile. Lizzie nodded, and grinned.

"I must be honest, Nicola. I do not enjoy some of them." Lizzie looked at the ring on her finger. "But each one has brought me to the one thing I thought I would never have." She kissed her ring and smiled happily. "Lord Braggio loves me. I can scarce believe it."

The ladies left their room and walked down to the courtyard. It was filled with men rushing back and forth, loading down pack horses. Neither Bruce nor Braggio were anywhere to be seen. The ladies handed off their bags to one of the men, then wandered around the gardens, trying to stay out of everyone's way. While they walked, Nicola spotted a well. "I wonder if we should take a flask of water with us." Nicola turned to Lizzie. "We had a flask in our room. We should have brought it."

"I can run and get it. That is a good idea." Lizzie started off. "Stay here, I will be right back."

"The sun is shining; I will stay right here, letting it warm me," Nicola called. As soon as Lizzie was out of sight, Nicola walked to the well and gave the bucket's handle a gentle swing. It moved easily. Looking down into the well, Nicola could see nothing. Turning the handle used to raise or lower the bucket, Nicola made a quick decision. There were no castle windows looking down on the well; the gardens were deserted. Nicola picked up a large stone, forced it into the pouch with the symbol, and tied it tightly closed, with several knots. Looking around one last time, she leaned over the well, stealthily slipping the pouch with the stone and symbol secure inside over the side. It took a long while before she heard it hit water. The pouch was her last link to her father. Sad but greatly relieved the pouch could no longer place her in danger, Nicola let her father go. *I did it, Father. I did exactly what you asked of me. I could never get to Lady Margaret, but Tudor is on his way to the throne.*

Lizzie hastened around the corner of the castle at that moment. "I brought both, but Lord Bruce took them from me. He said he would see they were filled with fresh water for us. Everyone is nearly ready to leave. We should go now."

"Yes, we should. We have another trip to get through, my friend." Nicola grasped Lizzie's hand, and both hurried toward the group of men and horses now beginning to line up.

Braggio appeared when the ladies were mounting. He stopped at Lizzie's horse and smiled up at her. Giving her foot a quick squeeze, he walked to his horse. The sun was beautiful, the day was brighter, and Nicola knew she had done well. It was finally over. Drue nudged his way into her mind, as always, but Nicola shook him off. Nothing would mar this day.

DIABLO SAT ON HIS HORSE, studying the building and grounds below. The two younger daughters played in the courtyard while Queen Elizabeth strolled around the grounds. It seemed strange that Elizabeth was quite comfortable with her lodging arrangements, although she was still clearly under house arrest. No doubt King Richard intended to keep her closely observed. Just when he was about to ride down, he saw her glance back at the people working the yard, then quickly pick up something from the ground. Watching, he saw her slip something from her pocket and slide it into whatever she picked up. She glanced around again, dropped the item back onto the ground, then called to the little girls and they all went inside. Diablo smiled to himself. *So, Queen Elizabeth, you have not given up either. Good for you, lady. Help is coming to you.* He kept watch until he saw a young man appear and begin picking up the fruit from the tree where Elizabeth had stood. He picked up every piece, tossing them into a basket. Until he found what he was looking for. That piece he slipped into his trousers. Again, Diablo smiled. He rode down to the house.

Diablo waited patiently for the dowager Queen Elizabeth to receive him. Elizabeth walked into the room, still every inch a queen. Diablo bowed when she entered.

"The duchess wishes to remind you what she is able to offer," Diablo started.

"And what would that be?" Elizabeth asked, watching Diablo.

Diablo glanced around before answering. "Safety and shelter for all in need of these things."

Elizabeth smiled. "We are well cared for here. I cannot leave, as I am under King Richard's protection."

"Surely, there are those in your household who grow weary of this protection?" Diablo noted.

"Perhaps." Elizabeth walked around the room. When she had circled it twice, she stepped closer to Diablo. Very softly, she spoke. "Tudor must be weary. I hear he is."

"Did King Edward ever grow weary of fighting for the throne?" Diablo asked.

Elizabeth smiled sadly. Even now, her eyes grew bright with tears. "Never," she replied.

"You answer yourself." Now Diablo decided to press her. "The king will be hampered by what he is rumored to have done. The people, for the most part, thought well of King Edward. King Richard disposed of his only sons. There could be more support for a challenger than King Richard believes."

"That is *one* view." Elizabeth stopped. Speaking deliberately, she continued, "Even if the king were to be killed, his son would rule after him. I doubt the people of this country would tolerate another murder of a prince."

"Do you really believe politics would stop at two?" Diablo asked quickly. He knew her answer might be the opening for him to step inside her ring of confidants.

Elizabeth was a very astute politician. To his exasperation, she replied calmly, "The people of this country have a strange way of deciding for themselves what they will or will not tolerate." Again, she held him at arm's length. Diablo realized he would be forced to ask her directly if she knew where young Richard might be. He had begun to speak when one of her ladies knocked at the door.

"Your Majesty, I bring news from King Richard's court." The woman waited for Elizabeth to ask her in. Elizabeth hesitated, glanced at Diablo, then waved the woman in.

"What is your news? No . . . wait." Elizabeth had changed her mind, and Diablo understood her motivation—it might not be in everyone's best interest for the duchess's man to hear the news. "Will you join us for our meal, sir?"

When Diablo hesitated, Elizabeth immediately asked one of her attendants to escort Diablo out. Turning to a stunned Diablo, she spoke firmly. "Sir, our visit is concluded. Please tell my sister-in-law I shall look forward to hearing from her again and am happy she remains in good health." Not giving him a chance to argue or speak, she nodded to him and left the room, motioning for the news carrier to follow her.

"Does your mistress always dispose of visitors so carelessly?" Diablo demanded angrily of the attendant.

"I know not, my lord. You are the only unknown visitor she has had." The attendant bowed and motioned toward the door. After leading Diablo outside, she waited while someone fetched Diablo's horse, then stood by while Diablo mounted.

"Tell the dowager queen our visit is *not* over. I shall see her again, soon." Diablo jerked his horse around and left the courtyard.

ELIZABETH STOOD AT A WINDOW and watched him leave. *He may be a messenger for the duchess, but he has his own agenda. Ah, old woman. Why do you not help me? Tell me if my Richard is in the care of my mother's people. Tell me if he is safe.*

Turning to the lady waiting to talk to her, Elizabeth said, "Tell me what I already believe I know."

"Court gossip talks of Richard's attentions toward Princess Elizabeth. It is said he plans to set Queen Anne aside and take the princess as his wife." The lady waited for a response from Elizabeth.

"And you? What do you see as confirmation of this rumor?" This was no longer a rumor. The affair was moving much too quickly. Elizabeth worried. If her daughter did indeed marry King Richard, and lay with him, even if he were killed by Tudor, Tudor would never take her as his wife. Her own daughter would be the destruction of the plan to unite the houses of York and Tudor and keep a York on the throne.

The messenger bowed her head. "I see how he looks at her, Majesty, how he dances with her and how she . . ." The woman stopped.

"Go on," Elizabeth ordered.

"I have seen how the princess looks back at him, keeps close to his side, and touches his hand. I think Princess Elizabeth loves King Richard."

Elizabeth sighed. "Leave me." She sat down heavily in a chair near the fire. With her eyes closed, she rocked slowly, back and forth. "She will be the queen of England. If they have children, Edward's line will remain on the throne of England. Can this be the plan? His line stays on the throne through incest?" She could hardly think about it. Rising, Elizabeth called for her steward. When he arrived, she spoke quietly to him. He bowed and left. One of her ladies watched him, but he only walked back to the building where the rest of the stable men slept.

CHAPTER 54

DRUE STIFFLY STOOD AT ATTENTION, watching his brother struggle to maintain his composure. Lila lay in the galleria. The line of subjects that filed past her seemed endless. Cicero, dressed in black, sat in his chair on a raised platform somberly watching the procession, Lila's empty chair beside him, a single deep purple rose in the seat. Recent rains and the burning sun made the air heavy. Drue wondered why Cicero stayed sitting, watching over Lila. Given a choice, Drue would have not come. *Lila knows we loved her, and she knows we came to see her while she lived. Cicero was a model husband. Never a harsh word with her, never strayed. Could I be as true?* After a long moment, he admitted to himself, *For Nicola, yes, and I too would stay sitting with her body.*

The next day, Lila's funeral procession surpassed that of her father-in-law, the king, in numbers. The air was stifling as the service dragged on. She was carried in a black coach, with Cicero and Drue following, both of them dressed in full regalia. Lila was laid to rest next to her father-in-law.

Drue joined his brother for a somber evening meal. Neither man ate. After several moments of silence, Drue spoke. "What does a king do when his queen dies? Do his obligations change? Do the problems of his realm disappear?"

"You know the answer to your questions, Drue. Why do you even ask?" Cicero's voice was weary. "I feel as if my very soul is dead." He looked at Drue. "I loved her. More than you can imagine."

"I can imagine," Drue replied quietly, more to himself.

It took a moment for Drue's answer to register with Cicero. Suddenly, he was alert. "You can imagine? You are not just playing with me, brother."

"No," Drue answered, turning to face Cicero.

"Tell me," Cicero said. "I need some distraction. These past days have been far too long and too sad. Tell me."

"I cannot." Drue shook his head. "Not yet, anyway. I must finish with Tudor first. I have to pull an army out of the air for him." He shrugged. "There will be no other place to find one."

Cicero's eyes narrowed. "Tudor has not lived in England for any substantial time. Perhaps it might be easier than you imagine to garner support for him in other countries. Mercenaries, certainly, but we both know those can become some of the best armies."

"True," Drue admitted, adding, "especially when you offer freedom as part of the payment, *if* the battle is won." He looked at Cicero thoughtfully. "Dare I go to the prisons for soldiers? Could that type of man be trusted in battle?"

Cicero pushed. "Think, Drue. What kind of man is in prison? Every crime known to man is punishable by prison time. Pick your friends carefully."

"You make a great point, Cicero. A great point." Their father had once advised them of just such a move. "I knew Father was not speaking about us, nor our army. Still, the idea is sound."

The rest of the evening passed with the brothers remembering their father and Lila. It felt good to speak of them from untroubled memories. Back in his room, Drue began planning.

Early in the morning hours, Drue was awakened by knocking at his door. Vincent stood outside, his face serious. "Sorry to disturb you, Your Grace, but a messenger is here for you."

Drue could see Jon standing behind Vincent. Drue nodded toward his chamber and stepped aside for Jon. "Thank you, Vincent. That will be all."

"A messenger came to me today, bringing news of Tudor and Lady Nicola," Jon began.

"Together?" Drue asked, frowning.

"No. You know Tudor attempted to meet King Richard in battle, but both sides were forced to turn back because of the weather." Jon stopped for a moment. "King Richard fields a large army. Tudor, not so much. There is no talk of when Tudor will try again. Most think it is over."

"And the lady?" Drue asked. He held his breath.

"Diablo, the henchman for the Duke of Burgundy, now works for the duchess. Diablo knows Lady Nicola lives. Diablo is hunting." Jon's voice was level and calm, but it was clear that he was bothered by his report.

Drue straightened. "There is no mistake?"

"None," Jon replied. "The messenger is one of our men."

Drue felt his heart drop. He had not felt such a sharp ache since the day his mother left for England. "Do you know where Lady Weldon is? Is she still with Lord Bruce?" Drue asked.

"I believe she is riding with both Braggio and Bruce. The lords are preparing to sail for England, before the storms come again. My last information on Diablo had him in England already." Jon waited, then cleared his throat. "Pardon my intrusiveness, but it seems that you and Lady Nicola love each other, despite the fact that neither of you would admit to such a thing. That said, I have given you what information I have."

Drue motioned to object, but resigned himself to leave Jon's observation alone for the time being. He left his room to speak with Cicero.

Drue hated to face Cicero, but the time had come . . . again. Cicero always knew Drue would leave, though he hoped Drue's stay would last longer, and Drue frequently found himself pressured to do so. He hated to disappoint his brother, especially when his choices were not altogether clear to Cicero.

"We all have our part to play, Drue." Cicero stood to embrace Drue one last time. "My will is written clear and all understand. At my death, you will fulfill what our father longed for. You will sit where I sit, and my council will be yours. I know you're leaving. I only ask that you keep me informed of your whereabouts and how you fare."

When Drue and Jon rode out, darkness was throwing shadows across the land. Neither man spoke, each lost in a private world. Drue knew he had let his pride overshadow Nicola's safety. He thought about what Nicola had said to him. *She may not want to take on the role I have planned for her, but I do not give up so easily.* The image of Diablo flashed in Drue's mind. Diablo was a deadly adversary.

I pray I find you before Diablo does, Lady Weldon. This time, you will not talk your way from me.

CHAPTER 55

Over much of England the day opened under a full sun and soft, voluminous clouds. For the first time in days, Diablo was able to ride comfortably again. His visit with the dowager queen had been useless. Either young Richard was no longer alive, or Elizabeth had already found a safe haven for him. Diablo made the decision to focus on the missing Lady Weldon. Although wary of becoming entangled with any of King Richard's men, Diablo knew his quest to find Lady Nicola Weldon would be nearly futile without moving in more public circles. Desperate for information, Diablo headed for London in spite of the dangers.

Leaving his horse in a stable, Diablo walked to Kelly's business. She knew he was looking for Lady Weldon. If there was any recent news about Lady Weldon, Kelly would have heard.

As soon as he entered the foyer, he knew Kelly was no longer running the brothel.

It was unkept and seedy. Descending from one of the rooms upstairs, a graying woman approached Diablo. "If you're looking for companionship, there will be younger ladies coming down shortly. While you wait, I can feed you." Without waiting for any response from Diablo, she walked to the kitchen. Diablo followed.

"Is Kelly no longer here?" Diablo asked.

"Not for a long time, now. I sold most of her things." The woman began stirring a pot sitting over the fireplace. When Diablo did not respond, the woman turned around. Diablo was watching her. She did not know what to say, so she simply turned back, filled a bowl with what food remained, and set it on the table.

Diablo did not sit down. "I think you know where Kelly is. Tell me." He kept his voice low as he stepped toward her. His eyes bore into hers, and he reached to shut the door to the foyer.

Clearly frightened, she replied, "I never knew Kelly. They tell of how she walked away and left everything. Her room is still open; no one sleeps or works there. You can look if you care to."

Diablo changed tactics quickly. If Kelly had simply left, she must have known more than she admitted to him. There could be others who knew something about Lady Weldon. "I would speak to all your ladies," Diablo ordered. "Now." He stepped to the door and opened it.

The lady started to speak, but Diablo held up his hand. "Just bring them down. It is early afternoon. They cannot be that busy."

"They do not work for me. No one came to run this place, so we just work here. The ladies come and go. Please . . ." She hurried away to gather the few women still in rooms. As the women descended the stairs, Diablo realized he did not recognize any of them. While he had never utilized the services Kelly provided, he had been in her building enough to see most of the women working for Kelly. He had never seen any of these women, until the last one stepped onto the landing.

When Diablo made eye contact with her, she smiled. "You have not been here in a long time, my lord." She walked across the room to him.

"Is there a quiet place?" Diablo asked.

"Certainly. This way." She led Diablo back up the stairs. She stopped at the first door, but Diablo nodded toward the hall's end. Shrugging, she continued until they were at the last door. "Here?" Diablo nodded. He followed her into the room, then locked the door behind him. He watched as the woman visibly shuddered, her hand placed on a chair as if to steady herself.

Diablo walked across the room and removed his long sword. Without looking at the woman, he asked, "Did Kelly leave?"

"Yes," the woman answered. She edged toward the door.

Still not looking at her, he ordered, "Stop. You will not leave this room until I allow it."

The woman continued to tremble. Unmoving, she stood and waited.

Diablo let her stand there for a long moment. "When did Kelly leave?" He finally turned to look at the woman. She stepped back, nearly falling.

"I asked you a question." Diablo remained still.

"I am not certain. We have been on our own for many days. Several Sundays have come and gone."

"Where would she go?" Diablo asked.

"I do not know. She did not tell anyone she was leaving. We came down to eat in the morning, and she was gone. In the beginning, we believed she was at the market. But she never came back. Her room has remained unused. Most of the ladies left to work at other brothels."

"And you? Why did you stay?" Diablo took several steps toward the woman.

She looked directly at Diablo when she answered. "Most of the men coming to this place pay nearly twice as much as men going to other brothels. The money was good. But since she has been gone, the business has begun to die." The woman stopped talking and watched Diablo. "You could look in her room, if it would help you."

"It is strange she did not make friends with any of you," Diablo noted.

"She did have a friend. It was a younger lady who worked with us a long time ago. She left when a lady with money hired her to work at her castle, as a companion. The younger lady came back some time ago. With another lady . . . who never worked with us. I believe they only needed a place to stay."

Diablo stood very still, his eyes never leaving hers. "This is important. How long ago?"

The woman tried to think back. "I am not certain. They left a long time before Kelly left."

Diablo smiled slightly. *Now I understand. Kelly left because she knew I would soon find out Lady Weldon had stayed with her. So, Lady Weldon lives. Where would she go from here?* "You are doing well so far, lady. Just who was with Kelly's friend?" He watched as she tried not to divulge too much.

At last, she seemed to give up. "I do not know. I did not see her often, and never heard her called by any name. I only knew her father had been killed. I never heard her father's name." She gripped her hands together tightly, her forehead forming tiny beads of perspiration.

"Do not lie to me. That is not a good thing for you to do. Not to me. Once again, who was the second lady? Think before you answer."

"Please do not hurt me. I have told you all I know. I have helped you. You gain nothing by hurting me. Just let me go, please."

Diablo did not answer. He simply walked toward her. The woman swung around and dashed to the door. Before she even had time to touch it, he reached her and, with one powerful twist, broke her neck. The motion was quick and fluid. She collapsed, her lifeless eyes looking back at him. Diablo retrieved his sword from the bed and left the room. After taking the door to the back staircase, he was gone from the building. He would rather have not left a body lying around, but the body would be less trouble for him than the tale this woman could have told King Richard's men. Diablo feared Richard would connect Weldon's death to the duchess. To have Richard's sister involved so quickly would be Richard's first proof that King Edward's son, young Richard, might be living. It could also alert Lady Weldon to his presence. A body, on the other hand, would never talk.

Diablo roamed around the town for the remainder of the day. Not one soul knew anything. Everyone was still reeling from Richard's rapid ascension to the throne. Diablo toyed with the idea of speaking to the dowager queen again, but decided instead to spend some time roaming the various docks along the Channel.

At the first dock where Diablo stopped, the talk was of Tudor's retreat because of the weather. He learned Richard had ridden out to meet Tudor, but neither man had been able to handle the torrential rain, gale force winds, and viscous mud that made the ground nearly impassable. That fight never happened. The general opinion was that Tudor would not try again. Diablo shook his head in disbelief. *These are people badly in need of a strong leader. A fighting king. Perhaps Richard should be king.* It was clear King Richard knew Tudor would mount a second attack. The king had continued rounding up as many men as possible.

Diablo began to think about changing his plans. It would seem neither young Richard nor Lady Weldon mattered at this point. Perhaps it was time to return to Burgundy. Diablo stopped at an inn to eat and rest. Earlier, he had arranged passage on a ship leaving the next morning, back to France—from there, he would continue to Burgundy. If he were the duchess, he would send men to King Richard—better Richard as king than Tudor. But he was not of the same mind as the duchess. She would watch what happened, then decide. After he finished his meal, he stayed on, watching the men wander in and out. Suddenly, one man caught his attention. That man looked to be one of the men with Lareau when Lareau met with the duchess. He was sure of it. Lareau had not been seen in some time.

Diablo strode up to the man's table. "Can I sit here?"

"Not my table," the man replied, shrugging, then went on eating. Diablo sat down. For a while, he simply watched the crowd and sipped his ale.

Finally, as the man finished his meal, Diablo spoke to him. "You are one of Lord Lareau's men, are you not?"

The man studied Diablo for a moment before answering. "I was. He sailed for Burgundy over a week ago." He did not volunteer more.

Diablo casually noted, "But you did not go with him?"

The man just mumbled, "No." Then drained his mug. "More ale over here," he called to the man waiting tables.

"Why?" Diablo persisted. At this point there was a difference in his voice. He spoke with more authority, not just a casual conversation.

"Why are you asking me these questions? I have done nothing wrong. Leave me be." The man started to stand as his tankard was refilled.

Diablo put a hand on his arm. "Stay. I am from Burgundy, also. I have been sent to find a lady—Lady Weldon—for the duchess. After searching without success, I doubt she even lives."

The man sat back down. "She does live. Her father was tortured to death. No mother, and then no family." The man paused to take another drink. He looked at his tankard, then up at Diablo. "He thought Lord Weldon knew some great secret about Henry Tudor. The man died not saying a word about that rumor. And that is what it was . . . a rumor. Lareau would have tortured the girl, too, but she disappeared. Lareau always believed she fell from the cliff behind the castle." The man looked intently at Diablo. "I walked her down to see her father for the last time, in a cell deep below the castle. She is a strong woman. I never believed she jumped from the cliff. She has lived there all her life, and would not have fallen by accident. I have been stranded in England for many days. I have asked around, especially in London. She was there. From the description, I am sure it was her. She is with another lady. They were seen sailing from here, not long after she left London."

"She left here? How long ago is not long ago?" Diablo asked, frowning.

"Not so long." The man watched Diablo. "Maybe several weeks. Have not heard where she might be now, but do know the boat she sailed on was in the middle of a bad storm."

Diablo was watching the man carefully. This man did not seem like the kind to sit around and make up tales for a drink. The man was serious, and was still talking. "Men say Tudor will not come again. They say he was forced back to Brittany by God Himself. The weather was a sign he should give up." The man leaned back in his chair. "I do not think that way. Tudor will come again, and again, until he is successful or dead. Only then will he stop."

Diablo had to agree. *Perhaps I should not return to Burgundy yet. Instead I will stay on a little longer. Tudor's run needs to end. King Richard needs good fighting men. King Richard will likely keep his crown, if he can defeat Tudor. If Tudor were to take the throne, certainly young Richard, if he lives, will never survive. Someone will find him.* Long after the man left, Diablo sat deep in thought. The duchess had ordered young Richard, if alive, and Lady Weldon to be taken to Burgundy. Unfortunately, the dowager Queen Elizabeth would not cooperate. Diablo now believed her youngest son had indeed been safely removed from sanctuary before King Richard came for him. Diablo's gut told him Elizabeth knew her youngest was safely hidden away. Why else would she not talk with him? She was trying to protect her last son.

Perhaps Lord Weldon was innocent of all the charges against him. But the daughter . . . could it have been the daughter all along? A sudden chill passed over Diablo. Queen Anne searched for the wrong lady. Lady Weldon was the lady with the visions.

I will find Lady Weldon. There will be no more visions.

WITH NICOLA AND LIZZIE SURROUNDED by Lord Bruce's men, the group rode steadily toward the ship awaiting them. It was difficult to hear anything over the noise of the soldiers' gear and the horses. No one spoke. The general mood was solemn. Knowledge of the coming battle with such an uncertain outcome weighed heavily on Braggio and Bruce. Their unspoken outlook spread through the men.

Nicola, however, felt a sense of freedom. For so long, she had moved beneath the cloud of a promise that seemed impossible to keep. Nicola had forgotten what it felt like to just be herself. This morning finally held promise. Even the usual sounds of the riders and their gear were comforting. She knew Kelly would let her work. Perhaps her father's castle was still unoccupied. *No matter, whatever comes, it comes.* She smiled to herself—her father's words were always the same, if Nicola ever was worried about anything. *Whatever comes, it comes.*

The long, steady rides were becoming easier than in the beginning. The warm sun and the swaying movement of her horse soothed Nicola. Then, abruptly, she felt an iciness wash over her. The dark feeling of danger and fear was overwhelming. Surprised, she looked around, but nothing had changed. The men, the horses . . . everything was the same. *I am finished with Tudor; why is this happening?* The image of a man came to Nicola. It was not a man she knew. He was dressed like a soldier, armed and intense. He was riding through a forested area, away from the roads. The image filled Nicola with foreboding, but she could not understand why. The image faded, but the uneasiness stayed.

I fear this is not over. But what else? She immediately thought of Drue. There was no one else to talk to about how she felt, what she saw, or what it might mean. *He is gone. I will have to do this alone. I need to know where this man rides, and why. He must be here, but he cannot be riding after Tudor–I never felt afraid when I saw men pursuing Tudor. I must get to England, where I will be safe.*

Nicola gasped. Images of the land around the man flooded her senses—it was land she knew well. He rode into London. *He is in England. He looks for me.* As that realization struck her, Nicola felt as if she had been plunged into an icy lake. Her breathing became difficult. Fear gripped her yet again.

I need you, Drue. I need you once more. You would know why he seeks me and where he is. She tried to recapture the images in her mind, but they were gone. *Relax, let her speak to you.* Drue's words came back to her. *She cannot speak to me. She is dead.* Nicola closed her eyes for a moment. When she opened them, she glanced at Lizzie. Lizzie had moved, slowly but surely, until she was close to Braggio. No one watched Nicola—she tried to relax. *There is no one left to help me. I must understand what the message is by myself. I cannot put those with me in danger.*

The remainder of the ride was a blur. Nicola was unable to see the man again. When they arrived at the ship enlisted to take them to England, Nicola's uneasiness grew. Nicola felt certain that whatever was happening was happening only to her. She needed desperately to find a quiet place.

Lord Bruce escorted the ladies to their quarters, then returned to the deck. It took little time before they were moving away from the shore.

"Nicola, let us go outside and watch!" Lizzie suggested. Her eyes were bright, her face was flushed, and Nicola could tell she could barely contain herself. At first, Nicola thought to stay inside, but that would not look so well for Lizzie to wander around alone.

"Yes, let's do that. The air will help." Nicola followed her friend to the deck. Braggio was not around, or Bruce. "I think Lords Bruce and Braggio are working with the maps, or whatever it is they do when we sail. We can still watch from here, out of the way," Nicola suggested. "They might come on deck soon." Lizzie brightened, but as the boat moved farther from shore and the waves began rocking them, her face fell.

"Oh, Nicola, I am going to be sick again," Lizzie moaned, shifting toward their quarters.

"Look at the horizon," Nicola reminded Lizzie. "Watch it closely." Both ladies stood clinging to the stair railing leading to the upper deck, staring at the horizon. It didn't help. They gave up and hustled to their room.

Braggio knocked on the door just as they had both made their way to their beds. He stepped inside, insisting that they join him. "Come on, you two. This will be a better trip, I promise. Come with me." Lizzie stood up gamely and pulled a shawl over her shoulders.

"I think I shall stay here. I have some things on my mind. Please, go on." Nicola waved to the door.

Braggio nodded, closing the door behind Lizzie and him. Nicola lay on her bed, closed her eyes, and let her mind empty. The sounds outside faded.

The motion of the ship was lost. The images began to reappear. The man was no longer riding. He was in a village. People moved away from him when he walked by them. He turned to look down the street just before the image faded. Nicola now knew what he looked like.

Without Drue, that was little consolation. *If I tell Braggio or Bruce what I know, they will never understand. Worse, they could label me a witch, like poor Jacquetta Woodville.* Jacquetta, the wife of Lord Rivers and mother of the dowager Queen Elizabeth, was widely reported to have visions and was rumored to have the ability to foresee the future or conjure up events to change the course of lives. Even after Jacquetta's death, the rumors persisted. Nicola's own experiences made her uncertain of Jacquetta's ability to change anything, except perhaps by sharing what she saw. Additionally, Jacquetta's relationship with queens, including her daughter, protected her from prosecution. Even when she was on trial, her friendship with a royal kept her safe, and the charges were dropped. Nicola had no such protection. Sharing what she could see with anyone but Drue was a step Nicola was unwilling to take.

Nicola was certain the man she had seen in her mind's eye was looking for her, and she realized that could threaten Lizzie's safety also. Nicola would have to know exactly where the man was. Drue had told her it was far better to be the hunter than the prey—Nicola would become the hunter. *I must be alert to signs of the man who looks for me.*

Nicola continued to lie on the bed, trying to clear her mind once more. For a long moment, it seemed useless. Slowly an image formed. As it came into focus, Nicola recognized Drue. He was on a ship, with one companion, Jon. They were not coming to the usual port, where the ocean received the waters of the Thames. They were sailing southward, along the coast. She could not tell why, but a powerful feeling told her Drue needed help when he landed. Nicola sat up. She was forced to tell someone. After considering both Lord Bruce and Lord Braggio, Nicola got up and went looking for Braggio. She found Braggio and Lizzie standing near the bow talking.

"Lizzie, this is a much easier trip, is it not?" Nicola asked, as she approached. She knew Lizzie noticed little but Braggio. He was gentle with her, kind and protective. Lizzie had never been treated so well. At Nicola's voice, both turned to her. Lizzie's face was beaming. "Love suits you well, Lizzie," Nicola murmured. Lizzie blushed. "Might I have a word with Lord Braggio? Nothing is a surprise if you know about it," Nicola hinted. Lizzie laughed, as Braggio took her hand and kissed it. "I will be back in our rooms shortly." When Lizzie had gone, Nicola was quiet for a moment, uncertain what she could say to Braggio. If he doubted her, Drue could be in real danger . . . as could Nicola. Few people would understand.

"Lord Braggio, I do not know how to begin my tale. You know about my promise to Lord Weldon." Braggio nodded, waiting for Nicola to continue. "Lord Weldon had visions that gave him ideas about the beautiful pieces he created." Again, Braggio nodded. "The visions became more . . . prophetic. The last one he experienced was just such a vision. He never had an opinion whether the vision was right or wrong—he only realized the message of the visions." Braggio was frowning. Very carefully, Nicola continued, "I never had visions or anything like that until after Father died. Then, well, then it started." She prayed Braggio would hear her out.

"Are you telling me you have messages, or whatever you call it, as well?" Stepping back, Braggio was now watching her intently.

"Yes. Tonight, I was lying down and saw Drue. He will sail on a particular ship, but the ship will not dock at the port at Thames." Braggio frowned, but Nicola continued, "They will travel southward, along the coast. I cannot tell where, but Drue will be in danger. The captain of that boat is evil and he has other plans for Drue. You must help him. Please."

Braggio stood up straight and looked off toward the horizon. In the silence that followed, Nicola's eyes began to fill. "Please, Lord Braggio," she began, quietly.

"Stop," he commanded. "I have to think on this." He looked back at her. His face was stern. "Does Drue know about you?"

"Yes," Nicola answered. "He helped me when it started." Nicola watched Braggio digest this information. She could tell he was not certain what he should think. "Drue taught me to trust what I saw. Remember our search for Tudor?"

"You knew where he was, and Drue listened. I remember," Braggio finished.

"We found Tudor," Nicola added quietly. "I do not expect you to under-stand, but I pray you will trust what I say enough to help Drue." Nicola touched Braggio's arm lightly. "There is no one else I know on that ship, only Drue and Jon. The ship they sail on has a full crew of men, all against Drue. Please, Lord Braggio—"

"I know nothing of the things you speak about, but I will help. You must tell me what you saw. I need to know where they are headed, and when. Do you know when they sailed?"

"I do not believe they have sailed yet. The ship they are on is large, armed, and the men are not English. I see Drue on that ship." Nicola's voice dropped. "I do not know how or why these visions come. I do know I could be in grave danger because of them."

Braggio looked at Nicola. "You will never be in danger because of me, Lady Weldon. Come to me when you have more to say." He turned back to stare at the sea.

"Thank you," Nicola murmured. "I owe you much."

Braggio did not look at her, but he shook his head. "No. You do not owe me. I do not intend to tell Lizzie, but we will ride with Drue. He will ride for Tudor. The fight is coming." As Nicola turned to walk away, Braggio spoke again. "Lady, please let Lizzie know we will dock this evening. I will see that you both have safe quarters. We will unload quickly." When Nicola turned to listen, he smiled at her. "I am accustomed to changes in plans, lady." Braggio would have time to send a message to Drue when he arrived at Deal, as well as suggest the ship be inspected.

"We dock so soon?" Nicola frowned.

"We were not blown off course this trip. The winds usually blow from east to west. Winds are on our side." Braggio turned to resume watching the horizon.

It took little time for both ladies to pack. Lizzie never asked what Nicola and Braggio might have spoken about.

Nicola lay down on the bed trying to rest, but she was afraid to relax. Braggio would see to Drue's safety, somehow. There would be none to see to her safety. As she lay in the darkness, the man's image appeared before her again. His face was void of expression as if he were dead. As the image moved toward her, Nicola quickly opened her eyes. The image was gone. Too fearful to remain alone, Nicola pulled a shawl about her shoulders and left for the deck. The wind blew slightly and the ship's rocking was gentler. Evening was near, and land was in sight. As the crew made ready to dock, Nicola watched the land grow in size, much like the fear inside her. She felt herself sailing into the devil's lair.

CHAPTER 56

JUST AS DRUE fEARED, he and Jon arrived at the docks to depart
for England one day after Bruce's ship had already set sail. Jon was easily
able to secure passage for Drue, himself, and their horses, on a ship leaving in
several hours, although the dock master informed Jon the ship would dock at
Deal, south of London. Not as close to London as Drue hoped, but it would
have to do. Both men were already on board. Unfortunately, the time he was
aboard ship would be time without communication from any of his many
spies. Drue paced the deck.

Late the next evening, Drue was walking the deck again when the captain approached him near the bow of the ship, away from any crew. He
proceeded to ask if Drue knew of any work for him and his crew. "I find it
necessary to dry dock this vessel at Port London, for routine repairs. If I keep
my crew busy, they sail with me again and do not look for other work. They
are a good bunch of men. I would like to keep them."

Thinking while the captain talked, Drue decided to explore the captain's
offer. From what little he had seen, the men clearly worked hard for the
captain. "What kind of men do you have?" Drue asked. "Are they seasoned
sailors, fighting men, runaways, what?"

The captain laughed. "They are both seasoned sailors and fighting
men. I sail to all manner of ports, and have been able to fight off pirates on
more than one occasion. This vessel is well armed. Would you care to see
for yourself?"

Drue immediately accepted. When they had toured the ship, Drue and
the captain sat in the captain's quarters. Pouring a tankard of some of the
best wine Drue had ever tasted, the captain proudly asked, "Have you seen
such a ship as this?"

Drue smiled. "Only mine, but yours is even more discreet. Tell me, do you fight pirates or take pirates on?"

The captain laughed. "You are a wise man. Both. We look for their ships, and when we are finished with them, we share with whatever country whose waters we sail. We share well. Very well."

"Whose waters you sail?" Drue asked, puzzled.

The captain smiled slyly. "Yes. If we are in Spain's waters, we bring 'gifts' to Spain—if we are in waters of the Holy Roman Empire, gifts to Rome. When sailing in French waters, gifts to France. No one bothers my ship." He took a long drink of wine. "We have accurate information regarding what shipments are going where." When Drue's brows raised, the captain added, "Even honest men talk when they are drinking and whoring. The pirates talk too. They are men, you know. Well, nearly all of them are men." He smiled at Drue again.

With narrowed eyes, Drue asked, "Why are you telling me these things?"

"As I said, I would like to find work for my crew. I have sailed with these same men for five years now. They are getting restless." The captain paused for a moment. "I am quite good at judging people. You are not just on a pleasure trip. How can I and my crew help you?"

Drue twirled the wine around in his tankard. "Good wine, Captain, very good wine." Drue stood and walked around the room. The furnishings were those of a wealthy man, not a struggling seaman. He could use good help, and good fighting men. *Can I trust this man? Probably not, but could I use him for a short while?* After thinking on the captain's behavior and the feeling he got from the man, he made a decision. Drue stopped before the captain. "Any man worthy of his title could use good fighting men. How do I know they will not simply step over the line and change sides?"

"Look at the men. They have no country. They remain free only as long as they fight and stay with me," the man argued.

"And their crimes?" Drue asked.

"Pick it. You have it. The only crime they have not committed is assault or abuse of women or children. The rest . . . well, they are here." The captain waited a moment before adding, "Each of these men may only have one special skill. But that single thing they possess, they possess with remarkable expertise."

Drue asked shrewdly, "And what is your crime, Captain?"

The captain smiled. He studied Drue before answering. "I have never assaulted nor abused any woman or child." He offered more wine to Drue, who waved it away. He refilled his own tankard. "You should know, you would be commanding Captain Pilbik."

Drue extended his hand. "Captain." The men shook hands. Drue set his tankard on the table and walked toward the door. Turning, he caught the glint in Pilbik's eye and the look on his face. "How long before we make land? I may have work for you and your crew." Drue gave no indication he had seen anything unusual. Indeed, he had not. He expected treachery from the man who had just offered his service and the services of his men.

"We dock soon," was Pilbik's only answer. Drue closed the door behind him. Walking to his quarters, he made certain his face and carriage gave no indication of his final assessment of the captain. Several of the men working on the ship nodded as he passed. Others paid no mind. Not seeing Jon gave Drue pause, but upon opening his door, he found Jon busy packing.

"Going somewhere?" Drue asked.

"No, Your Grace. Only preparing," Jon replied. "I find the men aboard this vessel are prone to talk about what they plan on doing after we are 'gone.'"

"You are sure?" Drue asked. He had not expected the crew would be so aware of Pilbik's intentions.

"They all speak Portuguese. As do I," Jon replied. "Do you know how to swim, Your Grace?" Both men were speaking in very low tones.

"I do, but did not intend to show you . . . or anyone else. My plans included getting out with our horses." Suddenly, Drue put his finger to his mouth. Pointing to the door, he watched as someone's shadow moved to block the sliver of light at the door's base. "This trip is much smoother than our last one. The weather in the Channel is very unpredictable, it would seem."

"At least we do not have to ride in the rain. It will be warmer months in England, now," Jon replied, his eyes on the shadow. Eventually, it moved away.

Drue clasped Jon's shoulder. "Now the game gets interesting."

JUST before darkness fell, Drue and Jon slipped, hand over hand, along the anchor rope before they slid from the anchor into the water, barely causing a ripple. Moving alongside the ship's side, they made their way to the stern of the vessel, staying beneath the protrusion of the captain's quarters. As darkness enveloped the waters, they swam the short distance to the shoreline. On shore, Jon emptied his boots. "I must say, I cannot see how we are going to get our horses now."

Drue smiled at him, but remained silent. Jon shook his head and followed Drue's lead toward the nearest building. A man stepped to Drue and gave him a message from Braggio. Inside, a dock master and Drue had a short conversation. The dock master immediately sent for the authorities. When several men arrived wearing badges, the dock master spoke with them. Men were dispatched to the dock at Deal.

CAPTAIN PILBIK WAITED A SHORT TIME before calling for his quartermaster. "Well?" He waited expectantly. He doubted the man would have much to report, as Drue was unaware of the danger he and his retainer were in. Just as he thought, the quartermaster had little to report.

"They spoke of the last crossing and the cursed rain in England. Nothing important," the man reported. "We should drop anchor soon. Port London is quiet just now. Plenty of room for us."

"No. They believe we are to dock at Port London. After they are both asleep, sail for Deal. Scotland's ship will meet us at Deal. It would not help to have our passengers suspect we're taking gold to support Scotland. The waters are smooth so far. While asleep, they will not notice. I have made arrangements to have a 'reception.' Our guests will be taken prisoner after our cargo is unloaded and on its way to Scotland. The money Richard would pay for our hostages will be welcomed, and I will act surprised, of course."

"I do not look forward to riding for King Richard, sir. But you have always steered us well."

The captain smiled. "Do not trouble yourself, my good man. Neither you nor any of us will be fighting for Richard. Tudor will not try again. I have information from a valuable source that he will not try again until possibly next summer. However"—and he paused for effect—"providing our passengers to Richard will suggest a strong allegiance that will get us into the port without question . . . or inspection." Both men smiled.

When Pilbik docked that night, the authorities demanded they be allowed to board. Upon inspection, the cargo he carried was confiscated and he was arrested. Drue and Jon retrieved their horses and rode away, leaving Pilbik to his fate. Jon glanced back in time to see that Pilbik was bound and being loaded into a barred wagon, along with his men.

CHAPTER 57

THE PORT OF LONDON WAS BUSTLING as people scrambled
to load, board, say goodbyes, and make ready for the next ship docking. Most were of no interest to Diablo. As he scanned the harbormaster's
posting, two ships scheduled to arrive caught Diablo's interest, one from
Normandy and one from Burgundy. The Duchess of Burgundy may have
sent information. Of greater interest was the possibility that Lady Weldon
may well have sought passage with the vessel from Normandy—she may not
have been aware of the ongoing search for her and considered it safe to return
to England. She was wrong.

Diablo knew patience was a great weapon. To capture Lady Weldon
would be worth biding his time. He smiled to himself. *She will talk to me. She
will tell me everything and more, just to have it all end.*

Waiting specifically for those two ships to arrive, Diablo hung around
the docks, wandering in and out of the inns and listening, yet always standing to the side. Gossip held that Richard was preparing for another battle
with Tudor. Most still believed Tudor was through. Fighting was expensive,
and the common man paid for fighting in the worst way, with all he owned
and frequently with his life. Yet the fighting was not over. There were still
pockets of resistance in both the northern and southern lands. Diablo knew
this and relished the thought of watching the few men Tudor might be able
to raise on the field of battle. He had no intentions of joining Richard, but
he would be there to see Richard take Tudor.

Noise alerted him to the arrival of one of the ships—it was from Burgundy. There was no message for Diablo. The captain was arguing with the
dock master. Burgundy was being taxed heavily for the duchess's refusal to
openly support King Richard. True, the Duchess of Burgundy was the sister

of King Edward, but she was King Richard's sister, also. Edward was gone. Richard hoped his sister would speak out in his favor. So far, she had not done so.

Diablo knew the Duchess of Burgundy would not ever actively support King Richard. He was rumored to have murdered his nephew, Prince Edward, and may have done the same to Edward's younger brother, Prince Richard— an act the duchess could neither forget nor forgive.

That the dowager Queen Elizabeth was able to get her youngest son to safety was still entirely in the realm of possibility. Diablo had never believed young Richard lived in the beginning, but after his failed attempts to get Elizabeth to discuss the boy, he now believed young Richard did indeed live. Kingdoms were much like the waters of a mountain stream, ever changing in direction and strength.

The ship from Normandy docked, causing a second flurry of activity in the port. Diablo stood at the opposite end of the shoreline and moved to approach the ship, which would remain at port only as long as it took to reload supplies. They planned on leaving before morning. Diablo would need to move quickly, if he were to watch for passengers leaving. He stepped up his pace, but most of the crew had already disembarked before he got close enough to see who was aboard.

DOCKING, BRAGGIO INSTRUCTED Nicola and Lizzie to ride on into London and stay with Kelly instead of staying near the port. Bruce and his men would come for them after they had met with Drue, if at all possible. "I will see to his safety," Braggio assured Nicola. Braggio then bid farewell to Lizzie. "I will come to you as soon as I can. We will be with Drue and what men he might have. Stay clear of any fighting. Remember, I love you, my Lady Lizzie." He held her closely, kissed her, and left.

CHAPTER 58

Ａfter arriving in London, the ladies immediately went to the stable they had used before. The stable master, aware of their connection to Lord Bruce, eagerly took the horses in. "You look well, ladies," he told Nicola and Lizzie, and Nicola could see he was happy to have their business.

Nicola and Lizzie left the stables, warily watching the people around them. Changes in London's populace provided easy cover for men of dubious intentions. There were few women on the streets without male accompaniment, and many of the businesses were barely hanging on or closed. The feeling of an unseen threat hung in the air. The two hurried to Kelly's, and Nicola was anxious for the safety she could offer.

At Kelly's, a few women still worked the nights, though none lived there and everyone was frightened. An older woman who had always cleaned for Kelly agreed to talk with Lizzie and Nicola when she recognized Lizzie. She told of a mysterious man who had come to speak with Kelly. When he had gone, Kelly had hurriedly left that same night, taking few of her belongings. The man came back weeks later looking for her. One lady took him upstairs. She was found dead the next morning, which led to a mass exodus of the remaining women. Only the older lady still lived in the building. "I stay hidden as much as possible. Have shelter here, I do, but food is hard to come by. The man seen with the dead girl was the man Kelly had talked to the night she left. Kelly was afraid, and she was not afraid of anyone." The woman shuddered. "You'd best move on. 'Tis not a safe place, this London. Everyone is suspicious of their neighbors . . . even of their own kin." She briskly pushed both ladies toward the door. "I never had company on this day. Saw none. None here to work. I have not seen you. Go."

Nicola stood firm. "Wait. Please tell me what the man looked like." When the woman turned away, Nicola persisted. "We have to know who it is that might do harm to us."

The woman hesitated briefly. "He was a soldier, but wore no lord or king's colors, dressed all in black. His face had no expression. His eyes made one want to turn away. I do not know what name he goes by." The woman shivered.

Nicola felt a chill that bode unspeakable danger. It was the man in Nicola's vision. She pressed coins into the woman's hand. "God bless you, and stay safe. We will leave out the back." Nicola led the way from Kelly's into the alley.

With their hooded cloaks pulled tightly around them, locked arm in arm, Nicola and Lizzie hurried away. "Where do we go now?" Lizzie whispered.

"I know not where we might be safe. We must find shelter, soon. We are easy prey for the likes of men now roaming the streets of London," Nicola whispered. "I fear every town will be the same."

"I wish we knew where Kelly went," Lizzie said, gripping Nicola's arm tightly.

"Perhaps we would be out of harm's way if we left this town," Nicola suggested. She felt herself being drawn to her home, as if by invisible strings. She turned toward the stables. She could not explain it to Lizzie, but she knew they could be safe there. She felt it.

"Alone?" Lizzie whispered hoarsely. "Surely you jest, Nicola! We have no protection. In case you have not noticed, we do not have a guard. It is getting dark."

Nicola kept walking. "I know of only one place where we might be secure. It is not, I think, a place where anyone would look for us." Nicola knew the man looking for her was not in London . . . yet.

"Where is this place?" Lizzie asked.

"My home," Nicola replied.

"Is there no one living there?" Lizzie pushed. "Surely you cannot expect it to be unoccupied, Nicola. You know King Richard has taken most of the estates from those he deemed disloyal." Lizzie's voice softened. "That would be your family."

"Yes, I know. But I believe it to be abandoned. I remembered something Drue told me. He said it was feared haunted, because of the stories claiming I had just disappeared." It wasn't the entire truth, but she was afraid to tell Lizzie how things came to her. She had never spoken about such things except to Drue and, reluctantly, to Braggio.

Lizzie followed Nicola, but it was clear she was still not convinced. Nicola felt fairly confident that her sweet friend now wished she had insisted on staying with Braggio. And Nicola would have let her go, if she had known how this would turn out. But it was too late for that.

As they neared the stables, Nicola felt an icy sensation grip her. She stopped walking and pushed Lizzie deeper into the shadows. With her finger at Lizzie's mouth, she stood still. Lizzie froze. They waited. The sounds of a horse approaching grew louder. The rider stopped at the stables. In the dimming light of evening, they could easily tell it was a man. He called to the stable master. When there was no answer, he dismounted. The stable was dark, its doors pulled tight. To awaken the stable master would likely awaken the inhabitants of the inns and homes sitting nearby. The rider mounted and rode on. There were more stables, much farther in London.

Nicola watched as the dark figure and his horse rode out of view.

To prevent theft, the stable master always slept in the loft. He left out the back and slipped around to see who had tried the door, appearing behind Lizzie. The ladies recoiled until they recognized the man. "'Tis not a good time in London," he warned them. "Best you leave before the likes of him comes back. Come back he will."

In short order, he had their horses ready to ride. Directing them to the discreet side exit, he opened the door, soundlessly. "Keep it oiled, I do. Times call for speedy departures. Travel safely, m'ladies. God keep you." His voice was sad. Nicola tried to pay him, but he refused. "Wouldn't do well for me to have coins around. Leave the door as you can. Stay off the streets 'til you get out of town." He looked around nervously.

Nicola slipped coins into his hand anyway. He tried to refuse again, but Nicola closed his fingers around the coins. "You have always been there to help me. The dock is not far from here. We will be safe there." She and Lizzie slipped out the door, and waited until the door was closed and the bar securing it was in place. After carefully navigating darkened alleys, they finally left London behind and rode toward the docks.

After a moment, Nicola stopped and sat quietly, thinking. "Where do we go?" Lizzie asked. "Are we not going to your home?"

Nicola sat with her eyes closed. She knew to keep Lizzie with her could put Lizzie in danger if Nicola were seized as a traitor or heretic. Where else could they go? Nicola looked at Lizzie. "Toward Bosworth," Nicola replied firmly, as she turned her horse. "We will go toward Bosworth."

"Where is that?" Lizzie asked, frowning. "Why would we go there?"

"Because Tudor will be riding that way," Nicola replied. "Lizzie, you must go to Bosworth now."

"Why? I do not understand, Nicola." Lizzie sat still, staring at Nicola. "Why do you say *I* must go? You would send me alone? What is happening to you?"

Patiently, Nicola replied, "Tudor will fight somewhere near Bosworth. Lord Braggio could be injured, badly. He may not die, but he will need you."

"When?" Lizzie reached for Nicola's arm. "When, Nicola? How do you know these things?"

"Soon. You must go there. Stay away from the fighting, but stay close. When it is over, you must go to Lord Braggio. Tell anyone who asks that Braggio fought for Tudor and is injured. Tell them you are his betrothed and would care for him. You must do this soon, before the unrest with Tudor's reign begins, as it always does with a new king." Nicola reached out to touch her friend.

"How do you know these things?" Lizzie repeated. "How is it you know what is coming?"

"I cannot explain it now. There is not time. You must trust me. Drue trusted me, as did Lord Braggio. When we next meet, I will tell you all you ask. But not now. You must leave now."

"And you, Nicola? What will you do?" Lizzie asked. "Come with me," she pleaded. "I am afraid to go alone. Where is this Bosworth?" Lizzie began to weep.

"Ask for Derby. Derby is north of Bosworth. There are small villages where you will be safe. There will be others following King Richard, so do not pick sides. The news of the fight will spread quickly," Nicola replied, adding, "I cannot go with you. I bring danger to you. The man we saw in

London looks for me. He would surely kill you, Lizzie, if he were to catch us together. I must go alone."

Lizzie shook her head. "I cannot leave you, Nicola. I will stay with you."

"No. Lord Braggio will need you, Lizzie," Nicola insisted. "If you are not there to care for him, he may not survive."

Lizzie gripped Nicola's hand. "And you, Nicola? Are you certain you will be safe?"

"Of course." Nicola smiled. She spoke with more conviction than she felt.

Whisperings in London had not gone unheard. Nicola knew that King Richard had reached an agreement with the dowager Queen Elizabeth, allowing her to leave in safety, though she would remain under Richard's rule and "guidance." A portion of that agreement indicated he would assure her daughters married well and were kept in good stead. Further, by Christmas of 1484, rumors were rampant about Richard's amorous pursuit of the eldest daughter, Elizabeth. Nicola knew the houses of York and Tudor were destined to be united. Following Queen Anne's death in March 1485, to quell the unrest over the possibility of such a union, Richard was forced to make a public announcement that he would not seek to marry his brother's daughter. Nicola knew that anyone aware of even the possibility of such a union would most certainly support Tudor's coming invasion.

"Nicola?" Lizzie broke into Nicola's musings.

"Lizzie, neither side may even know yet where they will fight, but you know it will be near Bosworth. You must not tell anyone why you go to Bosworth. Your life will be at risk if you even hint at it. No one else can know what is coming. You should ask how to get to Derby. Derby is beyond Bosworth, but it will not be evident that you go to be near the coming fight. You will know when you come to the place where Tudor and King Richard will meet." Nicola squeezed Lizzie's hand. "Braggio will need your care, but he will survive. Take him back to his home."

Lizzie started to speak, but Nicola's raised hand stopped her. "Take the road until you come to the houses on the left. All will surely be abed at this hour. Knock at the first house anyway. Just tell them you have lost your way."

Lizzie sat staring at Nicola, ignoring the tears trickling down her cheek.

Her voice broke. "I feel like we will not meet again. I . . . I cannot find the words to say all I feel."

"I know, Lizzie. I love you, too." Nicola's voice was soft. "I will never forget you, my dearest friend. Take care, Lady Braggio." Nicola turned her horse and rode deeper into the forest.

As Nicola rode away, she felt drawn to a different place. *Wait . . . I cannot go home yet. What happens now?* Images came to her slowly at first, like the sprinkling before a hard storm. The images grew in size and began moving rapidly. In an instant, Henry Tudor was before her. He was pacing inside a tent, his face registering the anxiety and uncertainty he was experiencing. Nicola felt as if someone or something was pulling her. *I must get to Tudor this night.*

Though unfamiliar with the land, Nicola turned her horse and followed where her mind took her. She rode through a forested area until she came to a road whose tracks struggled to move from under the vegetation covering them. Without hesitating, Nicola took it. The feeling grew stronger. Knowing Lizzie would stop for the night, Nicola was careful to stay away from people. The feeling that she must reach Tudor drove her onward. Drue's voice came to her again: *Trust your instincts.* Though she had no knowledge of the land or where she should ride, she felt strangely sure of herself. It was pitch-black all around her, but she rode without hesitation. Her father's horse carefully picked his way along the seldom used road. *I am coming, Henry Tudor. Take heart. You will take the crown.*

CHAPTER 59

Diablo had stood behind the tables of lords and dukes while they plotted battles over lands and titles for as long as he could remember. He always stood quietly, doing the bidding of whoever paid for his services. His last master was the Duke of Burgundy. Though the duke had died, Diablo never doubted the duchess would take up the duke's own cause to favor England's rise as a powerful nation. As King Edward's sister, she had ambition surging through her veins. She called on Diablo just as her husband had so often requested his services.

When news of King Edward's death reached Burgundy, Edward's mother begged her daughter, the duchess, to refrain from stepping into the ring, but the Duchess of Burgundy walked to her own tune. That she would enlist his help came as no surprise to Diablo. She had no one else to trust with such a mission. Edward was dead, his sons missing at best, and Richard's son was now deceased. The throne was ripe for the picking. The duchess would use every resource to keep a York on the throne.

The dowager Queen Elizabeth's behavior, and all she left unsaid, swayed Diablo to believe persistent stories that young Richard lived. Lady Weldon would know just where the young prince was being kept. He, Diablo, intended to be the one to bring that information to the duchess. He had grown weary of his chosen business. He thought to retire quietly in Burgundy. That could happen if he could find Lady Weldon. Perhaps her secrets would provide him with knowledge useful enough to pay him well. Getting Nicola to divulge her secrets would prove easy for a man of his special skills.

Riding through the streets of London, Diablo passed a smaller stable. Diablo knew if he stabled his mount in one of the larger stables, there would be questions. His horse was well cared for, his riding gear the best—both indicating an owner with considerable funding. Upon finding the door locked, his first inclination was to rattle the doors, trying to wake a stable hand. He decided against the noise, for fear of drawing unwanted attention. He rode on, passing groups of armed men roaming around wearing Richard's colors. Intent on avoiding any command to join King Richard's forces, he kept moving westward through London.

Diablo passed a second smaller stable. The location was perfect. As he paused, he could hear men talking behind the building. He turned his horse around and dismounted. The doors opened easily. Diablo led his horse inside to a vacant stall, but left the mount saddled and the stall open. Walking through the stable, he stepped into the light of a rather large fire. Several well-armed men sat around the fire on barrels or leaned against a short rock wall built near the river's edge, eating and drinking. The men were dressed in Richard's colors and wearing his badge, a bristled and armed white boar. Immediately, every man stood. Not a word was spoken as both sides evaluated the other.

Diablo spoke first. "I have traveled from the port at Sandwich. I ride for the Duchess of Burgundy, the sister of King Richard. She sends me to ask if King Richard has need of additional arms. I see you ride for him." He calmly walked toward the stone wall, speaking as he moved. "Who is the commander? I would ask where I should take this request. The duchess is expecting an answer quickly, before the storms begin and make crossing the Channel difficult." He stretched his hands out to the warmth, taking care that nothing in his movements or words gave cause for concern. One man alone stepped away from the fire to stand near Diablo.

"You're in luck, m'lord. We are to gather in the early morn, to hear from our commander. Meanwhile, we have been about, recruiting additional men." The speaker was younger. Diablo could tell he was anxious to show his authority.

"How goes the call to arms?" Diablo asked casually.

As the soldier started to reply, another interrupted. Glaring at the man, he ordered the soldier to refrain, adding, "You are so experienced you are certain this man is who he says? He wears no badge of Charles the Bold, Duke of Burgundy." Turning to Diablo, he said, "Why don't you tell us what you are really about?"

At that moment, Diablo knew he could be forced to fight the five men. Keenly aware of the man standing near him, he stepped toward the speaker. In a soft but deadly voice, he spoke. "We will all be better served to stay calm. I did not come here to fight anyone, but will do so if need be. It is true, I do not wear the badge of the duchess. These are not easy times in your fair England. One is never certain just where another's loyalty lies."

He continued to circle the fire. Then, without warning, he drew his sword. As he whirled, he struck down the man nearest him. Lunging toward the man behind him, he killed him too. The rest of the men were scrambling to get around the fire and the barrels surrounding it. They fanned out and moved in on him. Diablo pitched a burning wood piece onto one man's face. That man fell into a barrel, which tipped, sending him into the fire. Flames caught quickly. The screams and smells of the man burning panicked the horses inside, trapped in stalls. One animal kicked his stable door down and ran toward the opened back door. The rest followed, as the flimsy stalls crashed. In the confusion, Diablo whistled for his own horse and mounted as the horse ran past him. *Damnation!* Diablo's work was now much more difficult. Because of this, he would be forced to continue his search for Lady Weldon in the dark of night, when King Richard's men would be less likely to recognize him. *Should have killed them all.* He reined his horse in. *I still can. No one can be left to identify me.* He turned his horse around.

After returning down the alley behind the stable, he dismounted and edged along the wall toward the fire. The two men left were just returning their horses to the stable.

The younger of the men was arguing with his companion. "I still say we say nothing," he said. "How do we tell this story? One man kills three of us and rides out?" His companion, an older soldier, remained silent, though his anger was palpable. He led his horse into the stable, while the younger man stood aside, holding his horse. Diablo waited until the first man was well inside the stable before he struck. Stepping up silently, he quickly slit the younger man's throat.

"Are you coming? Get in here!" the older man ordered. When his companion did not answer, Diablo could hear him draw his weapon. Diablo did not enter the stable—instead, he stepped aside to prevent a silhouette from the fire behind him. After waiting, the man cautiously stepped forward, but Diablo could hear the subtle sound—if this man thought he could take Diablo, man to man, he was a greater fool than Diablo had even thought.

The man never felt the knife that opened his neck. Diablo looked around. All was still. After returning the way he had come, he mounted and left, riding to the very end of the alley, then crossing the street. He rode through town, out in the open and with a relaxed demeanor, projecting a general lack of concern. Several men were headed to the stable with the runaway horses. They only glanced at him.

He checked every inn, cluster of men, and brothel he could find. There was no sign or word of two ladies unescorted or even one lady without escort. *Perhaps my belief was wrong and Lady Weldon stayed at port.* As Diablo rode slowly through the streets of London searching, he tried to think where the ladies might have taken refuge. Two women riding alone would be in danger on the roads of England. They would not be safe . . . unless they were never on the roads. It was time for Diablo to explore the vicinity in greater detail. He needed to hear unguarded conversations. He reached a larger stable and gave the man several coins, warning him not to sell the animal.

London was in chaos. Men hid to keep from being forced to ride for a king rumored to have killed his own nephews. Other men, hoping to garner monies in exchange for fighting, gathered and drank. Hours passed, ale ran, fights broke out, and men were killed. Meanwhile, Richard's guards roamed throughout the city, recruiting for a confrontation with Tudor certain to come. Diablo noticed one of the more seasoned guards watching him as he left his horse and strolled onto the street. Diablo knew he had the pronounced look of a fighting man. He carried weapons, rode with confidence—like one who would not easily back down.

"You there, come with me," the man ordered Diablo. At first Diablo took no notice, but when the man called again, he turned just as the soldier reached him. "Come with me. King Richard has need of good fighting men and you look the part."

Diablo answered in French, hoping that if he were not from England, he could not be expected to fight for either side. "I do not understand what you say."

The soldier smoothly replied in French, "I say you are to come with me. You will be fighting for our Richard."

Diablo persisted. "I would refrain from any fighting. I am not from England."

"But you are *in* England now," the soldier pointed out. "You will come with me." The man stood still, his stance clearly indicating he would fight if necessary. While Diablo had no doubts about winning any fight, he knew where a fight in the middle of the street with one of Richard's men would lead. Several more soldiers stood around, watching the exchange.

Switching to English, Diablo grinned amiably. "You have made your point. Where are we bound?" The soldier nodded and, clasping Diablo's shoulder, he turned him around. They both walked back toward an inn where men were lined up. Skirting the line, Diablo and the soldier entered.

The rest of the evening was spent talking with other men and eating. Everyone spoke with confidence for a win in the coming battle. The entire troop of men were to head out early the next morning. Diablo knew if he were going to avoid this twist to his plan, he would have to leave during the night.

Several times during the evening and into the night, Diablo left the crowded inn, returning shortly. The first time he left, the soldier who recruited him and another both watched him leave. Both appeared ready to follow after him. As hours went by, the two watched him less and less. Diablo wandered in and out, always careful to be seen leaving and returning. By this time, neither soldier was watching him at all. It was near dawn when Diablo wandered out again. He walked to the stables and rode out of London.

Diablo had not ridden far when he heard riders behind him. After edging into the surrounding forest, he stopped his horse and waited. The riders all wore Richard's colors and carried his standard. While listening to talk during the night with the king's guard, he knew these men were riding to join Richard and his army at Nottinghamshire. Diablo had no intention of being seen by Richard's men, or by Tudor's, for that matter. His focus was on finding the elusive Lady Weldon.

Richard's men were long out of sight before Diablo continued riding toward the western coastline, staying within the forested areas offering cover. Unfamiliar with some of the terrain, he took great care to avoid the roads.

He rode for the estate of Lord Weldon. From comments made by several of the men recruiting, Diablo believed that Lord Weldon's castle was one of the holdings listed that had not sent anyone to ride in support of King Richard. Diablo believed that could mean the current residents rode for Tudor or no one. He knew the Earl of Blackgrove would certainly not willingly fight for Richard or anyone else. More likely, Diablo reasoned, it meant the castle was unoccupied. Blackgrove would have left rather than risk losing his life in a battle. Unoccupied would please Diablo—he needed someplace to stay unnoticed. When he finished with Lady Weldon, he would press dowager Queen Elizabeth to speak of her youngest son. Tudor would have difficulty fielding an army of substantial size. Winning would not improve King Richard's popularity with the cloud of murdering his own nephews hanging over him. In Diablo's mind, neither contender belonged on the throne of England.

CHAPTER 60

RUMORS OF KING RICHARD'S intentions toward Princess Elizabeth troubled Henry Tudor a great deal. Henry's mother and the dowager Queen Elizabeth had already reached an accord, promising Elizabeth's hand to Tudor. Such a marriage would go a long way to bring supporters of King Edward to his side. Tudor needed Princess Elizabeth. To take a bride no longer a maid was a bad move in itself. To take a bride who was believed to have lain with King Richard would never garner the backing of Edward's supporters. Worse, if she became pregnant soon, there would always be speculation over the child's father.

"One battle at a time, Henry," Jasper advised. Events in England were quickly becoming more volatile. Tudor recognized his time to claim the throne was now. So began his move onto the pages of history.

After taking counsel with Jasper and other leaders in exile, borrowing a modest amount of money from Charles III, and outfitting a small fleet, Tudor set sail. Henry and his fleet left Normandy, from Honfleur, at the mouth of the river Seine. Sailing with him were only four thousand men, including men from the prisons of Normandy.

Henry followed his plan to land at the western tip of Wales, where his father, Edmond, and his uncle Jasper had a strong stand during Henry VI's reign and from where he and Jasper had fled when Edward IV took the throne. Henry would not face opposition on those shores.

It took six days before his ships sailed around the southern tip of England. Every day at sea, Henry and his uncle thought on and talked about what they were undertaking. The size of his army was a constant topic. He had to find more men once he reached Wales.

Henry's thoughts wrestled with the knowledge that men sailing with him had plenty of time to think on what they had agreed to do. They would know their numbers were small, as were their chances. Somehow, Henry had to find a way to light the fire of conquest for England's throne in the very souls of the men following him.

On Sunday, August 7, 1485, Henry and his men landed at Mill Bay near Milford Haven and Pembroke Castle, the place of his birth. After wading ashore, he knelt and kissed the wet Welsh sand. Standing, he gazed at the lands before him and, turning to look into Jasper's eyes, he nodded resolutely. Turning to the men behind him, he yelled, "Your freedom awaits you!" The men cheered and scrambled ashore with enthusiasm, but Henry knew this would be tempered—their ride to battle would not be an easy one.

In his heart, Tudor prayed for guidance and success. He was about to embark on a quest for which he had prepared his entire life. From a thick golden chain at his neck, beneath his doublet, hung the symbol given to him by an old woman that foretold Tudor's odyssey and success. Tudor gripped the symbol. "I pray she is right," he whispered.

Jasper answered his nephew's unspoken question. "We ride to claim England. Do not forget your stepfather's men, rumored to be well over two thousand. Lord Stanley will bring his soldiers to you, all seasoned fighting men. Stanley's brother will bring his men also. Margaret has assured me she has gathered others to our cause. Take heart, Henry. No battle is easy, none with more at stake. When the fighting is over, one man will be left standing— you, King of England."

Crossing to England through Wales was Jasper's idea, and a smart move. There would be no hostilities against Henry Tudor from that region, but there would be the possibility of adding to their forces from the people living in the area. Tudor's army was an odd mixture of Frenchmen, a few Scots, Welsh, and English exiles, some prisoners, and anyone else Jasper could convince to step to Henry's cause. Henry glanced back at the mob behind him. Fear that the coming battle would still prove too easy for Richard plagued him.

Banking on gathering additional forces as they moved across Wales, the Tudors stayed close to the shoreline. Although initially few of the men his army passed joined his force, word of his movement quickly spread throughout the countryside, giving heart to more and more of the Welsh men. Slowly, greater numbers of men stepped in with Henry's army.

Henry and his men traversed the mountains of Wales and sloshed in and out of the marshes to reach England through the plain of Shropshire. Although it was the middle of summer, the countryside made for rugged and difficult travel, which gave his men something to occupy their thoughts besides the fight they moved closer to face.

Henry went over and over the details of the coming battle. His hand gripped the symbol beneath his tunic. He could still see the old woman, her painful movements adding to the credibility of her message.

"Your mother would say the old woman was sent by the devil," Jasper noted one afternoon.

Henry nodded. "Yes, but I do not believe that. If she was sent by the devil, would her message be the same as my mother's? I think not." After a while, Henry spoke again. "Uncle, I do not know my mother. My memories are of watching her wave goodbye." He looked off in the distance. "I pray, Uncle, if I ever have sons, I will be to them all you have been to me." Henry spurred his horse ahead, moving to the front of his army.

Jasper watched Henry ride away. "You are the son I could never have, Henry. I have loved you well. I have loved your mother all these years, though she knew it not," Jasper said under his breath.

IT TOOK THREE DAYS OF PUNISHING TRAVEL, dragging guns and each other through the high grounds, to reach the small settlement of Shrewsbury. Initially, the city shut the gates to Tudor and his men, but a messenger bearing letters from Henry's mother—and money—convinced the mayor to open the city gates. From this site, the Midlands of England stretched below them. Here lay Henry's chance to seize the throne. Again, he gripped the symbol beneath his tunic.

The banners Henry flew were met with excitement and favor. Henry added the cross of St. George, patron saint of England, to his badge. He next added the dun cow of the Beaufort family, which spoke of royal intent and his Lancastrian ancestry. It was still rumored that Richard had murdered his nephews. When his wife died, rumor added Queen Anne Neville to the list of Richard's victims. With such rumors flying, Henry attracted more men to his side. Tudor's army grew, but he knew from Jasper's spies that Richard's army was also growing.

Jasper Tudor wore the Draco Rubius as his badge. Taken from a legend, the Red Dragon represented the British people. Legend told of the defeat of the White Dragon, representing the invading Saxons. Yorkist propaganda merged this myth with their own tale of an angel that appeared and foretold of the death of the Red Dragon by the White Dragon. Cleverly, Tudor reversed this interpretation so that he was the Red Dragon and King Richard III, an outsider, was the White Dragon. Tudor quickly adopted the Red Dragon Dreadful as his principal standard, took on the mantle of the fair unknown, the heir, raised in obscurity only to emerge and claim his crown, just as King Arthur had. Jasper kept in contact with the Welsh bards who spread the stories of the defeat of the White Dragon by the Tudor Red Dragon. The Red Dragon, set against a background of green and white, connected Henry with ancient kings of the Britons. Thus Henry's invasion had become a holy crusade. Momentum was building.

After a week of arduous travel, Henry and his men reached the Dyfi Valley. They stopped at the small town of Machynlleth that in earlier times had been a center for the rebels of the whole country, their capital of sorts. From here, Tudor sent official letters requesting the support of the surrounding lords, letters whose language, tone, and signature bore the feel of an English monarch. Henry Tudor was playing his cards—he knew Richard was doing the same. He also knew Richard was proven in battle. Tudor had never been in a battle or even led men. He had never strategized for defense or for attack. He was going to take the men with him into a desperate push for the crown. Doubts were beginning to crowd other thoughts, and he knew he could never allow his men to see the uncertainty he felt. The load upon his shoulders was great indeed.

CHAPTER 61

B Y AUGUST 19, Richard's army was massive, though he wanted more men. Richard knew Lord Stanley and his brother could add at least five thousand men. Richard wanted those men. Stanley, as usual, had not committed his support, so Richard summoned him to his court. Citing illness as the cause, Stanley failed to meet with Richard. In times of conflict, Stanley and his brother were known to switch sides at any point, based upon which side was expected to win.

When Stanley did not show, Richard was furious. One of his commanders was able to find and capture Lord Stanley's only son, Lord Strange. King Richard now held Lord Strange as a hostage with the threat of execution if Stanley failed to support the king, insuring Stanley's support.

WHEN STANLEY MET WITH HENRY TUDOR and informed him of his son's predicament, Henry knew Stanley would not commit to him. Although Lady Margaret had assured Henry of Stanley's backing, Henry now knew he could not count on Stanley.

More troubling, Henry knew that King Richard continued to gain men as he moved with his army northward through England. Henry had been surprised when Richard arrived at a small town, Sutton Cheney, northeast of Bosworth Field, where Henry himself camped. Richard set up camp outside the town. He arrayed his vanguard, expected to secure ground in advance of the main force, along the hill overlooking the fields. It was clear that King Richard hoped the sheer number of his vanguard, spread along the hill overlooking Tudor's men, would be intimidating. The vanguard could be seen for miles. Henry and his small army were camped below. They watched that vanguard silhouetted atop the hill.

Situated at equal distance from King Richard's men and Henry's men, Lord Stanley camped with his men. Between Lord Stanley and his brother, their men totaled approximately six thousand men. Henry desperately needed Stanley's men in order to stand any chance of defeating King Richard. Stanley's battle position confirmed that Tudor's chances of counting on Stanley for support were nonexistent. Tudor would fight King Richard with only his few men. He felt the weight of doubt. *How can I possibly win? The old woman said I would win. I must win.* And so the argument in his mind raged, as he paced.

Late that afternoon, Tudor's mother, Lady Margaret, arrived. She stepped inside his tent, and Henry immediately went to her. He held her closely.

She was clearly anxious to see him before the coming battle. He could sense that fear filled her heart, but she refused to let it be known. She was of the mindset that, for her son to win, he must believe he would win. And Henry could agree with this logic—there could be no doubt. And it was true that his hodgepodge army had by now become more orderly. Yet the dimming sunlight filtering through the trees displayed the overpowering numbers of Richard's vanguard to Henry where he stood with his mother. Still in his embrace, she looked up at him with a smile intended to comfort him and spoke. "God did not bring you all this way to have you defeated. He knows that you need Him now, more than ever before, and He will stand by your side."

"Yes, but am I truly going to win this battle, Mother? Is this the reason I have trained?" he asked, whispering into her hair.

"It is God's will; you will be king of England. He brought you this far and will not see you fail now. You must not lose heart, son."

NICOLA RODE WITHOUT STOPPING, desperate to reach Tudor before he and King Richard met in battle. Henry had to believe with every fiber of his being that he would be king. Again, Drue visited her mind. *Because of you, Prince Drue, I ride at night, alone, without fear. You did not intend to leave me with such knowledge, but I have kept it all.*

At last she reached the Tudor camp. She announced herself to one of the posted guards. "I come alone. I have a message for Henry Tudor."

After a brief pause, the guard nodded and allowed Nicola to ride on. She made her way through the crowded space teeming with men, horses, and tents. Tudor's tent was marked with his standards. Another guard was posted outside. Again, Nicola requested to speak with Henry Tudor. "Tell him I have a message from the old woman who once visited him not long ago." The guard nodded and entered the tent. He came out shortly and motioned to Nicola.

When Nicola dismounted, the guard stepped closer. "You are alone, lady?"

"Yes," Nicola replied. She spoke quietly, infusing her words with a sense of calm. Henry Tudor required tranquility. The man frowned, studied Nicola for a moment, then stepped aside.

Inside the tent, Nicola felt the familiar knot of fear. Henry, his uncle Jasper, and his mother, Lady Margaret, were talking. Henry was watching the tent entrance. Nicola bowed low to Henry. Before she could speak, Henry challenged her. "Who are you?" he asked, frowning. "What is your purpose?" He looked past Nicola, hoping to see the old woman.

"You will find yourself in the Tower when Henry is king," Lady Margaret haughtily interrupted. "Take her away—she could be part of the York uprising. She is now a prisoner." Lady Margaret's face was filled with worry and fear. "I have spent every waking hour preparing for the coming confrontation—and any distraction is unacceptable. She could be a spy. You must act quickly, Henry. You cannot think on whatever she has to say. Your future is before you. Guard! Take her away!"

The guard entered the tent, but Henry's upraised hand halted him. When Henry shook his head, the guard stepped back out. The tent was quiet while Henry studied the lady standing before him. He ignored his mother's advice. "I ask again, why are you here?"

Nicola knew that she did not appear aggressive or threatening. She lifted her head, confident and untroubled.

"Answer when you are spoken to," Lady Margaret stated.

"Your Majesty, I do not know all that has been done by either house, York or Tudor. I only know what the old woman knew to be true." Nicola met Henry's eyes, unwavering.

Lady Margaret gasped, her head spinning toward her son. Henry stepped forward.

"I do not understand all that has happened. I know little of either side of this coin, only that you, Henry, will be the king. And I know you always were meant to be king," Nicola finished quietly.

"And what makes you so certain? How do you know?" Henry asked, his manner intense. "How?"

"An old woman with a symbol came to you, before you sailed to take the throne of England," Nicola said, and Lady Margaret stepped forward aggressively.

"Guard! Take her away! She is a heretic . . . the witch Queen Anne spoke of!" She pointed at Nicola, her hand trembling.

The guards were inside the tent at once. "I must speak only to you," Nicola interjected. Her eyes never left Henry's, so that he would feel her strength of conviction.

"Let her be," ordered Henry. When Lady Margaret started to protest, he added, "Mother, you and Jasper leave us. I will speak with her alone." Lady Margaret turned to glare at Nicola, but Henry's voice was firm. "Jasper will walk with you. I will call for you when we are finished."

Jasper nodded, stepped to Lady Margaret's side, and led her away.

Waiting to give Jasper and his mother time to walk out of hearing, Henry turned to Nicola. "How do you know the old woman?"

"You were near a settlement of huts, larger and better made than those of England. There were pins for livestock and fields of crops. Beyond were mountains. Nearby a stream ran freely. Millers and their families were living there before the killing began and the fires were set." Nicola paused. Henry listened intently. "The old woman came to you in a small clearing of the forest, away from the burning settlement. Your uncle was the only other man around and he was in the hut where you stayed. You did not want to hear what she came to say, but she persisted." Nicola continued, "You were given a symbol. The stones of the symbol bore colors predicting the deaths of King Edward, his two sons, King Richard's son . . . and King Richard. It also had a red rose with the white rose at its center. There was only one unbroken crown on that symbol."

Nicola was quiet for a moment. "The unbroken crown of the red rose. This battle is necessary, but you must take heart. You will be the king of England. You know well the story the old woman spoke of. You have retold that same story to yourself, countless times." Nicola said gently. She could tell from the emotion filling Henry's eyes that she was right.

"How do you know these things? Did you dream them?" Henry's voice was intense. "The old woman told me the symbol was created because the symbol maker had a vision, or dream. Are you the symbol maker?"

Nicola hesitated a moment. "Your Majesty, I am the symbol maker's daughter," Nicola replied. "I know all that the old woman said to you, because that old woman was me, disguised. It was the only way I knew to get to you and deliver the symbol my father made for you. My father made me promise I would bring the message and symbol to you alone. He died shortly after he spoke with me. I kept that promise, but your mind is filled with many thoughts. Problems you think could end your quest."

Henry stood still in silence, watching Nicola. She continued, "You must never doubt your right to the throne of England. You will be a good king, Henry Tudor. The battle you are preparing to wage will take many lives, but not yours or the life of your uncle." Her conviction felt powerful and compelled her to continue. She spoke words that came to her as if from a whisper in her mind. "You will have support from men you hardly know, support from other men who will turn against you in the future, and from still others who would die for you. You will learn to tell one from the other." Bowing low, Nicola finished. "Now, your time is nearing. You will be King Henry VII." She curtsied low, then turned to leave.

Henry stopped Nicola. "Thank you for your message—I feel a calm filling me and am grateful for the strength it gives me. You will leave my campsite safely, but do not stay close. The marshes will make this a difficult battle. Richard has many more men than I, but I have destiny with me." Henry bowed slightly. "Thank you, lady."

Nicola nodded, curtsied again, walked out of the tent, and retrieved her horse. Without looking at anyone, she left the war camp of Henry Tudor, the man who would be king. Her work was done.

Nicola rode to Stoke Golding as if led there. The stable was small and empty. There were no horses within its corral. The stable master was the son of an older lady. Alone and unescorted, Nicola felt her situation stir sympathy from the man. She was welcomed to their home. The old woman offered her own bed, but Nicola refused, saying she would rest near the fire. As night deepened, the house fell silent but for the sound of the gentle breathing of the woman and her son. Sleep evaded Nicola. Her mind was filled with memories of treasured moments with Drue. Could she leave without knowing if Drue survived?

Waiting until she was certain both were fast asleep, Nicola left a small pile of coins on their table before she slipped out of the hut. Struggling to saddle her horse, Nicola was startled when the stable master spoke to her. "Let me, m'lady. 'Tis too heavy for you." After he was done, he stood watching Nicola. "You do not have to leave. You would be safe here."

"I thank you and your mother for your kindness to a stranger. I must not stay. I would bring danger to you." She pressed most of the coins she had left into his hand. "Stay safe. There will be a great change, but this is not your fight. Soon it will be over."

Without waiting for a reply, Nicola rode away. Drue was going to fight for Henry Tudor, and she intended to be close by, praying for his safety. Try as she might, she could not tell what would happen to Drue on this day. She only knew that once more, before their story ended, she would look upon the man who now held her heart in his hand.

CHAPTER 62

K ing Richard stood staring at the fires from Tudor's small encampment. His own camp spread out, covering a hilltop just south of Bosworth, near Dadlington and Stoke Golding, both smaller villages. Below his camp, near Tudor's, was a marsh filled with reeds and thick mud that stuck to anything touching its surface.

Richard turned his thoughts back to the defeat of Henry Tudor. By the best counts coming to him, Henry had barely three thousand men, if that. Richard commanded a field of at least fifteen thousand. His leaders, including the Duke of Norfolk, a very able though aging commander, believed the odds were overwhelmingly in favor of Richard. Despite these assurances, Richard was tired of spending every waking hour trying to keep his crown. He knew well how King Edward had struggled to keep his throne, but Edward had had Richard to help him win those battles. Weighed down by the inexplicable disappearance of his two nephews and the pain of his son's death followed by his wife's, Richard knew he would have to win this battle. Popular opinion was turning against him, especially since his wife died.

Richard never assumed a victory. Having led the charge in many battles before, though he always won, he recognized small things could turn any fight. He paced inside his tent. Lord Stanley's son, Lord Strange, was Richard's ace—no father would abandon his son, his only son, to support someone attempting to usurp the throne. Richard knew Stanley and his brother, Sir William Stanley, could muster a large army of men. Those men could increase Henry's odds considerably. Angrily, he strode to the corner where Stanley's son sat awaiting his fate. Richard grasped Strange's coat and jerked him close. "You will be dead at the first hint of your father's move for Tudor. You will be dead—do you hear me?"

Lord Strange nodded shakily. "Yes, Your Majesty. My father and his men will come to you. I am certain of it." Desperately, his eyes searched the tent—the young man surely knew the king made no idle threat. Lord Strange's life would be over.

King Richard's mind wandered to his dead wife. They were so happy in the beginning. How he had loved her, and how sad she had become believing he might set her aside to take the Princess Elizabeth as his wife, to secure a successor.

Richard needed a son, an heir, to keep the throne safe. However, public opinion made such a move impossible. With a stab of guilt, Richard knew he had caused Anne deep pain and sorrow. *Look, Anne. Look down on me, and tell me how I will spend tomorrow's eve.*

There was no response, only silence.

JUST BEYOND HIS CAMP, Henry Tudor stood watching the silhouette of King Richard's vanguard, spread across the hill beyond. This battle would tell his story, the story of his crowning victory or dying defeat. *There can be no defeat. I am meant to be the king of England, and so I will be.* Turning at the sound of footsteps, he waited for his uncle. Jasper had just returned after taking Lady Margaret to safety, far beyond the two camps, closer to an escape route. It was well known by all now that she had provided funds, rounded up men, and encouraged her son in his quest to be king. If King Richard won, Lady Margaret would be tried as a traitor and put to death.

"Henry, your mother has requested I secure a safe escape route for you, should this battle look to be lost. You cannot chance being killed. I am leaving now to do just that." Jasper spoke quietly, for fear they might be overheard.

Henry was surprised. "You will not be with me in the morning?" It would not be the first time Henry had to run for his life, but this time, he intended to stay. More, he counted on Jasper staying with him.

"I will return before morning," Jasper promised as he grasped Henry closely. The two men embraced. Henry thought he could see uncertainty clouding Jasper's eyes, but now was not the time for such conversation.

"Go, Uncle. Make haste, I need you back with me," Henry replied. As Jasper rode away, Henry whispered, "I leave this battleground as king or die trying for the throne. I will run no more."

The sounds of men entering camp roused Henry from his reflection. He turned and walked back toward his tent. The new men were dismounting, laughing, and greeting Henry's men. With surprise and relief, Henry recognized his friend Prince Drue Vieneto. Lords Braggio and Bruce were with him, as well as more men. Drue met Henry near the command tent. The men greeted each other warmly. Henry spoke first. "I see you have men with you, Drue. And two able leaders as well. I owe you much, my friend."

Drue smiled. "Not just men, fighting men, every one of them! I see you have the Earl of Oxford. He is one of the best commanders. 'Twill not be easy, but you take the crown tomorrow, Henry." The men entered the tent.

Drue spoke with such conviction Henry nearly asked if he knew the symbol maker. Before he could, Braggio, Bruce, and the earl joined them. Talk took on a heavy note. With so few men, they each would have to do more than their part. Someone called out toward the tent, and Henry rose and stood at the entrance. David Owen, the illegitimate son of Owen Tudor, Jasper's younger brother, strode toward Henry. Upon landing on England's shore, Henry had knighted David. Now, true to his promise, David had come. He led a small group of men whose sole purpose was to guard Henry Tudor. Henry clasped David's shoulder and led him inside the tent, introducing him around.

WHILE THE NIGHT MIST THICKENED, Drue stepped away from his men and pulled Jon aside. "Tonight, Lord Strange must be rescued, and Lord Stanley must know he is safe. Without Lord Strange safe, neither Lord Stanley nor his brother can be counted on to take Henry Tudor's side. We need their men. Take care, Jon. I need you. You have an important duty meant for you alone, when we return to our homeland."

"You need not worry—Strange will be safe and I will be at your side again with morning's light."

At the Tudor camp, to Henry Tudor's obvious delight, two royal captives, imprisoned in the Tower on suspicion of plotting against Richard, had escaped while being moved. They both joined Henry with the few men they had mustered. Henry discussed plans for the first moves with his team of commanders—Drue, Bruce, Braggio, and the Earl of Oxford.

Drue had no thoughts on the upcoming battle. He knew what was expected of him, knew how battles could swing at any time, and knew his men would do whatever was needed. Instead, all of Drue's thoughts were on Nicola. In reality, if he survived the coming battle, he was expected to return to his homeland and his brother. He knew he loved Nicola, but could he pull her into his life? There would always be assignments, and that could not be a good thing for Nicola. He wrestled with the decision. Should he go for her? At last, shaking his head, he admitted it would be best for Nicola if he let her go. He knew he must do what was best for her, though she still possessed his heart.

As he sat waiting for the sun to display the fields beyond—fields that would soon belong to another king, King Henry VII—he turned his mind to the upcoming battle.

JON REMOVED ALL HIS WEAPONS, changed into dark clothes, and left everything but his short blade in Drue's tent. Moving unnoticed around behind Henry's camp, he faded into the darkness. Knowing King Richard's camp sat atop a small hill above Henry's camp, Jon chose to move away from both camps. He knew that however King Richard had positioned his soldiers, their attention would be upon the Tudor camp itself. The inhabitants of both villages to the rear of King Richard's camp had all abandoned the homes closest to the king's tents and men. When Jon had moved well away from the perimeter of Henry's camp, he stealthily worked his way back until he reached the rear of the king's camp, which dwarfed Tudor's camp below. The king's tent, set along the rear, was by far the largest tent, allowing the king a full view of his camp and vanguard. His standard billowed in the evening breezes. Surprisingly, there were few guards watching the area. Jon furtively inched his way closer. He lay flat on the ground watching as various men moved in and out of the king's tent. Eventually, the traffic of battle tacticians ceased.

Edging nearer, Jon studied the tent. It was structured in two sections, each with a fire burning along with several lamps hung throughout, projecting silhouettes onto the tent from the inside. Jon could make out a bed and table in the smaller section. He crept around the tent. The light was enough to provide faint silhouettes of King Richard's armor, weapons, and other items leaning against the center pole of the larger section.

Jon stole along the tent base until he found the silhouette of a man sitting against a side support for the larger section. He held his breath when he saw King Richard approach the man, jerk him up, then shove him back down. *Ah, you reveal Lord Strange. Thank you, Your Majesty.* Jon smiled to himself, but still he waited patiently. The night slowly gave way to daybreak while Richard paced, then tossed and turned on his pallet, unable to sleep. Jon waited and watched, knowing that, unnoticed by King Richard or his men, Henry Tudor's men had begun moving in the shadowy darkness between night and early dawn.

As the sun's first light shone, fractured by the surrounding trees, Jon watched King Richard ready himself for battle. In full armor, the king paced, grumbling impatiently about the priest being needed to say morning mass. Exasperated, he stormed out of the tent, looking for the priest himself. Before he could reenter, a man ran up to him, reporting the priest was available.

Mass had just finished when the king was informed that Tudor was already moving. He called for his horse and his commanders. Jon lay frozen against the tent. While the king's men were moving toward the field of battle below the king's camp, Jon quickly stole nearer Lord Strange, slit the tent, and grasped Lord Strange's bound hands. Lord Strange sat motionless, no doubt unsure where this turn of events would lead.

Strange managed to worm his way through the opening Jon provided. In silence, both men slithered farther from the camp, then crawled cautiously toward Lord Stanley's camp, set a considerable distance from both King Richard and Henry Tudor. Well beyond King Richard's camp, the men stood, moving through the trees. Jon stopped near Lord Stanley's camp and watched as Lord Strange entered his father's tent.

NICOLA HAD NOT RIDDEN FAR FROM the stable before she saw the fires from both encampments. The largest one was situated atop a hill across from her. That camp was overlooking a much smaller camp at the base, near the marshes where she had just spoken with Tudor. Her heart dropped. Nicola knew Henry Tudor would win somehow. But looking at the difference in manpower, she momentarily doubted her intuition—how could any of Henry's men survive? She was drawn to watch the coming battle, to know in her heart Drue was safe, before she could leave. The battle would mark the beginning for Henry Tudor, his cause and his men. She could not tell what might happen to the one man she knew she loved. There were no messages for Nicola.

When she heard rustling nearby, she held her breath. A woman walked toward her, leading a horse. "Lizzie?" Nicola's voice was soft. "What are you doing here?"

"Nicola!" Lizzie rushed to Nicola. Nicola slipped from her horse and the ladies embraced. "I could not stay away. I am so afraid. There are so many men with King Richard, Nicola. How can Henry Tudor ever win? How can Braggio survive what I see coming?" They stood, side by side, staring at the fires beyond. Nicola turned away and Lizzie followed. They led their horses within the sheltering forest and tied them. Hand in hand, they returned to stand just out of sight but with a wide view of the fields below.

"I do not know how this will finish. I only know Henry will win and Lord Braggio will survive. I pray Drue is safe," Nicola whispered.

"You told me Braggio would not die—can you not tell if Drue will be safe?" Lizzie asked.

"No. I have tried, but nothing." Nicola sat down. Lizzie sat next to her without comment. They leaned against each other. Tomorrow would be a terrible day, of that Nicola was certain. Eventually, Nicola rose, and Lizzie with her, to find shelter for the night. Securing a room for one night, they spoke little, preparing for bed. During a night that felt as though it lasted a lifetime, neither of them slept.

In the early morning light, they returned to the hill, looking onto what appeared to be a quiet scene. Anxiously, they scanned the marsh and fields below. To the right, King Richard's men were just beginning to stir. They could make out the dark forms of men leaving Henry Tudor's encampment to the left. Tudor's men were already afield, moving around the marsh toward the king's camp and men. Suddenly, Lizzie's hand went to her mouth, and Nicola scanned the rows of men. In the growing light of daybreak, Bruce and Braggio stood out at the head of yet another contingent of Henry's men. They too were on the move. Desperately searching the field, Nicola could not find Drue, though she knew he was there somewhere, leading his own group of men.

Nicola gasped when a sudden rain of arrows from the king's men fell onto the men below. Tudor's men had been spotted. Fear filled her every fiber. She struggled to follow Bruce and Braggio, but was unable to keep them in view. She kept searching for Drue as she went.

CHAPTER 63

KING RICHARD HAD SLEPT VERY LITTLE, and the morning mass before battle had caused a delay. He was fearful of betrayal, and his fitful dreams during the night had put him on edge. The Duke of Norfolk reported that he had awoken to find a crude note on his tent, warning him that a master was bought and sold. The duke understood the message was to hint that one of the king's commanders had changed sides. Richard believed the most likely to sell out against him would be the Stanley brothers. The message hinted Stanley would fight for Tudor. To make his morning worse, he'd had no time for breakfast, as one of his commanders called out an alert that Tudor's men were already well on the move, marching in battle formation. There was still no sign Lord Stanley's men had joined his side. Richard gave the command to execute Stanley's son, as he mounted and rode to a vantage point.

Richard's men had to scramble to be ready for the oncoming assault. He first ordered a deadly shower of arrows on the movement below, but it was clear that the Earl of Oxford and Lord Bruce were expecting just such an attack. They quickly positioned their men in a wedge formation, used their shields, and withstood the charge. Between the two forces lay the impassable marsh. Oxford and Lord Bruce, with planned precision, managed to navigate their men around the marsh, keeping it on their right. Joined by Lord Braggio and his men, they launched an attack against the king's vanguard being led by the Duke of Norfolk. The morning tension was broken by the sounds of serpentine guns and bombards. Caustic smoke and deafening booms rose from the field. The fighting was vicious.

To Richard's great dismay, Henry's troops fought in tight clusters close to the standards. This caused some confusion for the king's men, uncertain where to strike. Oxford and Bruce pushed forward, and Richard observed as men fighting on both sides were felled.

In the savage fighting that followed, the Duke of Norfolk was killed. When Norfolk fell, his men backed toward the marsh head, with Oxford and Bruce in hard pursuit.

Richard's rear guard, seven thousand men strong, was led by Henry Percy, now the Earl of Northumberland. Northumberland held his men still. No blows were given or received. They appeared to be unable to cross the marsh, but Richard believed that some other issue was afoot. Though always loyal to King Edward, Percy had delayed mustering for King Richard. He had been raised alongside young Henry Tudor, when they were both made wards of William Herbert by King Edward IV. Richard understood now that Percy's loyalty lay with his friend from his youth.

Richard still had numbers on his side. The fierce battle raged on as hand-to-hand combat now broke out all around. Yet neither Percy nor the Stanleys had elected to engage on either side.

Drue's men, alongside other men belonging to Tudor, were fighting between Henry Tudor and the bulk of men King Richard sent to the field. Richard, from the higher elevation near his camp, saw Tudor in the clear, toward the back of the fighting. Tudor rode with his standard, surrounded by only his bodyguards. Richard knew that if he could kill Tudor, the battle would be over and the crown would stay with him—he had won many victories by seizing opportunities quickly, as they were presented. Making his move, his full calvary thundered down the hill right toward Tudor.

HENRY COULD SEE RICHARD COMING toward him and dismounted to meet him, sword drawn. He watched as Braggio called out to Drue and both men joined the pikes and foot soldiers moving into position near Tudor.

Richard's initial charge hit with incredible force. Tudor's standard bearer was pierced by a vicious pike thrust. The Red Dragon fell. Tudor's men began to fear defeat—when a standard fell, that usually meant the man beneath it was dead.

Henry clung on, refusing to give way. His actions spread among those of his men near him. Henry's force stood firm, encouraged by the skilled fighting and shouts coming from two men wearing foreign colors, Drue and Braggio. Henry's spirits rose at the sight—these men who were fighting side by side with his men were from another country, just as most of his own men were. They all fought for him as he fought for his crown, the crown of England.

With some of his best men, Richard fought his way toward Tudor. But he was so intent on killing Henry that he misjudged the distance and formidable blockade provided by Tudor's guard, backed by the men with Prince Drue. Pikes were replaced by axes and swords.

DRUE WAS IN HIS ELEMENT NOW. His sword moved with speed and precision, cutting a swath through the men surrounding him. Drue could see that Braggio did the same, until he suddenly found himself through Richard's line, fenced in. Braggio dropped three more men before he went down, and Drue no longer had his friend in his line of sight.

A rumble, scarcely heard in the distance, crept through the noise. That sound slowly gained volume until it rose over the din of the battle below. A large cavalry was bearing down the hillside toward them—it seemed the very ground shook. Drue knew only a large mass of horses could produce such a noise. Stanley's men, perhaps. He closed his eyes and thought of Nicola.

He vowed that he would not go down easily—somehow, he would stand as long as he had life. Looking around for Braggio, Drue's eyes found Henry. Henry no longer looked as though his end was near as he stood watching the oncoming barrage. The calvary, now near enough to be heard over the sounds of fighting, were chanting, "Tudor! Tudor!" Henry raised his sword, yelling, "I take this battle!" Drue caught only a flash before losing sight of Sir William Stanley and his men, as Richard's men continued fighting toward Henry. The clash was fiendish.

HENRY, PREPARING HIMSELF FOR RICHARD'S assault, heard the uproar of the approaching calvary and felt a crushing despair. As he glanced toward the sound, he saw it—a flash of red. Sir William Stanley and his men were coming full speed, but toward Richard! They were coming to his aid, after all.

The conflict changed decisively, with Sir William's calvary smashing into the side of Richard's men, shoving them into the marsh. Men and horses closest to the marsh began to flounder and fall into the muck, unable to escape before the men and horses behind and near them plowed into the mess. King Richard's standard bearer had both legs severed, but somehow he clung to the standard. It was evident that Richard's only hope at this point was to escape. Henry watched as Richard pulled hard at his mount, attempting to turn back. Then it happened—Richard's horse stumbled trying to turn sharply, and fell. Richard was able to escape a crushing injury by jumping from the animal, but he was now on foot. His helmet and crown lay on the ground. A cry went out around him. "He needs a horse! Get the king a horse! The king needs a horse!" Henry could hear the king yell, "I will neither quit nor run, but will live or die the king of England."

Realizing Richard was aground, Henry's men launched a savage attack. From behind the king, a powerful swing with an axe smashed into the back of his skull. It was done. The entire battle for the throne of England was over by noon.

AS THE SOUNDS OF KING RICHARD'S last battle faded, Nicola turned and slowly walked away. Her one prayer was for Drue's safety. For days now, she had not discerned his presence. When last she sensed him, she could see he was aboard a ship, whose captain was bent on turning Drue and his companion over to King Richard's men. They would have been in grave danger from a king fighting for his crown. Today, Nicola had one quick glimpse of Drue after Richard fell. She felt he was safe. *It is time for me to go home. My job is done, my promise kept. I long for the comfort of my father's house.* She paused for one last look at the scene below her. *In truth, I long for Drue's touch, but it is not to be.* The sadness and ache of loss made her feel as though she could barely function. Alone, she was not certain she could move through life. Drue would be her last glimpse of a deep love. All was gone.

LIZZIE RAN DOWN THE HILLSIDE, her one thought to find Braggio. She began looking where she last saw him. He was not there. Through tear-filled eyes, she struggled to find him. She was terrified he would die before she could find him, if he lived at all. All the carnage around her only served to heighten her panic. Stepping over dead men, body parts, dead horses, and all manner of weapons, she doggedly searched for her love. She had been looking for an hour when she heard her name. Looking around, she saw Drue coming toward her. Running to meet him, she begged, "Please, Drue, please. I must find Lord Braggio."

"I too have been looking for him. I saw him go down, and dread what we may likely find."

Lizzie's heart sank. She followed Drue as he began to move among the dead and dying, making his way toward the area where he had last seen his friend. It took another half hour, but Lizzie eventually saw Braggio's still form. "There, he is there," she cried. As Lizzie started to run, Drue held her back. "If you watched this fight, you know he may not still be with us, Lizzie. You must prepare yourself."

"He is alive!" Lizzie interrupted. "Come, Drue, I know he is alive. I need help to get him home."

She ran to Braggio. He was alive, just barely. Gently, she spoke into his ear. "My love, it is Lizzie. I have come for you. I will take you home." She tried to tell which wound was the worst, but they all looked lethal to her.

Braggio's eyes opened. "My Lizzie." His voice was raspy. With great effort, he turned to see Drue. "Please, Your Grace. I have need of your help." He paused with the effort it took to speak. "I would ask your permission . . . to go home. If it please you." He closed his eyes again.

Drue knelt at Braggio's side. "Braggio, I will see you and Lady Lizzie safely aboard, bound for home, on this night. Stay quiet—we will do what is needed, my friend." Drue looked at Lizzie and back at Braggio, then around the battlefield. "I will need a cart and horses to move him," he said, and then he left Lizzie at Braggio's side.

Drue returned more quickly than Lizzie had expected. He had found Bruce and what was left of the men with Bruce and Braggio. They had searched until they found a cart and team. After padding the cart bed, they brought it to Braggio, who was lifted onto the cart, followed by Lizzie. Having gathered their weapons and supplies, they were gone, heading east toward a coastal inlet called the Wash. Lizzie worked to keep Braggio comfortable and alive. Darkness fell before the sea became visible to Lizzie, and she prayed for quick passage.

THE MEN WHO HAD FOLLOWED HENRY TUDOR to England and survived were now free men. They chose to stay in England with him. Henry would spend his first night as England's ruler in York, making plans to travel to London the next morning. He was given the crown that fell from Richard's head and had acknowledged the cries of "Long live King Henry Tudor."

For the first time in his life, he did not have to run, hide, sail to distant shores, and dread the future. The future was his. Riding away from the battlefield, Henry turned to look back once more. The ugly sight and smells would remain with him for years. He knew the cost of becoming England's king and would never forget how rapidly and gruesomely Richard had slid from king to a mere dead man. Turning to move forward, Henry again grasped the symbol still hanging beneath his tunic. *I would talk with the woman once more.*

DRUE HAD SENT JON TO MAKE ARRANGEMENTS for the surviving men to leave from the dock at the Wash. Now, Jon walked the dock, impatiently waiting for news. Word had begun to spread that King Richard was dead. Jon felt some relief. The struggle for Henry Tudor was finished. Jon would not feel the full relief of victory until he saw his lords and their men returning.

Stopping to search the street leading to the dock yet again, he caught sight of a cart carrying what looked like someone who had been wounded. The men wore the colors of Bruce and Braggio. He could see Drue riding along-side the cart. Relief washed over him. As the cart approached, he sent word to the ship's captain. It was obvious at least one man was badly injured. With another surge of relief, Jon caught sight of Bruce. Silently praying Braggio was in the wagon, Jon hastened to assist in boarding the men.

DRUE SUPERVISED AS HIS INJURED FRIEND was taken to the captain's quarters. He talked briefly with the captain and Bruce before standing near Braggio's bed. His wounds had stopped bleeding, and he appeared to no longer flounder between life and death.

Lizzie, aided by one of the older men, was tending to his wounds. Drue pulled her aside. "You will be well cared for, Lizzie. Braggio has asked permission to marry you and I have readily granted that request. Braggio and you are going home. You have a gentle touch—he will be grateful for that. The weather promises to let you pass easily." He kissed her hand before turning to Braggio.

Braggio was more alert as Drue bade him goodbye. "I will be home as soon as possible, Braggio. You are in good hands." Braggio weakly clasped Drue's hand. "Remind my brother: I always come home," Drue added and, smiling, walked from the room.

He next approached Bruce, who stood at the plank looking out at the land beyond. Bruce turned to him and observed, "You are not coming with us?"

Drue shook his head, but Bruce persisted. "You should not be in this place alone, after today. Let me come with you, Your Grace. There is still a great deal of unrest in this country. You have my services and the services of my men."

"The men need to see their families and stand on their own soil. They should enjoy a freedom won. No, not this time, Bruce. See to Braggio and Lizzie. I will take Jon and my guard with me." Drue paused, looking back at the weary men behind him. He realized that, given the chance to leave, he could not. It mattered not how he had tried to convince himself otherwise. He would not leave alone. "I am going for Nicola." The two men embraced. "I have not the words to express my gratitude, Bruce."

Bruce's voice was filled with emotion. "Nor I. Take care. I expect to stand for you at your wedding."

Drue walked down to the dock, Jon at his side. "The guard?"

"They wait where you sent them. Are we going for Lady Nicola? Do we know where she stays?" Jon asked.

Drue looked at the young man walking with him. Ignoring the question, he instead noted, "We need fresh horses."

Jon flashed a quick grin at Drue. "Right this way, Your Grace." He led Drue to a well-kept stable, where two horses stood saddled and waiting. Both looked to be horses made for speed. Drue gripped Jon's shoulder in approval.

CHAPTER 64

Nicola rode until she reached Gloucester. Early the next morning, she veered south, staying along the shoreline as much as possible. Many of the inhabitants in that area were not fond of Richard—most of them favored Tudor. Nicola prayed she could move safely among those who lived on the fringe of disputes over the crown. Unfamiliar with the land and its many treacherous forests and hills, Nicola let her horse pick his way, only making certain he headed in the direction she hoped was southwest. Each time she rode out of the thick cover of trees, she studied the sky. Her home would provide a safe haven where she could rest and heal. With Richard dead, one could not tell how the feeling of England's people might yet swing. Henry Tudor was a stranger to most of the populace. Persistent rumors of the escape of young Richard fed into the unrest. The times would be difficult and tempers explosive.

All the nights riding with Drue gave her some confidence now. To stay safe, Nicola would have to stay out of sight. Progress was slow. As darkness began to blanket England again, the land around her seemed to take on an ominous personality. The feeling that she was in danger had left her two days ago but returned with the darkness of this night. The thought of the safety of her father's castle made her push forward. The impulse to stop until dawn teased her, but the idea of sitting alone in the middle of the forest all night was frightening.

At morning's first light, Nicola finally stopped. After dismounting, she knelt to drink clear, cool water from a small stream. She was startled when her horse abruptly raised his head and stood alert. All at once, she heard the sound of something or someone approaching. Nicola tried to move the horse and herself into the surrounding forest, but it was too late. A voice stopped her.

"Lady Nicola Weldon?" When Nicola did not answer, he laughed. "No matter, lady, you will have more time to talk later. And believe what I say: You *will* talk." When Nicola turned and saw the man dressed in black coming toward her, she dropped the reins and ran, but he and his horse were upon her before she could even run beyond the glen. He slid off his horse and walked quickly toward her. Again, she tried to run. She stumbled and fell hard.

He reached her just as she grasped a fallen limb. She swung hard, striking his face. His cheek began to bleed as he staggered slightly from the unexpected blow. He stepped to her and jerked her up. "You will not try to run again, or I will tie you behind my horse and you will keep up or be dragged." His voice was cold and threatening. Nicola looked into a face without expression—the face she had seen in the vision. The face that evoked the sensation of danger in her.

Nicola remained silent. Gripping her arm, he returned her to her horse and shoved her up onto her saddle, pulling a leather strap from his belt and tying her hands to it. He picked up the reins to her horse, mounted his own, and moved out. Nicola felt a wrenching fear grip her. She was helpless. Almost immediately, she was slapped in the head by brush limbs, nearly unseating her. Struggling to right herself, she leaned forward on the horse's neck.

This man was the reason for the cloak of dark danger she felt. His face was the one she had seen in the vision while sailing back to England with Bruce and Braggio. That was the first time she had ever felt a vision was about her. She was in real danger. What he wanted from her was beyond any reasoning she could think on.

The two of them rode for hours. He stopped every once in a while to allow the horses to drink. During the stops, Nicola sat up. Her head hurt, her hands were numb, and fear grew inside her, making rational thought impossible. She knew she could not fight this man and that she might not live to tell anyone what he did to her. She was going to die. There would be no help.

Evening breezes pulled the daytime temperatures down. Darkness grew. Diablo stopped for the night. After pulling her from the horse, Diablo dragged her to a tree, where he tied her and threw a blanket over her. "It won't do to have you freeze before I finish with you," he told her. Nicola had remained silent, but she knew that the fear in her eyes betrayed her. He ate what was left of the food rolled inside his blanket. She assumed that the need to avoid discovery kept him from lighting a fire. With his cloak and saddle blanket, he passed the night.

After lifting her up onto her horse in the morning, he tied her again. Nicola had no idea where they were. It would not matter anyway. Her short life was going to come to a horrible end. After they had traveled for several hours, Diablo announced, "Tonight, our journey ends." So be it—she would gladly trade death for release from the man leading her horse, and so she prayed for it.

As the light was beginning to fade, Nicola, leaning on her horse with her eyes closed, could tell the horses were no longer walking through the forests, but onto hardened ground. Their footsteps began to echo off walls. An eerie silence encircled everything. The feeling of evil enveloping her tightened. She felt her journey was nearly over. There could be no help, no rescue now.

When Nicola looked around, she gasped, nearly falling from the horse. They had ridden into a deserted courtyard. Her father's courtyard. Terror racked her. She opened her mouth, but no sound came. Her heart beat faster. Signs of neglect clearly indicated it was uninhabited. Nicola's last sliver of hope disappeared. *This cannot be happening,* her mind screamed. She felt faint.

The man untied Nicola and jerked her off her horse. Stumbling, she could barely stand. He pulled her up and shoved her toward the castle. Her home. It was a place of horror when her father died and now it would become a place of horror for her, as she died.

Moving along the castle wall itself, the man pushed a door open, exposing the stairway leading down to the cells beneath the castle. It was obvious he had been here before. Nicola was so frightened she could not walk. Sinking down against the wall, she began trembling, but the man yanked her up, forcing her ahead of him down the stairs. Stumbling, she leaned against the wall, numb. In silence, they eventually came to the very cell that had held Nicola's father when he slipped away from life.

He pushed the door open, then cut her wrists free and shoved her inside.

"Why do you do this? What have I ever done to you? Who are you?" Nicola cried.

He looked at her, then announced coldly, "I am going to find a bed and sleep. I suggest you rest, too. You will need it. Tomorrow will be the longest day of your life, my little witch." With that, he slammed the door, locking it from the outside.

At his comment, Nicola sank onto the floor. She knew then that he must have come because of the rumors about her father and, by association, about her. She knew Queen Anne had searched for her. But Anne was dead. Was this man one of Richard's men? Was he fueled by Richard's death? No matter, her time on earth would not end well. She began to weep, as hopelessness engulfed her.

WANDERING AND RUMMAGING THROUGH the first-floor rooms, Diablo could find nothing to indicate what kind of man Lord Weldon was. There were no remnants of him. After spending time with the last occupant of the castle, the Earl of Blackgrove, Diablo was certain Blackgrove knew little if anything. Diablo was just as certain that Blackgrove would have taken anything of value when he abandoned the castle. Valuable items were not what Diablo sought. He needed food for himself and evidence for the Duchess of Burgundy. Evidence that would tie Lord Weldon to the turmoil engulfing the English crown. Evidence that could effectively tarnish Tudor, and perhaps restore the crown to the house of York.

The kitchen and the pantry had been cleaned out—only empty pots and utensils remained in the cabinets. Diablo spent several hours combing through a cellar room. He found wine and some moldy cheese. After unwrapping the cheese, he cut the mold away, ate the cheese, and drank the wine. There was nothing else left. Diablo headed for the stairs. He entered Weldon's study, then stood for a moment, surveying the mess. There were books and papers strewn about, dried ink wells and writing feathers on the floor. Methodically, Diablo tried every drawer and searched behind every cabinet door. Nothing.

He knew the earl had been called into service by King Richard. The vacancy and condition of the rooms indicated the earl had chosen to run rather than serve. His exit had certainly been a hasty one. Among the items Blackgrove had missed were precious stones, several drawers of them, in colors Diablo had never seen. Making a mental note to retrieve the stones after he finished with Nicola, he moved on.

Diablo searched what he believed were Nicola's rooms. Empty. Diablo could find nothing to warrant interest in Lord Weldon or his daughter. Frustration set in. The Duchess of Burgundy was seldom wrong. Her spies were among the best. The information she received was usually accurate. *Not this time, duchess, not this time. However, I may have found a way to bring information to you.* Diablo smiled to himself. Tomorrow might prove to be most interesting. He wondered how long Nicola could hold out. Briefly, his mind returned to Kelly. Kelly . . . his only mistake. *Kelly knew more than she shared. Could have saved me time.* With a pang, he thought how she would have loved a ring made from any of the stones.

CHAPTER 65

Days of riding, with little sleep, and now several glasses of wine, began to have an impact on Diablo. He was exhausted but, at the same time, exhilarated. He had managed to find and capture the elusive Lady Weldon. Tomorrow he would learn all she knew. He felt certain Nicola must know the woman with visions, the woman Queen Anne had tried so hard to find. The Duchess of Burgundy's command to bring Nicola back to Burgundy unharmed had been tossed aside from the beginning. With everything he would get out of Lady Weldon, the throne of England would go to the rightful heir, the son of King Edward rumored to be living. *He must be living–else why would the dowager Queen Elizabeth agree to leave London? Lady Weldon will tell me what she sees coming and who will have sons. I will know where young Richard is hidden. I have wrestled dark secrets from strong men. That tiny creature will not hold out long. I must keep her alive until I know all she knows. Then what is left of her burns.*

In keeping with his usual habits, Diablo set out for the best room in the castle—Lord Weldon's. He would rest in luxury as a lord, not as a mere henchman. He opened the door to the lord's chambers. The moon was full, its light spilling across the floor. He stood at the door a moment, surveying the grandeur. Though simple, it was far above anything he possessed. Blackgrove had left most of the linens and blankets where they lay, such was his haste to leave.

Diablo crossed the room to light a fire, then one of the candles. When Diablo heard the door behind him close, he stopped. Turning slowly, he stared. The man standing at the door carefully slid the lock bar in place, while watching Diablo. He was dressed in close-fitting clothes, armed with a sword and shorter knife. Diablo started to move when the man spoke, smoothly drawing his sword. "You have something that does not belong to you, Diablo."

Diablo swiftly drew his weapon. "We meet finally. The famous Drue Vieneto. I have always wanted to face you. Too bad for you, I am by far the better with our weapons of choice—all of them." Diablo lunged at Drue.

Sidestepping the thrust, Drue deftly swung his sword, making Diablo move backward. Diablo recovered quickly, forcing Drue around the room. Diablo was an expert with the sword, but he knew that Drue wielded his weapon for a greater cause than defense—this man fought for Nicola's life.

Chairs and tables were overturned and tapestries were slashed as the men fought. Both were cut and bleeding, when Diablo kicked a heavy stool into Drue. Drue slipped and fell backward onto the bed. Diablo lunged toward him, with his sword steady. Drue rolled sideways at the same time he drew and thrust his short blade. It penetrated deeply into Diablo's chest, the pain searing through him and causing his sword to miss Drue—it plunged harmlessly into the mattress.

Diablo stood rigid, blood flowing out of the wound and beginning to drip from his mouth. He turned his head slowly to stare at Drue. Drue stood and swung his sword at him as hard as he could, and the world around him turned black.

DIABLO'S HEAD FELL ONTO THE FLOOR with a thud, followed immediately by his headless body. Drue collapsed back on the bed.

For a long moment, he lay winded with his eyes closed. Standing slowly, he retrieved his short blade, then cleaned both weapons. After tearing pillow coverings, Drue bound the deeper of his wounds. He left the room, closing the door behind him.

CHAPTER 66

SWEEPING THROUGH THE CHAMBERS, Drue looked for anything that might tie Nicola to the house. Nothing was left, not even clothing. Lord Weldon's rooms had been ransacked. Papers and books were strewn about. There was not a thing that spoke of the young lady who had once lived in the castle. Only Lord Weldon's stones could ever hint at Weldon's past. Drue took them. He was reasonably certain Diablo had acted alone, but to protect Nicola, he carefully checked every room. There must be no sign of Nicola for anyone who might find Diablo.

I should have kept Jon with me, not with the horses. Unfamiliar with Weldon Castle, Drue began hunting for Nicola. He knew she would not have been kept in the living quarters or in the hidden stable. Not all bergs had a dungeon, and certainly not all dungeons were kept in the same area. He moved to the bottom level of the castle. Every door led to a service room. There was no sign of the people who had once lived in Weldon Castle. The hours slipped by.

With a stab of panic, he considered the possibility she was dead. *No, Diablo brought her here for a specific purpose. He was trying to get information.* Drue's next thought was how Diablo may have tried to get Nicola to talk. *Am I too late? No! She is not dead yet. She cannot be dead.* A heightened sense of urgency possessed Drue. The only area left was below the main structure. With every attempt at finding a door leading under the castle unsuccessful, Drue began searching the exterior of the castle, thinking of how a prisoner would have been brought in. He remembered the entrance to the stalls hidden behind a pillar. How could he not have remembered sooner? As the first hints of dawn spread, he slowly walked around the wall, examining the structure.

Eventually, he found a large door supported by two great hinges. Once open, a passageway revealed stairs leading downward. The stairwell was musty and cold—he knew he had found the dungeon. The stairs came to a level walkway deep beneath the castle. Drue followed the walkway until he came to the last door, closed and locked. The key was still inside the lock. He turned the key and the door swung open.

AS THE SOFT RAYS OF FIRST LIGHT CREPT THROUGH a small opening at the top of her cell, Nicola heard footsteps. She began to shake. She knew she would suffer greatly, then die. In her weakened state, she prayed she would die quickly. She stood pressed into the farthest corner of the cell. The heavy door opened. When a man's silhouette filled the door-frame, she collapsed.

"Nicola."

It was not the voice of her captor. It was Drue. Unbelieving, she stared. As he moved closer, she saw it was indeed him.

"You came for me!" Nicola cried. She struggled to stand upright.

"I told you I would," Drue replied softly, as he knelt down to help her. When they stood, she leaned against him. Supporting her, Drue lifted her chin and looked deep into her eyes. "You can never dismiss me, lady. You will not be allowed to do so. That is not a privilege I will ever extend to you." His gaze moved over her face, her disheveled hair, and back to her eyes. "I will always be with you." He bent down and tenderly kissed her lips.

Brushing her hair from her face, he held her closely. She shivered, less from the cold damp cell than the knowledge she had escaped the probable horror that had come so close. Her eyes were swollen with dark circles under them from crying all night. Dirt, scrapes, and blood covered her face and arms, and her clothing was torn and filthy. Her feet were bare. Drue removed his cloak and wrapped it around her. Within the warmth and steadiness of his embrace, Nicola gradually stopped shivering. "How did you find me?" she asked, her face searching his.

"I am my mother's son," he gently reminded her. Nicola remained still, within the safety of his embrace. He waited for a long while, holding her close to his heart, before speaking. Time was getting away. "Can you ride, lady? There's something we must do."

Nicola's eyes revealed panic. "We are leaving? What if—"

Drue interrupted. "There is no 'what if,' Nicola. You are safe now. That man will not come after you again. You are safe."

"Are you certain?" Her voice broke.

"Unless he knows how to magically reattach his head and mend his black heart, I am certain. He is dead." Drue lifted her chin again, looking into her eyes. "Listen carefully—there is something we must do, Nicola."

"Just tell me. I will do anything you ask."

"You must finish with Henry Tudor," Drue replied.

Nicola leaned back, frowning. "I have. I spoke with him before he and King Richard fought. What more?" she asked.

Drue shook his head. "It is not over yet. Margaret ordered a search for the lady who spoke to Tudor that night. There are those who would feed on the uncertainty surrounding you. We will find a way to speak with him, one last time. We ride to London. Henry must be certain of the course he now takes. More importantly, he must command your safety. His mother is attempting to damage your reputation. Worse, she plans to have you executed." Drue paused for a moment before adding, "She is not happy that she was told to leave and was unable to hear what you and Tudor discussed. I've been told she has labeled you a heretic. You will clear that up. If I thought he would settle for me, I would do that for you, but I cannot."

"How can I possibly do that?" Nicola asked. "How can I stand up to her?"

"You will find the words, my lady. You will," Drue insisted. "You know what you shared with Tudor before. You must remind him again. Not Lady Margaret. King Henry. He is the one who will unite the houses of Tudor and York, uniting England." Drue's hand caressed Nicola's face. Looking into her eyes, he spoke quietly. "You can do this, Nicola. Do this and it is finished. We leave and do not look back."

Nicola looked at her dress and wiped her dirty hair from her face. The last two years and the dramatic final days were burned into her heart. "I do not care to live my life looking over my shoulder for Lady Margaret's vengeance. How do I do this thing? I look like I belong in one of the lesser brothels of London." Drue's faith in her gave her courage, but she realized how important Henry's first court would be to him and to all who came to see the new king. "I cannot go to court looking like this." Nicola shook her head. "I cannot, Drue. Look at me."

Drue took her arm. "I ask again, are you able to ride?" Drue's voice was firm but kind. "If we are to have peace in our lives, Henry must order your safety in England and abroad. I am sorry to rush you, but there is little time. We will first escort you to Jon's sister's home in London. She can help you with a new gown. You will be at Henry's court by tomorrow night." Drue led her out of the cell and up the stairs. He walked with her to the horses, where Jon stood waiting.

Nicola could think of nothing to say. It would make no difference. She knew Drue well by now. He would have his way. It mattered not. Nothing else mattered. He had come for her. He would protect her. All was not lost.

As he lifted her up to the saddle, she rested her hand on his. "Only once more. Pray I can think of what to say. I fear I have said it all already."

Drue squeezed her hand, and looked into her eyes.

The riders pushed their horses. Concentrating on staying in the saddle left no time for Nicola to think about what was to come. As night fell, Drue finally stopped them. Nicola could barely stay upright. Drue lifted her down and led her to a fallen log. "You may rest after you have eaten." When Nicola started to speak, Drue shook his head as he lifted her chin. "I am quite certain you have not eaten in a long time. It would not help your cause to faint before King Henry . . . or his mother." Drue smiled. He kissed her forehead, then turned to his men. A fire was soon blazing. When all had contributed, there were hard chunks of bread, pieces of cheese, and a pot with a stew bubbling.

The smells made Nicola's mouth water. She walked to where Jon squatted stirring the pot. "Where . . . how did you do this?" She pointed the pot.

Jon grinned. "My mum could make a meal out of anything. With five boys, it came in real handy. She insisted we learn. Hated it then. Blessed for it now."

Everyone ate well, and then Drue fixed a spot for Nicola to lie down. For the first time in days, she slept well.

When they entered London, it was early afternoon. Drue escorted her to a small but refined home in London. "I must leave you now," he told her. "You will be safe with Jon."

Nicola gasped. She started to speak, but Drue interrupted. "I know you can do this. I will come to you when it is appropriate. I will take you to safety, Lady Nicola. I promise." Drue lifted her off the horse. His hand lingered on her face. His touch was gentle. He looked exhausted and pale, his wounds dark and crusted over.

"What if something happens to you?" Nicola whispered, trying to shake the fear from her mind. "You do not look well, Drue. Is there no other way?"

"I will be fine. I will be close," Drue assured her. "Before the sun sets this night, I will be with you, my Nicola." Raising her hand, he kissed it. Then, once he mounted up, he was gone. Nicola watched him until he was lost in the street's activities.

Without any indication that Nicola looked a mess, Jon's sister, followed by ladies in attendance, graciously led Nicola to a room where a bath awaited. Placed on a bed nearby were several beautiful gowns along with everything Nicola might need for a court appearance. Nicola hesitated. "My lady, I cannot pay for these things. I think to not continue, as—"

The lady interrupted. "Fear not, Lady Nicola. Everything has already been paid for by His Grace, Prince Drue. And, truth be known, I doubt he asked you to court. He ordered you to go. He has a gentle way of giving orders. Perhaps to make it feel more like a favor." Smiling, she instructed the ladies to make haste, as the time for King Henry's first court reception was rapidly approaching.

After bathing and washing her hair, Nicola felt better, yet unable to shake the uncertainty that clung to her. Standing at the bed, Nicola looked at what was provided for her approval. She wanted something proper for court, but the clothing looked too beautiful to even touch. Her father had made certain Nicola was always well dressed, but she had never seen attire this elegant. Even the gowns from Eny were not like these. *I should dress accordingly if I am to be in the presence of the king, but what is accordingly?* Remembering how she looked when she spoke to Henry the first time made Nicola smile in spite of her hesitation. *This is better, I think. Time is wasting.*

The ladies in attendance waited, anxious to finish with the special assignment of preparing her. "I do not know which to choose. They are beautiful, but . . ." She looked to the ladies, frowning. "What do you think?"

Surprised to be asked for an opinion, the women were silent. One lady, an older woman, stepped closer. After looking from Nicola to the gowns and back at Nicola, she picked up one gown and removed the stiff material around the neck, exposing a softly draped neckline. She pulled another gown out, freeing a great swath of material. She held it close to Nicola's face.

"Now, m'lady, we will use this softer material as a perfect drape. Quickly, now."

Nicola dressed. The result was a gown with a feel of richness all its own, not because of jewels or stiff laces, but layers of soft material that flowed around Nicola as she moved. The gown was a dark navy with a draped neckline and long, gathered sleeves. At the shoulders, a train was attached with pearls. The train was a soft gray and flowed to the gown's hem. Nicola's eyes became the focal point. She turned around, astonished. "This is . . . I am . . . I cannot describe how this looks!"

"We are not finished, Lady Weldon," the older lady admonished. Quickly pushing another of the ladies toward Nicola, she said, "Fix her hair. Up, it needs to be up. Now, this will go on top."

When her hair was finally arranged perfectly at the top of her head, a tiara covered in pearls was secured.

"No, I cannot wear this." Nicola reached to remove the tiara.

The older lady held her arm. "His Grace insisted you wear this."

What was he thinking? For certain Lady Margaret will be afire when she sees this. Nicola dropped her hand. "If His Grace wishes me to wear this, I shall."

"He also left this for you." The lady handed Nicola a small soft bag full of coins. "Here, put it in there," she said, pointing to a small pocket elegantly tied at her waist.

Nicola looked at the glass again. "I fear he may have made a mistake this time." Nicola could hear the gasps behind her. "None of you are going to face Lady Margaret," she told them. "Pray you never have to."

When Jon came for her, he stood and stared. Nicola stepped forward, as

Jon's sister wrapped her in a deep gray cloak. "This was the easy part, Jon. How do I get an audience with the new king?" She could not think about Lady Margaret without trembling.

"I will get you there, lady. Though it will be no easy feat to slip you in unnoticed looking as you do, I will see you safely to King Henry." Jon helped her outside and into the waiting carriage before climbing up with the driver.

Staring out at the street, Nicola shivered. So much depended upon her conversation with King Henry. Knowing his mother would be present made this night a bargain with danger.

When Jon opened the carriage door for her, she almost refused to exit. She had never been to any court. The grandeur was at once exciting and fearsome. The new king's flags waved in the evening breeze. Men dressed in Henry's colors were everywhere. Taking a deep breath, she stepped down. Just as Jon reached to assist her, she felt it. It was as if fingers of ice brushed her face. Her chest felt tight, and the familiar sensation of fear gripped her once again. Slowly, her eyes moved upward. Above the crowd, a window gave view to a room beyond filled with light. Nicola gasped. In the window, Lady Margaret stood watching the people. Just then, she turned her gaze onto Nicola. It seemed, even at that great distance, that their eyes locked. Lady Margaret turned away immediately, and Nicola felt Jon urging her forward.

The entrance into the castle was crammed with people anxious to see the new king and be a part of the new court. Others seemed less enthused about the new king. They wanted to see for themselves what manner of king Henry Tudor might become. Jon and Nicola were soon swept along with the people swarming into the castle proper. Just before they stepped under the large eaves, Nicola looked up at the window again. Lady Margaret stood watching her again. At her side, a guard nodded and disappeared from view. Jon had followed Nicola's gaze. "Jon," she spoke softly, "Lady Margaret and a guard saw me as we entered. I am certain her men come for me, even as we speak."

Jon leaned to Nicola. "I saw the same. Lady, slip back through this crowd, and get away from here. I will get word to His Grace. Stay in the shadows as much as you can. Go!" Jon stepped in front of Nicola, pushing her away from the entrance toward the outside as he was swept along with the bodies crowding to get inside.

CHAPTER 67

Lady Margaret stood at her window, watching the people arrive to attend Henry's first court. So long she had prayed, plotted, and worked for this moment. Her son was the king of England. He had claimed the throne with a hard-fought battle. In spite of overwhelming odds against him, he had won. How could anyone doubt he was meant to lead England? As she thought on all that had led up to this night, she remembered, with a painful stab of guilt, some of the dark orders she had executed on her son's behalf, in order to get him to the throne. This was a night of victory. She refused to allow any negative thoughts to sneak into her mind. Every action taken had been necessary to bring Henry to where he was now. Had she not prayed daily for just this night?

Several ladies stood nearby, waiting for Margaret to dismiss them. They were not allowed to attend the events this evening, but could watch from a landing above the great hall. Margaret could see they were eager to claim a spot with a clear view, and was about to give them permission to leave, when something caught her eye, making her startle. She leaned closer to the window.

"Guards!" she cried. "Call the guards at once." She turned, not willing to wait, and dashed into the hall, calling for them herself.

While Lady Margaret waited at her chamber door for assistance, Beth stepped to the window to see the cause of her lady's anxiety. As the daughter of one of King Edward's lords, Beth had witnessed her share of royal politics. Surveying the crowd below, she caught sight of a slight lady dressed in a deep gray cloak. Her escort wore the same colors as the man Beth had stayed with the previous night. Beth was told the colors belonged to a Prince Vieneto, from some other country.

Stepping back into the room, Lady Margaret was speaking with the guard. Beth quickly stepped away from the window. Lady Margaret crossed the room and hastened to the window. "Her! And the man with her. I want them both taken to the Tower. Now! They cannot be allowed near Henry. Go!" Waving everyone from her chambers, she hastened to her armoire and pulled down a wrap.

As the ladies left, Beth stole away using another route. By this time, Margaret's reputation was well known. She had already dismissed several ladies for simple mistakes. The rest of the ladies assisting were fearful whenever called upon to help her. How much of the gossip swirling around Margaret was true mattered little. With the lady and man ordered to be seized, Beth knew it could not bode well for either. Perhaps the two were lovers? They were certainly of a similar age. Touched by how kind her lover had been during the night, Beth was moved to help the two people Lady Margaret ordered removed to the Tower.

It was not that she was often tempted to disobey or naturally rebellious. In fact, she risked her own safety by lending a hand. But she had already seen so many innocent people injured by Lady Margaret . . . it was too much for her to simply stand by, yet again.

Moving through the crowds, Beth left the court and hurried toward the inn where she had spent the night. She could not remember where the men and Prince Vieneto were from, but knew they had fought for King Henry and were here to protect some lady. Beth realized the order given to take those two people to the Tower would mean probable death for both. She never had anyone treat her as harshly as Lady Margaret had when she discovered Beth was from Scotland. Beth would help the two strangers, then return to Scotland. Staying in England was never her idea anyway. In Scotland lived the man she loved—he had begged her to return, and she had promised to do just that. Tonight would be the night she kept her promise.

Rushing through the darkened streets, she caught sight of the inn. Beth flew up the stairs to the soldier's room, pounding on the door frantically.

It quickly opened. The man she had spent time with stood staring at her. Before he could speak, she began, "The lady you protect was ordered to the Tower by Lady Margaret, the king's mother. She called the guards to take her and the man with her. You must help them."

The soldier grasped her arm. He pulled her to Drue's room and opened the door. "Your Grace, Lady Nicola had been taken to the Tower, along with Jon."

Drue had been in the middle of dressing and spun around. "What? Who tells you this?"

"I do. My name is Beth. I am one of Lady Margaret's ladies-in-waiting," Beth replied. She related what she had just seen and heard and described the two people.

Drue gave quick orders to his men. "I am going after Nicola. Find Jon. If we are separated, meet at the dock." Drue grabbed his sword and handed off a package sitting on his bed to one of his guards. Pausing before Beth, he spoke quickly. "Thank you, Lady Beth, for what you do this night. You are saving someone of great importance." He started to leave, but Beth called to him. "Your Grace. Might I stay here? It will not go well for anyone to know what I have done this night. I wish to return to Scotland; I must not return to Henry's court. His mother has a long memory." Beth continued, "I have seen firsthand how she deals with those who cross her. I am certain she already knows I am missing. Please, Your Grace. I would return to Scotland to be with my people."

"I will see you safely there, lady," Drue promised as he left the room.

ALREADY PUSHING THROUGH THE MASS of bodies, Nicola worked to separate herself from the crowd, a crowd far too large to fit into the grand hall near St. Paul's Cathedral. Those not accompanied by someone of rank were turned away but stood milling about. Weaving in and out of a group of men and ladies leaving, Nicola walked as quickly as she dared. The streets were still damp from recent rains and thunder rumbled, threatening more. Turning away from the cathedral, Nicola headed westward, toward the

Strand. Few men of ill means were about the Strand. Most of its inhabitants were people of wealth. On this night, the majority of businesses were already closed as people swarmed around, hoping to catch a glimpse of the new king. Fearing a lone woman would be noticeable along this street, Nicola changed directions and hurried toward the London Bridge. She crossed to the south side of the Thames.

Nicola realized the streets on the south side of the river were not crowded with couples dressed to impress a new king. With the news of King Richard's defeat and the expected meeting of the lords and knights to pledge allegiance, Nicola understood that brothels and inns hoped for a much-needed increase in traffic. She knew there would be men who traveled to protect the lords, but none of them would be allowed entrance to attend the new king's first court. Instead, they would wander to the southern side of the Thames, where establishments waited, knowing there would be money to be made as people left the court. She saw small groups of men standing at street corners or at the doors of inns, the conversations all revolving around Henry Tudor, while ladies hustled toward brothels that promised better earnings this night, with King Richard gone.

Nicola knew one place where she might be safe, if she could only get there without anyone seeing her and if the man would allow her to stay. She walked in the shadows, trying not to move too fast. Several times she heard shouting in the distance. Her breath quickened, as did her steps.

Passing a coach sitting idle while the footman and coachman stood talking in the street, Nicola glanced around. No one was looking. She stepped back and pulled the cloak from her shoulders, pushing it through the coach window. She paused a moment, thinking. Her train and tiara would attract attention in this part of town. After pulling off the tiara and train, she shoved them into the coach before moving on. She hoped the guards looking for her had only caught a glimpse of her as she turned to leave. They would probably remember the cloak. Shaking her hair loose, she kept walking. Several ladies stepped off the corner to cross the street, and Nicola crossed with them. The first spatters of rain began. Searching for anything she could use to cover up, she passed an alley where a woman was leaving from the back door of an inn. The woman was clutching a long black cloak as she paused before stepping out onto the street. Nicola offered to buy the cloak from her. The woman struggled to make up her mind but soon agreed when the man at her side encouraged her, saying it would buy food for their children. Nicola pressed coins into the lady's hand. "God bless you m'lady," the lady responded, handing over the cloak.

Nicola slipped the cloak on, pulled the hood up over her head, and stepped from the alley. Staying in the shadows, she walked as fast as she dared. *Please find me quickly, Drue.* Kelly was gone, but Nicola knew the master of the stable where Bruce and Drue kept their horses would hide her.

JON WAS IMMEDIATELY SURROUNDED by Lady Margaret's guards. One of the men stood with his sword pressed to Jon's throat, while another removed Jon's weapon from its scabbard. "The lady with you," he demanded, "where is she?"

"Do I look like someone with a lady of his own?" Jon replied. "You mistake me for someone of greater means."

The guard frowned. He examined the sword Jon carried, which was made of good steel, but without adornment.

"You should not have entered with a weapon," the man snarled.

"I was allowed to enter unquestioned. I can fight, and come to fight for the new king. Take my weapon—I trust I will get the same returned." Jon was calm and stood patiently. *I pray I am allowed entry, before Lady Margaret sees and recognizes me.* The guard hesitated, then stepped around Jon to continue his search. The rest of the guards were already nearly out of sight.

As soon as the guard left him, Jon slipped between a tight group of people and stepped into a darkened hallway, standing behind a pillar, hoping to see Drue or one of his men.

DRUE AND HIS GUARD ENTERED the courtyard. Dressed in the colors of Vieneto, he and his men looked official and were allowed to move through the mass of bodies still trying to catch a glimpse of the new king. It took little time to know Nicola was not among them. Turning to leave, he was surprised to see Lady Margaret only a few yards from him. She was angrily ordering the guards to search the city for Nicola. The guards scattered immediately. Drue knew it would be useless to try to stop the search. He would have to find Nicola first.

"Have you seen Jon?" he asked the nearest of his men. "Or Lady Nicola?"

"No, Your Grace, but we will find them." The man took several others with him, and Drue's guard began to search the alleys and streets outside the king's hall, moving quickly.

As Drue made his way through the crowd toward a wall, he heard his name. Looking in the direction of the sound, he saw Jon step out. Together, without speaking, the men wove their way toward the door.

"Lady Weldon?" Drue asked when they were clear of the guards.

"We were separated, Your Grace. I sent her back out while I tried to stall the guards."

"I'm going to the stables. Lady Weldon kept her horses there and hid there before, so she would feel safe there," Drue said as soon as he was close enough for Jon to hear.

"Which stables, Your Grace?" Jon asked.

"The stables to the west. Where Lord Bruce keeps his mounts." Drue and Jon had reached the entrance. "Stay near, Jon, in case she returns."

NICOLA KNEW THE STABLE WAS in the distance to the west, beyond the street's bend. She hastened on. Before she reached half the distance to the stable, she was taken. Roughly, a guard pulled her closer to the light coming from an open door. The spattering rain had become a steady drizzle. "Are you sure?" his companion asked. "She looks like a common whore." The guard pulled her hood off. Nicola stood still, without speaking.

"I am certain it is her. I saw her leaving King Henry's camp the night before we fought. It is her." The other man pulled the cloak from Nicola, exposing the exquisite gown she wore. "'Tis not the gown of a common lady." With that, the men each grasped an arm and turned back toward the castle. Nicola could not pull away and was nearly dragged along with the guards.

At the entrance of the court, they hesitated. "Should we not go on to the Tower with her?" one asked.

"Best we be certain 'tis the right wench," the second replied. "I am certain it is, but Lady Margaret has a bad temper. I would not like to turn her against us so soon." With that, the men pushed through the now thinning crowd. As if on cue, Lady Margaret was walking toward them. She stopped and took one quick look at Nicola, her face full of disdain.

"I see you have taken her. Good. To the Tower, quickly, before she can cause a disturbance," Margaret directed.

The men turned toward the entrance. Nicola twisted around so fast one of the men lost his grip on her. "King Henry requested my presence—you do know that!" Nicola told Lady Margaret as she tried to pull free.

Nicola could see that Jasper Tudor was now moving through the crowd of men surrounding her. It looked as though he was searching for someone, and it didn't take him long to spot Nicola. "Stop!" Jasper roared. The men responded, looking from Lady Margaret to Jasper, appearing uncertain as to who carried the most power. With Nicola again grasped firmly between them, they turned to Jasper, awaiting his command.

Lady Margaret's manner was one of authority. She nodded to the guards, ordering, "Take her." The two men hesitated, waiting for some response from Jasper. "You do not know who she is, Jasper," Lady Margaret began. "I know of her well."

"Do you?" Jasper asked quietly. Before Margaret could answer, a page gripped her arm.

"My lady," the man spoke quietly, but with urgency in his voice, "King Henry requests you come to his quarters immediately. It would appear he is ill. Come quickly!" To Nicola's surprise and relief, Lady Margaret raced after him, forgetting all about her.

Jasper ordered Nicola released. "Are you well, Lady Weldon?" he asked her gently.

Nicola nodded as she put the old black cloak back on. Jasper stood a moment, then reached for the cloak. "May I?" Again Nicola nodded as she handed the cloak over. She was soaked. Jasper covered her with his cloak, then began to escort her toward the grand room, but before they were able to reach the room, he was stopped by a priest.

"Lord Jasper," the priest said, taking Nicola's arm, "I am Lady Margaret's confessor. You must do as she requests, until we can determine if the lady is indeed a heretic."

"And how will you determine that, Father?" Jasper asked, trying to pull Nicola away from the priest. But the priest held firm, the pressure on her arm increasing, making her cringe in pain.

"We have ways, my lord," the priest replied, his tone dark and commanding. Nicola gasped.

At that moment, Jon shoved his way next to the priest, stating loudly, "King Vieneto and his brother will know how the court of King Henry VII treats those who fought by his side. Vieneto sent men and arms to the king's aid. Lady Weldon is with Vieneto's court, yet you think to endanger her? Do you not know King Vieneto has other men at this gathering to declare allegiance? The king will know how his envoy was treated before you can reach the Tower."

Silence filled the hallway, and Nicola felt relief flush her face. She might not be sent to the Tower yet.

Jasper turned to the priest. "I know you are not who you claim to be. I know what men like you did to reach this position. The Church was no part of that." Jasper looked intently into the priest's eyes. "It would be better for you and your future if you released this lady." The priest quickly let go of Nicola. Jasper offered Nicola his arm and nodded to Jon as he left the huddle of men behind.

Taking advantage of the confusion in the reception hall as men jostled for position, Jasper pushed his way through, positioning Nicola nearer the front of the crowd. When King Henry entered, the room quieted and everyone bowed. Nicola wriggled her way closer to the front. King Henry spoke briefly, of his gratitude to God and the men who had lost their lives to secure his throne. Soft murmuring behind Nicola indicated not everyone agreed his throne was secure.

As soon as Lady Margaret had determined that Henry was not ill but instead anxious about his imminent first appearance as king, she rushed back to the corridor. It was empty. After calling for the guards once more, she ordered Nicola again be apprehended. Hurrying down hallways, she searched for Nicola and Jon. The guards followed, and Margaret questioned several of them. She knew instinctively they were keeping something from her. Her anger grew. "Maybe the king needs new guards! Men who can actually guard," Margaret snapped at them.

When she heard the rumblings from the reception hall, she realized Henry was already at his court, receiving his knights. Margaret gave up the search, instructing the guards to continue. She pushed her way through to the front. Bowing low before her son, she stepped up to stand at his right.

Drue and one of his guards were stopped by Jon just as he passed the grand entrance. Jon described Nicola's rescue by Jasper. "She is in the court now, with all the others."

Drue released a sigh of relief. "Then we go back to our original plan." Both Jon and Drue's guard nodded. "I have no doubt Jasper will see she is able to speak with Henry and will see to her safety."

Jon and the guard returned to the great hall. The space was still as the king spoke to the assembly. Jon casually surveyed the room and its occupants, his mind working. *If indeed, some of the men here are not truly supporting Henry, they could already have a plan in place against him.* Jon knew all too well how quickly fortunes could change, and he prayed he and Nicola could get away from the unrest certain to come, before they were swept up with it. In keeping with his original plan to enter late, Drue had already moved away, waiting a short distance beyond the traffic of carts, horses, and people. Handed a package, Drue smiled as he took it. He reached beneath his tunic, locating the item he had kept near his heart since first he was given it. Carefully, he slipped a ring onto the middle finger of his right hand—the ring given to him by his mother.

MEN SLOWLY BEGAN PUSHING FORWARD without any special order, scrambling to get closer to Henry, to declare their support and obtain his favor. Forced further and further back, Nicola caught sight of Lady Margaret, who was watching her. While men spoke to Henry, Lady Margaret leaned to whisper to a man standing next to her. The man nodded and turned to speak to one of the guards. The guard looked at Nicola. Their eyes met. She knew he recognized her, and she knew she must make a move or lose the chance, and likely her life. Just as the man in front of her began to step forward, Nicola quickly shoved him aside to get around him. The startled man gave way as Nicola forced a path through the line to stand in front.

"Your Majesty, I must speak with you." She looked directly into Henry's eyes before bowing. Henry paused, frowning. She could see that he recognized her, but perhaps was not certain from where. As Nicola straightened, she ran her hand through her hair, pushing it from her face. She quickly realized that this unconscious movement on her part was recognized—Henry's face brightened, but at that moment, two guards grasped her arms and started to pull her away.

"Stop!" Henry demanded in a firm voice.

Margaret knew she must act quickly to keep Nicola from the king. "Henry, she is not to be trusted. She is—" Margaret began. As before, in his tent, Henry's raised hand stopped her.

"No, she is welcome in my court, always." His powerful voice stilled the room. Looking at Nicola as the guards quickly released her and stepped away, he continued, "So what do you have to say to me?"

"I would speak with you privately, Your Majesty," Nicola responded softly.

"Come, follow me." He stood, and over his mother's protests and the gasps of the astonished crowd, he led Nicola to a private room. After instructing the guards that he was not to be disturbed, he closed the door, walked across the little space, and sat down. "Now tell me, why have you come to me again?" Henry asked quietly.

"I made a promise to my father. I kept that promise. I gave you the symbol he sent to you. I spoke with you before Bosworth, reminding you what you already knew, in your heart." Nicola kept her voice low. Thoughts were coming. The words left her mouth as soon as they entered her mind. Trusting herself, she spoke what she felt. "Your firstborn will be a son. You will rule successfully. You already know you will unite the houses of York and Tudor. You are where you were always meant to be, Your Majesty. You *are* the king of England. My job here is finished."

Henry listened intently, and Nicola continued, "I come to you this time to ask for your protection. There are those who would accuse me of being a heretic or an enemy to you. You know in your heart that neither accusation is true." Nicola's voice betrayed her anxiety, try as she might to keep it steady. "Majesty, I request that you guarantee my safety. I have given up all I have for you—my home, my family, and nearly my life. I cannot stay here. You know I am not safe."

Henry leaned back in his chair. The fact that she assured him he would have a son and would rule successfully gave him the first real measure of comfort he had felt since the hard-won battle at Bosworth. He stood and walked around the room. "Where would you go, lady? Where would the symbol maker's daughter like to go?" he asked, studying a wall tapestry. He was not keen to have her leave his side just yet.

"I think to live at my father's house, if it please you, Your Majesty." Nicola had not really thought about it, but it occurred to her that she had no idea where Drue was. She needed to seek safety someplace besides London. Someplace Drue would look for her.

"It does not please me," Henry responded, turning to her. He studied her for a moment. "I see the surprise on your face and in your eyes, but it is true. I think I cannot allow you to live alone. You would not be safe living alone, away from court."

Nicola panicked. "You do not think to keep me here against my will, Your Majesty!" Nicola protested. "Have I not been loyal and true to you? I have risked and lost a great deal for you, Sire. Please." Her voice faded. The fact that he might not allow her to leave had never entered her mind.

Drue, you may come for me, but I think you come too late. Her heart sank.

"Lady, is there not someone who would vouch to care for you?" Henry stood looking down at Nicola, his chin on his fist, frowning. "I have several men I trust. Any one of them would be honored to care for you, I'm quite certain, if you were to agree to such an arrangement."

Nicola's heart broke. She had no idea where Drue had gone. She could not speak for him without him knowing. What if Henry went so far as to give her hand to one of his men? *Could my predicament possibly get any worse?*

"Come with me," Henry told her, making his way toward the door.

"Your Majesty—" Nicola tried again.

"The subject is finished, lady," Henry replied firmly.

It can indeed get worse. Nicola felt her world crumble around her . . . again.

Henry returned to his reception court. His mother was furious. She glared at Nicola. Nicola ignored her, knowing she had accumulated enough problems without worrying about Lady Margaret. Henry stopped walking when he reached the front of the hall, and stood near his chair. He took Nicola's hand and announced loudly, "Henceforth this lady, Lady Nicola Weldon, is named my cousin. As such, she is always to be given the respect and honor and safety that a relative of the king should be given." He turned to look directly at his mother, then at the crowded room.

The crowd fell silent. Nicola could hear Lady Margaret gasp. A soldier stepped forward and spoke to one of the guards, who approached the king and spoke quietly to Henry. Henry nodded. He glanced at Nicola, then continued, "Is there anyone among you who would speak for this lady? She is very important to me, and I would see her with one who could care for her." He looked pointedly at his mother. "In England and abroad." He turned to the crowd, waiting.

Nicola felt faint.

"I will speak for Lady Weldon, King Henry." A man spoke from the back of the crowded room.

At the sound of the man's voice, Nicola caught herself on the arm of the king's chair. The crowd broke away and allowed the speaker through. Nicola was stunned. His eyes found hers. He wore the colors of his realm. From his luxurious cape, nearly reaching the floor, to every piece of clothing he wore, the richness of the fabrics lit up the room. Upon his head he wore a crown, and at his side hung a sword. Both were inset with precious stones. A heavy gold chain encircled his neck. From it hung the symbol of his kingdom fashioned in thick gold. He looked every inch the king he now was. But none of this mattered very much to Nicola—she only knew he had come for her again, just as he promised. She wanted to run to him. His eyes held hers. With a slight smile and nod, he turned to King Henry.

King Henry stepped down and embraced Drue. "Ah, King Vieneto. I was told about your brother and am sorry for your loss. I am also grateful for your support. I know you lost good men for my cause, Drue. I owe you much. Your father was a good friend to me. I spoke with him several times during my travels. I am happy to entrust this lady to your care." Turning to Nicola, he said, "Lady Weldon, your father was a great man, in every aspect. I believe he would bless this match."

Drue stepped up and took Nicola's hand. His words came back to Nicola. *You will bow to me.* She squeezed his hand. He returned the touch. The moment was brief, because Henry announced quite suddenly that he was starving. Turning on his heel, he led the way out to a grand hall set with tables, benches, and chairs. Food was piled onto the surfaces of every table. Henry indicated chairs to his left for his mother and Jasper, then nodded to Drue and Nicola. They were seated on his right. Nicola sat very still. Life had turned once again. No matter, she was safe. She felt it. The feeling was intense. The symbol maker's daughter was finally safe.

When the meal was finished, Drue spoke at length with King Henry and Jasper before returning to Nicola. Nicola rose from where she was seated and placed her hand on his arm, and he led her between the groups of men and women gathered for the meal. As they left, his soldiers moved from the crowded room and followed.

ALL EYES WERE ON THE COUPLE as they left the room, especially Margaret's. She refused to give up. There were things she could make happen, and Henry need not know. At a touch on her elbow, Margaret turned to face Henry and Jasper. Henry spoke firmly again. "Lady Weldon is not to be threatened, followed, or harmed in any way, Mother. She is protected by my promise and the goodwill between myself and King Vieneto. She is neither a heretic nor a traitor. She lost her father, her home, and all she knew, to be certain her father's message came to me." Henry paused, and his voice softened. "Her message was for me not to give up, to keep moving forward, to stay the course. She is not a fortune-teller or a pretender. Her final message to me is that my firstborn will be a son. Your first grandchild will be a boy, Mother. All you have done for me bears fruit."

Margaret's eyes filled with tears. "I have spent so many years protecting you and find it hard to step aside and allow you the freedom to do what I know you can do, Henry. You have my promise; I will search for Lady Weldon no longer. She is protected by this throne and by this king, and by me."

Henry kissed his mother's forehead.

Outside, Drue assisted Nicola into a carriage, spoke briefly with Jon, then joined her. "I am quite sure I left a cloak for you. A gray cloak, and a crown of pearls. Were they not to your liking?" He studied her face, frowning.

Nicola began to smile. "On the contrary, Your Majesty. I found the cloak and crown were beautiful. However, when I became the object of the hunt, I chose to exchange both for something less noticeable." Nicola smiled. "I left your gifts on the seat of a carriage. I bought a lovely cloak from a poor lady, with the last of my coins." Nicola smiled again. "Lord Jasper Tudor would not allow me to wear it when entering the king's court."

Drue nodded. "I see. It was a good move." His voice was gentle. "I know you must be exhausted, lady. Is it possible you can ride this night?"

Nicola was startled by the question. "Your Majesty?"

"Drue, my name is Drue. There is no one to hear us." He took her hand in his. "I ask if you believe you can ride. We leave England tonight. I do not care for the drive Lady Margaret has, with regard to her fear of you. We will board ship early, before first light, and be long gone ahead of her next move. I think she will have enough to worry about, without thinking about you. Still, I would keep you safe."

"Of course I can ride. I will be fine, because I am with you, Drue."

"Do you know where you are going, Nicola?" Drue asked, while pulling a blanket from beneath the seat.

"Certainly. With you," Nicola softly replied.

Drue stopped what he was doing and turned to her. His head tipped to one side as he looked at her. Slowly, a smile filled his face. He opened the blanket, moved to sit next to her, spread it over her lap, and leaned back. Grateful for the warmth, Nicola gave in to the exhaustion she felt. She leaned against Drue's shoulder and let sleep overcome her.

EPILOGUE

As the sun warmed the air, flowers awoke to spread their perfume-laden petals. Butterflies moved from bloom to bloom, drinking sweet nectar. Stopping to rest on bushes whose branches sagged with the weight of berries and blooms, birds sang loudly to announce the new day to anyone near. Drue walked through the comforting surroundings of his mother's beloved garden, his thoughts scattering like leaves in an autumn wind. In his mind's eye, he could see his mother. That image faded to reveal his father. Lila floated into view, with Cicero at her side. His family . . . all gone. Through the fog of loss, Nicola's image became clearer. She was smiling, clutching flowers. Her gown flowed around her as she drifted beyond his view. He could never have imagined how precious she would become. From the confused and scared child to the confident and serene woman he would take as his queen. He had loved, yes, but never like this. He needed to see her, at least once more, before the next sunrise.

Drue felt himself sigh involuntarily, felt a strange flutter in his chest. He left the garden and headed toward her rooms.

When one of her ladies opened the door, Drue saw the look of panic that washed over her face. "I wish to speak with Lady Weldon," he announced. The lady curtsied, glanced behind her once, and left Drue standing at the door as she entered Nicola's bedchamber. Drue could hear unintelligible murmuring beyond.

A second lady came to Drue. "Your Majesty, if it please you, Lady Nicola has not returned from a morning ride." She bowed and would have stepped away, but Drue stopped her.

"A morning ride? Of what are you speaking?" Drue frowned. Before she could answer, he strode into the room and crossed to the bedchamber. The bed showed signs of having been slept in, but was now empty. His voice became quieter. "I asked a question. Someone please answer."

For a moment, the ladies looked from one to another.

One older lady stepped forward. She curtsied before speaking. "Lady Nicola was unable to sleep during the night, Your Majesty. Upon rising, she requested we accompany her on a short ride, to calm her nerves, I believe. I am not able to engage in such activity any longer, and asked to be excused. Others left with her. She has not yet returned." The lady stood, waiting for Drue's next order. He simply nodded and turned away.

She has no mother to speak with, no one close to her to help settle her nerves. It is a shame Lila is not here. Drue admitted he would really not know what he could say to her. While he had been with a woman, in truth more than one, he knew Nicola had never been with a man. That was not a conversation he wished to have with Nicola. She would find out soon enough what a man and woman did when they were abed together.

It was the first time she had ridden without him. He knew well the road she would have taken. It was a short trip. They would return by the time everyone broke fast.

Bruce entered Drue's chambers just as Drue slammed a book closed and tossed it aside—it had done little to distract him. "You do not look like a man who will marry his fair lady on the morrow." Bruce grinned as Drue's page fled and closed the door behind him. "Unless perhaps the man is having second thoughts?"

"That marriage may not take place if the fair lady does not return very soon. She should be here as we speak. Still no sign of any in her party. If she is injured or in some kind of trouble, I will make the cause of her delay wish he had stayed away on this day," Drue vowed. "I find it difficult to think she might be in danger. Surely even Margaret's reach does not extend here." Drue paced the room. "I sent Jon to look for her. He should have been with her."

Bruce poured a glass of wine and offered it to Drue. When Drue refused it, he drank it himself. "Perhaps she is lost. You know Jon is not that familiar with this land or with Lady Nicola's determination when she makes her mind up. It may take some time for her to return." Bruce's tone of voice indicated he too was concerned.

Drue glared at Bruce. "She did not take Jon with her—I had to send him looking for her." As he spoke, the door flew open and his page announced Nicola and Jon. Relief washed over Drue. "Now, we shall see what tale Jon tells. It had best be good."

"I am late, Your Majesty." Nicola bowed low, and Jon followed suit.

"I noticed," Drue replied, turning to Jon. "I will speak with you later, Jon. This is not now nor will it ever be acceptable. I expect you and your men to ride with her, if I am indisposed." After bowing, Jon beat a quick retreat. Looking down at Nicola, Drue continued, "Lady, you could not inform me of your departure?" He could see she was neither injured nor ill. "Surely you would never leave me waiting while you took a pleasure ride."

Bruce moved toward the door, but Drue stopped him. "Please, Lord Bruce, stay. This promises to be a most interesting finish to a long morning." His tone was sarcastic and challenging, as the anger he felt grew.

Nicola could feel her face redden, but she remained calm. When he at last allowed her to stand, she looked at him with innocence. "I am so sorry to have caused you any worry or agitation, and I beg you to forgive me, Your Majesty. We were on our way back when we passed an area where . . . where I left the road and entered the forest."

"Why would you do that?" Drue strode across the room to stand staring out his window, trying to control the urge to send her away. *How can she not know where my mind would go when she did not return?*

"Because I found it," she answered simply. At her reply, he turned slowly to face her, frowning. She could see he was at least going to listen now. "I came to a beautiful glen." Her emotions were evident in the radiance of her face and in her eyes. "There were all manner of flowers. A field of thick grass surrounded a small spring, its overflow trickling away into the nearby underbrush. There were birds everywhere. Their calls filled the air around us." She paused again. "Near the spring, there was a bench. Beyond the bench, a small stone hut stood. I walked to the hut and opened the door. Inside, I could see it had a bed and a chair near the fireplace. It looked to be long deserted, but time had not been harsh. Nothing appeared broken, overgrown, or ill-used." Her voice became softer. "I know this place, Drue."

No longer angry, Drue watched her. She was happy, so full of life. He listened as she told him of the place she found.

"I know it well." Again she paused. "I could feel her there. She told me I would find a place of peace and solace. I found it today." Nicola stopped for a moment, watching Drue. Gently, she continued, "This move has been unsettling for me. But I felt her there as if she stood near me."

Bruce set his second glass of wine on Drue's table, and left unnoticed. By now, Drue was listening intently. His heart softened as she spoke. Her eyes became misty. He walked to her and pulled her close. "I also know that place. Yes, she is there, and it is peaceful there." For a long moment, they stood just so. "I have to think about this, Nicola," he finally said.

Nicola pushed back to look at Drue. "I am so sorry to anger you. I could not stop, or leave immediately once we were there."

"I am not angry," he replied, looking into her eyes, "but I will not go through another time like today. You are too precious to me. Now, however, I would know why you have not talked to me about the dissatisfaction regarding your new home."

"I am not uncomfortable here, or unhappy . . . only . . . it is a different world. The customs, food, language, dress, and people. Often I have felt as though I do not belong. I feel I am beneath what you should have and what your people expect." Reaching to touch his face, she continued, "It was good to feel the peace of that place. I love you, Drue. I love you and all that you are. Your people will become my people, as will all things that are part of you and this place. It will just take time. I would beg your patience with me."

Drue lifted Nicola's face to kiss her. "You are already loved by my court and my friends and will be loved by my people. I would remind you again, you are so much more than you imagine yourself to be, Nicola. You have proved that time and again. I will be patient, but I pray there will not again be worrying and wondering where you are, something I have done before on other shores and something I care not to do again." His voice became gentle. "I am glad you found Mother's garden. My father spent many hours there after Mother left, as did Cicero and I. It is a good place for you. I will show you a shorter way from the castle. Now, I would like to dine with you. Then, I understand the custom is to be apart and not see you until we are wed tomorrow—a night I await anxiously." He kissed her, gently. As he released her, she laughed softly.

At his raised brows, she laughed again. "I remember you telling me one day I *would* talk to you and bow, too. I nearly screeched back I would *never* bow to you."

"You did screech," Drue noted smiling. His eyes narrowed. "I was correct. You now do both. And it pleases me well." He turned her toward the door. She headed out of the room, but stopped, turning back to him. "Drue, I am home. Truly home." Her eyes were bright.

"Yes, we both are," Drue replied, watching the keeper of his heart walk away. "And it is good."

ACKNOWLEDGMENTS

For all the late nights, when he patiently dragged my computer bag and research book everywhere and for his kind encouragement when I ran out of words, I want to thank my husband, Beto. I am so grateful for his love and support.

As it has always been, working with the crew of Greenleaf is a pleasure. The editors are always easy to work with, offering suggestions for improving the flow of the story. Most importantly to me, they have all allowed my story to remain my story. The staff of Greenleaf, including Jen Glynn, Sally Garland, Ava Coibion, Shannon Zuniga, and so many others, make each manuscript come alive, from cover, content, and beyond.

ABOUT THE AUTHOR

CLARE GUTIERREZ is a retired registered nurse who grew up on a cattle ranch in rural Colorado as one of four children. After living in New Mexico for twenty-eight years, she and her husband, Dr. Beto Gutierrez, now make their home in the Rio Grande Valley of South Texas. *Symbol Maker's Daughter* is her fourth novel.